THE BLUE ROOM

Published by David James Publishing 2014

This book is a work of fiction and as such names, characters, places and incidents either are products of the author's imagination or are used fictitiously. Any resemblance to actual events or locales or persons living or dead is entirely coincidental.

First David James Publishing edition 2014
www.davidjamespublishing.com

A CIP catalogue record for this book is available from the British Library
ISBN: 978-0-9928280-2-8

Don't be on the side of the angels,
it's too lowering
D H Lawrence

THE BLUE ROOM

by
Michael McKeown

PART ONE

Freedom in a Far Land

Chapter 1

Martyr's Memorial
(An observation by Pat Farland)

WHEN I ARRIVED at the prison I had no sense of fear or apprehension. I knew all about the place from my time on remand there. It was brief enough, I'd got out as I knew I would and I'd severed my links with the organisation immediately.

It was a hellish place but I could let all of its intimidating milieu wash over me now – the looming walls, the harsh lights, the jangling keys, the heavy gates, even the jeering taunts of the thugs in uniform.

The screws.

I didn't expect to recognise any of them now nor did I want to make eye contact in case I did. Their faces might as well have been lumps of plastic attached to their dark uniforms and their peaked caps for all the attention I paid them. They wore their sets of keys and their batons at their sides in the manner of gunslingers. I looked straight ahead as I went through the usual stringent security checks, doors hissing open on the way down the corridors to the prison hospital. It was a small clinic with eight single ward beds. As I went in one of the screws, a black-browed neanderthal with a Scottish accent, made some jibe about bringing my mate in a Mars bar. I ignored him.

When I saw Butler I could not believe how much his appearance had changed for the worse. Naturally tall, lean and wiry, he seemed to have shrunk in every direction and he was abnormally still. It was as though his natural athleticism and vitality had ebbed totally out of his body, leaving only an emaciated shell.

His dirty fair hair, long and matted, hung on either side of his skull-like visage and scant, uneven wisps of a beard showed like faint patches of dirt on his chin. His face was yellow and he was clearly in pain. His pale blue eyes protruded blindly from their sockets.

"I can see the shape of you," he said, "but I can't see your face."

It was a moment before I could compose myself to speak. When I did, my voice sounded strained and hoarse to my own ears.

"You knew I was coming, anyway. Special visit. I didn't think I was that special."

Butler was silent for a long moment before answering.

"Neither did I," he said at last.

He looked up at me and grinned like a corpse.

"But I suppose they might as well. They've tried everything else. Why not send my old mucker Pat Farland while they're at it?"

He paused again.

"You've been sent by the Great White, then?"

"Aye."

It was the nickname they all used for Father Brian Hunter, the prison chaplain.

"He's a conniving bollocks."

"Don't shoot the messenger. He says the rumours are true, there's a ceasefire imminent and it's going to last this time. There's a deal on but it may be too late for you if you don't pack it in now. That's the gist of it. Matt Slattery was in with him before me but he didn't say anything. He did offer me a job in his bar, mind you."

"You should take it. It's a good pub. You'll not see Matt; he spends most of his time playing golf these days. That's what I heard."

"Yeah, well, I have taken it. I haven't worked since I came home."

"You should have stayed in America. Plenty of work there."

"Maybe."

I told him about the meeting with Father Hunter. The priest was an old man, old enough to remember the last hunger strikes. He had a reputation for shrewdness. He said that the visit he was asking me to make wasn't just about saving one man's soul. I told him I wasn't religious.

"So I've heard," he said. "Don't worry. I haven't brought you here to debate theology."

He gesticulated towards a copy of the *Irish News* lying on the table beside him. The front page gave no hint of resolution. Half of it was about Butler, the other half about a loyalist splinter group that had taken to upping the ante, picking up victims at random for torture killings reminiscent of those carried out by the Shankill Butchers back in the nineteen seventies.

"My concern is, Pat, that your friend's death could undo everything that's taken so long to put in place. We are tantalisingly close to putting a permanent end to all of this."

"Why me? You know I'm out of the loop."

"It's because you're out of the loop that I am asking you. You were his friend. Will you at least talk to him?"

So I let him make the arrangements, though I knew it wasn't going to do any good. I told him so but he didn't believe me. It's difficult to argue with people who have faith.

Butler was silent as I related this, his head slumped into his skeletal hands. He was shaking slightly. When he spoke again his speech seemed weaker, slurred and slow. He talked incessantly for about ten minutes, almost compulsively, although he hadn't looked to have had the strength for it. He asked me about a lot of people but only briefly did he mention Heather.

"Heather Lockhart. What about her…what about Blondie?"

"You know the score. She went to Australia. Sydney. The city, not the bloke she went there with. I never knew him. She never came back."

I wasn't all that surprised that he remembered her; just that he'd bothered to ask about her. I had never stopped thinking about her, especially when I went off to America on my own and felt the predictable pangs of exile. I had acquaintances in New Jersey but I wouldn't have called them friends. I found myself surviving by getting labouring jobs on the building sites, sometimes lapsing into the maudlin comfort of an Irish bar in the evenings to avoid solitude. It was easy enough. What I did find hard, and relentlessly painful, was what I can best describe as a terrible sense of loss, for a girl who after all that time was still a mystery to me.

"So Blondie got away after all," Butler said. "Good for her. If you ever see her again, tell her Rhett said hello."

"I'll tell her Rhett said goodbye."

He was never much like Clark Gable in *Gone With The Wind*, but we'd all had nicknames based on old film characters once and some of them had stuck.

But Heather had never meant anything to Butler, even in the days they used to go everywhere together. They had met as teenagers - it wasn't that long ago – and for a time they seemed inseparable. More like brother and sister in appearance, they seemed to have a common chemistry going for them, a sort that you very rarely see. I don't think either of them fully realised that. They had their ups and downs, of course, like any other couple. Then suddenly, after an extended period with a lot more downs than ups, it was all over.

When Butler did give her the brush-off, it was cruelly done, in front of a crowd of us in a bar one night. His language was typically abrupt and abrasive and it stopped the conversation dead. She didn't react much, just a flicker of the eyelids, a barely discernible grimace, and then she was gone without a word.

She came to see me the next night, at my flat. She was looking incredibly good, dressed all in black with her ash blonde hair brushed back. She had green eyes, like those of some exotic cat, classical high cheekbones and a wide smile that showed perfect white teeth.

She was ditzy in a lot of ways, but I didn't care much because she was quick and intuitive in others and I appreciated that. She had a certain beauty.

"You'll have to get rid of that moustache," was the first

thing she said, "and your hair doesn't suit you like that either. Let me take care of that."

She wasn't long out of school, which she had hated, and she'd wasted no time getting a job, as a hairdresser in a place up the Newtownards Road. She was from the east of the city herself. I think that was part of the fascination she seemed to have with our crowd, the fact that we kicked with the other foot. But she never liked listening to 'love across the divide' jokes, or any of those old clichés. It was serious enough for her. Certainly she couldn't boast about the company she kept to her family or her contemporaries so she found herself leading, at a young age, a strange sort of double life.

As for Butler, he had left school at the first opportunity too. He was hyper-active, a perpetually animated character with a brash manner and a ready wit. He could never sit still and he was naturally a very disruptive influence in the classroom. These qualities didn't endear him to his teachers but they didn't handicap him much with girls his own age, who generally took to him.

Heather didn't like talking about him, shrugging her shoulders, usually, and changing the subject if I mentioned him at all. She genuinely didn't seem too interested and I couldn't tell if she was ever putting it on. It was uncanny and even unnatural to me that they had both assumed utter indifference to each other virtually overnight. When she did talk about it, and she hardly ever did, she'd tell me that she liked me because I was older and I had far more sense, but that she had always felt attracted to people who were wild and who didn't care about anything, and to people with a sense of humour who could make her laugh. That was about as close as I ever got to understanding it all because I found myself in jail less than a year into our relationship and although I wasn't long there, and I knew it wasn't going to be long, it happened that by the time I got out she had gone to live somewhere in Australia, with an Englishman. I knew it might as well have been the moon she'd gone to for all the hope I ever had of finding her or loving her again because she'd have shrugged off her memories of me by now, like hair clippings off a towel.

She had always had a wanderlust, a desire to 'get the hell

out of it,' as she put it, and we even had a spell over in Blackpool, where she worked as a waitress and I had a job on the fairground, to try to exorcise her nagging desire for something better and something different from what she knew. It was no sort of life. Long hours, low pay and collapsing in exhaustion more nights than enough in our cheap digs. In the end I persuaded her to come back to Belfast, though she wanted to stay on. I could tell her now, if I could see her, that there is no getting away from 'it', no matter what part of the globe you make your abode, that you always carry 'it', whatever 'it' is, around with you, but then I suppose we're all clever people with the benefit of hindsight. I wondered what she'd make of Butler becoming an international celebrity because at heart, underneath it all, I still felt that she was Butler's girl.

I had met up again with Butler after my release. He was just out of a young offenders' centre himself. He'd done a short stretch on a petrol bombing offence and he came out tougher, fitter, meaner and more anti-authoritarian than ever before, sporting a close-cropped haircut and brimming with a wealth of stories and new acquaintances. Looking at him now, I bitterly regretted ever enlisting him for the organisation. However, I reflected that if I hadn't then somebody else certainly would have. He was born for the front line, so daring that his nature always drove him beyond what others were contemplating, so lucky that he'd get away with it, maybe nine times out of ten. And the tenth time? Well, all cannon fodder is expendable.

Frequently, as I spoke to him, he would moan and say things I couldn't understand before regaining perfect lucidity. I nodded at the jug of spring water by his side and asked him if he wanted a glass. He shook his head, replying that he was very ill and couldn't keep it down.

"What about Jimmy McGuinness?" I said finally. "I never thought I'd see the day he got lifted. It's hard to believe."

"Believe this," Butler whispered. "They'll not hold him."

He coughed and spluttered and motioned to the water jug. I poured a little into a glass and helped him sip some. He kept it down all right.

"It tastes funny," he said. "I think they've been putting

something in it. Vitamin boosters, maybe. I know it's not right. I should know, I've been drinking enough of the stuff. You know what? I can't see this fucking glass."

"Well. No point in showing you the paper, then."

I pulled the *Irish News* out of my inside pocket anyway. The huge colour photograph dominated most of the page. It was the first the press had ever managed to get of Jimmy McGuinness. He was handcuffed between two policemen but you couldn't see their faces. In the centre was Jimmy, an ordinary looking man in his mid-fifties, slightly above average height, attired in a brown jacket, white shirt and grey trousers, a characteristically impassive expression on his long face. Even in the snapshot you could get a sense of the inscrutability he was known for. The image caught the gaze at the camera, the aquiline nose, the large ears, the strands of greying hair combed over his head from a low side parting in a desultory attempt at hiding creeping frontal baldness. It betrayed nothing of the man himself.

No one knew what lay behind that mask, not even, it was said, his closest associates. If you had met him you would imagine that great knowledge, almost omniscience, lay behind it, and an understanding kindness – that is if anything much did lie behind it, anything more than an acutely developed native cunning, for instance, or even some dark and unfathomed vacuousness, you just couldn't be sure.

"Jimmy!" Butler was muttering. "Jesus Christ…"

He shook his head.

"That man was like a father to me…"

He began talking again in a rambling monotone, as though inwardly hallucinating, about being in his teens again, his time on the run in Dundalk, being back at school, winning a junior championship medal at hurling and playing for the county minor team. He kept returning to the subject of Jimmy Mc Guinness again and again, repeating that they'd never hold him inside, that he'd get a good lawyer who wouldn't be long getting him out. The tout that grassed on him would get what was coming to him, he said. There would be no ceasefire. The rumours could not be true. He spoke of the futility of those who tried to crush the movement because even if they succeeded in crushing individuals they could never crush ideas. He spoke flatly, without any conscious trace of irony, of the inability of any oppressor to kill the idea of freedom because the oppressed would kill the oppressors rather than let that happen. He believed that the last battle wasn't far off, even if it didn't look that way now. He paid tribute to those who had died before him and to those who would die after him. He spoke so intensely and for so long that he finally lay back exhausted. He stared blindly at the wall, the bones straining through the pallid flesh of his face.

"They'll never break me," he said at last. "I'll show the bastards!"

"I know," I said quietly. "I know you will."

With a superhuman effort he lifted a stick-like arm, feebly, a few inches in the air and smiled a terrible smile like a death grimace, wider than before, gaps showing in the mouth where a screw had once kicked several of his teeth out during a wing shift.

"Tiocfaidh ár lá!" he croaked. "Hope for the best, Pat. Prepare for the worst."

"I'll be seeing you, Jim," I said.

I left, tip-toeing as gently as I could. I needn't have bothered because already he was drifting off again and oblivious to all but his own tormented imaginings.

I walked out later into the still evening and decided that I needed to get drunk more badly than I had ever needed anything else. I couldn't face the priest yet. I didn't need him to tell me what was coming in the days ahead, indeed I could have written the script myself. The show funeral with the lone piper at its head and the massive cortege... the graveside orations... the public grief, the inevitable reaction on the streets... it would all go to a pre-set, pre-ordained formula.

Then it was a matter of sitting back and waiting for the eulogising and lionising to start in earnest – the proselytising ballads, the poems, the books by journalists eager to turn a fast buck who would solemnly quote Butler's words on imperialism or ideology or whatever, as if he had ever known what the words meant. All accompanied by the polemics of political coyotes of varying hues, the sort of opportunists who would readily ascribe a fatuous nobility to anybody or anything that could be translated into electoral advantage.

I thought about heading into the Titanic Quarter of Belfast for a while. There were some interesting new buildings on the Belfast skyline that I hadn't seen close up.

I decided against it and went to the Cathedral Quarter instead, to a new bar in Donegall Street called the Pig's Trotter. It was a small enough place, a little too bright and synthetic for my taste but not too crowded. There was a low hum of conversation. The plasma television screen on the wall was showing an advertisement encouraging the public to volunteer information on any terrorist activity they were aware of. There was an e-mail address and a confidential telephone number. Joe Public was represented in the ad by some doe-eyed, slack-jawed local actor I hadn't seen before, masquerading as a concerned citizen who was traumatised by brutal events around him. His reaction was to dial the confidential line, presumably for the better future of his wife and young child.

The inexorable ending to the piece was for obvious reasons missing: the masked man on the doorstep, the sharp retort, the corpse in the hallway. Sipping a double Black Bush, I reflected on another snippet I had heard on a local radio station that morning – another plug for the confidential line, featuring the number being chanted moronically to the irritating beat of an advertising jingle. I speculated idly on the possibility of a republican mole having infiltrated the highest reaches of the world of broadcasting before downing the rest of my drink in one gulp.

On the screen an interrupted programme resumed. It was about the recent 'magic bullet' cure for lung cancer, a treatment that it was claimed would transform the disease into a chronic illness which could be managed, like diabetes, rather than an inevitable killer.

A leading specialist from Belfast City Hospital spoke excitedly of a 'paradigm shift' which had revolutionised medical science before railing against the government for relaxing the smoking ban in bars and restaurants. Two elderly men near me took up the argument.

“They’re bastards,” one was saying. “They’re taking backhanders from the tobacco companies. Bound to be.”

“You think everything’s a conspiracy,” said the other. “See me? I don’t give a fuck. I enjoy a smoke and it never did me any harm.”

There wasn’t much happening in the bar. One of the barmen was standing with his hands on the counter remonstrating with a customer who looked like he’d been doing the rounds of a few hostelries. There was a game of darts going on in the far corner between two young men, bad players or drunks or both judging by the number of darts banging onto the floor or missing the target altogether and thudding into the wall. A youngish couple came in, looked around them and went straight back out. I finished my whiskey and decided I didn’t want another one there.

I thought about the various clubs I knew and decided to visit the one on the Falls Road I used to go to in the early days when we all sat around full of Guinness and idealism, making impassioned conversation about politics and what we were going to do to change our world. Butler would sit on the periphery of the company, bright-eyed and attentive, a bomb of energy ready to go off. Now he stood at the threshold of his own immortality. I saw no reason, knowing him as I did, why I should seek to deprive him of that at the behest of the Great White or anyone else. I didn’t care about the politics of it anymore and I wasn’t privy to the games that were being played. If there was going to be a ceasefire, well and good. A permanent peace, even better. Failing that, the alternatives facing Butler were death or rotting in jail.

I knew he viewed prolonged confinement with a claustrophobic horror of an intensity that few could conceive. I knew too, as I clambered into the nearest taxi, that a myth of fearlessness would be created around his memory soon. To an extent the myth would be true because where physical danger was concerned, Butler was genuinely fearless. The reason he knew no fear was because he had no imagination. He would speed to a riot like a moth to a flame, revelling in the excitement of it all, no more able to imagine himself crippled by a plastic bullet than he could imagine an adversary maimed by a petrol bomb. I knew too how that brand of fearlessness has no defence against an inner assault on the mind and the spirit and that was why Butler had been so pathologically eager to volunteer for the hunger strike. I had no doubt in my own mind. Butler was infinitely better off dead, and a hero, than alive and deranged. Or the worst possible option – a hunger striker who, for one reason or another, had failed to last the distance and was subsequently doomed to eke out the increasingly demented days as one of the living dead, forgotten or despised by his own people, a ruined husk of a human being with faculties permanently impaired. There were precedents for that fate, few in number admittedly, but fortune didn't always favour the brave. What was it Butler had said? Hope for the best. Prepare for the worst.

I ordered a bottle of Guinness and a Black Bush at the club. I felt immediately uneasy in the dingy unchanged surroundings. At first glance I didn't recognise anyone there. Then I noticed big Turley in a corner, looking at me as though he had seen a ghost. I remembered some of the old regulars in the club as some of the best people I had ever met.

I remembered Turley as a psychopath who used to recount with relish how he dealt with touts, letting them have it in the stomach and then watching them bleed to death.

As I stood at the bar I saw him point to me, muttering something to one of his companions. I threw the Black Bush back in one go and then slowly poured the Guinness, making sure that the head was sitting just right. I had realised that it had to happen sometime and that it might as well be now. I knew that suspicions had been aroused when I got out of jail and cut my links with the organisation. Still, there was nothing concrete…they all knew I had no real bargaining power worth talking about and that even if I had sold Butler and some of the smaller fish down the river it wouldn't have been enough to get myself off the hook.

Jimmy Mc Guinness was a different matter entirely. The 'devil incarnate' was what the big goon who had originally interrogated me used to call him. I remembered how he could scarcely conceal his triumph when I gave him the information, though it seemed tenuous enough to me at the time and I feared it wouldn't be enough. I was adamant that I wasn't going to sign anything, under any circumstances.

"Maybe you won't have to," he told me. "You're a sensible man. A very sensible man."

In the mirror behind the bar I saw Turley and several of his henchmates edging their way through the crowd in my direction, like predators. Butler had, of course, been right about Jimmy. He would be back again. It would take a fool to deny that. For my own part, there was a limited mileage to be had out of thirty pieces of silver and I knew I had exhausted it.

I ordered another round of drinks and, spotting a vacant seat at a nearby table, inched towards it, Black Bush in one hand and Guinness in the other. Bleakly thinking of Butler for the last time, I sat down and silently awaited my own fate, an entirely different kind of martyrdom.

Chapter 2

Silent Music

"WELL, PAT! LONG time no see."

"All right, Carlo?"

"I'm all right. What about you? You're looking a bit rough. You're shivering like you've caught a dose."

"A dose of paranoia."

"What?"

"Ever get the feeling that you were dropped into a goldfish bowl, Carlo? Instead of you looking at everybody, it's changed. Suddenly everybody is looking at you."

Turley eyed him suspiciously, then grinned his minatory grin.

"What the fuck have you been drinking, man? Whatever it is, give me a shot of it quick, so I can understand this conversation. I hear you were up seeing Rhett earlier, by the way."

"News travels fast. He's at death's door. I suppose you've heard that too."

"He'll survive. No thanks to the Great White and useful fools like you, Pat. You shouldn't have listened to him. Everything's under control."

"I didn't go to please the Great White. Rhett's an old

friend; I went to see him."

"Aye. Not so much of the old – he's still in his twenties, for fuck's sake. Not like you and me. Are you going to drink that stout, or what? I'm getting thirsty listening to you."

"Go ahead, have it."

Turley grinned again, lifted the glass and downed the Guinness slowly. He licked his lips and set the empty glass down on the table.

"That's better. Watch the news on the hour, Pat. There's a cessation of military operations from midnight tonight. Maybe you should get yourself back to your sister's before then, keep yourself right. I heard you were dossing down there, before you ask. There'll be something about a certain Mr Branagan on the news as well."

"Who's he?"

"Short Strand tout. He grassed Jimmy up, no doubt about it. He was found hanged in his cell. Suicide, apparently. Long runs the fox, Pat. Jimmy will be out soon. They'll all be out soon. Are you working this weather, or what?"

"Aye. South Belfast. Slattery's bar – do you know it? I start tomorrow."

"Matt's place? Good man yourself. I'll know where to go for a free drink next time I'm over there. Why don't you hit the road, Pat? You look all in."

"I will do, as soon as I can get out of the goldfish bowl. I like looking out at people. I don't like people looking in at me."

Turley frowned at him, then threw his head back and laughed loudly. He slapped Pat heavily on the back.

"Always the joker. Good luck to you, Pat!" he shouted, moving off with his silent companions in tow. "I'll see you again. In Slattery's, maybe. Look after yourself."

Slattery's was a busy and popular bar with a youngish staff, students for the most part, trying to earn enough to keep body and soul together. One of them, Adam Conway, told Pat the next day that he'd never set eyes on Matt Slattery.

"He doesn't employ too many full-time staff," he said. "The pay's not great for the part-timers. You're lucky getting in full-time."

"I'm not worried about the pay. Bar work's a doddle compared with navvying on a building site. I'm lucky, all right. You don't know how lucky."

Pat felt relaxed in the bar. It was busy enough, the time went in fast and there was constant banter amongst the staff. They all got on well. After a couple of weeks he felt as though he had been there a lifetime. There were frequent lock-ins, for staff only, after the doors had closed on the last customer and on their days off groups of them would often socialise together.

He had taken an immediate liking to Adam, a thin dark-haired young man with a quiet intelligence about him. He had a natural shyness that you could see evaporating when he'd had a few pints. Like many young men of his age he was only starting to come into his own but hadn't the life experience to appreciate it. Outwardly he seemed diffident, a bit of a loner, but there was something resolute about him. He reminded Pat in some ways of himself at that age. He came from Poleglass, still an impoverished area blighted by petty crime and high unemployment, but he had a sensitive side to him and enough ambition to want to fly high if he could, he just didn't know where to. That was something he'd have to work out for himself.

It was Adam who had told him about a vacancy in a shared house he was in and Pat had agreed to fill it.

"It'll do me rightly until I can get a place of my own," he'd said. "My sister's been putting me up but I don't like imposing on her."

It was an untidy, poorly furnished place in Ireton Street off Botanic Avenue, noisy as well as dirty more often than not, but within a few minutes' walk of Slattery's.

It wasn't long after he'd moved in when he arranged to meet Adam for a drink on a night off in the Rumour Machine, a new bar in the city centre. Adam was accompanied by Dominic Gray, another of the house residents. He was a small intense individual who habitually dressed in faded denim and gave the impression of hurting all the time, for the slightest of reasons or none at all. They were sitting in a bright spacious corner of the bar, beside a window. There was a buzz of anticipation in the air, the sort of communal warmth and excitement that occurs spontaneously on a Friday night when the worries of a week are temporarily vanquished by bonhomie and loosened inhibitions. Pat waved a greeting and brought over three pints of Smithwicks.

"I'm just glad Belfast isn't burning anymore," Adam was saying. "I love this city. I want it to be everything it should be."

"Listen to your man," said Pat, jerking a thumb at him. "Are you thinking of going into politics, Adam? If you were a politician you'd get paid for coming out with that sort of bullshit."

"I couldn't care less about politics," Dominic Gray replied. "One place is much like another as far as I'm concerned. I have this theory – it's more of a belief really - that we're all going to burn, anyway."

"I didn't know you were a religious nutter, Dommo," Pat said.

"I'm religious enough," he snapped. "That's not what I meant, though. What I meant is that everyone has something out there that's going to burn them one day. It may be an unforeseen event, or a terminal illness, or anything. It's out there for all of us at some time, just waiting for us. It could be a woman. If you'd had to listen to Conway as long as I have tonight, you'd swear it's a woman for him all right."

"Leave her out of it," Adam muttered. "In fact, why don't you just stop being such a miserable bastard?"

"I'm a realist, that's all. You can't do anything about fate. Anyhow, you haven't shut up about Chelsea all night. If you're that convinced she's going to dump you, she will. Have you never heard of a self-fulfilling prophecy?"

Pat was glad when the two of them got up and left to go to another bar.

"Aren't you coming, Pat?" Adam asked.

"No. I said I'd meet someone here. See you later, maybe," he replied.

It was a lie. Silently, he sat watching an altercation at the door of the bar. Some big drunk had been getting lippy with the bouncers and was looking belligerent. A cool resolve was concentrated in his hooded eyes and a long cigarette dangled from the corner of his mouth. It took four bouncers to deal with him in the ensuing skirmish. He squared up to them when they approached him and when they tackled him he lashed out left, right and centre, his large fists flailing like pile drivers, catching first one on the chin, then another, before they finally pinioned him in a sort of writhing rugby scrum, still not managing to bring him to the ground, the long cigarette still dangling insolently from his sneering mouth.

Pat picked up a discarded copy of the *Irish News* that was lying in the cubicle beside him and read it with interest. Most of the main news was political and the editorial waxed lyrical about the ceasefires and the possibilities that lay ahead. Even the sports pages were not immune. An antediluvian journalist with a penchant for nostalgia had sought to link his column with the emerging new political reality.

SPIRIT OF IRELAND was the headline; beside it were pictures of Jack McGrath, the famous Irish tennis player who had once won Wimbledon and whose nickname it was, and Shaun Simpson, another famous but less successful Irish player of the same era. A smug caption read:

Sports fans love a trier and Shaun Simpson was always that. He was never less than a credit to his country. But Jack McGrath was a winner and he wasn't called the Spirit of Ireland for nothing. In a very real sense, Jack McGrath ***was*** *Ireland.*

Underneath the journalist wrote:

I penned the above words in my 'Looking Back' column a year ago today. How times have changed in a year. We are now, as today's editorial boldly puts it, emerging into the light of a brand new dawn. It is no longer a time for looking back. It is a time for looking forward.

The Ireland that Jack McGrath personified, not so much a place as a state of mind, has gone. It was an Old Ireland, where moribund tradition reigned supreme and a collective sentimentalism allowed us to turn a blind eye to the very public failings of one of our own living legends. We not only condoned the cod patriotism, the drunken buffoonery, the egregious gamesmanship that ultimately defined the career of the man we called the Spirit of Ireland. We encouraged it by our silence. Jack McGrath's subsequent battles with alcoholism and, almost incredibly, poverty, are well documented. They are our fault as well as his. We, his uncritical public, worshipped his success on the courts and made him our national hero. We laughed indulgently at his bad behaviour. It is no wonder he self-destructed in the end. Where's Jack now? No-one knows. We all stand indicted for our negligence.

It is Shaun Simpson who now carries the flame for the New Ireland we have come to inhabit today – a land where opportunity, growth and renewal are what our people aspire to. This is a man who never laid claim to the prodigious talents of his compatriot. He never won a major tournament, despite coming close on a number of occasions. He was nonetheless an exemplary sportsman, one who never courted controversy and who served as a role model at all times. His recent reincarnation as an entrepreneur has come as no surprise to those who know him well. He looks deservedly set to become as famous for his business acumen as he was for his sporting prowess and the revelation that he intends expanding his UK based sports goods chain, The Blarney Stone, in the directions of Belfast, Derry, Cork and Dublin in the near future is good news for everyone who cares about jobs and prosperity. There are also reports that he intends investing substantial funds in a new tennis project here in his native Belfast. Shaun Simpson, one of the two Belfast men who succeeded in putting Ireland on the tennis map, has shown that he is looking to the future rather than the past. For that we must applaud him, once again.

Beside the article, bizarrely, was an unrelated piece about an allegedly dangerous cult called the Vice Versa Society, whose leader was a guru with the improbable name of Keith Dalkeith, founder of an organisation called the Meltsonian Institute, to which it was linked. Several leading religious figures were quoted, warning people to give the cult a wide berth when it started recruiting in Belfast.

Pat threw the paper away and hesitated for some moments before going to the bar and ordering another pint. He thought about giving Maeve Lindsay a ring and decided against it. He knew it would be a mistake.

He'd met her the first night he'd moved into the house in Ireton Street, in the same bar he was sitting in now.

"You remind me of Heather," he'd told her drunkenly. "I don't know why."

"Who the hell's Heather?" she'd retorted. "I'm me, not somebody bloody else."

She was twenty one years old, about five foot four, with short red hair, a trim figure and a face that wasn't what you'd call beautiful but attractive and interesting nonetheless because there was something about it that suggested intelligence and humour and personality. She had a rich Derry accent and a dress sense that was casual to the point of carelessness. She'd been engrossed in conversation with someone she didn't know, a woman of about fifty who had been drinking alone, glass after hurried glass of champagne until she was almost incoherently drunk. The woman was the worst possible type of drunk for her own circumstances – an introspective one. Her drunkenness was a vain attempt to dull the horror of a recent divorce.

Predictably, it had just served to exaggerate her despair. Pat intervened, told the woman she needed to get home and took her by the arm to a waiting taxi outside. He returned and offered to buy Maeve a drink.

"I wouldn't say no."

"Is that a promise?"

"Just get me a Bacardi Breezer. Watermelon if they have it, pineapple if they don't."

They had left her towards the end of the night and gone back to Maeve's place, a cramped bedsit not far from Pat's. She had shocked him by producing some of the paintings she had done as part of her course at the Art College. Some of them seemed beautiful to Pat but the visual complexity was such that she'd had to explain most of them to him. Amongst them was a series of five paintings on the theme of Death which, suddenly serious, she explained to him in detail. The irony of a twenty one year old so full of life putting so much time and effort into such an exercise was something Pat thought best not to mention. It occurred to him that she had probably had little or no experience of death yet.

She said plaintively: "Well-do you think that I'm going to be a famous artist?"

Pat said that he did and kissed her before gently undressing her and embracing her between the musty smelling sheets of her single bed.

He had felt bad about leaving her the next morning. Even when she was sleeping there'd been a suggestion of energy and vibrancy about her, as if she inwardly resented having to spend any time asleep in case she might miss something. Her head was resting lightly on the pillow and her body felt warm and comfortable in his arms. Her mouth was curved slightly upwards in the corners in the sort of half smile that people with a highly developed sense of humour often have, even in repose. As the rain bounced off the skylight on the roof above, Pat got up quietly and dressed without waking her. He sensed that she would regard his presence as something of an intrusion if he overstayed his welcome.

He'd seen her on one subsequent occasion, down in Slattery's, and she'd made some disparaging comment about how sloshed she was that night. Pat had got the message and had felt all of his thirty eight years as well as physically and mentally slumped. He remembered a throwaway comment she had made, about how he would have been really good for her if time could change and he'd met her about ten years ago and she was already twenty one. The thought had disturbed him greatly. She was funny, rude and fiercely independent, with a natural warmth about her; all qualities that a lot of younger men were destined to appreciate more fully than he ever would.

Pat downed his final pint of the night in the Rumour Machine and reflected on the transient and turbulent years of his own youth. He went for a walk along an illuminated path down by the River Lagan, alone in his own recollections, immersed in the silent music of Belfast in the shimmering night.

Chapter 3

Irish Jig

ADAM CONWAY HAD dreamed about beating Jimmy Selby. In the dream he was made invincible by a unique cue, distinguished by a handle like the top of a polished wooden rifle, one that was infallible on the crucial long pots. One night it looked like he was finally going to do it; that was until he heard what he heard about Pat Farland.

It was Selby who told him about it. A laconic Geordie, he had worked most of his life in various jobs in his native north-east before marrying a Belfast woman and moving across the water to be with her. He'd almost immediately got a job as a prison officer. He'd quickly picked up a convincing Northern Irish accent that was betrayed only spasmodically by the curious colloquial inflections of Newcastle-upon-Tyne.

His wife was a dowdy frump of a woman from Tiger's Bay. Adam had never spoken to her, indeed he'd only seen her once, but he'd got to know Selby as a regular in Slattery's bar and played snooker with him whenever he'd got the chance. Selby was not what anyone would call an outstanding man – he was short, plump, roundy-eyed, with greasy hair and the sort of anonymous face that populates every crowd and that you'd never remember in a month of Sundays – but a wizard on the green baize, adroit at playing an almost impenetrable safety game.

"Pat Farland?" he said to Adam, surprised, as they paused for a couple of pints of Smithwicks in the snooker club bar. "He's one bad bastard. I'm telling you, you oughtn't to get mixed up with a man like that."

And the following night he showed Adam a copy of the personal file, for Selby had an unwholesome passion for his job and used to sneak details of prisoners' records home with him for private perusal and God knows what. Adam often suspected that he kept a scrapbook full of this sort of stuff, a sort of idolatrous rogues' gallery dedicated to those whom he secretly admired. Perhaps it took a particular stamp of person, Adam surmised, wayward wilful individuals who did things little Selby would never dare himself, to excite him in any way. Perhaps he just passed them on to paramilitary associates of his wife's family in north Belfast. Adam did not know.

The file was a revelation to him. All the personal details were there. Name: Farland, Desmond Plunkett. Also known as: Pat (Adam wondered why, because he had always thought his name was Pat). Date of birth: well, Adam had known he was thirty eight now. It seemed ancient to Adam but to be fair to Pat he never talked about his age. A photograph in the top left hand corner showed a face that had never really been handsome – the large nose, broken on more than one occasion in brawls and the lantern jaw were indicative of a set of features that were too rugged to be ascribed anything in the nature of conventional good looks – but it was certainly Pat Farland, a younger, less final version. The hair was back combed, black and plentiful, like that of a youthful Elvis Presley; the face of indeterminate age, as is often the case with big men, who seem to reach adulthood, physically at least, at a faster than usual rate of knots. But it was recognisably the man Adam knew. He was thirty eight now and age had improved him. The hair had grown and was now less severe, parted at the right and fashionably longish. A drooping bandit-style moustache of the type that had recently come back into fashion was a recent innovation. It undoubtedly did something for that craggy face which had a pitted, lived-in appearance that suggested maturity. When he smiled that slow lazy smile of his, his eyes would twinkle and his face crease up like a piece of cellophane on a hot stove and he would smirk indolently at you like one of those hollowed-out pumpkins you see in front windows at Hallowe'en, with a candle burning inside.

"What do we want with an auld lad like that in the house?" Dommo had demanded, when Pat had originally agreed to take the vacant room in the house that Adam had told him about.

He'd been won over easily enough in a short space of time, as had the other residents, Stevie Marlow and Jap Prendergast. On their first night out as a group they'd gone to a nurses' fancy dress party in a new hotel up the Glen Road, all dressed as priests. Pat had started the night with his party piece – sinking a pint of Guinness in one go – then he'd brazenly taken up a collection in his priest's hat in the public bar for the next round. Within half an hour he was dancing with a vacuum cleaner he'd picked up somewhere, hogging the middle of the dance floor, roaring some tuneless country and western standard at the top of his voice into an empty Guinness bottle he was using as a microphone.

It was just another drunken night. Jap was being sick into a hedge at the end of it, Stevie holding him up, when Adam and Dommo wandered out to join them.

"Farland's all right," Dommo was saying. "He's a sound man for a geriatric."

"I told you he was sound," said Adam, swigging from a bottle of Harp. "Where the fuck did he go?"

A loud shout from the driveway answered the question, the unmistakeable figure of Pat waving to a departing car full of girls.

"C'mon and we'll get a Chinky," Jap was pleading. "Eh? A fucking sweet and sour, that'd do me! What do you say, boys?"

"You'd only throw it up, you buck eejit," Dommo hooted. "Anyhow, where do you think we're going to get a Chinky at this time of night?"

"Here – how are we going to get home?" Stevie demanded. "Did any of you dicks think to order a taxi? No? For Christ's sake… they'll all be booked, we'll be here all night!"

Pat had solved the problem of getting home by breaking

into a parked car outside and driving it at breakneck speed, screeching and weaving all over the road, all the way back to Ireton Street. They'd stayed up playing cards the rest of the night, drinking watered down poteen and singing rebel songs, and at sunrise Pat drove the car back and left it where he'd found it.

Everybody in the house had a different perspective on him and none of them really knew him. Jap thought he was good at talking to women but that he had as much sensitivity about him as a pig at a trough. Adam thought that rich coming from Jap. Stevie liked the obtuse hazy perseverance he had when he was out on the town; he didn't care how often he got shot down, or how often his drunken fumblings were rebuffed; he'd just keep going until he got off with somebody or other. But Stevie thought he was smart.

"He's just having a laugh, coming down to our level," he said. "I'd like to think I could still get away with that sort of crack when I'm that age but I can't imagine that far ahead. Fair play to him, anyway. He's having a ball. Nothing could annoy the man. Either he's a warning to all of us or he's an intelligent man who knows how to play the fool. Take your pick. I think there are no flies on him."

"He's a sensible man," Dommo had conceded. "A very sensible man. He's interesting when he talks about things like literature and drama. He's writing a play, you know. Something set in a prison."

Adam agreed that he could sound deep enough when he wanted to. He just didn't seem to want to very often. He liked the low life.

Within a fortnight of moving into the house in Ireton Street, Pat got a weekend off work and took off on his own to a *fleadh choeil* in Sligo, attired in a Mexican sombrero and poncho he'd bought for a pittance in the Oxfam shop in Botanic Avenue.

"You have to get yourself noticed at these things," he told Adam cheerfully.

He got back, exhausted, the following Tuesday with a Dublin woman who'd attached herself to him. She was forty, you could see she must have been pretty once but her best days were definitely behind her. Pat went straight to bed. The woman mumbled something about being fed up working the streets of Dublin and wanting to start a new life before following him noisily up the stairs. Adam had heard all about it from another of the barmen in Slattery's who'd been there; the drinking and the singing and the revelling in the town, going on into the small hours...Pat collaring some of the traditional musicians and inviting them back to a party....the crowd gathering in the dancing, flickering light of the camp fire...the boys and girls, some shyly, some boldly, pairing off in the quiet of the woods, or in the exhilarating aphrodisiac of a four hand reel in the cool dark night...the instruments sizzling wildly from the fervour and enjoyment of the musicians wielding them, the crowd vociferous and ecstatic, and there, amid the cavorting couples, the tall, moustachioed figure in the poncho and Mexican sombrero, bounding and leaping and capering insanely around the blazing fire with some drunken floozy of Dublin woman to the infectious dizzying lilt of an Irish jig.

Dublin Donna, as they came to know her, had certainly managed the difficult feat of lowering the tone of the house in Ireton Street, bringing back new clients at all hours of the day and night. Nobody gave a damn. Pat in particular seemed to like the extra company, often inviting the punters to join a poker session or a hand of pontoon to pass the time. The police would drop in now and again to remonstrate mildly with Donna but Pat would always be friendly with them and offer them a beer.

One time he cajoled a couple of them into going into Dommo's room when he was comatose with drink and waking him up to tell him he was being arrested. Dommo had pissed the bed in fright and the rest of them hadn't stopped laughing for a week. Eventually Donna just disappeared one day and they never saw her again. Her new life had lasted all of ten days.

It was in the snooker club that Jimmy Selby had nodded towards Pat one night, when he and Adam had been playing a few frames. Pat often loitered around the pubs and the snooker club with Adam or some of the other lads in his spare time, like he was a student himself. Selby knew him from Slattery's anyway but didn't speak to him much.

"That barman – what's his name?" he asked Adam. "I've a

feeling I know him from somewhere. Not here, nor Slattery's. Somewhere else."

When Adam told him, he looked disturbed as well as surprised. He'd produced the file the following night. Jimmy's best friend, another prison officer called Hughie McQuiston, was there too. Adam just sat staring at Jimmy, his little screwed-up insignificant face working itself into an expression of distaste, as he talked him through the major incident on the file. It related to a bomb attack on a Shankill Road pub by a four-man team who machine-gunned an angry crowd as they escaped. Five people were killed altogether including two women, one of whom was pregnant at the time. Jim Butler, who was subsequently to come close to death on hunger strike whilst in jail, was alleged to have been the gunman. Pat Farland was described as the leader of the unit and the driver of the car, the burning wreckage of which was eventually found in Ardoyne after a high speed chase through a labyrinth of city streets. Hughie McQuiston was shaking his long grey face morosely, pushing his spectacle frames up his nose with his little finger from time to time.

"There's been too much death. Too much destruction," he said gravely. "I could never understand anybody doing the like of that. What's the sense in it?"

"None. It was a random attack," said Jimmy. "Five dead. Dozens injured, some seriously. They claimed certain people drank in that bar and Trevor McCaw was one of the ones killed. McCaw was a bad lot all right but you couldn't have said that about any of the others. There was no sense in it. None at all."

He added that the team involved all got life sentences, bar Farland who'd got off on a technicality and had a clean record. He reckoned they would all get out soon if the ceasefires continued to hold. It would be people like the prison officers who would pay the price because they would lose their jobs when the jails emptied again.

Adam could just see him in his crisply laundered warden's outfit, with his anonymous, tight-lipped little ferret's face under his little peaked cap, tut-tutting sanctimoniously as the gates were thrown open for the last time.

"You stay away from that man, son," was Jimmy Selby's solemn warning. "He's got the smell of sulphur on him."

Adam didn't tell him Pat was living in the same house as him and he didn't tell Pat or any of the others what had been said. All the papers and all the news bulletins and all the smarmy-voiced politicians were all telling people that the war was finally over this time, that a whole new era was opening up. He believed them. Besides, he liked Pat and he had other things on his mind.

Chelsea, to be precise. He knew things were coming to a head with her – again. He thought Pat was the best person to talk to about it so he arranged to meet him for a drink in the Rumour Machine after they'd finished a shift. Adam was in a sombre mood, Pat bleary-eyed from Guinness and whiskey, a bit worn out after several drunken nights in a row.

"She's a good looking girl," Pat said, "but there's plenty of them around. I've been in the house for what – a month? – and I could count the number of times I've seen her with you on the fingers of one hand. Maybe that's a slight exaggeration but you know what I'm saying. You should let her go."

"It was bad the first time," Adam said. "I don't want to be feeling like that again."

"I forgot. She dumped you once before, then? You probably told me before."

"I don't know if I did or not."

"Well, you're a slow learner, if that's the crack. Go looking for grief and you'll get it. Toughen up, kiddo – shit happens, don't obsess about it."

"It's easy for you to say that."

He recalled vividly how depressed and emotionally disturbed he had felt. How he couldn't stop thinking about her because he still loved her. He could not get the memory out of his head of the night she had told him, in a cold and formal voice, that she no longer loved him and that their relationship was over. He'd taken it all passively, like some poor proud stupid dumb beast.

That night he'd tortured himself, fruitlessly going through the scene again and again in his imagination. Everything he did, or saw, twisted up his nerve ends; as he knew little things, places, snatches of conversation would be destined to do for a long time to come. He hadn't slept all night, twisting and turning in his now solitary bed, and he felt suicidal. He'd staggered out into the early morning and walked aimlessly and unseeingly up Ireton Street. He'd spent hours roving the cold dusty streets before going to the Students' Union and proceeding to get blind drunk. It was a self-defeating pattern of behaviour he was to repeat many times over.

"You better grow up," Pat had said. "Get a grip. If you're sure she's going to ditch you again, ditch her first. You'll both feel better for it."

He made some remark about having been close enough to death once to love life and value every minute of it and said he wouldn't get hung up on any woman as long as the world was full of them.

"It's my ambition," he had announced grandly, dwarfing a pint of Guinness with one of his huge hands, "never to get married!"

Dommo and Jap and Stevie were in by this stage and they all heartily cheered this sentiment and concurred loudly. Pat Farland sank his pint of Guinness in one gargantuan gulp, playing to the gallery as was his wont.

"Women," he stated flatly and succinctly, "are vermin."

They'd all laughed and cheered loudly and banged their glasses on the table and another of the uproarious evenings that gathered their own irrevocable pace so frequently got underway. It was only in a quieter moment when the crowd was beginning to thin at closing time that Pat had told Adam that a year or two in another country might be the best thing for him if he got burned again.

"Not England," he said. "It's too close to home."

He'd worked in Blackpool on the fairground years ago and in bars and building sites in London and Liverpool when he was younger but said that he'd recommend something different to that if Adam wanted his advice.

"America would be good. Or Australia. Work for a while, earn a bit of money and then go travelling. You're young, you'd enjoy it."

"Australia, maybe," Adam had replied. "What could possibly be better than Australia?"

Pat had sounded sad and old when he'd mentioned Australia and Adam couldn't tell why. He knew Pat had been in America but never Australia, to the best of his knowledge. Adam told him he'd think about it.

He was still thinking about it when he got an offer of a job in the Civil Service, one he could defer taking until after his finals. It wasn't much of an offer – it was for a low paid administrative post in a new office in the city centre – but it was a job all the same. Adam reckoned it would keep him going while he looked for something better.

Also, it would mean he wouldn't have to work any more nights in Slattery's once his exams were over.

He went down there the following Saturday evening and ran into Jap and Dommo and about a dozen other people he knew.

"Anyhow, Joe drives her out to the formal. She was all dressed up to the nines, like," Jap was saying in his whiny Newry accent, "and as soon as they got there, didn't he say to her: 'Do you fuck?' She says something like 'Oh, really, don't be disgusting!' or some crap like that, so doesn't he leave her standing there and go and get drunk with his mates, and end up getting off with one of the barmaids in the hotel!"

Some in the company were laughing and looking embarrassed, others frowning in amazement, others simply shaking their heads, at a loss for words.

"Jap, would you ever take yourself back to whatever kindergarten you crawled out of? These people are laughing at you, not with you," Dommo said. "Ladies and gentlemen, I apologise for allowing this gormless, foul-mouthed big lig into your company tonight. As you can see, what we have here is a severe case of retarded development."

"Aye – but that's not the best of it," burbled Jap, impervious, smoking furiously whilst swilling a pint of Harp and grinning maniacally. "The next night we were all in the Union bar and we were all out if it. Totally blocked, boy. Next thing Joe pulls his dick out and shouts at the nearest wee dirty: 'Hey! You with the tits!' – she turns round – 'Suck this!' He nearly got us all thrown out. Crazy man, or what?"

"Prendergast, you are a total, utter and absolute disgrace. See if I caught my fourteen year old brother mouthing off like that? I'd slap his lugs for him and stick his head under a cold shower."

"For fuck's sake, get that beer down your neck, Gray, and stop your gurning. You're one boring cunt when you're sober, do you know that?"

There was more in this vein for about half an hour before Jap – or John Aloysius Prendergast to give him his full moniker – started bragging about his own adventures with women. Adam reckoned Jap was a virgin. He was always boasting about getting off with some 'wee dirty' or 'dirtbag' as he liked to call women, but Adam had never seen him with one. When he started describing what he'd done with his latest alleged conquest in the back alley behind the Rumour Machine, Adam decided to leave. Dommo said he would go with him. Dommo told him later that he'd gone to look for Jap on the night in question and found him at the entrance of the alley fumbling with the zip of his trousers.

"C'mon, baybeh," he was slurring to some shocked looking bleached blonde old enough to be his mother. "You know you want it – don't deny yourself!"

"She kneed him so hard in the balls it made me wince, never mind him," Dommo said. "I ended up having to get him a taxi home."

Adam told Pat Farland on the way out that he was heading up to the Botanic Inn for a change of scene. Pat nodded. He was quieter than usual and looking a bit distracted.

"What's up with Pat?" Adam asked Dommo on the way up the road. "He's subdued tonight."

"There was an altercation earlier on," said Dommo. "Your wee mate you play snooker with – what's his name? He had words with Pat earlier on. I don't know what it was about but Pat threw him out."

Adam never did see Jimmy Selby again. He heard from another source that the bouncers had had to intervene to stop him coming back in that night, the short squat silhouette of Selby finally being forcibly removed from the doorway when the obscenities started getting too loud. Someone else said that he'd decided to indulge his twin passions of drinking and playing snooker a bit nearer his wife's home territory in north Belfast, sticking to the local pubs and clubs instead of coming into town.

Outside snow was falling and starting to lie. Adam trudged on to the Botanic Inn with Dommo in silence. Dommo was in one of his morose moods.

On the University Road they passed a young man shouting something to another young man and a girl who were standing in front of Queen's University's Lanyon building, between the manicured lawns and the gateway. The one with the girl burst into some tuneless song, something about a good ship sailing down the alley, alley O.

"We're a collection of petrified empty vessels, the lot of us," Dommo said as they came to the bar. "You know what, Adam? None of us knows what we're doing or where we're going. Take away all that witless macho posturing and bluster we're all fond of and what are we? A bunch of frightened little boys."

"Dommo, would you ever stop whinging? I came out for a drink to cheer myself up, not listen to you slabbering like a fucking suicide jockey. Frightened little boys, my arse."

"Except for Pat Farland," Dommo said. "He's different. Pat's a frightened big man."

Adam went home later that night and again there were no messages from Chelsea. Without stopping to think what he was doing, he threw everything he had to remind him of her into a paper bag. Letter, notes, small presents, cards, photos – there were a lot of photos. He burned the lot out in the back yard and for a moment- but only for a moment- it felt strangely liberating.

Chapter 4

<u>*Down The Alley, Ally O*</u>

ALASTAIR O'LOAN HAD reached his summit. After five pints of cider and two brandies his extreme good humour was only a short step away from uncontrollable wooziness.

"It's time for me to go, boys," he said, getting up from his comfortable seat at the back of the Botanic Inn. "You can call me a fucking wimp if you want. The woman would wait for me all night if she had to – I've got her well trained. Only thing is, I don't want to keep her waiting much longer, if you get my gist!"

A short, sturdy, barrel-chested lad of eighteen, he looked considerably older with his firm features, flat nose and wrinkled brow. His short mousy hair was already thinning at the crown. His remaining friends were still quarrelling about whose round it was but Wesley Mc Master shouted back at him: "Well, give her one for me, Ally. Tell her she's a bitch for not being there!"

"Maybe she is a bitch," he grinned, "but if she is she's my bitch. Just remember that."

He left the Botanic Inn to the familiar chorus of:

"The good ship sailed down the alley, Ally O
The alley, Ally O
The alley, Ally O ..."

It was a bastardised version of an old rhyme which Ravenhill had resounded to only twenty four hours earlier when he had raced and wriggled and bludgeoned his way into the corner for the winning try of the game. It had become something of a theme song with the Methody supporters throughout the competition as he had gone from strength to strength, playing and scoring in every game all the way to the final. He valued the support and it had felt good to see his friends in the Botanic Inn on the Saturday. He knew they'd been there on Friday night after the game but there was no way he could have got away from the team celebrations in the hotel the school had booked.

Stepping out into the cold March air, flakes of snow still falling intermittently, he re-ran the match in the theatre of his mind yet another time, exultant with pride, bristling with elation at the chants of the supporters and the delighted reaction of his own team-mates. It was only a matter of time before he would be considered for representative honours for Ulster. Or maybe even donning the green shirt of Ireland. Why not?

It had been a hard match, harder than any of the others. The normally immaculate Ravenhill surface was treacherous due to a constant downfall of snow, unusual for St Patrick's Day. But he had done the business when it mattered, keeping his feet when others couldn't keep theirs and giving the crowd something to cheer about. Beating their fierce rivals, the Royal Belfast Academical Institution, added lustre to the crown. He remembered something a cousin who had gone to school there once told him, about comments in the school magazine that spoke of 'reclaiming' the Schools Cup from the 'outer darkness,' and he laughed at the pomposity of it.

He passed his own school, Methodist College, and paused on the opposite side of the road to the entrance to Botanic Gardens. He recalled fondly the day he met Chelsea there. He had always loved the park, having hiked off from school numerous times to go there and share a bottle or two of cider with his friends.

There's a magnificent Palm House at one end of the Gardens, an imposing cast iron and curvilinear glass structure with a glorious collection of flowers within and, in the fertile seasons, an equally kaleidoscopic view outside. He remembered a sharp bright day in early February, a cold breeze blowing. A few people were sitting on the benches dotted around the park, contemplating the world. Most were walking along fairly briskly and Alastair O'Loan was one of them, leaving Wesley, Mark, Trevor, Simon and one of two of the rest of the gang sharing another litre of Strongbow over in the bandstand. This was too cold a day for watching the grass grow, or even playing a leisurely game of bowls on the green across the way beside the Queen's University Physical Education Centre, the huge architectural monstrosity that everyone for as long as he could remember had called the PEC. It was not just a playground for students but a place where middle aged men with bodies thickening with age and minds fearful of it drove their cars of an evening to pay for the privilege of jogging a couple of painful miles, or chasing a squash ball around a court with apoplectic gusto.

Standing at the entrance to the Palm House, looking down at a mini-jungle of spectacular plants, was a girl. Five feet seven inches tall – that's in her bare feet, she was taller in boots with high heels such as she was wearing here – she was slim and graceful in appearance and had a rare natural elegance and serenity about her. She was dressed in a costly looking black leather coat that was unbuttoned, a red cashmere jumper with a white silk blouse underneath, a black skirt, black stockings and black boots. Her blonde hair, cut short, was partially covered by a red woollen cap.

Alastair recognised the perfect profile turned at a right angle away from him.

"Chelsea?"

He looked immediately, as she turned, into a pair of beautiful blue eyes and a smile of greeting that unnerved him.

And so it went. He had taken the opportunity to ask her out and subsequently worked hard at trying to impress her. Ever since he had started going out with her he had had to endure chants at school of:

We love you, Chelsea, we do
We love you, Chelsea, we do
We love you, Chelsea, we do
Oh Chelsea, we love you!"

That, as well as the usual rugby palaver about the good ship sailing down the alley, Ally O, but he didn't mind that, he reflected as he walked along, it wasn't malicious, it was more the stuff of hero worship.

Noticing a small queue forming at the mobile fast food van in Elmwood Avenue, from which the usual greasy fug is emanating, Alastair stops to bawl some ritual abuse at the proprietor. The old habits die hard.

"Yo, Gringo! You old thief! You still haven't paid me for those pigeons I gave you this morning, Gringo! Where's that money you owe me?"

The man in the van leers across at him, tombstone teeth bared in a grin that's closer to a grimace, swarthy faced and beady eyed, cynically at home with this sort of thing in his own rough-hewn way. He shouts back something along the usual lines, something about drunken children being better off in their beds at this time of night.

Across the road in the other direction Alastair spots the beanpole figure of Archie Mc Cloy, his face as ever a model of state of the art stupidity, his piggy eyes cast heavenward, his wide mouth with its big rubbery lips undulating in incoherent song. He has an arm around a plain looking thickset girl with curly auburn hair, whom he is steering uncertainly in the direction of the ancient doorway fronting the Lanyon building.

"Give me the moonlight...," he is warbling, *"Give me the girl – and leave the rest to me..."*

"Archie!"

The lanky figure staggers to a halt, looking round and swaying and grinning his typically silly grin.

"Ally O! What about you, wee man! You must have just missed us. We were up at the Bot earlier on. I suppose you're away to give Chelsea the message now, eh?"

"You said it!" Alastair shouts cheerfully, walking on. "I'm a bit late. Lucky I've got her well trained. Be seeing you!"

As he strode on he heard the cracked adolescent cackle of Archie Mc Cloy breaking into some tuneless rendering, a stray 'Ally O' featuring somewhere in the midst of it before he and the girl disappeared out of sight through the doorway, into the hallway and the quadrangle beyond.

He wasn't a bad fellow, Archie, Alastair thought indulgently as he walked on down Shaftesbury Square, the air pervaded as ever by odours from the fast food restaurants, the lingering smells of hamburgers, chips, pizzas, fried chicken, the huge electronic sign glittering high on the bank building on the corner extolling alternately the merits of Coca Cola and the *Daily Mirror*. He was always a useful lock forward, he won a lot of ball at the line-outs yesterday, even if he was a bit of a looper.

He thought again of Chelsea. She had been a couple of years ahead of him at Methody before getting a place at Queen's to study social sciences. He had always admired her but because she was older than him she had seemed inaccessible, never more so than when she went to university and started going out with another Queen's student. He couldn't believe his luck when she'd told him that day in Botanic Gardens that she was not in an exclusive relationship, as she put it, with Adam – that was his name – and was free to go out with anyone and everyone. He was elated when she agreed to go out with him. He knew he would devote all his available time to her. It wasn't long before he was telling her his sporting ambitions, his desire to get out of school as quickly as possible – summer couldn't come fast enough for him – and hopefully get a place at Queen's himself. He told her, too, of his love of travel.

Before a fortnight had passed he was tentatively suggesting to her that they spend a weekend in Paris. He suggested that they go there as soon as possible, taking in the sights and the atmosphere, banishing all their sorrows and their cares as they walked hand in hand down the Champs-Elysées as the evening shadows fell. He spoke excitedly of the gargoyles of Notre Dame, the vaults of the Pantheon and the singing nuns of Sacre Coeur. He promised to take her for a trip on the Bateau Rouge, where they would sip champagne on the River Seine. He knew the romantic imagery had captivated her when she took him to her bed for the first time in her room at the university halls of residence that night. He had never felt less like a schoolboy and more like a man.

But he hadn't seen her for a week now, since the previous Saturday night to be exact. He had taken her for a meal first, at a Chinese restaurant in the city centre. It wasn't great. The food was ordinary, the atmosphere not too special either, just the usual jaded blandness, the soft muted tones of some inoffensive 'musak' and not much of a crowd.

Things livened up afterwards when they went to Belfast's newest concept pub, the Gridiron. The tiled floor was marked out in prominent lines, like an American football field; fluted wall lights accentuated grotesquely bright murals depicting large crowds at a game, made to look even bigger and denser by the skilful use of strategically placed mirrors. Painted at either end of the long bar were giant yellow goal posts in the shape of an angular Y. The barmen wore football shirts with huge numbers emblazoned on them, while two bouncers at the door were kitted out in full uniform with armour-like padding, huge shoulder pads and metal helmets with face masks. Girls wearing cheerleader outfits flitted self-consciously around the floor collecting glasses and taking orders, blushing occasionally at the ribald comments of various loudmouths amongst the overwhelmingly youthful clientele.

Alastair kisses Chelsea fondly and makes some unctuous remark, which causes her to laugh her tinkling infectious laugh and tell him to behave himself.

It's only later on, in her bedroom, when he starts to undress her, as he loves to do, and as he reaches to unbutton her blouse, a light cream silk number that clings to her, and as she inclines her head, he looks at her, slowly, from head to toe and is struck more than ever by her sheer physical beauty. He looks at her soft, exquisitely groomed blonde hair, marvels at the perfection of her heart-shaped face and her slender, perfectly proportioned body and feels something infinitely more powerful than lust. He wants to tell her that he loves her, because she likes to be told, likes to hear it as frequently as possible, but the passion rises uncontrollably in him and he can't even murmur it because he feels the intensity of his own desire choking him. He longs to hold her naked in his arms and caress her all through the night…it is only when he reaches to undo her skirt that he realises the extent of his own tension and she whimpers with disappointment as she feels him spill himself uncontrollably. He shakes his head, exasperated. He apologises. He tells her he'll make it up to her. She tells him not to worry.

Lost in thought, Alastair had almost reached the spot in the city centre where he had arranged to meet Chelsea, large snowflakes spinning like pennies in the air when he saw something he was destined never to forget. He saw Chelsea standing in the middle of the street outside the Rumour Machine bar, kissing a man he knew he had seen somewhere before. The man was tall, dark haired, possibly in his mid-twenties.

The picture was to be forever vividly imprinted in his mind. Even though it was March, St Patrick's Day had only been yesterday, the vision before him was mysterious and dark and Christmassy; it could have made for him a valedictory Christmas card, decked in tinsel, the scene enhanced by real snowflakes and a doom-laden sky, the dim street coloured by the bare electric lights in the dingy shops which lined it, the romance of it all centred around one long, meaningful, erotic kiss, sensual in its utter negation of innocence, an embrace between a man and a young woman deeply enmeshed in the knowledge of each other's uniqueness and splendour.

Alastair O'Loan walks blindly down the other side of the street with tears trickling down both cheeks. He feels immeasurably sad. He experiences the pain of a consciousness abruptly emptied of all wishful imaginings and comforting distortions of reality and suddenly prey, his defences flung violently asunder with the speed and ferocity of a fairground switchback, to the illuminated nightmare of total clarity. He no longer feels drunk although he knows that he is. He has an uneasy remembrance of an old maxim about the gods first sating the desires of those whom they wish to destroy. He knows now that for him there is no Utopia, no Elysian fields.

Only a disgusted looking little old woman, shuffling along with a plastic carrier bag, sees him as he trips at the mouth of an alleyway, falling, banging his head against the ground as he does so, suddenly and violently sick, spewing up diced carrots, potato, little bits of meat smelling of rancid cider and brandy together with his hopes, his vanity, his illusions and the hitherto immovable rock of his own self esteem in one giant, heaving catharsis, a putrid monument in the blackened snow, a lone O'Loan alone again, down the alley, Ally O.

PART TWO

The Way That Young Lovers Do

Chapter 5

<u>*Chelsea Girl*</u>

CHELSEA SUGGESTED TO Adam that they finish their drinks and leave. He shrugged his shoulders and grunted his assent.

"What about the Common Room?" she said. "I'm not walking any further than that in these heels."

Typically, he had failed to notice her new shoes, or her new lipstick. There were many things he tended not to notice. Too many. He had had a dull resigned look in his eyes all evening. It had been complemented by a sullen anger when they found themselves surrounded in the Students' Union bar by a faction of the Queen's Gaelic football society who were entertaining themselves by throwing beer over each other and singing a discordant version of *The Wild Rover.*

"It was your idea to come here in the first place," she complained. "You know I hate the place."

"All right. We're going."

As they got up to leave Dorian Eaves, the President of the Students' Union, came over to speak to them. He was a tall, handsome young man who spoke in an almost exaggeratedly polite drawl normally but he had to shout to make himself heard above the boisterous caterwauling around him. He stooped down to speak, his long fair hair hanging over his forehead.

"Where are you two going?" he demanded. "Nowhere far, I hope."

"The Common Room, actually," said Chelsea. "Why do you ask?"

"There's been a murder. A student. They haven't released the name yet but it was really gruesome, apparently. They're saying it was sectarian, that it was that gang the New Butchers-"

"For fuck's sake!" said Adam. "Did nobody tell these people the war's over? You'd think their own side would deal with them, if the peelers can't."

"Well, I'm just going around warning people, that's all. The streets still aren't safe. They abducted him on the Cliftonville Road, by the way. The body was found up Glencairn way. They're saying he was tortured before he was killed."

"Okay, you've warned us," said Adam. "Now go and put the shits up somebody else. We're off."

They walked out of the Students' Union in silence, up the brief stretch of the University Road past the Ulster Bank to the adjoining College Gardens where the Common Room, a three storey building fronted with a line of French windows, faced Methodist College.

"You were very rude to Dorian," Chelsea said. "There was no need for that. He was only trying to be helpful."

"I don't like the guy. He's a poser. Totally full of himself."

"I think he's rather interesting, actually."

"He's good looking and he thinks he's God's gift to women. That doesn't make him interesting."

They showed their student cards to the doorman and entered the building. The Common Room had recently been renovated to mark its return to club status, following some years of usage as a pub and then a restaurant.

"It's a bit bunged in there," the doorman advised. "There was one of those 'Poems and Pints' events on earlier. It's over now but the crowd's still there."

"Yeah, I forgot about that," said Adam. "We'll try it anyway."

Inside, the room was packed with people, many standing around the occupied tables and stools or queuing to get to the bar. There was a small platform with a lectern near the door, presumably to facilitate the readings that were now over. There was a wide range of age groups represented, the middle-aged and the elderly mixing freely with a student element that was mainly postgraduate.

"We'll not get a seat here," said Adam. "Maybe we should go somewhere else?"

"I've walked as far as I'm going to walk. Let's try Writers' Block."

They walked upstairs to the small square oak-panelled room which was used as an extra bar at weekends and for functions. Its nickname derived from the proliferation of portraits of literary figures which hung on the walls. The far wall, visible on entry, featured only writers with a past or present connection to Queen's as alumni or teaching staff, former writers-in-residence in some cases. Images of the living mingled harmoniously with those of the dead. Here Seamus Heaney, Medbh McGuckian, Frank Ormsby, Bernard MacLaverty, Stewart Parker, Glenn Patterson, John Hewitt, Ciaran Carson, Paul Muldoon, Sinead Morrissey and Daragh Carville returned the stares of curious drinkers; there, on the wall next to the bar, other Irish writers not so connected vied for attention, amongst them Joyce, Yeats, Beckett, Wilde, Kavanagh and Synge. Most prominent of all was a huge new oil painting by a German artist with an unpronounceable name. The subject was portrayed as an old man, gaunt and ragged, staring into space. A glass and a bottle were sitting beside him on a circular table on which one of his arms rested. The colours were a passive blue and pinkish brown, but on the facings of the subject's coat and on the floor were slashes of blood-red. The forms were massive, oppressive, seeming to grip like clamps.

"Padriac Fiacc," Chelsea said, reading the caption underneath. "He certainly lived a long time. I can't say I've heard of him."

"He was a poet. A very great poet. He wrote poetry about the conflict here in the seventies and eighties when other poets wouldn't touch it."

"Not my sort of thing."

"How do you know? Why don't you try reading some of his work? Look – there's a couple of seats."

Chelsea snorted in exasperation as Adam claimed a couple of seats beside two lecturers they knew, Max Lovell and Glyn Moxley. Lovell was a lecturer in social studies, a wizened little man with an owlish expression and a tiresome tendency to ape the accent of whatever individual he happened to be talking to.

Moxley, a small bald Welshman with an Oxford background, taught politics and had achieved some recognition locally as the author of an obscurely titled book, *The Celtic Coelacanth,* published by one of the small presses around the time of the Good Friday Agreement.

The book, a speculative work which had sought to analyse future political trends, had proved eerily prophetic. Moxley had eschewed the optimism that was prevalent at the time and predicted that the peace process, built as he interpreted it on a foundation of lies, guilty secrets and amnesiac evasions, would collapse.

His assessment of possible factors that would lead to a return to a renewed armed conflict had proved in retrospect disturbingly accurate – the fall of the Assembly, the fresh pogroms, a marching season of unprecedented violence, political assassinations, revelations of top level collusion, the election of a virulently right wing Conservative government. He foresaw the rise of a new republican alliance which would have strong Marxist influences and of recalcitrant loyalist groupings that would be ready to prolong hostilities indefinitely.

There would, he suggested, be at least one more major political deal that would prove to be insubstantial before, eventually, Northern Ireland would be subsumed into a single political and economic entity with the Republic, effectively becoming part of something resembling a United States of Europe. *The Celtic Coelacanth* did not offer a likely date for that outcome.

Max Lovell got up as Chelsea and Adam sat down. Chelsea did not like the way he leered at her. She regarded him as an incorrigible lecher who, like Moxley, spent too much in time in bars frequented by students.

"I'm just going to the bar," he said. "Can I get you a drink, Chelsea?"

"Thanks. Could I have a glass of white wine, please?"

"Sure. What about your friend?"

"He's drinking Smithwicks."

Adam was deeply engrossed in conversation with Glyn Moxley who was gesticulating energetically as he spoke.

"It has to be all over this time, Glyn. That's what everyone thinks," Adam was saying. "Don't tell me it's all going to start again."

"I'm not a clairvoyant. I don't know what's going to happen but I would never say never. Things can change very quickly. The government at Westminster is the worst we've had for years. The international community, frankly, is bored with us. There's a single unionist party about to be formed here."

"Yeah, surely that's no big deal."

"If the Reverend Ichabod Cairns gets the leadership, we're in serious trouble. I don't think he will but he'll be a monkey on the back of whoever does. I'm old enough to remember Paisley at his worst, you know. One dies, one appears in his place. It's enough to make you believe in cloning."

Moxley's eyes were bright and his speech fast. He always became animated when he talked about politics, Chelsea noticed. It was clearly his passion. She'd never had any time for politics but she liked to see people being passionate about their interests.

"There's been another murder tonight," Moxley said. "A Catholic student in north Belfast."

"I know," said Adam. "We heard about it on the way here. You didn't hear the name?"

"No, but it's the work of the New Butchers all right. They won't claim it because of the ceasefires and they'll probably lie low for a while now. They'll only start rocking the boat again in earnest when they're confident the time is right. Be afraid of those people. Be very afraid."

"You don't need to tell me to be afraid of headbangers who slice people up with knives. They'll get sorted out soon, I would have thought."

"Who knows? They're not mad, though. They're making a point, as they would see it, by the methods they use. I have met their leader. He's an extremely dangerous man."

"What? You actually know these bastards?"

"I've met Billy McCaw. It's common knowledge that he runs that unit. He threatened me last year when I was up on the Shankill campaigning for the party in the council elections."

"What party are you in now?"

"Irish Labour. We've a few hundred members here now. We'll be contesting more elections in the future. You should join us – we're an all-Ireland party and that's the way things are going to go."

"I'm not surprised you were chased off the Shankill. You're lucky that's all it was. What's McCaw like?"

"Personable, but frightening at the same time, if you can imagine that. He's on the military wing of the ULDC-"

"I can never remember all these alphabet soups."

"The Ulster Loyalist Defence Coalition. They're growing, watch out for them. They have close contacts with the Reverend Cairns and a few others. Watch McCaw in particular. He wants to destabilise things and he has the capacity to do it."

"So you reckon the writing is on the wall, then?"

"The writing is literally on the wall. Look how many paramilitary murals were removed from gable walls during the last peace process. Gradually, they came back. The last few weeks, more have been going up. Peace breaking out hasn't meant a thing. That alone should tell you something."

Chelsea looked impatiently at her watch as she finished her wine. Max Lovell was sitting uncomfortably close to her, invading her personal space as he spoke to her about the employment prospects of social workers. His breath reeked of cigar smoke and alcohol.

"There'll always be jobs for social workers, don't worry about that," he was saying, "but do you really want to be a social worker? The money's not bad but the work is awful. Why don't you just marry a rich man?"

Chelsea tugged Adam by the sleeve and asked him to hurry

up and finish his drink.

"What's the rush?"

"I'll tell you later."

"I'll get these men a round first. They got us one."

"There's no need," said Glyn Moxley. "We're not staying, we're going to the Wellington Park when we finish this."

Chelsea took Adam's hand as they walked together up Elmwood Avenue.

"What is it?" Adam demanded. "I was enjoying that conversation with Glyn. He's an interesting guy."

"He's clever and he can rabbit on all night about politics. That doesn't make him interesting."

"Very funny."

"Max is just a sleazy old git. I didn't want to have him in my face all night. The Wellington Park is welcome to both of them. Anyhow, we have to talk."

"About what?"

"I think you know. That bench over there will do."

They crossed the University Road, quiet for the time of night with only a few cars passing, walked to the wooden bench beside the gates of Botanic Gardens and sat down.

"We both know what I'm going to say is true," Chelsea said. "It's over. Our relationship is over. It was a mistake, us ever getting back together again. I only did it because I felt sorry for you."

"Did you, now? How very caring of you."

"Don't be like that. It's nobody's fault, we just need to move on, both of us. A clean break is the best way. We can get on with our lives then, without getting in each other's way."

"There's somebody else, isn't there?"

"No, there isn't, not in the way you mean. I've been out with a few boys recently, yes, but nothing serious. Let's face it, we haven't been getting on for some time, have we?"

"You didn't tell me you'd been out with anyone else. Who?"

"It doesn't matter. The fact is I don't love you. I feel trapped."

"Trapped? With me?"

"Don't be angry, really, there's no need."

"I'm not angry."

"You are. You shouldn't be, though. You'll find a girl sooner or later that's much more suitable for you. There's absolutely no chance of me changing my mind this time, incidentally. For both our sakes, please don't ever ask me to again or I'll end up regretting ever going out with you at all."

"There's absolutely no danger of that happening. I can assure you I won't be back. Twice is enough. Once should have been enough."

She reproved him immediately and urged him not to be unpleasant. He was obviously agitated but she managed to calm him down. He was subdued enough as he walked her back to the halls of residence for them to exchange some formulaic promises about remaining friends.

She phoned him the following evening, just to make sure he understood everything. She had read a book about relationships once that recommended this, to make sure that there were no loose ends. She was taken aback at how tetchy he sounded.

"Is this a joke, Chelsea? If it's a joke, it's not funny."

"It's not a joke. I just wanted to know if there's anything you felt you needed to talk about, or if you understand everything."

"No, there's nothing I want to talk to you about. Yes, I understand perfectly what you said to me."

She didn't like the brusqueness of his tone or the abrupt way he hung up. She sighed, then checked her diary for the coming days. She was enjoying seeing other men again. Dorian Eaves tomorrow, Alastair O'Loan the day after, a Nigerian medical student called Frank at the weekend. None of it was serious, she wasn't in the mood for that, she just wanted some fun. It would be time enough to think about settling down with someone in a few years' time, when she had her degree and was starting her career.

"You'll be met and married in a month," her mother had often said to her. "That's the sort you are. In the meantime – if you can't be good, be careful!"

Her mother knew her better than anyone. She had warned

her from the outset that Adam wasn't the one for her, that he wasn't really her type.

Enda was a very different proposition. She met him in the Crown Bar one night after she had been to see a play in the Grand Opera House with Alastair O'Loan. When Enda walked in she was instantly attracted. She didn't know he was Adam's cousin then. Alastair had not noticed her interest as she made slightly prolonged eye contact with the handsome stranger; then he smiled at her and she smiled back. He sat down in the snug opposite her and closed the door, having stepped aside to let his two companions in first. One of them was a tallish keen-eyed man with ginger hair, the other a much older grey-haired individual in a long black overcoat. The latter stayed for just one drink and spoke in a low, almost inaudible voice to the ginger-haired man about something that must have been important to judge from the seriousness of their expressions.

"I've a feeling I know him," Alastair remarked to Chelsea when the man had left. "I think he might live somewhere near me on the Malone Road."

"That's where he's from," the handsome stranger said, having overheard him. "He has a big house up there. His name's Wilson."

Chelsea was immediately captivated by the soft Dublin accent.

"What's his first name?" Alastair asked.

"That is his first name. He's called Wilson Squires. It's one of those strange names you get here in Ulster, you know the sort. Two surnames together. Maybe his mother's maiden name was Wilson. I don't know," replied Enda."I must ask him sometime."

"My uncle Thom got his name that way," Alastair said. "He's Thompson O'Loan. But everybody calls him Thom."

"Is that the one that's gone a bit dotty?" Chelsea asked. "The uncle that goes about in a Lone Ranger outfit?"

"Yes. He's all right most of the time, when he takes his medication. It's when he doesn't take it that you have to worry about him. He's got involved with that Vice Versa sect now, you know the one. The family's very concerned about him. It's a shame. He used to be one of the best teachers in the country."

"Aren't you going to tell me you know this man as well?" Enda said cheerily, clapping his companion on the back. "Even if you've never played tennis, you must know this man."

"I think I do. Shaun Simpson?" Alastair said. "I used to watch you when you played at Wimbledon."

The ginger haired man looked ill at ease, as though embarrassed at being the sudden centre of attention.

Chelsea hated sport and having to listen to men who talked about it incessantly. But Simpson's name rang a bell with her.

"Even I've heard of you," she said. "And I know nothing about tennis. There was you and that other guy from Belfast – Jack Mc Grath. What was it they used to call him? They had some name for him."

"The Spirit of Ireland," Alastair rejoined. "Everybody knows that. He was some champion. Some character, too. You two must have had some great times in that era."

"It wasn't so long ago," Simpson said, gazing abstractedly at the stained glass windows of the pub.

"Of course it wasn't," Enda chipped in. "But Shaun's even better at making money these days than he was at playing tennis. He has a chain of shops all over the UK now. Sports goods. I run one of them for him in London, in Covent Garden."

It transpired that Simpson had been considering opening a shop in Belfast and that they had been looking at a couple of potential locations, one in Royal Avenue and one in Cornmarket.

"I really think the peace is going to hold for good this time. People want it. It's good for business," Simpson opined. "Look at the crowd in here tonight - at least half of them must be tourists."

"They come here all the time," said Alastair. "It's a very historic bar, very famous. A beautiful building. Look at all the stained glass and the wood carvings and the gas mantles. Just look at that ceiling, too. And the snugs. We take the likes of the Crown for granted but that's just because we live here."

"Anyway, we better be getting on, boss," Enda said, finishing his drink. He winked at Chelsea, having slipped her his mobile and London telephone numbers while Alastair had been up at the bar. "We've things to do. People to see."

“If you do open a shop in Belfast,” Alastair said as they were leaving, “you should bring your old friend the Spirit of Ireland over to open it for you, if he ever shows up again. He would still be a big draw. I read something in one of the papers about him going missing again. Is he alive or dead, do you think?”

Simpson paused at the door of the snug.

“I neither know, nor do I care,” he said, speaking very deliberately. “And I can assure you that he’s no friend of mine. Jack Mc Grath was a shitbag.”

The two men left, Enda putting a finger to his lips and affecting a comical expression as he turned towards the exit. Alastair still didn’t notice when he held Chelsea’s gaze all the way out the door. There were many things Alastair didn’t notice.

Too many.

Chapter 6

Spirit Of Ireland
(An observation by Shaun Simpson)

THEY CALLED HIM the Spirit of Ireland and it was a name he revelled in, hyping it up for all it was worth. He got it after he won Wimbledon for the one and only time and his fame, both on and off the courts, was at its zenith. Predictably enough the soundbite came from his own mouth. He was always ready with an abundance of quotes for the ubiquitous posse of journalists that was forever at his heels; that was one of the reasons he achieved as much fame and infamy as he did.

SPRING-HEELED JACK! bellowed the press when he won the title from the Swedish kid Nilsson, the latest teenage wonderboy, over a cliff-hanging five sets, surviving six match points and coming from 5-0 down in the final set before going on to win it in the most spectacular way possible, with a volley that looked physically impossible. He wasn't just a big serve and volley man, Jack, though that was his fundamental game. He had other qualities as well that all the great players have, like a naturally lucky streak and the ability, when the chips are down, as they frequently are at this level, to pull off a shot that seemed unplayable. I've pulled off a few shots in big games myself that have been described like that but what happened that day put my own achievements into perspective. I had the ideal vantage point on Centre Court, sitting on the edge of my seat, close enough to the action to play every ball mentally as if I were out there myself. Nilsson was back in the ascendancy, moving effortlessly, hitting the ball perfectly, ready to assume control again. Jack needed to deliver a miracle to stop him. That's exactly what he did to seal the Wimbledon final, leaping like a man possessed, somehow reaching a lob that looked well beyond him to hammer the ball past the unbelieving Nilsson, who had previously sent him scurrying back and forth to both corners of the base line with a series of precision lobs for what seemed like an eternity.

The crowd went wild. He was the first, and to this day the only Irishman to win a singles final at Wimbledon and he was probably the most popular champion ever. That was always what he had wanted. It was what I had always wanted too but it wasn't to be for me.

I had known him for ten years, since we were callow teenagers leaving Belfast on sports scholarships, learning our tennis in the alien heat and humidity of Florida. Jack wasn't the Spirit of Ireland then, just a tough big Belfast lad with a bloody minded attitude. In the fiercely competitive new world we had entered, he was the fiercest competitor of them all. He was a quick learner and soon looked destined for great things. He was good for me then. He forced me to raise my game, to work harder and harder to keep up with him. I got on better with the coaches than he did. They could never change his contempt for the bland conformist image the game had nor his tendency to unruliness. They tolerated a lot from him because they knew he was good and could always channel his energy and aggression the right way when he was on court.

Off court, he liked to spend most of his spare time in a bar not far from where we were based. It was a home from home to him. The bar was owned by his uncle Vincent, who had emigrated to America as a young man and eventually set up his own painting and decorating business. The business thrived and when he was sixty he sold it and bought the bar. The Irish Mist was the name of it. It was a big building at the end of a street, a popular meeting place for the area's growing Irish diaspora, festooned with Irish tricolours and with pictures of past Irish sporting heroes adorning the walls. They were all there: soccer players, golfers, Gaelic footballers, hurlers, snooker champions, rugby internationals, cyclists, Olympic athletes, boxers, almost everything you could think of. There were no tennis players.

"Ireland's never had any, Shaun," Vincent told me the first time we visited. "You boys can change that. You've got the opportunity of a lifetime, so you better not blow it. You gotta knuckle down, work hard. See those two guys?"

He gesticulated at pictures of Sean Kelly and Stephen Roche, two famous professional cyclists from the nineteen eighties who had won numerous top honours.

"They were the best. We'd never produced world class cyclists before…those guys were inspirational. It was their time, boys. Maybe this is yours."

The bar provided a lot of sports related entertainment, sometimes beaming in live Gaelic football matches from Dublin, sometimes showing old footage of previous Irish sporting greats. Vincent had a particular fondness for the 'singing boxers', as he called them – old champions like Jack Doyle, Rinty Monaghan and Barry McGuigan who would lead their audiences in song after a winning fight.

"People pay their hard-earned money and they want to see a show," Vincent explained. "Those guys gave them a show. People appreciate it when you give them what they want."

Other nights the bar would put on live sessions of Irish traditional music, or host Irish dancing classes, or show ancient films with an Irish theme, the likes of *The Quiet Man* or *Darby O'Gill and the Little People* or anything with Errol Flynn in it.

"Flynn wasn't really one of us," Vincent said. "He just told everybody he was so the marketing boys sold him as an Irishman. Worked wonders for him in the early days. You boys, you're the real McCoy, so don't let anybody ever claim you as Brits or Yanks. Never forget where you came from."

It would have been easy for me to do just that. I knew I could never go home again and settle in Belfast, not now that I'd tasted something richer and better. Unlike Jack, I lost my accent fairly quickly and I was only too eager to adapt to the new American culture I was experiencing and to the strict regimes of the tennis coaches.

Jack despised all of that. He liked nothing better than to disappear into the Irish Mist. He was an anomaly, an anachronism, a visceral populist with an old head on young shoulders and a passion for the history and histrionics of a mythological Ireland that had long gone out of fashion. Crowds queued up to sample what he offered and watching that final, it was obvious why. Apart from an imposing physical presence – he was six foot four, a heavily built man with short black hair and a black beard - he provided his audience with a medley of non-stop entertainment.

Any measure of sympathy that Nilsson elicited, because of his youth and his superlative skills, was eroded by his cold fish demeanour. His utter lack of emotion contrasted sharply with Jack, whose every reaction was written all over his face and expressed in every other demonstrable way possible. Adept at unsettling opponents, he would keep up a constant barrage of jokes, taunts, arguments and antics throughout a match, roaring with anger when he made a mistake, jumping with joy when he did something extraordinary. He would engage in a fierce dispute with an umpire one minute, then have even the most rigid and frosty-faced of them giggling with coy amusement at some characteristic off-the-cuff witticism the next. Whenever he won a tournament his face would split from side to side in a big happy grin and he would punch the air and shout to the crowd as it stood in unison to roar its approval.

At Wimbledon that year he did his usual party piece, somersaulting the net at the end and circling the court with his spring-heeled strut, his racket balanced in the air on the tip of one finger. He paused only to run after the distraught Nilsson and, draping a massive arm around the boy's shoulder, persuade him back onto the court, raising his arm aloft with his own, the tumultous cheers drowning with immediacy the memory that only minutes earlier the newly acclaimed Wimbledon champion had reviled and berated the same player who had tried so vainly to convert just one of his six match points into the celebration of his own immortality.

The party afterwards went on well into the night, following a familiar routine. Jack would always end up at his favourite Irish pub in the heart of London's West End, surrounded by his usual entourage of hangers-on, some from the tennis world but the majority from outside it, some famous, others wanting to be famous.

Eleanor, his girlfriend of nine years standing from Lisburn would be there, fighting with him as always before the night was out. Invariably some musicians would appear, amongst them Joe Beaney, a white-haired old tramp Jack had encountered one day in Hyde Park giving a mournful rendition of *The Fields Of Athenry* on a battered banjo to a sparse gathering of uninterested loiterers. Jack's eyes had lit up.

"Do you know *The Wild Colonial B*oy at all?" he asked him.

They were Jack's two favourite songs. Mad-eyed old Joe smiled a toothless smile and launched into it, Jack joining in with his loud resonant voice until a crowd had gathered around him and it seemed like half the population of London was singing with him.

But most persistent of all the entourage was the ever present press gang, a veritable swarm of sports hacks and paparazzi, notebooks in hand, bulbs flashing, questions firing, microphones hovering, the intrepid newshounds and tough investigative reporters of Fleet Street's throwaway mythology, always first at hand with a round of drinks or of noisy sycophantic laughter, whichever happened to be called for.

"How do you really feel about winning Wimbledon, Jack?"

"Is this the Institute of Silly Questions annual night out, or what?" growled Jack, a stein of Black Velvet in his massive fist (the bar manager, a man called Gerry Sheehy from Waterford, had got in a collection of the huge beer mugs specifically at Jack's request). "Who are you with, pal? *The Sun*? Tough. Why not try and get yourself a job on a newspaper? Next question!"

"How important do you think your victory is today for the folks back home in the Emerald Isle, Jack?"

The second questioner had an Irish accent which mollified

Jack's abruptly prickly mood a little.

"I'll tell you how important, my friend," he said magnanimously, standing up straight, beckoning over both Eleanor and myself. "Vital. That's how important. Sport can be a great unifier of people in divided societies."

He stopped and took a huge draught of Black Velvet before going on.

"You're an Irishman," he continued calmly. "Are you orange or green, boy?"

The startled reporter protested that he didn't consider himself either.

"But you are, my friend. You're one or the other if you're from Ireland. I'm green, I make no bones about that. Eleanor here - Eleanor is orange." He kissed Eleanor tenderly on the lips and the cameras whirred as she snuggled up to him. "So's my best mate here, Shaun Simpson from the Ballysillan Road. Don't let that red hair and Fenian sounding name lead you astray. The man's an Ulster Protestant. And do you know what I say to that?"

The sea of faces looked up expectantly.

"Who gives a fuck?" he shouted with a wide grin. "That's what I say to that!"

The assembled crowd roared in approval.

"Remember this, my friend, about what it means to people back home," Jack said thickly, looking around him majestically. "We've never had any big name stars in tennis before. Now we've two, Jack Mc Grath and Shaun Simpson. Why? I'll tell you why. Partly chance. But it's not all chance. It's policy too – taking talented kids who show a bit of promise and getting them American scholarships. It worked for me and it worked for Shaun. That's what I call thinking ahead. See that lad there? That's our next champion!"

He pointed at a gangling raw-boned youth who was clutching an orange juice at the edge of the crowd.

"Owen O'Sullivan from Cork, my friends. Just remember the name because he's going to be mega in a few years. He's a good kid."

The youth blushed furiously as he received a rapturous

round of applause.

"But at the end of the day," Jack concluded, "it's all about spirit. You can take the boys out of Belfast but you can't take Belfast out of the boys. I'm only an ordinary Belfast lad from Twinbrook at heart. Shaun here's a good Belfast lad too, despite that stupid American twang he's picked up, believe me, he's a sound man!"

Gales of laughter.

"So remember about spirit when you write about Jack Mc Grath," Jack mumbled on. He was obviously drunk by now and struggling for words. "I'm not just about tennis…"

He stared into the air vaguely.

"Tennis is just a boy's game. But they don't call us the fighting Irish for nothing. We'll sweat blood out there if we have to but there's one thing we'll never do and that's lie down. It's all about facing up to things, about spirit…spirit with a capital 'S'. That's the way forward for my country. It's not just about tennis. It's about the Spirit of Ireland!"

Amid the roars and the laughter and the mutual back slapping Ron Mendlicott, a veteran journalist I had got to know well over the years, had unobtrusively sidled up to me.

"There's a quote or two in that lot for the sports pages. And a few other pages," he said quietly. "Does he never tire of sending himself up? The press loves it, of course. Sometimes I despair of my fellow reptiles. Some of the papers will probably have their people dressed up in leprechaun outfits to treat him to a display of formation kow-towing by the time he steps off the plane in Belfast. But it's all a bit demeaning, don't you think?"

"I don't lose sleep over it," I told him. "He'll tell you that you can't stop the media stereotyping the Irish so you might as well give them the full caricature writ large and milk it."

"Indeed. I notice he didn't say anything about the doubles final."

"Well, he's just won the singles," I said defensively.

"He'll burn himself out inside a couple of years at the very most. I've seen it all before," said Ron grimly. "No professional athlete can afford to carry on like that. I don't count sports like darts or snooker. Being a drunk goes with the territory there. But the likes of footballers, boxers – they come a cropper fairly quickly if they don't look after themselves. I've never known it in pro tennis. I suppose there's a first time for everything. I hope you're not into mindless hero worship, by the way?"

He gestured towards Owen O'Sullivan, gawping open-mouthedly as the musicians ripped into yet another chorus of *The Wild Colonial Boy* and Jack tottered like a colossus through the crowd at the bar to demand another stein of Black Velvet.

"Have you ever heard a kid from Cork trying to affect a thick Belfast accent? How was it Shakespeare put it about Hotspur?

'And speaking thick, which nature made his blemish
Became the accents of the valiant...' "

"I didn't know you were a culture vulture, Ron," I said. "I thought you were just an ordinary vulture, like the rest of them."

He grinned sourly.

"We hacks aren't all illiterate yahoos with pea brains and no morals. We just think, write and act like we are. It's our job."

He finished his gin and tonic.

"I'm off," he said. "Don't put your shirt on the pair of you winning the doubles."

The comment disturbed me because I had learned to respect the accuracy of his opinions. I knew too that if Jack and myself were to win the doubles it would necessitate Jack being one hundred per cent motivated as well as on his game because if you were you take away his obsessive will to win, there wasn't all that much about his game that was all that special. In the event I mightn't have bothered worrying.

JACK ASS! was the sneering headline in the popular daily that was destined to decide the doubles final. There were pictures of Jack slapping Eleanor in a hotel bar during their inevitable nightly row and one showing him leaving the hotel with a glamorous blonde. Underneath a snide caption sniggered: *'Jack the Lad courts disaster on eve of doubles final.'*

Jack was livid at the press, even one newspaper, turning on him. There was even a jocular piece in the editorial under the heading *'Stick it up your Jacksie!'* suggesting that we were a certain bet for a *'paddy whacking'* in the final because of Jack's careless and dissolute behaviour. His temper wasn't improved when we watched a television interview with our opponents, the American Dick Reynolds and his partner Tony Davidson, an Aussie, two dour nasty bastards who had few friends on the professional circuit. Reynolds was a humourless patronising dried-up dog's turd of a man whose face would have cracked in two if he'd ever smiled, the sort of guttersnipe you couldn't possibly like even if you'd reared him. Davidson was a more vicious version of the same breed.

"I don't particularly rate Shaun Simpson," Reynolds was saying in his carefully cultivated Yale accent. "He's the sort of player who will always give a reasonable account of himself but not win anything. Basically, he's a ham and egger."

Bastard. It might be the truth. But it still takes a bastard to say it publicly about a fellow pro.

"McGrath's a good player," Davidson interjected grudgingly in his nasal Australian whine, "but we can handle him too. We have a game plan. We're not afraid of the Spirit of Ireland."

That was the last we heard of those two begrudgers spouting journalese for the time being as we both went off to prepare ourselves. My preparation was based on some tried and tested yoga exercises, Jack's on listening to some rousing Irish rebel songs to psych himself up.

On the day of the final, I had a momentary illusion that Jack was still stinking of drink, as he often did. He wasn't, of course, he was never stupid enough to drink before a match and risk failing a test and the truth was that his growing dependency on alcohol didn't concern me unduly. At that time he could handle it. He had a great engine in him, as the commentators liked to put it... the sort of ultra robust cardio-vascular system that could absorb a lot of punishment. More to the point, there was a steely determination about him that suggested he was more than a little interested in winning.

Posterity will record that we won the match, a tough, hard fought encounter over four sets, by 7-6, 3-6, 6-4, 6-4. What it won't record is that Jack virtually won it on his own. I didn't play well, I sometimes don't against the big serve and volley specialists, especially if they're particularly strong on topspin like Reynolds and Davidson both were. Jack was in unbeatable form, though, playing for every point as if his life depended on it. Throughout the match he never shut up for one minute, constantly cajoling, encouraging and bullying me whilst keeping up a fluent stream of banter and abuse which enraged Reynolds and Davidson. When Jack put his mind to it he could unsettle pretty well any opposition. In this instance both opponents were badly rattled, especially Davidson who was the more belligerent of the two. It was his succession of unforced errors, culminating in a nerve-jangling double fault that gave us match point. It was a tense finish to an unbelievably bad-tempered encounter but the winning shot from Jack, a carbon copy of the mighty leap and volley that won him the singles title, dispelled all that as the spectators once again whooped and roared and cheered until they were hoarse at the familiar sight of the Spirit of Ireland somersaulting the net and delightedly strutting his stuff down the length of the base line, waving to the fans, racket balanced precariously on the tip of one finger as he acknowledged the adulation.

"It's what we call the salmon leap," he told a television interviewer later when asked to talk the audience through footage of the final moments of the match. "It's being able to jump your own height from a standing position. It was one of the tests you had to pass to become one of Cuchulainn's warriors of the Red Branch. But I'll not bore you with old heroes of the Irish nation. Not when you've got a modern day one here in front of you."

Later that night in the Irish bar, Jack looked the happiest man in the world, joviality personified. He was surrounded as always by newspapermen furiously scribbling down his every comment.

"Whiskey, was it, Jack?" Gerry Sheehy shouted above the din.

"The very thing, Gerry, my friend. None of your foreign muck, mind – make sure it's Irish. Stage Irish, if you have it," he added to me with a laugh, draping a giant arm around my shoulder. "That's the sort they all love. I'll tell you something, Shaunie. If I could bottle the air from Twinbrook I'd sell it because there's more than enough dummies out there in the world who'd buy it. Give the people a dose of good old fashioned corn-on-the-cob shamrockery every time – they'll lap it up like sweet milk. Remind me to start saying things like 'Faith' and 'Begorrah,' by the way. It used to work all right for Errol Flynn."

He emptied the whiskey glass in one gulp.

"You know something else, Shaunie boy? Some people take this game far too seriously. You're one of them. You want to wise up, catch yourself on. Just remember this. Give the hacks and the paparazzi what they want and they'll always look after you, they'll never let you down. Get wise, my friend – tennis isn't sport, not these days. It's showbiz. Glitz with the mits off! Here – see that toerag over there?"

He changed tack suddenly, pointing to a small fat man with sandy hair and a snub nose who was ordering a drink at the bar.

"That's the wee shite who rubbished me in the paper today. Watch this."

He called Joe Beaney over to his side.

"Joe, do you know that tune out of *The Quiet Man*, you know the one, where John Wayne goes into the pub to meet the locals and they all start singing? Aye? Sound man. Start it up when I give you the nod."

He strode over to the unsuspecting hack, a man called Mungall, and engaged him in animated conversation. It all seemed amiable enough, both men laughing loudly and apparently in high spirits.

By the time I pushed my way through the crowd I realised Jack was telling a string of Irish jokes which had Mungall spluttering uncontrollably in fits of mirth.

"But do you know why Irish jokes are so simple?" Jack said genially.

Mungall shook his head.

"So the English can understand them. And do you know the first sign of maturity in any race?"

Jack wasn't smiling now and an expectant hush had descended amongst some of the group in that corner of the bar.

"I'll tell you," said Jack. "It's being able to laugh at

yourself. It's easy when you know how. I'll give you a free lesson. Play it again, Joe!"

Nearby Joe Beaney on the banjo, a Kerry man called O'Dwyer with an accordion and various stragglers with an assortment of acoustic guitars and other instruments struck up a grotesque improvisation of that "mush-mush-toora-li-addy, mush-mush-toora-li-ay" dirge from *The Quiet Man* ad infinitum. Jack lifted Mungall by the scruff of the neck and the back of his jacket and then, with his exaggerated spring-heeled strut, to the accompanying crescendo of the music and a host of drunken cheers and jeers, paraded the flabbergasted scribe twice around the bar, then outside to the back yard where he deposited him head first into a bin, his little legs flapping frantically in the air.

"That's lesson number one," panted Jack. "You rubbish me, my friend, and I'll rubbish you. Read the papers tomorrow and have a good laugh at yourself. Show your face in my company one more time and I'll treat you to lesson number two."

Amid the throng of people, mostly paparazzi who had followed the spectacle all the way outside with their cameras, Jack spotted me and again threw a giant arm around my shoulders.

"Shaunie boy, you're my best mate," he beamed. "See the like of that? It's well worth the fine. Gerry Sheehy! Where are you? Set them up-two more Black Velvets! Your best Guinness and your finest champagne, my friend. Only the best for the Wimbledon champions!"

Astonishingly, the fickle allegiance of Fleet Street survived even that incident.

JACK OF HEARTS crooned the tabloids, when on a whim Jack and Eleanor decided to get married two weeks later and took a flight to Jamaica for a quick and private ceremony. At least, that was the intention. I had the misfortune to be the best man and I've never put in forty eight hours like it. I hope and pray that I never will again.

The wedding photographs convey an over-riding impression of immense dignity with Jack immaculately dressed, standing tall and dignified, Eleanor looking suitably solemn but radiantly happy.

They don't tell the full story – such as why the best man is standing in the background sporting a black eye. They don't capture the scene in the hotel bar with Eleanor and Caroline Hall, an old flame of Jack's who by appalling coincidence had been holidaying in the same hotel, shouting and screeching at each other about abortions and whose baby was it anyway and lots of similar incomprehensible stuff. They don't see Jack slapping Eleanor at midnight, so hard that she went down and stayed unconscious for several minutes. They don't show Shaun Simpson walking in at precisely the wrong moment, unaware of what happened, actually stepping over Eleanor without noticing her.

Jack was standing at the bar, muttering to anyone who would listen to him: "Nobody calls me a Fenian bastard."

"Sure that's what you are, Jack," I said jokingly, not realising what was coming (he hit me so hard that my right eye closed up and didn't open for three days). And certainly no camera recorded me wresting the whiskey bottle from him only two hours before the wedding took place, as he swore repeatedly that he was going home, or throwing bucket after bucket of cold water round him to sober him up. But that's how it went.

And it's a matter of record how it went on from then on. Jack stayed at the top for almost another couple of years, much as Ron Mendlicott had said he would. He won a few more big tournaments, the last of them being the US Open at Flushing Meadows when he beat me in straight sets in the final. But there was no stopping the single-minded downward spiral into drunkenness, violence, more drunkenness and, ultimately, oblivion that he had so fatalistically embarked upon.

JACK IT IN, JACK! implored the anxious sports hacks, seeing the sands of time running out for their pet protégé only too clearly. The signs were all too obvious: the drinking binges, the fights, the matches lost in prestigious competitions to grossly inferior opposition… the embarrassing chat show appearance, when he had gone on television so intoxicated that the authorities sanctimoniously withheld his fee, whilst smugly watching viewing figures multiply for all the wrong reasons… the notorious occasion when he emptied a glass of champagne over a member of the royal family at a garden party, allegedly because she had gigglingly referred to the Irish as pigs. But he was far too far down the road ever to turn back. The final straw was when Eleanor left him, unable to take any more, for she was the person closest of all to him. Despite her own fiery temper and volatile personality she represented maybe the only chance there was of keeping his chaotic excesses even half in check.

I saw the Spirit of Ireland last night, for the first time in years. He was at a bus stop in Liverpool. I had spent the day on Merseyside looking at possible sites for my expanding chain of sports goods shops and was walking up to Lime Street from the city centre. The giant figure at a distance still had a measure of dignity; when I came closer I could see that the once jet black hair and beard were heavily shot with grey, the face ravaged looking. The black greatcoat he wore had seen many better days. He was talking to a tramp at the bus stop, a white haired old man who bore an uncomfortable resemblance to Joe Beaney, and as I approached I could hear the Belfast accent as he draped a giant arm around the old man, a whiskey bottle nestling in his other hand.

"If you're from the fourth green field you're all right with me, my friend. There's a wee wine lodge at the top of the street. Are you orange or green, boy? I'm green but I don't care what you are. Here, have a drop of this, it's good stuff. It's Irish. Stage Irish – that's the sort they all love…"

He didn't see me and I didn't want him to. I slowed down almost to a standstill and watched the unlikely comrades lurch off into the starry night, the old man not knowing that the swaggering good-humoured empathy of his giant companion could at any moment, at the drop of a hat, for no good reason, turn into a violent punch in the face or a savage boot in the guts.

You're all washed up, Jack. Nowhere to go. Over the hill, and far away. Where are all your friends and your army of hangers-on now, Jack? Disappeared. Like snow off a ditch. Where's your wife and your endless string of girlfriends? Gone. Living their lives with other men. Where's all your money from your days of fame and fortune? Squandered. Wasted without a thought. Where are your *Fields Of Athenry* and your *Wild Colonial Boy* now, Jack? Still being sung, in Irish pubs and clubs throughout the land. But never again in your honour. And where are your beloved press hacks and paparazzi, who did so much to create you in the image of your own cartoon machismo? Hyping other heroes. Buzzing like flies over a cowpat around the latest flavour of the month in braindead sporting apes, bloated with the flatulence of their own self-importance. There might be one final big headline waiting for you, though.

JACK IN THE BOX might be it, only it won't be the sentimental congratulatory slap on the back for the flamboyant showman on the brink of oblivion, showing at the final hour his legendary ability to bounce back, it'll be a reference to the wooden suit you'll be wearing when you're six foot under.

You might think I'm bitter and if you did then you'd be damned right. I've heard all the clichés, about how the flame that burns twice as bright lasts only half as long and all the rest of them, and I can tell you that there's no room for that sort of cracker motto sententiousness in the world I inhabit. You see, tennis for me never was just a boy's game. Or, for that matter, even a sport. And God forbid that it could ever have been showbiz. Tennis for me was my profession, my livelihood, what I did best. Tennis was my job.

Only if you've ever played the game at my level, as a professional, can you know the heartbreak and the depths of frustration and despair that come with reaching so many quarter finals, even semi-finals, in the toughest tournaments in the world only to falter at the last gasp. It's the agony of purgatory without the certainty of heaven at the end of it. Once – just once, in a career that spanned all those years on the professional circuit did I get to a major singles final and that was at Flushing Meadows where I played Jack McGrath. It was literally a once in a lifetime opportunity for me to realise the pinnacle of my achievements, to show the world that I could become – however briefly, however impermanently – the best in the world at my job.

It wasn't that Jack annihilated me so completely in the final, by 6-2,6-1,6-0 – I often did have bad days against the big serve and volley men – but the way he did it that devastated me the most. I should have known him long enough to realise that he wouldn't alter his timeworn tactic of total gamesmanship, no matter what the circumstance. Throughout the match he demoralised me, dishing out constant insults and abuse, cracking jokes, arguing with the umpire and the line judges over every triviality, never shutting up. If you've ever played the game at this level you'll know just how unsettling that sort of behaviour can be; otherwise you can only guess. At the start I had tried to vie with him, making my own jokes, bantering back, but it was out of character and just didn't work. I couldn't lose my temper with him there and then or that would have put the already partisan crowd even more on his side. All I could do, as he humiliated me on the most important day of my life in front of the vast crowd and the countless multitudes of television spectators, was to exhibit the perplexed incomprehension and mild consternation of an unremarkable little man in the presence of a god.

So don't be in a hurry to judge me if I shed no crocodile tears for the Spirit of Ireland. Think of the worst humiliation you've ever had to endure in your job, then multiply it a hundredfold. Chances are you'll not even get close, so maybe you'd better not judge me at all.

I walked on up to Lime Street, my heart heavy and as cold as the bitter wind blowing in off the Mersey, thinking of the financial rewards and security my years in the game had brought me with no satisfaction at all, and boarded my train back to London and the cushioned emptiness of my own future days.

Chapter 7

London Calling

CHELSEA HAD WASTED no time. She rang Enda two days after she had met him and they had chatted easily for almost an hour and a half. He told her he would be in Dublin to see his family on St Patrick's Day and would come up to Belfast to see her the following day.

Alastair had given her a problem by insisting on seeing her that night, even though she had avoided him for a week, not returning his telephone calls. In the end he left a message for her at the halls. She had not bothered to watch him play in the rugby final; she elected instead to have her hair done and spend the rest of the day shopping for new clothes and shoes. In the end, it had been easy enough to split with Alastair. When she rang him on the Sunday to make some spurious excuse for standing him up, he told her that he had seen her outside the Rumour Machine. He asked her to be honest with him if she didn't want to see him anymore. She had tried to be as diplomatic as she could in the circumstances but he still ended up getting very emotional and slamming the phone down.

In the beginning Enda made a habit of coming over to see her. She was surprised at how much time he seemed to be allowed off from his job but he told her that Shaun Simpson was an exceptionally good employer.

"More of a friend than a boss, really," he had said. "He trusts me with all sorts of extra-curricular stuff. Shaun's into everything. He has a finger in every pie. The sports goods chain is just the tip of the iceberg."

It was one hot summer night in June that he had first broached the subject of her going away with him. She was in the mood for relaxation after she had finished her exams and Enda's offer of a weekend in Portrush could not have been more timely. He had been offered use of a holiday apartment there by Wilson Squires, whom he described as a business associate of Shaun Simpson, and had borrowed one of Shaun's cars for the duration. It was a gleaming white Mercedes that purred as it moved.

"I don't bother with a car where I live," he told her. "Driving in London is terrible. The tube and buses are a lot handier and there are always plenty of taxis if you're out late at night."

Enda was restless that night and couldn't sleep because of the heat. He eventually woke her to ask her if she fancied taking a walk down to the beach. The seaside was five minutes' walk from the apartment but he suggested that it was a mild night and that she should go topless.

"I'll need something," she had protested. "What if someone sees me?"

"Here," he said, slipping a cardigan lightly around the top of her bare shoulders. "That's all you'll need."

They had walked through the darkened streets down to the seafront, Chelsea nestling close to Enda as they walked, passing only one courting couple kissing at a street corner and an elderly man stumbling drunkenly home. The town was quiet. They had made love tenderly on the beach for almost two hours, watching the waves, until the sun began to rise. Enda lifted the cardigan to put round her shoulders as they got ready to return but Chelsea shook her head and insisted that he carry it. With an insane pride she stuck out her chest and, hand in hand with Enda, walked slowly back towards the apartment, naked to the waist as he had previously desired. Already the blinds had gone up in many of the guest houses and blocks of flats overlooking the beach and Chelsea noticed with a strange narcissistic pleasure that several sets of prying eyes were trained eagerly on her as they walked. It was only when the top window of a small hotel nearby was flung open and she saw a man pointing excitedly at something to her far left that she realised something was amiss.

Enda was first to react, racing swiftly back in the direction of the beach towards the distant figure of a man walking straight into the water. He had gone under for the second time before Enda managed to save him, dragging him out and hauling him to safety over his shoulder. By the time Chelsea had reached the scene, panting and exhausted, the man was in the process of being led away by a solicitous looking middle-aged couple who had been out walking their dog.

"They knew him," Enda explained. "He's a local man, a schoolteacher. Tom Malone, I think they said the name was. I dropped your cardigan somewhere. Here, you better take this," he added, unbuttoning his soaking wet shirt and slipping it round her.

It was later, over breakfast that he suggested that she spend at least some of the summer in London.

"You'll love it," he said earnestly. "There's so much to do that you could never get bored."

"Isn't everything very expensive over there?"

"Not really. You could get a summer job dead easily if you wanted one, anyway," he replied. "But there's really no need. I'll look after you. We could maybe go on a bit of a holiday somewhere later on."

Chelsea needed only a week to make up her mind. By then she had secured somewhere to stay for her last year at Queen's, a promising place off the Stranmillis Road that her friend Belinda had already moved into. Belinda had got herself a summer job in a nearby restaurant.

Everything then seemed to happen very quickly; the plane to Heathrow, the train to Arsenal tube station, Enda greeting her delightedly before lifting her luggage into the white Mercedes and driving her the short distance to his three storey terraced house in Sotheby Road. He had always loved Highbury, he had told her, more than anywhere else in London. It was where he had stayed, in lodgings arranged by Arsenal, when he had signed for them as a hopeful teenager. He had been there long enough now to be considered one of the locals, something she was soon to find out whenever he took her into any of the local bars or restaurants or just walked around the streets, all around the area right down to nearby Islington in one direction or Finsbury Park in the other.

"Don't you ever regret not staying with Arsenal?" she asked him once, more out of curiosity about his motivations than through any interest in football. "You must feel some sort of disappointment."

"No, I don't."

It struck her that he was being totally honest. The more she knew him, the more she was impressed with what she could best describe as his self-possessed charisma. He gave her the impression that he already had everything he wanted and that his desire for her, gratifyingly powerful though it was in her presence, was not something to which he was subservient.

"The truth is–" he hesitated for a moment "- the truth is that I wasn't good enough. But that's not the whole story."

He confessed that the real reason he had been forced to leave the club was not that.

"I think I might just have got another contract out of them, with a bit of luck. Another year, maybe. But I was caught by one of the coaching staff with crack cocaine."

They had hushed it up and kept the police and the press out of it but his contract had been terminated and his career was effectively over once the word had gone out on the football grapevine.

"There were a few clubs in the lower divisions interested in me at first. Barnet. Southend. Peterborough United. I was on the verge of signing for Peterborough when they found out as well. I've never touched crack again since."

"I've never been attracted to anything like that," Chelsea admitted. "I'm surprised you were."

"I was very young at the time," Enda said. "It gives you an incredible high. Like every light in the world being switched on at the same time. But it only lasts a very short time. Then you're chasing that high again. If you had a month's salary on you, you'd spend it all to get that back. If you had a year's salary, you'd do the same, you're that stoned. Don't ever touch the stuff."

They were sitting at one of the wooden tables outside the Highbury Barn pub, a short walk from Enda's house, enjoying the evening of a glorious day in June. Chelsea felt an extraordinary sense of tranquility mingled with an inner pride that Enda had chosen that moment to tell her something so very personal, something that was so potentially damaging to him that he would have had to keep it a secret from the vast majority of people he knew. Later, back at the house, he told her that he would be taking a few days off to show her around London but that he had to go in to work for a few hours in the morning first. She was only half listening to him; tired from her journey, she was admiring the mainly cream and black décor of the house, the French windows, the elegantly upholstered furniture, the huge mirror with the ornate metal frame on one wall, the artistic prints on the others. Tucked away in a corner of the living room were a compact Bang and Olufsen television set and hi-fi while a glass topped coffee table in the centre of the room was covered with newspapers and magazines.

Chelsea reflected that while she felt that she was in love with Enda as much because of his constant desire for her as for any other reason, she had always been to some extent attracted by the idea of having a rich husband as much as by the thought of always having someone to love her. Before he took her to bed she looked deep into the darkness of his eyes and kissed him, conscious of something unbearably tender stirring her heart.

He took her to Covent Garden the next morning and showed her around The Blarney Stone, the sports goods shop where he worked. It was a bright, roomy building, with merchandise temptingly displayed throughout two floors. Several sales assistants rushed around frantically on both floors, attending to customers and replenishing stock. Enda introduced her to Jenny Isliff, his assistant, a pleasant well-dressed girl with long chestnut brown hair and a toothy smile.

"I suppose you're wondering why Shaun calls his chain 'The Blarney Stone', " she remarked to Chelsea. "I think it's just an Irish thing. He always likes to open shops in places that are going to attract tourists."

"I think it's his idea of a joke myself," Enda grinned, indicating a large black and white picture near the front door of Shaun Simpson frowning with concentration as he prepared to return a service in a tennis match. "He never had much in the way of blarney. He left all that sort of stuff to Jack McGrath. But he hated Jack McGrath. Still does, if truth be told."

Chelsea spent the rest of the morning wandering around the shops and the market stalls of Covent Garden, meeting Enda at lunch-time on the balcony of the Punch and Judy bar where they enjoyed the live street theatre taking place in the open space below, the chainsaw jugglers, the mime artists, the fire –eaters and the sword swallowers.

Later they travelled by boat to Greenwich, where they walked through the foot tunnel to bask in the sunshine by the Cutty Sark and wander at their leisure through the narrow winding streets, relaxing some time later in Greenwich Park, as they idled up Lovers Walk past the site of the old Roman building and the Royal Observatory, finally lying in each other's arms in the grass outside the deer park called The Wilderness. In the evening, on the way back, they visited Enda's favourite Chinese restaurant in Soho, where Chelsea was enthralled by the bright lights and the noise and the bustle, finally finishing up the Bank of Friendship, a bar close to where Enda lived, for a last drink.

After a couple of weeks Chelsea felt that she knew London intimately. Every few days she would ring home, chatting excitedly to her mother about where she'd been and what she'd seen.

"You'll be looking for a job over there sometime soon," her mother predicted on one such occasion. "Just make sure you finish your course at Queen's first."

"I'll definitely do that," Chelsea promised. "You might be right, though. I think I could be happy here."

"Anne George was asking about you," her mother said. "She said she hadn't seen you for a while. I saw that lad Dorian you used to go out with the other day. If he was made of chocolate, he'd eat himself."

Chelsea laughed loudly at her mother's pithy way of putting things.

It was one Monday morning shortly afterwards that the telephone rang in the living room just as Chelsea was getting out of bed at around mid-day. It was Enda.

"What are you wearing at the moment?" he enquired.

"Just my dressing gown. Why? I was just going to put the kettle on for a cup of tea."

"Take your dressing gown off."

"What?"

"Take it off."

Puzzled, Chelsea stood up and wriggled out of her dressing gown, letting it fall to the floor.

"Are you naked?"

"Yes."

"Good. I'm hoping to get away a bit early today and I want you to be waiting for me completely nude when I come home."

"You dirty dog! Don't you ever get enough?"

"There's just a few things I'd like you to put on. You'll find them in a cardboard box under the bed. Don't wear anything else. See you later. I love you."

He hung up.

Chelsea returned to the bedroom and peered under the huge bed. She pulled out a rectangular cardboard box and opened it. Inside were a studded black leather collar and cuffs with metal ring attachments and a black leather corset that looked more like a wide leather belt.

"You kinky devil…," she breathed, then smiled.

The collar and cuffs were exceedingly comfortable; they were adjustable and Chelsea fastened them so as to be tight against her skin. The corset was slightly more difficult, it would have been easier if Enda had been there to fasten it for her, but she managed to get it on eventually. It had the pleasing effect of pushing her bare breasts out invitingly while simultaneously helping her sex and buttocks swell out prominently.

She stood for half an hour in front of the full length mirror in the bathroom appraising her new look. Arms akimbo, turning first this way, then that, she tossed her honey blonde hair back behind her head, unable to help admiring the transforming effect that the shiny black leather accessories had created.

Outside, it was a swelteringly hot day, one of the finest of the summer so far, and Chelsea longed to go out into the back garden and sunbathe, as she loved to do when the opportunity arose. However, the garden was clearly visible from neighbouring houses and while she positively relished flaunting herself in her skimpiest bikinis on such occasions, her current attire obviously ruled out the prospect of her getting out and soaking up the sun.

She had a light breakfast of cereal, toast and orange juice and curled up on the sofa with a cup of tea, listening to an album of medieval music she had taken a fancy to. When she closed her eyes it was almost as if she could see the vaultings of a tall Gothic cathedral towering above her into the great beyond, and she felt a sense of awe. She felt also a certain exhilaration and jubilation at the vicarious nature of her own nudity. It felt oddly empowering to stroll naked about the house, knowing that Enda would be delighted to find her thus and bound by her promise to him as securely as if she had been chained to one of the living room walls.

She decided that she would clean the house while she was waiting. Enda sometimes got a cleaner in to do it, a woman who did the neighbouring houses as well, but he hadn't bothered since Chelsea had come to stay.

She spent the next three hours busily doing the chores she normally hated; dusting, cleaning, vacuuming, polishing surfaces, washing down walls, scouring the bath. The energetic activity absorbed her so much that she had not been conscious of time passing. It was three o'clock exactly according to the nearest clock, a small carriage clock in the corner of a worktop, when the sound of the front door being opened alerted her to Enda's return. Chelsea was on her knees at the time, vigorously scrubbing the kitchen floor. Dismayed, she caught sight of herself in the hall mirror as she rushed to the door. Her hair was tousled and greasy, her naked body streaked with sweat and household grime. Still, it was much too late for a shower or bath now. Enda was carrying a couple of large shopping bags and grinning broadly.

"You're looking lovely," he told her. "I knew you would."

"I feel very scruffy," Chelsea confessed. "I've been doing a lot of housework and I simply haven't had time to have a shower yet. I feel so dirty."

"Well, let's make sure you're really dirty before you get in the shower then. Close your eyes."

Chelsea obeyed and felt something soft being tied around her eyes.

"It's a silk scarf," Enda told her. "I've been buying you some new clothes. But you'll not need them for a while yet. Let's see if we can't get that waspie a little tighter on you. Breathe in as deeply as you can and hold it."

Chelsea did as she was asked, then gasped as Enda wrenched the corset even tighter and fastened it.

"That is so tight - " she began, but Enda put a finger to her lips.

"Shush, darling. Give me your hands."

He folded her arms gently behind her back, snapping the leather cuffs together with a padlock through the metal ring attachments. He took her in his arms and she immediately kissed him so enthusiastically and so passionately that she straightaway felt his erection straining at his trousers, pressing against her.

He took his time, fondling her naked body thoroughly, his mouth roving at will over her breasts. He fingered her slowly, moving in and out of her until she was panting and moaning. She moaned again when he pressed his now exposed member against her, quickly pushing himself in as far as he could go. He now went more roughly, thrusting inside her full force as he pinned her up against the wall, holding her bare buttocks tightly in his hands. He then raked his nails down her naked shoulders and back as he drove himself into her hard and then held her locked tightly until he shot his gift with one thrust, then another, then more. Chelsea was moving in rhythm, savouring it all, letting her own body simultaneously shoot with a wild finish. All in all, he had taken just over half an hour, using her at will.

Enda undid the blindfold and freed her hands. He kissed her gently.

"You look like the cat who just got the cream," he commented wryly.

She giggled.

"That's one way of putting it. I'll enjoy my shower now. What is it you've bought for me?"

"I'll show you in a little while. We're going out later so you can wear it then. We're meeting some people in that new Asian restaurant in Upper Street we passed the other day. Shaun and a man called Toby Venables, a business associate. And a couple of girls, Heavenly and Paula. Paula's from Northern Ireland. Donaghadee. You'll like her. I've a taxi ordered for us for seven o'clock."

Round about six, Enda asked Chelsea to strip and close her eyes. When he told her to open them again, he had her presents in his hands. He bade her stand still, naked, while he slipped on the black leather quarter cup bra that latched at the front and left her nipples prominent and free.

"That's the underwear taken care of," he told her. "I don't want you to wear any panties tonight."

He watched intently as she put on the suspender belt and black seamed stockings, then the see-through black lace blouse that felt so light that it was like wearing nothing at all. The rest of the outfit consisted of a black business suit, an immaculately tailored jacket which fitted her perfectly and a very short skirt, and an expensive looking pair of shining black slingback shoes with stiletto heels.

"What do you think?" Enda asked.

"It's good… I've never worn such high heels before."

"You'll soon get the hang of them. You'll not be walking much tonight, anyway."

"What about the blouse? I can't go out wearing this, can I?"

"Of course you can. This is London. You can do anything you want here, things you wouldn't dare do at home. You can be whoever you want to be. Anyhow, you'll have the jacket over it."

When they arrived at the restaurant, Chelsea felt a sense of arousal as Enda held the taxi door open for her. She was conscious of the driver's fascinated stare as she pulled her skirt down before taking Enda's hand.

From the outside the restaurant resembled one of the sleek architects' offices further down the street. A wall of black –framed glass panels led into a surprisingly spacious restaurant, stretching back to an attractively lit, white –walled garden of elegant bamboos. Swathes of wall were painted a strong golden yellow, the floors were tiled in antique terracotta which along with the pervasive wood panelling added a warmth and natural colour to the surroundings. The tables were bare apart from lime green paper mats which doubled as menus and the occasional packet of chopsticks. The basic bench seating emphasised the minimalist ambiance.

At a table at the rear of the restaurant, where tantalising odours of soy, sesame and chilli wafted from an open kitchen, sat Shaun Simpson and his three companions whom Enda introduced as Toby, Heavenly and Paula. Toby was in his forties, a man of medium height and build with thick hair greying at the temples and a kindly, friendly manner. Heavenly, who stood up to greet them in a loud American accent, was well over six feet tall even in flat sandals. She had long blonde hair, brilliant blue eyes, lips even more prominent than Chelsea's and the widest smile Chelsea had ever seen, revealing dazzlingly white teeth. She wore a light pink camisole and tight blue jeans which complemented her stunning figure. Her magnificent bosom, small waist, shapely hips and long legs gave her the appearance of some Amazon-like supermodel.

Paula was about Chelsea's height with regular, pretty features, sparkling brown eyes and dark hair expensively cut and carefully arranged. She wore a low cut strappy back red dress which stopped short barely halfway down her thighs, a visual effect enhanced by her bright red lipstick and a striking pair of silver earrings, large and crescent shaped and encrusted with a myriad of tiny ruby-like stones.

"I'm glad to hear another Irish accent here tonight," she told Chelsea cheerily. "We're making Toby feel like a foreigner in his own country. It serves him right."

Enda insisted that Chelsea should take off her jacket.

"It's far too hot to wear that," he said smiling.

He brushed her nipples lightly with his knuckles as he helped her off with it and she flushed a bright crimson when they stiffened in response. For a moment Chelsea felt her composure going and she made a strenuous effort to keep her eyes downcast and her hands by her side. Enda noticed her initial discomfort and squeezed one of her hands tightly under the table. Her embarrassment quickly faded as everyone complimented her on her appearance. Toby Venables appeared particularly appreciative.

"Enda told us he was going out with a gorgeous Irish girl," he said admiringly. "He wasn't kidding. You're looking extremely beautiful tonight, Chelsea."

As they fell to studying the menus, he suggested that they steer clear of the wine list.

"Stick to lager, or one of these pulped juice drinks they do," he advised. "It's tricky getting wine to go with anything spicy at the best of times and a lot of the best dishes here are curries."

"I don't fancy a curry. I had one last night," Heavenly said. "I think I'll start with the Malaysian green beans with blackened baby corn tossed in sesame oil – sounds good to me."

"Anyone fancy sharing some dishes?" Paula asked.

Eventually they settled on shared plates of crispy fried squid, vegetable tempura and the tender rare beef called bulgoggi with a pickled radish. Shaun Simpson alone insisted on a warm chicken salad with a lime and coriander dressing and drank only a mild green tea whilst the rest of the company sipped glasses of lager.

As the restaurant gradually filled up, Chelsea looked around in wonderment at the diversity of people around her, the cosmopolitan mix of the young, the middle-aged and the old, blacks, Chinese, Italians, Scandanavians. And even in her own corner Northern Irish, southern Irish, cockney and American accents reverberated effortlessly around the table. She couldn't quite categorise Shaun Simpson's accent; it seemed a curious hybrid of Belfast, London and America. Enda told her that Shaun had learned to play tennis years ago in Florida, as a youngster on a sports scholarship. It seemed to Chelsea that there was an unspoken hierarchy amongst the three men, with Enda and Toby being almost reverential in their respect for Shaun's opinions. That evening he spoke only fleetingly to the three women, even then regaling them with tales about a young Russian tennis player called Khusainov of whom Chelsea had never heard.

"Keep him in mind. There'll be good odds and plenty of serious money to be made in some of the tournaments this year," Shaun was saying. "Getting to the semis in the French Open last year was a great achievement. But that win in the Australian Open…that took me back. That's the way to handle a big serve and volley merchant like Pountney. Get ten feet behind the baseline to get focused on the serves coming at you, then clip the ball past the bastard when you know he's moving to the net. Wear him down when you have to."

"You make it sound easy, Shaun," said Heavenly, stifling a yawn. "Is this guy going to be as good as you were, huh?"

"He's already better than I ever was. That sort of game puts your body under enormous strain to compete. I only kept playing as long as I did because I was very fit and was lucky not to get too many injuries. But that Australian Open final was awesome. Did you see it? Did you see the way Khusainov was standing right up near the service line at the end, picking up serves of a hundred and thirty five miles an hour practically on the half-volley? I've never seen Pountney outplayed like that. He tried to blast the ball through the kid and ended up chasing passing shots and lobs all day."

Chelsea found Heavenly and Paula more stimulating company. Heavenly talked and talked, smiling incessantly and breaking into howls of gurgling laughter when anything funny was said. She told Chelsea that she had been born on Christmas day and her mother was going to call her Noelle, but it happened to be a beautiful bright sunny morning after a spell of horrible weather that had lasted for weeks.

"It's a heavenly day," her father had said to her mother, and her mother had decided upon that instant to christen her Heavenly instead. Her father was a preacher, an evangelical minister who had once had his own television slot on Sunday mornings. Her mother was a teacher at the local high school.

"I don't know where they went wrong with me, honey," Heavenly told Chelsea. "I guess I was always a bit wild. I got married when I was seventeen, to Jerry. Jerry was a jazz musician, my parents didn't like him because he was black and anyhow, I was only seventeen. I ran away. It didn't work out and I got married again a few years later to Roy, he was a lawyer. That didn't work out either. I came to London eight years ago and I've never looked back, I just love it here."

"So do I," Chelsea agreed. "It's early days now but if I'm still with Enda in a year's time I'd think about coming to live here myself. I'm hoping for a career in social work but I want to finish at university first."

Heavenly smiled broadly.

"Very smart of you, honey," she said. "You do that. Always have something to fall back on. What I do is a kind of social work, I guess."

"What do you do?"

"That's enough about work!" Paula interjected quickly. "We're out to play tonight. Anyhow, we work for Toby and he's here so we better not wind him up."

"Don't worry about me, darling," Toby said affably. "Anyone fancy another lager? I'm going to have one."

"Yeah. Get us all another, honey," said Heavenly. "These summer nights make a girl thirsty."

Chelsea found herself warming greatly to both the other women as the evening wore on, as they chatted together in one little group and the men engaged in some serious discussion in another. She particularly enjoyed Paula's quickfire wit and earthy manner and at the end of the night they agreed to meet up again as soon as possible.

"We'll have some great crack," Paula told her. "It's brilliant meeting someone from home. It means I don't have to talk dead slow, like I'm talking to an idiot."

"Though half the time that's what you are doing in this town, honey," Heavenly added.

As she got up to leave, Chelsea affected not to notice the

glances she was attracting from the various men around the tables in the restaurant. She held her head high and tossed her hair confidently as Enda held her jacket for her, then buttoned it and brushed a speck of dust from the top of a lapel.

Outside, taxis were waiting and they said their farewells. Enda and Chelsea got into the first taxi. When they got back to Sotheby Road there was a message on Enda's answerphone. It was from Chelsea's mother, asking her to ring her.

"It's late for her to be ringing me," Chelsea said worriedly. "It must be something important. I'd better ring her back."

Enda went to the kitchen to make coffee while Chelsea rang home. When he returned he found her sitting down, her face in her hands.

"What's the matter?"

"It's my aunt Sharon. She's dead. It was a heart attack. Totally unexpected. She was only in her early fifties."

"I'm sorry. I suppose you'll have to get back for the funeral…?"

"If I can. I'd like to. She was always very good to me when I was a child. My uncle Fred is taking it very badly, apparently. It's a hell of a shock."

Enda sat down and put a consoling arm around Chelsea as a few tears trickled down her cheeks.

"Leave it to me," he said gently. "I'll get you a flight. No point in going online trying for it now; it'll be okay tomorrow. We have an arrangement with that travel agent next door to The Blarney Stone, they look after us really well if we need to go anywhere in a hurry."

"It's such a shame," Chelsea said wistfully. "I've been enjoying myself so much here."

"You can always come back over," said Enda. "Anytime at all."

"I really like your friends. Shaun's a bit strange, though. He goes on a bit about tennis, doesn't he?"

"Shaun's all right. Tennis was his job, that's why he's so interested in it. There's another reason, though. He runs a spread betting syndicate that invests a lot in sports events. He makes the forecasts for tennis tournaments and he's very good at getting them right. He's a very driven man, that's all. He's fabulously rich but he's always looking for more."

"Paula and Heavenly were great fun. What do they do? Are they social workers?"

Enda threw back his head and laughed loudly.

"In a manner of speaking," he said at last. "They're call girls. High class call girls. They don't minister to the poor, just the extremely wealthy."

Chelsea sat bolt upright, shocked.

"You're joking!"

"I'm not."

"But they seemed so nice - "

"They are nice. You couldn't meet nicer women anywhere. Especially Paula, I've known her since she first came to London. She was originally only going into it for a year, to get her own house and car - "

"What? After a year?"

"Sure. Do you know the sort of money these girls get paid?"

He whispered in her ear. She looked at him, stupefied.

"You're not serious!"

"I am. That's for an hour, by the way, not for a night. Anyway, Paula's totally comfortable with it now and she enjoys it too much to quit. Her current boyfriend's a doctor and she's a bit dubious about telling him yet, so she's effectively part-time at the moment. He's working tonight so she's going to meet someone later at a casino. A regular. 'Belle de Jour' she gets called now, after the woman in that film – did you ever see it? Toby's idea of a bit of banter. But he's very relaxed about it all."

"What's Toby got to do with it?"

"He runs the agency. Shaun's a sleeping partner but Toby does all the work. He looks after the client base and won't take anyone remotely dodgy. He makes a point of meeting them all first, before the girls do, and looks after the finance. Even then the girls get to choose their own clients."

Chelsea shook her head.

“I don’t believe this. Toby was so nice as well.”

“Toby’s as decent a guy as you’ll ever meet. He only ever takes the best for the agency, mind you. But he looks after them superbly. He won’t have any junkies or alcos, or anyone like that on the books. You need character as well as beauty to get a look in.”

“I’m having trouble getting my head round this,” Chelsea said slowly. “I’m.... well, I’m flabbergasted, to tell you the truth. How could someone like Paula..?”

“She thought about it for a while first. There was no pressure on her; she had a job as a sales assistant in the Marble Arch branch of The Blarney Stone. It didn’t pay very well, though. She got to know Heavenly and some of the other girls through me and was very friendly with them well in advance of her deciding to ask Toby if he’d consider her.”

Enda finished his coffee and put down his cup.

“I used to go out with Paula, you know. For almost a year. I introduced her to Toby. She always had this fantasy about being a call girl. I told her what I told you earlier. This is London. You can be whoever or whatever you want to be. It’s not like at home. You can take your favourite fantasies here and actually act them out.”

“How did you feel about what she did?” Chelsea demanded.

“Great,” Enda grinned wolfishly. “Just great. I found it very exciting. She learned so many ways to please a man. But you know a bit about my fantasies. And I know a bit about yours.”

Chelsea nodded. She knew it was true. She had confessed to Enda on her first night with him that she had always had an exhibitionistic streak and thoroughly enjoyed the thrill of exposing herself intimately in front of a new lover.

He had responded to that in several imaginative ways, encouraging her to go topless that morning in Portrush, urging her to sunbathe in the back garden at Sotheby Road in a tiny bikini whenever possible, having her wait naked in the house for his return, finally that evening taking her out in public to a crowded restaurant dressed so provocatively that he knew she would be stared at with curiosity, desire and envy by other men all night.

He had correctly reckoned on her acquiescence in all of

those things. She stood up and kicked off her high heeled shoes.

“It’s going to be a long day tomorrow,” she said. “Let’s get some sleep.”

Enda smiled and took her by the hand. He turned off all the lights one by one and led her, mute and compliant, through the softly creaking bedroom door and quietly into the darkness beyond.

Chapter 8

Cast Your Fate To The Wind
(An observation by Adam Conway)

"WOULD YOU LOOK at the state of that?" said Tom Bellingham disgustedly.

The girl he had been staring at was about eighteen, with long unkempt hair, heavy make-up, a large ring through her nose and studiously tattered clothing. She brushed contemptuously past Tom at the bar.

"She's not bad looking, Tom," I said. "She'd clean up nicely, I'd say."

"I'll tell you what – if I had a daughter who turned out like that, I'd let her have a damned good belting before I'd let her out of the house looking like that," he growled.

He was a drab looking man in his forties, always conservatively dressed. He had a heavily boned face with a square jaw, a long straight nose, fierce eyes and a perpetually cantankerous expression. His short brown hair, parted neatly at one side, somehow always contrived to look like a wig. He seldom laughed and when he did it was invariably at things that weren't funny, in the rhetorical way of people who neither want nor expect others to laugh with them.

"Same again, Pat. And a pint of Smithwicks for Adam," he called to Pat Farland, finishing off his glass of stout as he did so. "I'll tell you another thing - this pub's gone to the dogs. Full of brats day and night. They think they can intimidate the regulars out. Well, they'll not shift me."

Pat came back with Tom's usual order, a bottle of Guinness and a Powers whiskey, and a pint of beer for me. He drummed his fingers impatiently on the counter as Tom, frowning, meticulously counted out his money from a purse until he had produced exactly the right change.

"Aye. Brats. I hate them," he continued, sipping the whiskey and warming to his theme. "The lot of them. I'd put them all in boot camps. Teach them manners. Anyhow – what do you make of that woodentop Stanley making the promotion list?"

"He's a clever lad, Tom," I replied with a shrug. "You have to admit, he's very well qualified."

"Qualified?"

He laughed mirthlessly, his face contorted as if in pain.

"You think I'm not, after twenty-five years in the Civil Service? That wee bastard's not much older than you and now he's going to be my boss. You're bloody lucky you're getting out. The whole system is rotten to the core when a pup like that gets promoted ahead of people like me. The wee gobshite's never done a proper day's work in his life. He's barely out of nappies, for Christ's sake. I'll tell you what. Your man King Herod out of the Bible had the right idea. Cull the bastards. He might have had his faults but he was sound enough when it came to social policy."

He looked around morosely, visibly cheering up only when he saw some of the regulars pottering about. I knew the clientele well enough to recognise the patterns of attendance. The early evening, just after work when people tended to drop in for one or two drinks, attracted a diverse mix of customers; contemporary youth mingled uneasily with old-time regulars who remembered the spit and sawdust days, before the bar was grudgingly and not very convincingly modernised.

Numbered amongst the latter were some of the most outlandish drunks, grotesques, pub bores and misfits the body of the city had ever thrown up, people who in other countries wouldn't have been allowed into a bar never mind served drink in one. Tom was never more comfortable than when in their company.

"It's the characters that come in here at this time of night," he would often say smugly, "that make Slattery's the best pub in Belfast."

Looking around him that evening, he looked almost happy.

"They're all in tonight," he crooned, sipping his stout. "Old Nob…Lily… Parky…Terry and Cheesy…Intergalactic Bob. By Jesus, it's the Lone Ranger! Old Thom O'Loan himself. He hasn't been in for a while."

A small, slightly tubby man grinned shyly at the bar, showing dirty uneven teeth. He wore a cheap cowboy outfit which included a studded holster with cap guns, an ill-fitting white stetson and old-fashioned boots with plastic spurs attached. A black cardboard mask, like something you'd get in a lucky bag, sat perched on his turned-up nose, held over his startled eyes by elastic bands secured behind his ears. Tom nudged me.

"Wait till you hear this," he sniggered conspiratorially. "Hey - masked man! Lone! Where's um injun tonight?"

"If you mean Tonto, Mr Bellingham, he's camped several miles up the road," the man replied calmly. "Shot of redeye, please, bartender."

Pat Farland resignedly poured a bottle of tomato juice. The man knocked it back quickly and turned to go.

"Wait a minute, Lone," Tom urged him. "What's the hurry? My friend here doesn't know who you are. Who is that masked man, he said to me."

The man grinned shyly again, then pulled something slowly from his pocket, displaying it in an outstretched grubby palm. It was a plastic silver bullet.

"Perhaps this will help answer your question, sir," he said, almost apologetically.

Tom went into noiseless hysterics. I didn't think it was funny. I just nodded at the man and he smiled back and turned to go again.

"Don't go yet, Lone," pleaded Tom. "Stay and have a drink

with us. I'll buy you another shot of redeye!"

"No, thank you, Mr Bellingham," he responded solemnly in a crisp, minty voice. "I've got to go now. Anyway – meeting a new friend is all the reward I need."

We followed him out to the door where a little crowd had gathered to watch him mount an ancient battered motor cycle and shout something that might have been "Heigh ho, Silver, h-away!" before chugging off slowly into the distance.

"Characters!" Tom was chortling. "This place is coming down with them!"

It was coming down with something, I thought. Parky, so-called because he had Parkinson's disease, sat shaking uncontrollably in a corner, sipping lager sporadically from a straw because he couldn't hold the glass. Old Nob, a smelly, half-demented old alcoholic with thin wispy hair, unusually bright eyes and a constant toothless grin, tottered amongst groups of irritated customers, accusing some of them of being Fenians in a high pitched, squeaky Ballymena accent. Lily, a wrinkled old woman who habitually wore a pink coat, was regaling Terry Parcury and Cheesy Ring, a couple of tedious barflies who were seldom out of the place, about the price of rum. She drank a particularly foul brand that no other bars would stock and that no-one else there ever touched. Intergalactic Bob, a bald man with a beard and a totally blank expression, was gibbering something unintelligible to one of the long suffering bar staff. The bar began to buzz with conversation, the atmosphere enlivened by the steady influx of office workers against the backdrop of the usual early evening shift, lowlifes, no-hopers and hate-the-worlds for the most part, shambling through the pub doors to take up their accustomed positions.

"I'm going to have a pint with Old Nob," Tom said grandly. "He knows what's what. Give me a shout when your cousin comes in."

I stood silently at a pillar, drinking my beer, watching Tom up at the bar as he produced his pipe and half-closing his eyes, jaw jutting forward, nodded sagely at whatever inanities Old Nob was spouting, for all the world as though some nuggets of unspeakably profound wisdom were being dispensed. It was then that my cousin Enda walked in. As always, he saw me before I saw him.

"Get that into you, Adam," the soft Dublin voice behind me said. "We're not staying. I've a little treat arranged for you and believe me, you don't want to drink too much."

He was a tall, handsome man, in his mid-twenties and still possessed of remarkably boyish good looks. He had a gentle voice and a charming smile that concealed a darker side to his nature. I encountered it first as a child when he came to stay with us; he was always getting into trouble of some sort but he just didn't care. He enjoyed it. He had his uses, though. He loved fighting and was extraordinarily good at it, taking the opportunity whenever it arose to thrash some of the most feared bullies in our housing estate. I revelled in the power of being able to use him as a deterrent. He was an outstanding footballer as well and several top English clubs tried to sign him as a schoolboy. He ended up going to Arsenal but it hadn't worked out for him and he had drifted from job to job since, the latest as a manager of a sports goods shop back in London.

"Is this the lad, then?" Tom Bellingham said loudly. "Enda, is it? I've heard a lot about you, son. I believe you used to play for the Gunners."

"Only the youth team. And a few games for the reserves," Enda said modestly.

"Fenian...you're a Fen-i-an!" babbled Old Nob, grinning and tugging at his jacket sleeve.

"Piss off," said Enda mildly. "Yes- I've been finished with football for a good while now, though. I never fancied dropping down into the lower divisions. I only play for fun these days. You can enjoy it that way."

"Off the field activities wear you out, did they?"said Tom with a wink. "That's what I heard, anyway."

"No. I just wasn't good enough," said Enda. "Clubs don't care much what you do off the field as long as you don't embarrass the club. I was never going to be good enough for that level. They told me so but I knew it anyway, so I got out. It wasn't the end of the world."

"You're a Fenian, Fenian, Fenian," crowed Nob, poking him now, still grinning away.

"I thought I told you to piss off."

Enda had this trick of never raising his voice, no matter what sort of mood he was in. He grabbed the old man by the scruff of the neck and hauled him to the door of the pub. There was a moment's silence, then a loud, clanging, clattering noise. Enda sauntered back in.

"I threw the old cunt in amongst those empty beer barrels round the side," he said cheerfully, rubbing his hands. "That'll quieten him down for you for a while. Are you finished that pint yet, Adam? Good, let's go. I told you I'd got a treat for you. You never set me up with a girl when I come to see you in Belfast, so I've set one up for you tonight."

"Fuck off! I'm not going out on a blind date with some dog I don't even know just so you can shag the good looking one."

"You're certainly not. O ye of little faith…."

"Well , then – what's the crack?"

"The crack is, just come with me and ask no questions. It has to be a surprise. Trust me."

"All right, I will. Surprise me."

"Good man. Let's hit the road."

I bade Tom goodnight and told him I'd drop into the pub to see him sometime next week before I left for Australia but he was shocked into silence, his brow furrowed with outrage and his mouth transfixed in the shape of an involuntary 'O' at the sacrilege of one his revered characters being treated in so cavalier a fashion.

Enda told me we were going to the Stranmillis Road. It was a short walk from the pub and a pleasant one. It was a mellow summer evening. We passed the magnificent Ashby Institute, the huge white university building where engineering was taught, towering benignly above the row of spotlessly clean shop fronts of Stranmillis village, the lower part of the area which some of the residents liked to refer to as the Chelsea of Belfast. Several couples strolled hand in hand down the sloping side streets in the direction of Botanic Gardens.

"This street," said Enda. "Just down here, round the corner

from the off licence."

I was glad we had arrived. It had been a strange conversation on the way up the road. Enda had talked a lot about Australia, where he'd spent a season on loan from Arsenal to a club in Melbourne once. He said I was lucky to be going there and I believed him. He was always more of a wanderer than me.

"I feel it's something I have to do," I told him. "I've tried the Civil Service and I don't much like it. I don't want to end up like Tom Bellingham. I need to spread my wings while I'm still young enough to do it."

Enda nodded vigorously, saying I was dead right.

"Cast your fate to the wind," he said. "It's the only way to live."

Then he quickly changed the subject.

"Have you ever read *The Story Of O*, Adam?"

"No," I said hesitantly. "I don't think I have."

"You haven't then," he responded quickly. "You'd remember it if you had. It's a brilliant book, Adam, a very sexy book – read it if you ever get the chance. It's about a girl, you see – her lover has her tied up and whipped, and used by lots of other men, and the thing is, well – she loves it, you see. She loves all of it, all of that sort of thing. Can't get enough of it. It's hard to explain. Read it if you get the chance. But I'll tell you something."

We had come to the door. Enda rang the bell and we waited. The pupils of his eyes were dilated and he looked excited.

"I've tried every drug there is, Adam. You know I have. Some of them have been great. But there's some things that give you a better hit than any drug and are more addictive than any drug."

A pale dark haired girl in a white t-shirt and black jeans opened the door.

"Hi, Enda," she said, smiling briefly. "She's upstairs. She's expecting you. The door's open."

We went upstairs. There was a separate flat there and Enda asked me to wait in the living room, telling me he'd call me shortly. I looked around the nondescript surroundings; the place was neat enough but somewhat colourless. There were a lot of books on the shelves by the far wall, sociology and psychology textbooks for the most part, and a smallish television in the corner. I tried to read a copy of the previous day's *Belfast Telegraph* that was lying on the sofa but I couldn't concentrate. It was over half an hour later and I was halfway through the crossword when Enda re-appeared. His shirt was unbuttoned and hanging over his jeans and he was looking elated.

"Come on," he grinned. "The bedroom's this way."

He watched the shock on my face with undisguised glee. Lying naked on the double bed in the centre of the room lay a stunningly beautiful girl with shoulder length honey blonde hair, high cheekbones and regular features except for a larger than usual mouth, with pouting lips and perfect white teeth. She had a voluptuous body, gloriously curvaceous, with a small waist that emphasized the enticing swell of her hips and long legs that seemed to go on forever. Metal rings hung heavily from the pierced nipples of her superbly rounded breasts and her labia, lewdly on display as her legs were flung widely apart, were newly shaven. Here and there on the inside of her white thighs a pearly drop of semen glistened in the soft shafts of evening sunlight that invaded the room through the half-drawn Venetian blinds. Her wrists were handcuffed to the top bedposts on either side and she wore a red velvet blindfold.

Enda kissed her and caressed her breasts for some minutes before propping her up on two pillows and guiding her mouth to a glass of Evian mineral water he had poured from a bottle on the bedside table. The bottle was three quarters full. Beside it lay a box of tissues.

"I'm leaving for a little while now, darling," he whispered softly. His eyes were shining. "My friend's here now, like I said he would be. I'll see you later – okay?"

She had nodded confidently, smiling. She had sipped the last few drops of mineral water. Enda got up and grinned at me.

"She's all yours," he murmured to me on the way out the door. "Enjoy, as the Americans say. If you're fastidious about stirring my porridge – well, it's up to you, as I say, she's all yours – but she's got a beautiful mouth…"

I didn't let him back in for over an hour. It was the first time I'd seen Chelsea for about a year and I knew it would be at least another year before I saw her again, if I ever did see her again. I managed to get through the hour without once speaking to her or removing the handcuffs or blindfold.

I was consumed with a fire that night, something close to a supernatural energy. The initial shock and confusion I had felt had surrendered swiftly to temptation when Enda left the room, closing the door softly behind him. I was convinced that she would recognise my touch but if she did she betrayed no obvious sign of it. I tried to vary things I normally did in the hope that somehow I would become anonymous, a cipher, any man, a phantom lover who took his pleasure selfishly and then was gone. She seemed to enjoy it too much, more than I had ever been used to witnessing with her. When I was finally finished I got out quickly enough.

Enda was sitting in the living room sipping a can of lager. I spoke to him briefly on the way out.

"You can go back to her now," I said. "By the way, you're a bastard. Did I ever tell you that?"

He just laughed.

"Don't tell me you didn't enjoy that. You were in there long enough."

"Do I look like I'm smiling?"

"You don't look like you're fit to raise one."

I was in a sombre enough mood when I left. I decided to go down to the Students' Union as I knew Dommo or Jap or Stevie or some of the gang would be down there. We still frequented the place even though we had all graduated and were in employment of some sort. Like many another, university hadn't prepared us very well for anything except, maybe, a lifetime at university. Most of the faces in the Union bar had changed, though. Most of them were younger.

But the decision to go to Australia was born out of something other than the boredom of a poorly paid job and a social rut. I was comfortable enough with those things. But none of the women I'd gone out with recently had interested me much and vice versa. None of them had lasted long. I still hadn't got over Chelsea.

I'd had a coffee with Anne George, her best friend at Queen's, one afternoon a couple of months previously. I was off work and wandering around the shops in Belfast city centre when I bumped into her.

I liked Anne. I knew a lot of people who didn't – she was considered vain, spoilt and catty by some and I suppose she was all of those things to some extent, but in an innocent sort of way – but I had spent a lot of time in her company when I was with Chelsea and had become fond of her. She wasn't a bad looking girl then; she had long blonde hair, a nice enough face and she could certainly fill a blouse. She wasn't quite tall enough to carry off the big, busty look she aspired to as strikingly as she might have nor was she ever likely to be compared to Marilyn Monroe, whom she idolised and whose films she never tired of watching. But I thought she was sound.

She was in surprisingly good form considering that she had just split up with Malachy, a law student she had been going out with for as long as I knew her. I'd always thought she would marry him. His professional status when he qualified would have been a big attraction to her.

"These things just run their course, Adam," she said, blowing smoke rings into the air and sipping coffee alternately. "We're still friends. That's the best way to be."

She told me that Chelsea had become a bit of a stranger to her lately. She'd found it hurtful because she had been her best friend at school, right through to Queen's.

"She moved out of the halls after her second year," she added, referring to the halls of residence. "She's sharing a house in Stranmillis now with Belinda Smith. Do you know Belinda? She's doing the same degree as Chelsea. They're both looking for jobs in social work next year. Except Chelsea's looking for work in London."

She told me Chelsea had taken up with a man who was based there and had been travelling across to see him at every opportunity. She had been socialising very little in Belfast as a consequence and had been working hard for her final year exams whenever she was here.

"I've never seen this guy," Anne said, "but apparently he's older than her. Very good looking. He's from Dublin originally, I think."

My expression must have said it all because she quickly reached over the table and held my hand. The sunlight was streaming through the window of the cafe and her blue eyes, already glinting from the contact lenses she always wore, glittered even brighter.

"You're better off without her, Adam," she said gently. "Believe me – she's not for you. She's not for anyone around here. She's grown apart from all of us."

At heart I already knew that. I knew too that Australia was no solution for me. The whole idea was driven by anger and depression and frustration rather than any deep-seated ambition or wanderlust or anything like that on my part. By the time I got on the plane I realised that I no longer wanted to go.

My fears turned out to be well founded. Australia was a mistake, a nightmare, an unforced exile that brought it home to me once and for all that I was a homebird, happier in Belfast than I could ever be elsewhere. But once I'd landed on the other side of the world I couldn't very well click my heels three times and wish I was back. I'd cast my fate to the wind by then. And I didn't much like the way the wind was blowing.

PART THREE

Lone Star State Of Mind

Chapter 9

<u>*Blue Heaven*</u>

IT WAS ONLY when he began *not thinking* that he began to be happy. This was the basic criterion for admission to the Vice Versa Society, though clearly if one were to progress and go higher within it one had to learn higher techniques.

"What is your name?" asked Zelda, a beautiful woman with long black hair, warm brown eyes and an infectious smile.

"Thom," he said. "Thom O'Loan."

"How did you find us?" said Richard affably.

He was a tall bony youngster with a forelock of fair hair falling over a box-shaped forehead.

"Well, I wasn't thinking …."

"Of course you weren't."

Thom looked at the man who had spoken, tacitly admiring his strong enthusiastic veneer. Keith – for that was his name – shook Thom vigorously by the hand.

"That's one way of finding us. Of course you still think -" he made an expansive gesture - "… but you have pushed one sort of thinking away from your consciousness. The sort that clings to what cannot be changed … the 'if only' thoughts, the thoughts of what 'would have been'. The sort that hurt and torment. You have attained a state of mind beyond the past - " he shrivelled up and folded himself up like a telescope, compressing his neck into his torso – "beyond loneliness" – he glanced bird-like around in exaggerated paranoia – "and beyond the anxieties of the near future."

His face took on a comically concerned aspect.

"And so," he concluded briskly, relaxing, "you are here. You found us by manipulating your insights, your visions, your memories, your carefully structured fantasies, until you arrived here as though by accident. Correct?"

"Yes, I suppose –"

"But above all –" Keith raised his voice, instantly capturing the attention of the ten others crammed into the little sitting room "- you arrived here by *not thinking*. In this way you have become a full member of the Vice Versa Secret Society. You are now our twelfth," he concluded with genuine pleasure.

The ten beautiful people nodded blithe approval. Thom observed how everyone was like a barometer for Keith's words and feelings.

"May I ask a question or two?" inquired Thom. His calm tone suggested that he was interested and appreciative, without the slightest trace of fear, which was indeed the truth of the matter.

"Of course, of course," Keith answered, waving his hand then looking away and tapping his foot.

"Must you have twelve members? If so, how did you manage before I came?"

"Yes, we must. Before you came we had someone else. He has since dropped out." Keith's voice became sad. "It's unfortunate, but we're like any other team, we have to change our line-up from time to time. You may regard yourself as a substitute. Like Philip there. And Leonora." He motioned towards two beatific disciples.

"You are about to ask," he continued, marching slowly up and down the little room, "if all of us – like yourself – arrived here by *not thinking*."

Thom nodded.

"Not so, not so at all. Leonora, for instance, came here after a lifetime of looking after stray animals, and feeding birds in the early mornings. When the birds learned to eat out of her hand and she learned the language of the birds, we knew it was time to send for her before some other, some less subtle team did. We play a subtle game, we of Vice Versa. Finesse, that's what we pride ourselves on. All right, it doesn't always pay off, but it's a joy to the heart to play." He sighed. "Anyway, as for Philip, he woke one morning to discover a brass handle protruding from his bedroom wall. Directions were engraved upon it. 'Turn to the right if your allegiance is to the world; turn to the left if your aspirations reach beyond the stars themselves. Should you desire death, simply do not turn at all.' The poor fellow probably would have settled for the world, only he always had such trouble telling his left from his right."

Keith had been directing his gaze steadfastly at the ceiling but suddenly looked sharply at Thom.

"Now you are going to ask me why our previous members left?"

Thom nodded.

"The Sickness," said Keith simply. "You understand?"

Thom was about to reply that he did not, how could he, when into his opened mind flashed an instant awareness of what 'The Sickness' was. It was emotional plague, his thought patterns told him, sweeping the world. Bad atmosphere. Negative energy. Mysterious forces absorbing energy from the earth and from human beings, harming both. Mass neurosis. People who chose the hard way; unable to love, sheltering behind dirty jokes, tough talk and second-hand attitudes. So long used to hate instead of love that they thought hate was love, to the extent that they were prepared to defend it as such. Prepared to defend and protect The Sickness, to become channelled into cruelties and perversions and fears, to become part of the gigantic conspiracy against life, all because they were afraid to love. As abruptly as the thoughts had entered his mind, they left.

"We of the league", Richard said, resorting to verbal communication in a friendly way, "have one purpose: to combat The Sickness and the powers that spread it."

"There are better teams than us," added an angelic looking

girl called Sian. "At the top of the league there are teams composed entirely of Masters. Whereas we're struggling against relegation. To the next division."

"We have one undisputed Master and that's Keith", the woman called Zelda said. "That's why he is our leader."

"Our style is based on the modern Occidental approach", and Keith, promptly walking through a wall and back again as though to demonstrate. "Though we try to leave as much room for individual flair as possible. I look upon myself as a sort of player-coach."

Thom shook off his initial surprise. "How many divisions are there?" he asked.

"Seven", replied Keith. "Richard – the league tables, please."

Richard solemnly pressed a circular orange button on an armchair and two pieces of wallpaper unpeeled to reveal a large list of tabulated names with points totals and some unfamiliar symbols beside them. The names were strange to Thom. Even those in English, or semi-English, seemed distinctly odd. At the end of the list, third from bottom and in heavier type than the rest, lay Vice Versa.

"We're threatened with relegation to the next division," explained Keith, "and that carries penalties. One of the more obvious is a partial return to everyday reality."

"The lower you go," said a tall man called John, "the harder it is to get back. The next division is a right dogfight."

"I could always get a transfer to another Premiership side," said Keith. "But the rest of you …" He shrugged his shoulders.

"What now?" asked Thom.

Keith levitated himself, floated across the room and indicated a map hanging on the wall.

"This is our next assignment. If we can get the points here, it will see us through the present season. We have been instructed to cross Cullacandy Mountain."

An uneasy silence fell upon the group. Thom thought it appropriate to ask a question. "Why are you talking about seasons? Isn't time an illusion?"

They all stared at him as though he were an intruder.

"Of course it is", said Keith in wonderment. "I thought everybody knew that. Don't stare," he added to the beautiful people, "it's a sign of The Sickness to stare. Now.."

Just then the doorbell rang. A crystal ball sitting on a table in the middle of the room suddenly clouded over, then revealed the shapes of three men with sallow complexions, wearing dark business suits.

"Here already," Keith muttered. "I didn't think they'd be on to us so soon."

For the first time Thom felt scared, but was immediately reassured by the angelic Sian, whose kind green eyes communicated confidence and strength. She laid a small feminine hand upon his shoulder.

"Don't worry. Our leader will protect us," she said.

Thom noticed for the first time that everyone, except Keith, was wearing what must have been the official Vice Versa regalia: a long, pure white hooded robe with a single mystic symbol printed on the back. Keith alone wore a tent-like overblouse with zipped cuffs, fastened up the front with peyote buttons, with matching plus fours and boots. All his garments were coloured a unique shade of blue.

"Meltsonian blue," Sian whispered, holding Thom's hand and reading his thoughts.

Thom had never heard of such a thing but searched his mind for a memory of that beautiful shade. Where had he seen it before? He had seen it in many things, he thought, but he could label them only vaguely and unsatisfactorily. In the delicate little vase in his aunt's Chinese pottery collection, perhaps. Or was it in the beautiful eyes of his niece's recent baby, in the simple trusting eyes of a young child, that that unique colouring lay? He did not know.

He felt certain, however, that the universe itself was in some way tinged with meltsonian blue, that in some shape or substance or form it was all around them and part of them.

The doorbell rang again. Keith immediately raised his hands in an arc, then chanted something incomprehensible as a force like a whirlwind lifted them from their surroundings, the little house and the men in dark suits dissolving into tiny distant specks. Momentarily weightless and suspended in space and time, Thom felt no fear. Rather, he found it an agreeable experience, as though he were suddenly gifted with the ability to fly while others were fated always to walk.

They found themselves at the edge of a wood in a gloriously pastoral setting. Keith pointed straight ahead.

"Look at the heart of that tree," he said.

They all looked and, sure enough, Thom felt that he could discern something in the shape of a heart at the centre of the tree with little luminous thread-like lines emanating from it, carrying the life-sap to and from the softly pumping heart. They admired the spectacle with a reverence that did not notice the passing of time.

Suddenly, from within the wood, there appeared a shimmering figure of shining gold, a golden boy. His radiance was such that some of them could not look at him but Thom was transfixed by his beauty as he felt his senses heighten almost unbearably. The apparition spoke to Keith, mouthing its words silently, then slowly disappeared, merging with the fading sunlight. John asked Keith what message had been given.

Keith, his own eyes shining with a divine light, replied, laughing, "On, on, on, on! That is the message. On, on, on, on, to the breach, to the breach!"

For three days and three nights they journeyed through the wood sustaining themselves only on fruit, berries and water. Simple fare indeed but such was the communal spirit, such was the immense personal power of their leader that everything they touched, everything they saw, or ate, or drank, seemed imbued with a magical, restorative quality.

On the fourth day they came to a vast glittering lake, so massive that it looked more like an ocean.

"Show us the way, Master. Guide us," appealed Grainne and Griselda, the identical twins, speaking together like the chorus in some ritual. In an around the lake there was no sign of life and the silence was absolute.

"I have a message," stated Keith.

"What is that message?" chimed the twins.

"The message is –" Keith paused, then laughed fearlessly at the vast expanse of water – "the message is – farther on and farther in!"

He plunged into the water. Hesitantly, the rest of them followed, struggling all the while to keep up with the powerful strokes of their leader. They came to an island where Keith beckoned them to sit. Resting on the dry land, several of them pointed to a tiny cigar-shaped object high in the sky.

"I know," said Keith quietly. "They've been around for some time. You can feel it. Didn't you notice how sparse the grass was at the end of the wood? They're feeding on all the good energy in the atmosphere."

Some distance away a periscope jutted out of the water with a terrifying slowness, stopping several feet above the surface. A harsh voice barked.

"Your attention, please. Stay exactly where you are."

The hooded figures stood silent on the island.

Keith motioned his followers to be still and pointed to a muddy pool of water at his feet. They looked into it and watched as it changed, as if inveigled with the powers of a crystal ball, to depict the progress of the underwater craft. They realised that the confrontation had had nothing to do with chance; they had been followed. The phantasmagoria in the pool conveyed fleeting impressions of past and present. The craft bore no resemblance to a conventional submarine but looked more like a huge, grossly mis-shapen trapezium. Inside was a vast engine room with impassive men dressed in black operating heavy machinery.

Keith raised a hand to freeze the picture in the pool.

"I know who you are and what you represent," he called out angrily. "You are not going to arrest anybody! There is no need for you to know my name. But let me tell you that I am a cosmic soldier, and that I command the Vice Versa battalion of the League of the Temple of the Stars!"

Keith suddenly arched his body and made a force field with his hands. It seemed as though he were encased in a wobbling aura of meltsonian blue. The periscope in the water emitted an intimidating whine and Keith shouted a series of instructions to each of his followers in turn.

Thom watched as Richard crouched some five yards to his right in a grotesque parody of an Oriental martial arts fighting position, his usually amiable face and benign forehead, with the lock of fair hair hanging over it, contorted in an agonised grimace. Thom moved to the left, motivated by some intuitive force, and stood in tense imitation of the grim-faced team, which was splayed out in a star-shaped formation. All were holding themselves in a stiff, alert stance, right arm outstretched, left arm on left knee, right foot beating frantically on the ground.

"You're warriors!" yelled Keith. "You're Samurai warriors!"

Immediately it seemed to Thom that the team had changed into huge, hulking figures of tremendous bulk; then Keith screamed: "You're Mongols! All of you, you're Mongols! You're the Mongol hordes under Ghengis Khan!" and the Vice Versa ensemble mutated into beings with slanted eyes and savage bloodthirsty expressions as the sonic attack from the periscope withered from a sustained deafening screech into a distant buzz.

Keith's body had taken on the appearance of a transparent, luminous shell of multitudinous little ropes and fibres of meltsonian blue, although his head remained intact. He led the warriors in a loud rhythmic chant, escalating in volume until he raised a glowing palm and, in the space of a second, the periscope in the water cracked and disintegrated. In the still reflection of Keith's impromptu crystal ball, Thom saw the weighty machinery within sway and tumble.

Something, a stone or some other small object, splashed in the water and the picture vanished. Thom looked up and saw Keith's head floating off into the sky like a fireball, shouting as it went, "Farther on and farther in! I will be with you at Cullacandy Mountain!"

Obediently they continued onwards, the battle for the moment halted, across land and through water, for what may have been months or may have been years. Despite occasional guidance from Keith's disembodied voice, Thom now felt himself somehow crucial to the expedition. This feeling intensified when he detected an impostor impersonating Keith, who had not been seen since the battle on the island. It happened on a deserted wasteland, when a man looking like Keith approached them in the night. Edward was the first to see him.

"Keith!" he called out as he ran towards the figure in meltsonian blue, arms outstretched in welcome.

"Stop!" shouted Thom "That isn't Keith!"

The others also instinctively knew this, but only once Thom had pointed it out. Before they could rush to Edward's assistance he had been hauled off, screaming, by three men in dark suits and taken away in a black limousine which had been hidden behind some trees.

"What happens now?" Thom asked anxiously.

"He goes back to his job as a railway signalman," said Richard sadly. "It's a tragedy. Keith had such high hopes of Edward. He always thought he'd go far."

"But we're down to ten now –"

"Not really. Keith is still permitted to guide us, though he'll be doing it more and more infrequently now. Until we get to Cullacandy Mountain. If we ever do get there."

"Of course we'll get there!" Thom asserted vehemently; then gasped in astonishment at the unquestioning agreement which his stout rejoinder had occasioned.

"It seems to me," Sian said to him, "that you must now assume command."

And so it was. Without knowing where Cullacandy Mountain was, or what crossing it was supposed to accomplish, Thom led the band of wanderers through unknown hidden ways and secret places, constantly startled and dismayed by the blind faith his comparisons had placed in him. All the time he was obsessed by doubt, by the feeling that he was somehow courting something unpleasant. Yet whenever these thoughts threatened to overwhelm him, Keith would appear to him alone in the form of an apparition, the very existence of which he would begin to doubt the instant it disappeared, exhorting him ever onwards.

Often now there was disorder in the ranks, but always it

would be quelled, uneasily, before it could amount to anything.

"It's The Sickness," Sian said to Thom after a particularly bitter row between John and Zelda on a jungle trail. Even in the sweltering heat Sian's face was pale.

"We almost lost another two just then," she said.

"How can you tell?" Thom wanted to know.

Sian bit her lip and would not answer.

Another time, in a lonely valley, Thom inquired about his predecessor.

"Oh, you mean Alexander," said Richard. "Keith had very high hopes of Alexander once."

"What sort of a man was he?" asked Thom.

"He was a man. Like you or me." Richard seemed puzzled by the question.

"He was a very nice boy," Vanessa said wistfully. "Quiet, always cheerful, very popular with all of us. There was never any discord when he was here. We all miss him."

"Very much," concurred Leonora.

"Now that's enough of that," warned Richard. "Let's not forget that he ended up getting a free transfer. Not such a prestigious thing, when all's said and done. Not in this game."

"How did he join you?" said Thom.

"He came from a hospital. They thought it was secure. It wasn't."

These conversations were scarce, for generally they did not speak. Thom was anxiously aware of the contrast between the social unease of the present compared with the unselfconscious camaraderie of the past. Tirelessly and unfalteringly they journeyed on, however, until one grey and sunless evening they came to a rocky, mountainous country, dotted with high plateaux.

Keith, smiling, stepped out from behind a boulder.

"Hello," he said. "We're here."

This time all the members knew that their leader had returned. They flocked like white sheep around their shepherd, who was resplendent in his characteristic meltsonian blue.

Never did a hero receive such a rapturous welcome, never was any man the centre of such tumultuous unrestrained adulation.

Thom alone viewed the arrival with unknown trepidation.

The others jostled and vied as though in competition to receive their leader's magnanimous blessing. Keith promptly admonished them.

"Competition," he said sternly, holding up his hand for silence, "is a sign of The Sickness. We must co-operate, not compete, my brothers and sisters!"

He greeted each of them in turn, finally shaking Thom's hand after kissing Sian gravely, then slapping Richard solemnly on the back.

"Do not desire to speak all at once," he continued in a loud voice, "for all the desires of man weigh like millstones around his neck. Praised be they who expect nothing; for they shall not be disappointed."

Keith indicated with a crooked smile that in his final observation he was indulging a rare facetiousness, which the happy group applauded like school children in receipt of an unexpected half-holiday. He then extended a finger to point to a faraway hill.

"Yonder lies our goal. Let us endeavour to score it. Cullacandy Mountain!"

They cheered loudly.

"Let us proceed," said Keith calmly.

They took a long time to reach their destination. They struggled through a punishing deluge of hail, then a freezing blizzard, during which Keith, always to the forefront, exhorted them on with shouts of "Farther on and farther in!" to which the joyful travellers responded as though possessed, fighting against the elements with ever renewed vigour.

They came to within fifty yards of the mountain to find the ground inexplicably covered in a widening expanse of smooth even lawn. The sun shone and the grass was green. Thom tested the flawless grass surface with a tentative foot and found his ankle almost immersed in thick mud. But Keith, already wading halfway across, yelled: "Come in! What's keeping you? Don't be afraid, brothers and sisters! Farther on and farther in!"

The white-robed figures, momentarily hesitating on the brink, then plunged into the vast expanse, encouraged by the example of their leader. The grass turned to bog beneath their feet and every step became a dangerous strength-sapping exercise; never before was the presence of Keith, always in front, always roaring encouragement, more inspirational. With the mud clinging to their feet, they emerged at last at the foot of Cullacandy Mountain. Like the lake before, it had no sign of life around it; no animal or bird betrayed its presence if, indeed, any were about. Thom thought that the mountain had no particular presence or power, it was merely there. Yet this was the goal for which they had laboured so long and so unceasingly.

Silently they began to climb. The ascent itself was not difficult but extremely tiring in the heat and the glare of the sun. It was only when they reached the summit that the enormity of the mission became apparent. Keith was saying something but Thom, swaying with fear, was only half listening. He had never climbed so high before.

"It's all plain sailing now," Keith was saying crisply. "The points are as good as in the bag. All we have to do is slip down the other side …"

Thom looked down and saw on the one side a black bottomless tunnel, on the other a sheer drop of infinitely greater proportions than the relatively brief ascent would have suggested. The tunnel, a pillar of blackness within the rock, was of indeterminate depth. The descent showed little in the way of footholds or regularity, indeed there seemed no way down except by plummeting to a certain death. Thom broke out in a cold sweat as he realised just how little space lay between the strange tunnel and the horrifying drop. He fell to the ground oblivious to the little bumps of rock which lacerated his hands and knees. The sun felt hot on his back.

"I'm not going down there!" he screamed. "What is this, anyway? What the hell's the point of this lunacy?"

Nobody answered.

He looked up into the face of Keith, which suddenly looked sly and unfriendly.

"You! You're nothing but a bloody nutcase!" Thom said viciously.

Trapped and helpless, he squirmed awkwardly to his feet.

"A bloody nutcase!" he repeated, looking wildly around.

"It's a pity it's come to this," Keith said softly. "I regret that Vice Versa is no longer in a position to guarantee your safety."

"I want out of this. Do you hear me? Out of it!" Thom shouted hysterically. "Will some of you for God's sake do something?"

"Certainly," he heard Keith saying gently. "I had such high hopes for you, Thom. It's a pity you won't be with us in the next division …"

He watched the dust particles dance indolently in the rays of the morning light as he jerked the duster back and forth the little blackboard. The classroom was empty and he felt tired and depressed, as he tended to more and more frequently these days. He often questioned the value of trying to teach history to adolescents; attempting to communicate his vision of the splendour of ancient Rome, for instance, to such an audience was, he reflected, a forlorn task. Hopeless, helpless and wasteful.

He did not notice the broken lock on the classroom door or the smashed window panes or the absence of children as he reached for the half bottle of gin in his breast pocket. It was the one sure way of blunting the edge of his myriad of disappointments and constant depression. Various things preoccupied him, weighty matters. His disintegrating marriage, his own juvenile delinquent son, his increasing dissatisfaction with the rut his life had become since he had been forced out of teaching and onto a regime of medication.

And yet it wasn't always like this. Sometimes, in idle moments, reading a particularly evocative account of a battle in ancient times, or looking at the flowers in his garden, or simply sitting alone, thinking, he would be stirred by feelings and forgotten memories of times, and things, and events, victories and defeats, somewhere experienced but not retained by his consciousness, preoccupied as that was with such important matters as family harmony, keeping the car serviced, taking the right pills at the right intervals. At other times he would meet someone, on a train, in the street, on the beach, anywhere, who would jolt his very being, making him aware in his heart that that person was somehow, or had been, a comrade or an acquaintance, a kindred spirit. But these times were nowadays easily pushed to the back of his troubled mind.

Finishing his gin, he stood and put on his drab overcoat. He drove through the deserted streets of the little seaside town, the warm air heavy with a brackish smell, the sky hinting at another bright new day to come. The stillness was broken only by the cawing of gulls.

Thom walked steadily until he came to the beach, continued walking and paused at the edge of the water. He looked straight ahead and walked farther on and farther in, oblivious to the shouts of the middle-aged couple walking their dog to one side and the distant figures of a young man and a half naked blonde girl to the other, the young man already racing urgently towards him as he immersed himself thoroughly in preparation for the blue heaven that was out there waiting for him, as he paddled hesitantly and softly, cat-like, farther on and farther in to the meltsonian blue.

Chapter 10

Trial And Error

THE RAPE TRIAL had been a harrowing experience for Adam Conway. He had turned up at the Courthouse nursing a hangover. Some people were rushing around like headless chickens, others were gloomily sipping insipid tea or coffee from plastic beakers. An old man and a solicitor near to him were having a conversation about some dreary case involving a dispute over land boundaries.

It was some time before he realised that he wasn't supposed to be sitting outside.There were still some people who were, though. One of them, a heavy featured oaf with a face that looked like it had been hewn out of a lump of blubber and topped with a thatch of greased brown hair that resembled a smearing of excrement on his fat head, was smoking nervously and speaking rapidly with a fake jocularity about a recent drinking bout in the Westbourne. Adam immediately placed him as being from east Belfast because it was a Glentoran supporters' club he was talking about, and correctly surmised that the unnatural cut of his attire – an ill-fitting cheap brown suit and two-tone brown and white shoes – suggested that he was up on some charge.

Before the day was out Gary Algernon Dornan – for that turned out to be his name – was to hear a judge sentencing him to six months in jail for driving over and seriously injuring a five year old child whilst drunk.

Adam found out at last where he was supposed to be, courtroom No 2. As he walked towards it he passed some chinless idiot in full regalia – the powdered hairpiece, black gown and all the rest of it – strutting towards an adjoining court, pausing only to purse his lips and gesticulate imperiously at a middle-aged couple behind him to come along. They trudged meekly in his wake, heads down, following the peremptory wagging finger like obedient puppy dogs.

Adam arrived in courtroom No 2 just in time to hear a distant judge slap a fine on him. The judge revoked it when informed that 'No 437' had just arrived but continued to fine others who had not turned up whilst berating them in their absence via a plummy-voiced tirade.

The real circus started when the jurors were being selected for the various trials. It was a lottery of a system with numbers being called out and people traipsing up to the front to be sworn in, or traipsing dejectedly back to their uncomfortable seats when they were objected to by various counsel. The juries for Gary Algernon Dornan and some other drunken driver, an emaciated whey-faced wretch who looked as if he hadn't slept for a week, were despatched first.

Then it was the turn of a forlorn looking loner, Lloyd George Taylor. He was a man of about fifty with a stern face, heavy black glasses, a bald head with fuzzy patches of hair sticking out at the sides and a tatty crew-necked jumper covered by a shabby grey overcoat. If you were to hazard a guess as to what he was up for you'd have to go for the popular stereotype, Adam thought: a flasher, or maybe a child molester.

As the numbers were called out Adam felt increasingly agitated, his head pounding and his mouth dry from the over-indulgence of the previous night. It was a strange feeling. He would have liked to have been able to walk out into the fresh air outside but at the same time he didn't want to miss participating, having come this far. Looking around, he sensed a similar feeling behind the anxious faces of most of the other potential jurors.

Adam noticed that the legal representative for Lloyd George Taylor was exercising his right to object to almost the maximum permitted number of prospective jurors. Most of those objected to were women. The Crown representative was also doing his share of objecting. Both of the legal eagles were appraising all the would-be jurors very carefully, scrutinising a long printed sheet in front of them. When Adam's turn came there were no objections.

The oath was an old fashioned nonsense, rooted in another time, but Adam dully went through the motions of being sworn in anyway. He stared back into the glittering eyes of the hard faced, raven haired girl who was saying the oath for him to repeat it. He smiled at her and kept his voice firm and steady but was disappointed not to get any glint of a response from her as she moved on to some trembling over-awed jackass who was next in line.

The final juror was a tall, intellectual-looking, bald man with keen eyes and a pointed beard and a cultured Dublin accent. He refused to take the oath on the grounds that he didn't believe in any of it but indicated his willingness to make an affirmation instead. There was something of a minor furore of raised eyebrows, pursed lips, clandestine mutterings and clucking consternation before the man was eventually allowed to take the stand.

The jurors were finally shepherded into a back room where there was nothing much except a table and a dozen chairs spread out in a rectangle in the middle of the floor. The walls were bare and there were some very basic toilet facilities at the back. It might as well have been a jail. The men and women looked curiously at each other.

"Maybe one way of getting out of jury service," the bald intellectual remarked with a smile, "would be to bring back the old Diplock courts for everything. That way there'd never be any need for a jury."

Conversation was sparse for the next hour as most of the jurors sat staring vacantly into space. Those who had newspapers with them buried their heads in them. The intellectual pulled out a book entitled *Women At War* from a jacket pocket and studied it intently. Eventually a voice from the door summoned them from the depths of their own stupor.

As they trooped into the courtroom they saw Lloyd George Taylor sitting at the back, flanked by policemen. A woman, frail in build and with one of those serene, finely defined faces that always seemed to be smiling, was sitting on the far side beside an elderly couple, presumably her parents, and a well dressed, heavy jowled, middle-aged man who was glaring ferociously in Taylor's direction. One of the jurors whispered that it was a rape trial.

The introduction seemed to drag on forever as the judge, a rotund little man with a voice like rich port, meandered on endlessly about the role of the jury. He was stating the obvious for the most part.

When the woman eventually took the stand, she came across as an impressive witness. She was attractive, younger looking than her forty nine years. Her demeanour suggested a simple and unpretentious honesty. The details were upsetting enough; she had known Taylor for twenty years, having befriended him through her work with the Samaritans, frequently employing him for odd jobs, mostly gardening at her Malone Road home, helping him out when times were especially hard for him. They were to see exhibits later where the rape took place. The house was a luxury mansion to the jurors, with shockingly expensive furniture and ornaments inside and Persian rugs rather than carpet on the floor. The woman had to endure a belligerent approach from the defence counsel.

"Mrs Singleton, is it not a fact that you discussed your sexual problems with Mr Taylor prior to this alleged incident, problems such as difficulty in lubricating, and details about the hysterectomy you had?"

"That is untrue."

Her voice was unwavering and she bore herself with a deliberate dignity, though at times she had difficulty looking at the jury. Adam felt progressively more uncomfortable as it went on, thinking that nobody should have to suffer being grilled in front of strangers on top of being raped.

The jurors looked at the documents presented to them, the exhibits – internal photographs of the house... physical details of the rape, which had been preceded by an attempted but unsuccessful rape…statements made to the police by Taylor afterwards, including a particularly disingenuous remark to the effect that he was very sorry and that it was all a misunderstanding.

Next in the witness box was a burly detective who had taken the various statements from Taylor. He dismissed the first statement, denying the incident, as a pack of lies, citing forensic evidence including DNA tests. He referred to the second statement, in which Taylor spoke of the 'misunderstanding' between himself and Elizabeth Singleton, whom he claimed to be 'head over heels in love with', in similar vein, all the while displaying in an obvious contempt for the defendant whom he confirmed he had known for around ten years.

When Lloyd George Taylor at last took the stand he denied knowing the rape victim. The jurors gasped and murmured amongst themselves. Eventually he was asked again if he knew Elizabeth Singleton.

"Aye…Betty Squires," he said doggedly, using her maiden name. "I didn't recognise her from here. My eyesight's not the best."

It got worse. The prosecution had a field day, cutting him to shreds on all the inconsistencies in his statements. He was a forthright enough speaker answering the questions but none too clever. In the background the judge sat back taking notes, serious faced and nodding occasionally. He'd know the Lloyd George Taylors of this world intimately enough within his legal jurisdiction, Adam reflected. He wouldn't have met too many of them socially.

It was left to the defence to make the best of a lost cause. The representative was a tall thin man with a country accent, Tyrone maybe, and a stiff manner of standing. He asked the defendant to tell the jury exactly what had happened. Taylor promptly claimed that on the night in question he had bolted into Mrs Singleton's house to avoid wild animals, then locked the door. His counsel's jaw dropped. He had not prepared, nor been prepared, for such a response.

"Wild animals?"

"Aye. The Malone Road's alive with them. Foxes, badgers, everything. Many's the man sleeping rough has got savaged by them. So I ran for the door out of fear and locked it behind me."

"Where was Mrs Singleton when you did this?"

"I let her in after about a quarter of an hour because she was hammering so much. It was against my better judgement that I let her in at all," he added weightily. "It was then that she jumped on top of me."

"You let her into her own house – after leaving her hammering at her own door for fifteen minutes – then she assaulted you?"

"Hold on – one thing at a time, now!"

The voice was suddenly menacing and when he removed the thick black-rimmed spectacles his eyes were mean and frightening.

"She jumped on top of me. That's what happened."

The voice was self assured again, there was a slight swagger about him.

"The sweat was lashing off both of us, whether it was pleurisy, or a brain haemorrhage, or whatever it was, and we ended up on the floor together for a while."

He had no fear about him then. He was trying to manipulate the jury into thinking he was insane, Adam thought. It had emerged during the trial that he had a brother who had been in and out of psychiatric care and it seemed that he was playing on that. On the far side of the court Elizabeth Singleton was sitting with her head bowed, staring at the floor. Her husband's eyes were popping out of his head like a bullfrog's and various onlookers in the gallery were staring at Taylor. The members of the jury sat transfixed, temporarily forgetting their own discomfort.

It was all over bar the formalities. The jurors had to listen to a pedantic lecture from the judge on the necessity of objective judgement based solely on available evidence. He explained the difference between a unanimous verdict and one that wasn't before the jury went through the motions of unanimously finding Taylor guilty. The newspapers were to claim later that they took only half an hour to reach the verdict but that wasn't true. It took them five minutes. The other twenty five were spent eating a tasteless meal of fish, chips and peas that was provided for them. The four women on the jury were the least perturbed of all by the proceedings, giggling about the case like it was an episode out of a soap opera and speculating about the cost of the Persian rugs and other opulent trappings in Elizabeth Singleton's house.

They all trooped back into the court to witness Taylor, who it transpired had a lengthy criminal record for burglaries and indecent assaults but had been given a clean bill of mental health by an expert, sentenced to twelve years. The jury foreman, a factory worker one year away from retirement who was nearly deaf and hadn't heard a lot of the evidence, had first delivered the guilty verdict in a vapid Belfast accent reminiscent of one of those ancient 'I-speak-your-weight' machines.There was an air of grim exultation throughout the courtroom, a welcome sense amongst those present of a just retribution having been achieved. Except for Lloyd George Taylor.

Adam had had enough. Outside, snow was beginning to fall. He headed straight for Slattery's, rapidly, on foot. A small crowd of regulars was gathered round by the jukebox at the far corner of the main bar, standing bolt upright and saluting whilst simultaneously clinking their beer glasses together in a solemn toast.

"Pint of Smithwicks, Joan," Adam said to the nearest barmaid. "Is Pat Farland working today?"

"You've just missed him. He left about five minutes ago with some rough looking customer, I don't know who he was. Pat looked white. You'd think to look at him that he was going to be taken out and shot."

"What's all this carry-on at the back?"

"It's bad news."

Adam sauntered towards the crowd at the corner, where the jukebox was blasting out the fast paced finale of the William Tell overture. He recognised several regulars amongst the group. Terry Parcury was there, a malevolent looking dwarf with long black oily hair, along with his constant companion Cheesy Ring, a taller, crinkly haired, pear-shaped individual with a long nose and chin, a perpetually supercilious expression and a bemused smile. Tom Bellingham was there too, clutching a glass of stout and shaking his head morosely as he read the front page of the *Belfast Telegraph.*

"Have you heard, Adam?" he demanded. "Have you heard what those bastards have done? They've killed old Thom. They've murdered the fucking Lone Ranger!"

Adam reached for the newspaper in shock.

NEW BUTCHERS CLAIM LATEST VICTIM was the headline; underneath was a none too recent photograph of the man described as Thompson Leonard Hugh O'Loan, a former schoolteacher and Methodist lay preacher. The finger of blame was already being pointed at the shadowy loyalist grouping known as the New Butchers, which had been active up until the previous ceasefires and had taken to stalking and inflicting gruesome deaths on random innocent victims once again. Five had died in the last two months since the attacks had resumed.

Adam read on.

STRANGER ON THE SHORE was a sub-headline which attracted his attention: beneath it was a photograph of Thompson O'Loan being rescued from the sea at Portrush during a failed suicide attempt several years previously. The amateur snap was fuzzy, taken by a holidaymaker from a hotel window, but the rescuer bore a curious resemblance to his cousin Enda. A Portrush couple, a Mr and Mrs Gillespie, confirmed in an interview that they had looked after the victim after the rescue incident. They knew him as a local man who had returned to live in his native Portrush following early retirement from his employment due to mental illness.

His wife and son were too distraught to speak to the press but others who knew him spoke of his involvement with the ultra-secretive Vice Versa cult, an organisation composed entirely of former psychiatric patients under the hugely controversial tutelage of Professor Keith Dalkeith. Professor Dalkeith, described variously as a clinical psychologist, motivational guru, hypnotherapist and mass illusionist had sprung to prominence in recent years with what he liked to call his popular principle of meltsonian dynamics, an all-embracing philosophy encompassing elements of eastern mysticism, cognitive science, cosmic string theory and spiritual transmogrification. His books on the subject included bestselling titles such as *The Old And The New Magic*, *The Illusion Of Time, Kind Of Blue* and *The Paradigms Of Eternity*.

Professor Dalkeith could not immediately be contacted for comment on the murder.

"He was a good man, old Thom," Terry Parcury muttered, staring misty-eyed at the newly painted wall beside him. "All right, so he was a nutter. But he was our nutter. He was a Slattery's man through and through. If he wanted a drink and a bit of crack, this is where he'd come to get it. 'Shot of redeye, bartender!' That was his watchword."

"You're right there," Cheesy Ring intoned. "You said it. The words are yours, Terry."

"We'll not see the like of the Lone Ranger in here again," Tom Bellingham said lugubriously. "He was a good man, all right. One of the old school. Salt of the earth. The sort of man who knew what was what. Put it this way – he was a character."

"If he was half as brilliant as you make him out to be," Adam said, "how come you were always taking the piss out of him when he was alive? It was you who got that bloody William Tell music put on the jukebox so you could wind him up every time he showed his face here."

"Sure, that was only a bit of sport," Tom said defensively. "This pub is a broad church -"

"A cathedral of characters," Terry Parcury chipped in. "Old Thom enjoyed a laugh as much as anybody."

"Of course he did," said Cheesy Ring. "He'd be the first to tell you that himself. If he was here. "

"Pity about his nephew," Tom commented. "You know that young lad Ally – Queen's student? Comes in here of a Saturday night with the rugby crowd? He's taking it very badly, I believe. Anyhow – this is depressing, lads. Let's change the subject. What are you drinking, Adam?"

"Pint of Smithwicks."

"Where are you working these days? I've hardly seen you since you came back from Australia. "

"Rates office. Dull as dishwater. Not for much longer, though. I got some great news the other day. I've got a job I applied for with the union. I start next week."

"Nice one," beamed Tom. "Up with the suits in the White House, eh? Cushy number, if you ask me. Beats working for a living."

Adam nodded. The rape trial had drained him and he couldn't be bothered arguing. He decided after the second pint that he might as well stay on a while. The previous night's hangover was beginning to dissipate already. After a while, for want of something better to talk about, he told the company about the day's events at court.

"You what?" Cheesy Ring said incredulously when he heard the story. "You're responsible for sending a man to jail for twelve years? Why didn't you do like your man Henry Fonda in that film *Twelve Angry Men* and argue the bit out – convince the rest of the jury?"

"Aye!" said Terry Parcury, the drunker of the two, already squinting truculently about the bar, eyeing the women. "She was probably gagging for it anyway. Nothing these snooty Malone Road huers like better than a bit of working class rough." He laughed his loud, squawking laugh. "Anyhow, at least you know where she lives now, if you fancy a bit yourself."

Tom downed his Powers whiskey and reluctantly fingered his empty stout glass.

"I'm going to have to go, boys," he said sorrowfully. "I was on a half day today but I have to go home. The mother-in-law's coming for dinner tonight. Here – isn't that old guy that's just come in the ex-policeman, what do you call him – Wilson Squires?"

"That's him," said Cheesy Ring reverently. "He was one of the ones who knocked about with the original Shankill Butchers, way back when. Undercover man. Doctor Dolittle, they used to call him, because he could talk to the animals. We should ask him about these bastards that done the Lone Ranger."

Adam looked up and realised with a jolt that the man in the gabardine coat sidling up to the bar was the father of the rape victim Elizabeth Singleton. He quickly averted his gaze.

"Hey – Wilsie boy!" gabbled Terry Parcury. "Did you hear about the Lone Ranger being murdered by those New Butchers cunts?"

"Wilson. Not 'Wilsie Boy'," said Wilson Squires. "Mr Squires to you. Yes, I did. Give me a rum, Joan. What do you call the one Lily the Pink drinks?"

"It's rocket fuel, that stuff. Seriously, Wilson. It would rot the brass plate off a coffin. You don't want to drink that," Joan protested.

"Understand this, Joan. I tell you what I want to drink. Not the other way round. Give me one of those. Make it a double, in fact."

Joan shrugged and poured the drink. Squires handed her some money and told her to keep the change.

"What would you do with those murdering bastards if you caught them?" Terry Parcury persisted.

"I'd shoot them," said Squires quietly. "I'd shoot the lot of them. Terrorists, rapists, paedophiles – I'd start with the rapists. People have to be protected. The innocent have to be protected."

"That's a typical policeman's perspective," Cheesy Ring said pompously and with some difficulty, "but I have to say I agree with you. Somebody has to clean up the streets. I'd go further than that. I'd send their families the bill for the bullets, like the Chinkies used to do."

"It said in the paper that Thom O'Loan had over a hundred knife wounds to his body," Tom said, frowning. "What sort of animals would do a thing like that? Eh? Were the original Shankill Butchers as bad as that – Lenny Murphy and the rest of them?"

"Lenny Murphy certainly was," replied Squires. "He was a very arrogant, very domineering man. I knew him personally. I knew all of them personally."

He sipped his rum tentatively with a look of great distaste before suddenly knocking the remainder of the drink back with a grimace and a shudder.

"It was a hundred and fifty four knife wounds, by the way," he added. "The papers never tell you the full story."

"Who the hell are these bastards?" said Tom vehemently.

"Are they from the Shankill? Are they trying to outdo Murphy's lot, or what?"

"Oh yes, they're from the Shankill," Squires said, buttoning up his coat and turning to go. "Though it's a very different Shankill these days from what it was in the Murphy era. Tens of thousands less people, for a start. And these guys aren't participating in a war. They're trying to start one. So they can't make the excuse that their actions are dictated by the behaviour of their enemies. Otherwise the similarities are there. They're products of their time. Just like their heroes."

"Well, they got a Prod this time," mumbled Terry Parcury. "The Lone Ranger was a Prod. Fucking own goal, or what?"

Adam gave Squires a couple of minutes leeway before leaving the pub himself. He dropped into the betting shop next door to do a few bets on the night racing at Doncaster. On an impulse, he decided to put most of the money that was left in his pocket on a horse called Lloyd George at 12-1 in the 7.30. He kept just enough change for one more pint.

"It's still running," a punter told him with a grin when he went back half an hour later to check the result.

As they say in racing parlance, it always was a no-hoper.

Chapter 11

Shankill Butchers

"I HAD A dream last night," the boy said. His ebullient mood had evaporated and he was suddenly and inexplicably sombre. His head was bowed. "I dreamt that I saw the reflection of my own face high in the sky, with dark storm clouds around it and rain, not dank, drizzling rain but heavy, steady, cascading streams of water. I was parallel with my own reflection. I was talking to it. I could sense intuitively that my reflection wanted to hear nice things. But I was drunk with my own power and I wanted to hurt my own reflection."

He sipped his pint of lager while his girlfriend listened silently; then he continued.

"I could see its gentle, trusting, sensitive face and I wanted to hurt it and watch it change expression. I said some terrible things to it. I knew I had a moral duty not to say those things but I said them anyway. I hurt my reflection."

He closed his eyes for a moment, then opened them. Still he stared down at the floor of the bar.

"One of the things I kept telling it was that it was going to die sometime. I kept repeating this. 'You're going to die! Don't you realise that?' I kept insisting in a horrible goading voice. My reflection grew puzzled looking first, then more and more vulnerable – it was very vulnerable looking to start with, and obviously in need of the most confident reassurance – until finally it looked as though in pain, and terribly, terribly hurt, hurt beyond all redemption and forgiveness. Finally it just faded away, like a mirage."

His girlfriend took his hand as he went to reach for his pint glass, squeezed it and held it. The boy didn't raise his head.

"I worry about you when you talk like that," she whispered. "I really worry about you. Come on, cheer up for me. You were in brilliant form ten minutes ago. Remember we've a party to go to tonight."

In other parts of the city the party is already beginning. It's Friday night and it's Belfast and the town smells like a pub, with a pallor of gloom spreading over it like a shadow across a shroud. On the Shankill Road four men are huddled in a corner in the Lawnbrook club, drinking together and discussing murder.

In a police station not far away the senior police officer nicknamed Control and another much younger man, scruffily dressed and with a three day stubble adorning his sallow cheeks, are talking about the same thing. Control has a thick file lying open on his desk and, rarely for him, a look of febrile agitation. The two interrogators, Teer and Lamont, are sitting taciturnly beside a table in the room.

"If that's the truth on that one, Doc, and not just drunken nonsense …. what we need tonight is a break. If there's even a shred of truth in it we need a statement."

"Getting one is going to be a problem," Wilson Squires said gloomily. "I've been undercover now long enough to know the score. It's the loneliest job in the world." He paused to light a cigarette. "It gets to me sometimes, going to some of these places. The Lawnbrook. The Windsor. The Long Bar. I'm only human. Unlike some of the punters we're interested in. Anyhow, the mob we're talking about operates mostly out of the Brown Bear, as you know."

"All we need," Control said dully, staring at the window, "is one breakthrough."

"It's difficult to the point of near impossibility," Wilson

Squires insisted. "Hearing the things I've heard is one thing. Getting anybody to testify is something else and I'm not just talking about the paramilitaries. There are still plenty of decent people on the Shankill. The point is, they're all scared shitless. I've never seen anything like it. They all know there's no hiding place for them if they start singing. We can't protect them for the rest of their lives."

"Doc's right," Teer remarked. "Everything's been tried."

"You can never say that," said Control quietly. "Defeatism isn't an option. Just stay focused on what you have to do. Remember that very shortly you'll be interviewing someone who has claimed – albeit when drunk – to have been a witness to this one."

He picked up the file and watched his fellow officers recoil at the photograph of the corpse with the head hanging off.

"It was a Saturday evening," said Control, "towards the end of February."

It was in the Long Bar we met Lenny. He was drinking with Billy Moore and Basher Bates and another man who's well known on the Road but I can't remember his name.

Outside, it's a sharp evening for February, with the sun hanging low in the sky, blind and unforgiving as a gouged eye, spilling its soft shafts of crimson light onto the dank wastelands and brittle glass grass of the Shankill where little grows and only the flowers of evil flourish, only as time melts away it won't be light that's being spilled but the lifeblood of an innocent screaming impotently to the heavens. Red sky at night, butcher's delight.

Lenny says there's a war on and the only way to handle a war is to go all out to win it. Lenny says all Taigs are the same. It doesn't matter how many you take out because they're all animals and scum.

In the Long Bar, as the evening wears on, Lenny Murphy is holding court about the political situation to a captive audience and concluding that the only way to change it is to instil a state of constant fear in the enemy. He has a way of talking that commands attention, the air of a man used to giving orders and having them obeyed.

He's not very big – but then neither was Napoleon, was he? They're all afraid of him, including Basher, and he'd stick a glass in your face as soon as look at you. Even Big Sam, he's another thug and twice the size of him. It's his reputation, all the things he's done. He's ruthless. You don't argue. You know not to. You just don't mess with him.

It's well past midnight when the five passengers accompany Billy Moore into his black taxi, which then careers off down the Shankill Road towards the city centre, via the darkened mazes of side streets as silent as the grave. The Butchers don't have long to wait for their next victim.

A youngish man with long fair hair is walking up Upper Donegall Street when the taxi pulls up menacingly beside him, a black harbinger of death. The man senses danger, tries to escape, but Lenny Murphy is wielding a wheel brace and hammers him to the ground from behind with a brutal blow to the back of the head. Bates leaps out of the taxi and helps Murphy drag the man, dazed and helpless, into the back seat where he is repeatedly beaten and abused as the taxi speeds back to sanctuary in the black womb of the Shankill.

The car stops at Brookmount Street and the vicious beating continues while Murphy darts into his house, to return brandishing a butcher's knife in the back of the cab. As the taxi swerves in the direction of the Lawnbrook club Murphy taunts his helpless victim with the knife, cutting him about the throat and sides of the neck while his torturers jeer at him and tell him he is going to die.

They stop at Esmond Street, at the entrance to an alleyway. The victim is moaning with pain as he is dragged up it, then mercilessly kicked by three men before Murphy hacks through his throat with the knife until the blade touches the spine. The last sight he ever sees in the hellish infinity of his last night on earth is the frenzied visage of Murphy, features contorted with hatred and elation, glowing blood red in the searing agony of his final moments.

Lenny, Basher and the other guy took the Taig up the alleyway to finish him off. He'd already got a bit of a digging.

"It was round about that time that the papers started talking about the 'Shankill Butchers'," Control went on. "They recognised the pattern. Random victims and particularly barbaric killings, even for these times. As sectarian murders go, you'll appreciate that these are in a different league."

"Maybe," said Teer, "except that the end result is the same. How many officers have we lost, even this year alone? What difference does it make whether you're killed with a gun, or a bomb, or a knife? You still end up dead."

"Which would you prefer?" asked Control. "Being blown up or shot – or tortured to death?"

Teer was silent.

Lamont said: "You could be mutilated by a bomb or a bullet, and take years to die …."

Wilson Squires said that he had read a book about the French Revolution once. There was a theory that the guillotine was a gruesome way to die even when it worked properly because it wasn't instantaneous. The brain still functioned for some instants after the head was severed so the victims could actually still look at their executioners briefly after they had been guillotined, absolutely helpless to stave off the horror of that final consciousness.

Control retorted that there was no point in moping about the way things were because nobody knew when it was going to get any better, least of all the politicians. He added that the police had a job to do and it was a matter of them all knuckling down and getting on with it.

Outside in the cold October night rain fell in heavy parallel lines, beating the ground with a relentless ferocity. The boy and the girl left the party at Jerusalem Street at two o'clock in the morning, together traversing the tight knit little streets of the neighbourhood, streets with names like Cairo Street, Palestine Street, Damascus

Street … the dark and narrow perspectives of Belfast's Holyland. They debated whether to stay at Jerusalem Street overnight and decided against it, because she was supposed to have been home two hours ago and her parents would be worried.

When they realise they have no money for a taxi they walk hurriedly and silently towards the city centre, to the wasteland of Millfield, a bleak and lonely area between a rock and a hard place. There are no houses there. Two side streets lead into the Shankill; two more lead into Smithfield shopping precinct, a lively place by day and a dead and foreboding one at night.

A short time earlier four men had left the Lawnbrook club, heading purposefully towards a beige Cortina which Billy Moore, leading the group, would drive. In his company are a tall teenager called John Townsley; Artie McClay, a burly man with long dark hair and behind them, stamping ponderously and belligerently along the soaked pavements, the hulking brutish figure of Big Sam McAllister, his bullet head bobbing on top of his bull neck and massive torso like a captive ping pong ball on a jet of water. The rain had stopped temporarily and the dark sky was curdled by starlight above them as they bundled into the car and drove down the nether world of the lower Shankill, past houses with bricked-up windows in deserted streets. They stop the car at Brown Street, on the corner with Millfield. They leave Townsley, a boy several months short of his sixteenth birthday but already sporting a moustache and looking more like a man than a boy, to look after the car. The other three stand at the corner. The boy and the girl hear something shouted at them but they do not know what it is. They try to avoid looking at the men but almost immediately they are dragged violently away from each other, the boy to the waiting car by McAllister and McClay, the girl to the ground by Billy Moore who orders her: "Don't move. Don't scream."

In later years the girl will speak of having looked into the eyes of another human being and seen the face of the devil.

In the car the boy is subjected to an horrific beating as Moore speeds towards the Shankill to pick up a butcher's knife and a gun from an accomplice. On the way to the crystallisation of all his grim forebodings and darkest premonitions the boy is strangely calm, even when being taunted that he is going to die and cut around the neck with the knife by McAllister, who hands it to Moore as they drag the boy out of the car to face his own demise.

When the body is found early in the morning at Glencairn, near the Community Centre, it is motionless. A bullet has been put through the head, which has almost been severed from the body by the knife. The body is lying on its back with the legs bent back underneath, arranged so as to make the throat wounds immediately visible.

Lenny says prison's no problem to him. He's killed a man in prison before, a grass who was ready to fit him up on a murder charge. Lenny says most of the screws are all right, they know what side their bread's buttered on. He can still control his team from inside. They'll carry out whatever orders he gives them. And soon enough he'll be out again to take over.

In the police station later that morning, two detectives are discussing the latest Butchers murder and the prospect of many more to come.

"Control is taking this one very personally," one of them commented. "It's goodnight to his theory that Murphy's behind them all. He couldn't be. He's doing twelve years. Possession of firearms."

"Six," grunted his colleague. The bastard will be out in six. Half remission. I see your woman's out."

He nodded at Jennifer Teer through the glass door. She was shaking her head bleakly at him. Behind her, Wendy Lamont led out the girl. She was tall, with a good figure, dark hair and a seemingly permanent pout that suggested amusement, though inwardly she couldn't have been anything other than frightened. To his disgust, the second detective felt the beginnings of an erection.

"According to Doc," he said, "that bitch and another wee millie sat in the front of the car, watching, the night they killed the lad Rice. Murphy picked them up in the Long Bar. But if Murphy did that one, and the others, then who sawed that kid's head off last night?"

"Lenny certainly knows how to show a girl a good time," the first detective remarked drily. "In my day we used to take them to the pictures. Still, I'm not surprised the wee huer's not signing any statements. She'll have sobered up since Doc heard her slobbering about it. She'll not want to spend the best years of her life looking at the world through the bars of a cell. Or get her own throat slit from ear to ear."

"Control's not going to be too pleased."

"No. I don't know why he's so uptight about Murphy. The loyalists were cutting up Taigs in the Romper Rooms long before anybody ever heard of the Shankill Butchers, for fuck's sake."

"Magic mirror, tell me today .... did my friends have fun at play?" the second man mimicked. "Well, it's only another drop in the ocean. We're looking at plenty of other murders this year. Look on the bright side – it's plenty of overtime for the boys."

"I've never met Murphy," the first man said, "but I've seen his file, and the photographs. He doesn't look anything out of the ordinary."

The other man snorted derisively.

"Do they ever? What do you expect, the mark of Cain? I don't know what goes on in the heads of people like that, nobody does. Start thinking about it and you might conjure up a few demons of your own, but you're not going to see the shape of anybody else's. Take my advice and leave that sort of thinking to the shrinks and the social workers. They get paid for it, we don't. I'll tell you what, though. I saw the body of that wee man Quinn, one of the first ones they did. Throat cut through to the spine. Not a pretty sight."

He took a sip of his coffee, then added thoughtfully: "It's the banality of the thing. You see a broken, crumpled wee body like that, that's all that's left at the end of it, and you wonder what the hell .... it's like switching off a light. That's what it's like."

He finished his coffee with one more gulp.

"Mind you," he said, getting up, "I'll say one thing for Lenny."

"What might that be?"

"His views on Taigs. He's on the ball there. Thinks they're

all scum and animals."

His companion looked at him, and laughed shortly.

"Aye," he said, "You're right there."

The two men walked on down the corridor together, laughing.

Chapter 12

Steal Softly Through Sunlight,
Steal Softly Through Snow

"SNOW AT THIS time of year! I've seen it all now," Pat Farland commented as he left the bar, gazing at the falling flakes and rapidly whitening pavements.

"The seasons are all fucked," Turley said. "Global warming or whatever they call it."

They walked silently up University Road, past Queen's University and on to Botanic Gardens. Pat had been shocked when he had seen Turley lumbering through the front bar of Slattery's, scowling at everyone around him. It was rare for Turley to venture anywhere other than the two or three clubs he frequented on the Falls Road. He had nodded curtly at Pat when he caught sight of him.

"I've a message for you," he said. "Jimmy wants to see you. He's up the road in the Ulster Museum."

Pat thought it imprudent to hesitate. He made his excuses and left, saying he would be back as soon as he could.

They arrived at the Museum, a huge imposing building at the front of Botanic Gardens which had undergone a recent renovation, and entered.

"He's in the café," Turley said. "Third floor. We'll take the lift."

They negotiated the narrow corridors past a collection of stones, fossils, stuffed animals and various display boards, passing close by the skeleton of a giant deer with huge antlers, a species that had roamed around Ireland thousands of years ago, on the way through to the little café.

Inside, only a few customers sat around the fifteen or sixteen little tables arranged around the room. Two young children, a boy and a girl, were staring with wide-eyed attention through the big window overlooking the park, chattering and squealing with excitement at the sight of the snow outside.

At the back of the café, at one of two tables overlooking the ancient Friar's Bush graveyard at the bottom of the Stranmillis Road, sat a lone figure, a cloth cap pulled down over his forehead, peering intently at a newspaper crossword. The man looked up as Pat and Turley approached, revealing a thin bearded face and a shy smile.

"Sit down, Pat," said Jimmy McGuinness. "It's been a long time."

"I didn't recognise you there for a minute, Jimmy," Pat said. "That's a cheerful view you've got there."

McGuinness looked down into the bleak graveyard, dotted with old headstones, a rugged collection of gnarled trees combining with the snow to obscure the visions of the towering white Ashby Building and the smaller but equally striking Keir Building nearby looming in the background on the Stranmillis Road beyond.

"I like this little café," he mused. "It's as good a waiting room for the grave as any other. I don't get to wander among the leafy suburbs of south Belfast too often. I haven't been to this place for donkey's years. Not since they put on that 1798 exhibition on the United Irishmen. Anyhow – sit yourself down, Pat. Carlo, get Pat a cup of tea and a bun. Same for yourself."

McGuinness sipped his own tea as he watched Turley plodding to the service area, then jabbed a finger at the crossword in the copy of *The Times* newspaper he was studying. All but one clue had been completed.

"This is about all the old Thunderer is good for these days," he remarked. "There's always one that beats me. '*Killed for his bad verses.*' Five letters."

"Cinna," Pat said. "C-I-N-N-A. It's Shakespeare. The mob scene in *Julius Caesar.*"

McGuinness smiled thinly.

"Of course. A capricious lot, mobs. The worst beast in any arena is always supposed to be the crowd. Isn't that what they say? You always were a literary man, Pat. It just took a little enforced education to bring it out in you. I enjoyed that play of yours they put on at the Arts Festival, by the way. Best prison drama I've seen in a while. Not very ideologically sound, mind you."

He filled in the final clue with a black biro as Turley returned with the tea and buns.

"Though I've heard, Pat," he continued as Turley sat awkwardly down on the chair beside him, "that writing wasn't the only accomplishment you were noted for the time they lifted you for that Shankill operation. I understand you also discovered a talent for singing."

"Like a fucking canary," Turley said.

Pat felt his hand tremble slightly as he quickly put down the tea cup. He could sense the colour draining from his face. He looked towards the entrance and noticed for the first time that two men dressed in working clothes had positioned themselves at the table nearest the door.

"Relax, it's all right," McGuinness said in a low, soothing voice. He looked Pat straight in the eye.

"There's men been shot for less," muttered Turley.

"We all know that, Carlo. But that was in the war years. Nobody's going to shoot Pat. I could do with another cup of tea."

Turley looked at McGuinness for a moment, then rose to his feet with a sigh and made off towards the service point again.

"What's this all about then, Jimmy? You didn't ask me to come here for a sociable chat. What about that Short Strand man they found hanged in his cell? He was the one who grassed you up. Carlo told me that himself."

"Branagan? That was suicide. Allegedly."

"Why would he commit suicide?"

"A guilty conscience affects some people that way. Give some people enough rope …."

Turley returned with a fresh cup of tea and sat heavily down again.

"Don't get melodramatic about what you did, Pat," McGuinness said quietly. "There were no strings pulled on your behalf. The Lord Justice ruled your statement to be inadmissible because it was beaten out of you. That's the only reason you beat the rap. The information you gave them about me wasn't a consideration. It really was as simple as that."

The three men turned as an elderly man in a gabardine coat approached their table. Pat recognised him as an occasional customer in Slattery's, a tight-lipped individual who never stopped for more than one drink.

"Sit down, Wilson," McGuinness said. "How did it go in court?"

"The bastard got twelve years."

"Good," said McGuinness. "I'm glad to hear it. This is Pat Farland, Wilson. You'll know him from Slattery's. Unfortunately there's a few other people probably know you from Slattery's by now, Pat. Undesirables, people you wouldn't want to know you. That's why I asked you to come here today. We have some information for you. It's very, very important. You might even say it's a matter of life and death."

"Do you want a cup of tea, mucker?" Turley asked. "I'm offering before Jimmy does."

"Wilson. Not 'mucker'," said Wilson Squires. "Mr Squires to you. No, I don't. I have had a deeply unpleasant day and I want a drink. The sooner I get this business over and done with, the sooner I can go and have one. Have you seen this?"

He slapped the copy of the *Belfast Telegraph* he was carrying down on the table in front of Pat, the front page headlines facing him like an accusation. Pat nodded briefly.

"I knew that man. Thom O'Loan. He used to come into the pub in a Lone Ranger suit."

"He rode well out of his territory this time," said Squires.

"The way I heard it, he pulled the same stunt in a certain Shankill Road club. The place just went quiet. Then all you could hear was the sound of chairs being scraped back. They rompered him for five hours in a back room. One hundred and fifty four knife wounds, including an attempted castration. Eventually they finished him off by dropping him repeatedly on his head. They had him stripped and suspended upside down from a rope attached to a roof beam."

"I take it this place doesn't enjoy much in the way of passing trade," remarked Pat.

"I wouldn't waste my time acting the smart aleck if I were you," Squires said grimly. "They thought he was a Taig. The way he pronounced his name might have had something to do with it. But if they'd do that to some harmless kook in a fancy dress outfit for trying to buy a tomato juice, I wouldn't like to surmise what they have in store for you."

"They don't know me. And I'm not in the habit of boozing up the Shankill."

"They do know you," Squires said, "and it doesn't matter if you're not going to walk into their club with a tricolour wrapped round your neck. They know you work in Slattery's. They've probably had some of their people watching your movements already."

"I haven't noticed anyone …"

"You wouldn't have. These fellows don't go around sprouting horns and tails, you know."

"Nobody would pass any remarks if they did," said Pat. "Have you been in Slattery's lately? Maybe you better get to the point. Who are these bastards, and what would they want with me?"

Squires stared at him for a moment before answering.

"They're the New Butchers," he said. "That's what the scandal sheets dubbed them when they first came to prominence, around the time your friend Jim Butler was on hunger strike. They've been back in action recently for a number of reasons. One is that they're cruel sectarian thugs with a bloodlust who enjoy torture killings. Another is that they don't like the way things have been going politically recently and would like nothing better than to entice your lot back into all-out war."

"They're not my lot any more. I left."

"Mr Farland, I would appreciate it if you did not interrupt again," Squires said brusquely. "Your history is well known to me. Unfortunately for you, it's well known to them as well. Courtesy of a gentleman named Selby."

"Who?"

"Some English fool. You barred him from Slattery's some time ago. He was playing pool in a club in Tiger's Bay a while ago in a competition. The other team was from the Shankill. Based in the same club I just mentioned. Anyhow," he paused and looked out over the old cemetery, "the Shankill boys managed to persuade him to part with some files he had in his possession. Don't ask me where he got them. He was only a low grade screw, one of the ones that were put out of work when what your lot would call the political prisoners were released. But he had access to some very compromising material."

"It gets worse, Pat," McGuinness said gently. "Just make sure you're taking all this in."

"I'm taking it in all right."

"Then get this," said Squires. "You and your friends who were responsible for that gun and bomb attack on the Shankill some years ago are top of the New Butchers' hit list. One of the men Jim Butler shot dead was Trevor McCaw. Brother of a certain William Putnam McCaw, also known as Billy the Kid. Also known to the police as the leader of the New Butchers."

"Trevor McCaw was a well-known loyalist killer," said Pat. "I heard a rumour once that his younger brother was a psycho …."

"I don't think many outside the Shankill know just how much of a psycho. At the moment he's ruling the road by fear. But he'll turn into a folk hero if he takes out your team, after what you did. He's already come close to capturing Mr Butler."

"I heard nothing about that."

"Maybe your friends will tell you why."

"Elementary diplomacy," said McGuinness. "We have to look at the big picture, Pat. You understand that."

"I don't," said Turley. "Neither does Rhett. They near took

the head off him with a wheel brace. Tried to abduct him in broad daylight in Castle Street."

"A group of young lads from Lenadoon were nearby. They recognised Rhett and pitched in. That's what saved him," McGuinness continued. "The Butchers managed to get to their car and sped off. There were three of them. What they had in mind for Rhett was pretty gross even by their standards."

Pat stared at each of the other three men in turn.

"How could you possibly know what they had in mind for him, Jimmy?" he said at last. "Did they consult you about it?"

"A Shankill source told me about it," Squires interjected. "I was born and bred on the Shankill. I've still got friends and relatives there. I risked my life years ago to go undercover to provide information on the original Shankill Butchers. McCaw and his friends know of me as a former friend and associate of Lenny Murphy."

"All right. I'll buy that for the time being," said Pat slowly. "Tell me, then. What were they planning to do to Jim?"

"They were going to starve him to death."

"He had a pretty good shot at doing that himself."

"That was different," said Turley indignantly. "That was politics!"

The other men looked at him.

"Go and get the motor. I'll be down in a few minutes, Carlo," McGuinness said, handing him a set of keys. "Take the lads with you."

The three men remained silent until Turley and the two watchers at the door had disappeared from sight.

"They were going to lock him in a little-ease," Squires said.

"A what?"

"A confined space, one too small to either stand up or lie down. I don't know how long he would have lasted without food or water."

"It's those bastards that ought to be locked up. In a padded cell," said Pat bitterly. "Where's Jim now?"

"You don't need to know that, Pat," said McGuinness soothingly. "He's all right. Or as all right as he's ever been since he came off the hunger strike. He's still a bit mad. But we got him to hospital down south and he's safe where he is now. Same goes for the rest of your unit. Cleaky's in America. Franco's lying low with his new girl in a particularly obscure part of Kerry. That leaves you and you're a sitting duck. It's entirely up to yourself, of course …but if I were you, I wouldn't go back to Ireton Street. Or Slattery's. If you do, it'll be a matter of time before we're reading about you in the papers."

"Their normal *modus operandi* involves hammers, knives, hatchets and meat cleavers," Squires added. "Sometimes they improvise. Pliers and a blowtorch were used on the last victim before O'Loan, the young lad they bagged on the Antrim Road. The one before that, that man O'Donnell, a red hot poker was involved. You'll not get every detail in the newspapers."

Pat shook his head in disbelief. Squires picked up the copy of *The Times* lying on the table and handed it to him.

"Read the international news," Squires said. "Read about what's happening in Africa at the moment. Or the Middle East. We live in a very violent world. Our own little difficulties don't really amount to a hill of beans. The Butcher boys aren't a million miles removed from some of the trash on your own side of the house. They're a bunch of brutal, bigoted, poorly educated nobodies trying to become somebodies. They have the arrogance of youth."

"Why don't the mainstream paramilitaries on the Shankill do something about them?"

"They don't have the bottle," replied Squires. "They know what McCaw is capable of. He blinded Tucker Beattie when he heard he was going to make a move against him. Acid attack."

"Why are you telling me about this?" Pat demanded. "What's it to you if they do cut me to ribbons? You're a Shankill man yourself. You've said so. You're an ex-peeler as well. You probably hate me more than you hate them."

"Not more," said Squires evenly. "I despise all of you equally. But I'm a businessman. A client I represent from London is committed to investing heavily here. A number of sports goods shops, a gymnasium, a private tennis club … various projects. It is not in his interests for war to break out again. It's bad for business.

Now, if that will be all -"

"Just leave us your new telephone number," McGuinness said. "The mobile. I suppose you're going to your daughter's house now?"

Squires nodded. He pulled out a biro and scribbled a number underneath *The Times* crossword, tore it off and handed it to McGuinness.

"I'm proud of her," he said simply. "She was very brave today. I'm going for a drink first. I think I deserve one."

Without looking backwards, he strode away from the table and exited swiftly.

"One's all he ever has," Pat commented. "I don't know why he bothers."

"We don't all share your enthusiasm for pub culture," said McGuinness. "A cup of tea was always good enough for me. I think it's a throwback to his undercover days. He would have needed to have kept a clear head."

"Each to his own. What now?"

"Take this."

McGuinness wrote an address on the other side of the piece of paper Squires had given him.

"It's a safe house. Lower Ormeau Road. Ring Squires in a few days. He may have something to tell you."

"Why?"

"The Prods were sickened by that last one. Thompson O'Loan. He was one of their own. They'll not take on McCaw themselves but some of them would be glad enough to assist if somebody else volunteers to do it. That's how Lenny Murphy was dealt with. Squires could tell you all about that. He was in on it. But it would be a blatant breach of the ceasefire if we did it officially and claimed it. It would spark off the very return to war that these dissidents are trying to goad us into. God knows how many more wasted years we'd be looking at then."

"Don't look at me," said Pat. "You know I've left it all behind me."

McGuinness gesticulated in the direction of the graveyard behind him.

"Look over there, Pat," he said. "There's a headstone over there, somewhere, a memorial. Dated 1847. To eight hundred victims of the Famine. Cholera, dysentery, God knows what. Would that kind of thing inspire you at all?"

"No."

"No, I didn't think so. What did motivate you to join the organisation?"

"Imperialism – " Pat began.

"Imperialism my arse," said McGuinness. "They don't even call it that any more. It's all euphemisms. 'Ethical universalism' I heard some boffin call it recently, on the radio. That sort of activity will always be with us. I seem to remember you were on the Marxist wing of the movement."

"Briefly."

"Marxism's just a recurring fashion. It's popular from time to time. But it can never work," said McGuinness thoughtfully. "If you want to know why, read Popper. If you want to know why we don't remember it can never work, read Althusser. A radical absence of memory. That's what he called it. He reckoned societies were just epiphenomena - is that the word? – of economic forms and lacked human continuity. It's probably true. Anyhow, Cleaky told me once that he swore you in the night of those crucifixions on Drumcree hill."

"He told you right."

"The Portadown brethren always did incline towards zealotry. But you understand my predicament, Pat. The movement can't be seen to have any connection with action on this. Trouble is, the hotheads in our ranks are getting harder to control every day. If they start a counter campaign now, it'll be the end of the present leadership. It'll be the end of me. And it will certainly be the end of the peace. That's where you come in. If you do the needful, fine. We'll disown it. If you get caught or killed, we can legitimately disown you anyway as an outsider. A dissident, or a maverick, or a tout trying to make amends off his own bat."

"What's in it for me?"

"Safety. Take out McCaw and the rabble around him will splinter and disintegrate. Cut off the head of the snake, Pat. The body will twitch about dangerously for a little and then die. The mainstream paramilitaries in the Shankill will slap his satellites into line fairly quickly if he's out of the way."

Pat shook his head.

"I don't want this, Jimmy. I'm through."

McGuinness put a hand on his shoulder as he got up from his chair.

"You're through if you don't, Pat. You're on your own. They'll get you. Or comrade Turley and the nutting squad might feel obliged to get you. Either way, your life won't be worth a penny candle. You could always go back to America. Snag is, you'd have to stay there. Forever. And that's how long the war might last this time. By the way, I forgot to tell you. That blonde bit you and Rhett both used to have the hots for. What was her name?"

"Heather Lockhart.What about her? She went to Australia."

"She's back. Divorced. I thought you'd like to know. She's living up Bloomfield way. You might like to renew acquaintance."

"I might. She must be staying with her mother."

"Get this other business sorted first," McGuinness advised. "If you're using a team, use lily-whites. None of the old crew, nobody connected. If you want a shooter, get a clean one on the black market. The Whistler might be able to help you. Or Costello. If you need a bomb maker, I can let you have Dennis Linden."

Pat looked out the big window overlooking Botanic Gardens. Outside, watery sunshine broke through the grey sky to illuminate the thin covering of snow that had transformed the park unseasonably into a picturesque winter wonderland.

"*After Linden*," he said, "*all bloodless lay the untrodden snow ...*"

McGuinness grinned for the first time.

"I know that poem myself. Don't ask me what Dennis has done, by the way, because you don't need to know. Let's just say he's a fellow traveller in the same boat you're in. He'd jump at a chance to redeem himself. Just be careful, Pat. Be very, very careful. Do what you have to do. Know only what you need to know. Steal softly through sunlight. Steal softly through snow."

Pat did not even see him leave. Deep in thought, he stared out the window for a very long time.

Eventually he got up himself and left. He walked alone, oblivious to the pervasive cold, down the frightened white paths that twisted through Botanic Gardens, past clusters of snow-covered bushes and rows of silent trees that stood starkly in abeyance like frozen warnings, onwards to the gate at the far side of the park that led on to Agincourt Avenue and the sanctuary that awaited him on the adjoining lower Ormeau Road.

PART FOUR

Close To The Edge

Chapter 13

Part Of The Union

IT WAS A dream move for Adam Conway. He had always enjoyed the trade union duties that had been such a regular feature of his life in the Civil Service; the work was often challenging but a welcome relief from the repetitive grind of office life. He had often envied the kudos of the full-time officials, well known personalities who were generally well respected in the Civil Service branches, people who more often than not had come up through the ranks as lay officers initially. Now he was about to join them.

The location of the union's headquarters, White House, could not have been more auspicious. He had recently made his home off the Stranmillis Road, having bought a comfortable small terraced house in the same street where his cousin Enda had once led him to that unforgettable encounter with Chelsea. He knew she didn't live there now, she was in London; yet he couldn't help thinking about her every time he passed the distinctive green door. The union headquarters, named after its famous founding General Secretary Elijah White, was situated ten minutes' walk away on a splendid site on the Stranmillis Road itself. Beyond an open metal gate was a very long driveway, flanked by green lawns and bordered with shrubs, laurel mostly, dark green and glistening from the recent effects of a little light rain. There were a lot of trees dotted here and there and a delightful odour in the cool summer air of flowers and grass.

At the end of the driveway was a large and imposing two storey building, painted an austere shade of white, with short windows on the ground floor and taller windows above, fronted by a pillared front entrance on either side of which an ornate lamp hung. On one side of the building, which looked magnificent in the emerging morning sunlight, was a grass tennis court; on the other, a huge bronze statue of the late Elijah White, stooping, brooding and bearded for posterity. Beyond the tennis court a towering fountain in the gardens below splashed water into deep pools.

As Adam walked towards the entrance an occasional car passed by, snaking round the building into the spacious car park at the rear. Adam pressed the bell at the door, over which the legend TUNICS (standing for Trade Union of the Northern Ireland Civil Service, though none but the initiated would have known it) was emblazoned. When he entered John Lennon was already waiting for him in the reception area. Adam knew him only slightly, as an official who was an affable lookalike of his illustrious musical namesake.

"Come in, Adam," he said, smiling and extending a hand. "I'll introduce you to everyone another time. Most of the officials are out this morning and the administration staff are all at a fire safety seminar."

Lennon pressed the button for the elevator and ushered Adam into it. He explained that there was a restructuring exercise going on at White House at the moment and no-one was quite sure how all the jobs were going to pan out.

"It'll take about another week to get everything straightened out," he said, as they stepped out into the first floor. "So what you're going to be doing until then is shadowing Tommy Ogdon. Do you know Tommy?"

Adam nodded. Tommy Ogdon had not conformed to the usual career path followed by most of the White House staff. A former stand-up comedian, he had cut his trade union teeth with the actors' union and had never worked in the Civil Service in his life.

He had a reputation for being crude but effective and for an often unorthodox approach.

"He's holding a training course in there."

Lennon pointed to a door at the end of the corridor, from which there emanated a frenzied cacophony resembling the barking of a multitude of rabid dogs.

"Just go in and watch. It'll be an education for you," suggested Lennon. "He's expecting you anyway. A word of advice – don't get too influenced by his methods. Tommy's a one-off. Whatever you do, for God's sake don't ever try to imitate him."

Adam tentatively pushed open the door and stood open-mouthed at the entrance. Tommy Ogdon, a big stout man in his forties with a large prominent mouth, wild staring eyes and longish brown hair that he was constantly slicking back from over his forehead, stood pointing dramatically at a group of several dozen trainee branch activists. Derek Greenslade, a veteran official who had previously worked for the Police Federation, sat unobtrusively behind him, arms folded.

"Oggy! Oggy! Oggy!" Tommy Ogdon was shouting.

"Ow! Ow! Ow!" came the Pavlovian response.

"Oggy!"

"Ow!"

"Oggy! Oggy! Oggy!"

"Ow! Ow! Ow! Ow! Ow! …"

The trainees even began to take on the appearance of a pack of slavering hounds as Tommy imperiously raised a hand to silence the din.

"I was walking down the town the other day. I saw a black policeman. *Coon*stable, I said to him - " he looked around the room, smirking "- *coon*stable, there's one thing that's never changed about the police in this country. You always were a shower of black bastards and you still are!"

An uneasy ripple of laughter spread around the audience, everyone eventually joining in. Tommy affected a reaction of incandescent rage.

"You laughed!" he shrieked accusingly. "You fucking laughed! You weren't supposed to laugh. Stand up!"

Sheepishly, they all stood up.

"Sit down!"

They sat down.

"After tea break," he continued solemnly, "we're going to be looking at race relations legislation. If there's one thing in this world that's not funny, it's racism. Some of you might have lived in England at some time, in which case you might well have experienced being called Paddy. It's no joke. If they can't even get your fucking name right, there's no hope for them. These days there's money to be had out of tribunals for that type of thing. Niggers, kikes, dagoes, Eyeties, gooks, Pakis, Frogs, krauts – you want to avoid using any of that sort of language. If you don't, you'll find yourself and your employers being taken to the cleaners. There's a huge big gravy train out there and every jabbering hoopdab in Christendom wants to jump on it."

"What about religious discrimination, Tommy?" asked one of the trainees, a young girl with an intent look of concentration on her face.

"That's different. Taigs and snouts and all that local sort of lark is covered by fair employment law," he replied. "Anyhow – bugger off and get a cup of tea. Be back here in fifteen minutes."

As the trainees filed out in the direction of the canteen at the other end of the building, Ogdon strode over to Adam and extended a massive palm.

"You always could work an audience, Tommy," said Adam, wincing at the bone-crushing handshake.

"You ain't seen nothing yet," he grinned. "I've been picking up a few tips. I was watching that Keith Dalkeith cove down at the Waterfront Hall the other day."

"He's a magician, isn't he? Isn't that the guy who's promising to make the Stormont Estate disappear in front of an audience sometime this year?"

"That's the one. Pity he wouldn't make some of the dickheads in it disappear. It'd make our job easier."

"He's an interesting writer," observed Greenslade. "I read his treatise on the souls of woodlice recently. Fascinating stuff."

"I've never read any of his books. But he's a motivational

guru among other things," said Tommy. "Some of the top brass in the Civil Service have been concerned with shrinking staff numbers and low morale lately -"

"That's our whinge," said Adam, "not theirs. What you mean is that they're looking at ways of getting more blood out of more stones."

Tommy and Greenslade looked at each other, grinning.

"You've got it in one, Adam," Greenslade agreed. "I like this boy's attitude, Tommy. He'll like it here at the White House."

"Yep. Anyhow, two Departments are already committed to buying in this five day course from the Meltsonian Institute called *Managing Your Mind*," Tommy explained. "It's for all the workforce. There's a lot of public money being thrown at it so I thought I'd sit in on Dalkeith's sales pitch, see what it was about and then rubbish it. It turned out to be a corker of a presentation, though."

They had walked as far as a door at the corner of the corridor leading to the stairs and Greenslade was fumbling in his pocket for a key. Adam noticed that the door was the only one in the vicinity without a number.

"Dalkeith was something else. He had the entire audience hypnotised – kept telling them to stand up and sit down, and repeat various mantras, all that kind of malarkey. Magic stuff," Ogdon went on as Greenslade forced open the door. "I still haven't sussed out how he worked that levitation trick in the middle of the lecture, though. Anyway – here we are. This is the Operations Room, by the way, in case you were wondering."

"Staff only," explained Greenslade. "You're one of us now, so keep this to yourself. There's a meeting of the Executive Council on downstairs today. We like to know what our ruling body is getting up to."

He flicked a couple of switches, activating a dim light and a television screen. The picture depicted one of the big conference rooms below. Twenty five elected members of the TUNICS Executive Council were shown seated round a large table, at the top of which sat the President, Yvonne O'Mara, flanked by the General Secretary Reg Hetherington and a couple of other anxious looking senior officials. There was no sound from the television but the animated behaviour of some of those present suggested that a heated debate was taking place.

"Care in the fucking community, this lot," said Tommy. "More brains in a false face."

"The arithmetic's worrying us this year, Adam," Greenslade added. "This one member, one vote nonsense was always dangerous. Time was, you could elect who got onto the Council at annual conference. Now, it's all at the whim of the membership. Most of them don't vote and the ones that do seldom know who they're voting for. Ballots go missing, too. Rumour has it there were hundreds nicked this year."

"The Free Radical caucus has a 13-12 overall majority this year. First time ever," said Tommy worriedly. "That's all this lot on the far side – you'll know some of them. Trots, mostly, and hangers on. Malcontents with bad sick records for the most part. On the right hand side they're all in the Beige Antelope faction -"

"The what?" asked Adam. "Why do they call themselves that? I know some of them too."

"Dunno. It's a variation on the Black Panthers and the White Wolves and all those lot, I suppose. They're an independent alliance, all political opinions and none. They were the dominant faction for years. Bloody good trade unionists, most of them - they do the actual work, the other shower are just messers. They hate everybody. Get the sound on, Derek. See that bug-eyed fuckwit that's slabbering at the minute, Adam? He's a candidate for the funny farm. Paul Stomper. The hatchet faced harridan beside him is Marjorie Guppy."

As Greenslade began to manipulate the remote control, Adam observed Stomper, a small fat man with a toothbrush black moustache and large bulbous eyes, standing up and mouthing excitedly.

"I don't care what you say, President," he was saying in a wheedling, sneering voice, as the sound came on. "I'll tell you now, the Executive Council is not going to gag me. The officials of this union will do what they're told to by this Free Radical leadership! I tell you now, the members will vote for an indefinite all-out, all-member strike if the situation is properly explained to them - "

"Yes!" screeched Marjorie Guppy, a woman in her fifties with a Welsh accent whom Adam thought bore a striking resemblance to the Wicked Witch of the West in *The Wizard of Oz*. "We must be open and honest with the members! But that's not all, comrades – we need a political arm as well as an industrial arm! A new vibrant mass political party, of the workers, for the workers - "

Greenslade pressed a button and the picture disappeared.

"They'll keep that bloody clown show going for at least an hour," he said, getting up. "There's no point in listening to it. We can come back later when they get onto the really mental agenda. Like electing full-time officials instead of appointing them, and cutting our salaries to the average working wage."

"Whatever the fuck that is. And that's just the fucking socialists," said Tommy. "You can see what we're up against, Adam. That's democracy for you."

"How did the likes of people like that ever get elected?"

"The silly name syndrome," explained Greenslade. "Nobody who knows Stomper would ever vote for him. But he gets the silly name vote. Like that nonentity Alan Aardvark that used to top the poll years ago. He never opened his mouth at a Council meeting but he always got elected because of his name. His was always first on the list."

"And there are more women than men in TUNICS. A lot of women vote only for other women, without knowing anything about them. So mad cows like Marge the targe end up here instead of in therapy, where they fucking well ought to be," added Tommy, switching off the lights. "Not a word about this, by the way, Adam. Those buffoons downstairs think it's security cameras we have in the conference rooms."

As they left the room and Greenslade locked the door, Lennon hailed them from the top of the stairs.

"There's a member in to see you, Tommy," he said. "A Mr Larmour. Says he has an appointment."

"Shit. I forgot about him," Tommy muttered. "Better see him, I suppose. He's a retired member. Some superannuation problem. I'd ditch these coffin dodgers if I had my way. They're not paying subscriptions anymore, so why should we bother?"

"Do you want me to take the class through the race discrimination law, then?" asked Derek.

"Bignose will do it. Won't you, John? You're in the office all day today anyway, aren't you?"

"All right," said Lennon. "You owe me one, then."

Tommy's office downstairs looked as if a bomb had hit it. Files and papers were piled high on the desk and around the floor and a bulging briefcase had been thrown carelessly on top of the waste bin beside a glass-fronted bookcase. The blinds were three quarters shut and the absence of light served to exaggerate the general disorder of the surroundings. Tommy pulled in a couple of chairs from a nearby store room and ushered Mr Larmour, a thin pale man in his sixties, into the office.

"I know you've written to me about your problem, Mr Larmour," said Tommy, "and I thank you for that. I'd be grateful if you'd just refresh my memory on the detail. This is Adam Conway, incidentally. He's a new member of staff. Ex-Civil Service man like yourself."

Larmour grew visibly more agitated as he began to talk. Adam's eyes glazed over as he rambled on and on about section four of the pension scheme and the injustices presented by paragraphs four six two and four seventeen two, or some such tripe. His problem seemed to have been caused by marrying the same woman twice, once after he retired, thus somehow losing out on over a decade's worth of widow's benefit. Or something like that. Adam was aroused from his half slumber when Tommy suddenly got up and shook Larmour's hand.

"Mr Larmour," he said solemnly, "we at TUNICS owe you our gratitude for raising this serious matter with us. Rest assured that we'll be giving it our utmost attention. Fortunately, in Adam Conway here we have one of the foremost experts in pensions that the trade union movement has ever been fortunate enough to boast of in these islands. You're in good hands. We'll be in touch. If you feel like winding down a little before you leave, why not take a walk around the grounds? It's a beautiful day."

Adam shook his head in exasperation as Larmour closed

the door behind him.

"Why did you tell him that? I don't know anything about pensions."

"Nobody knows anything about pensions. You just look it up, argue a case if there is one. But you're in luck."

"Why?"

"Because I've just given you a penalty kick, that's why. I actually did read the guy's letter. Pensions branch have got it wrong. They have discretion to over-ride the rules in a rare case like that. There's a precedent on file that they obviously don't know about. It goes back a long time. All you have to do is copy the papers to the pensions wallahs along with a stiff letter and bingo – you've won it. Come on, let's get a coffee. Have you ever been in the inner sanctum before?"

Adam replied that he hadn't. The staff canteen on the ground floor was out of bounds to the union's members, a rule that was rigidly enforced. It was a modest enough room with a scattering of tables and chairs. A kitchen area at the top housed a fridge, a microwave oven, a cooker, various cupboards and, on top of a long worktop, a kettle and two catering size tins, one each of tea and coffee.

"I'm just about ready for some caffeine," said Tommy. "This stuff is just about drinkable."

The door opened and Alma Walker, an official whom Adam knew only by sight, looked around her.

She spotted Tommy taking a couple of mugs from one of the cupboards but didn't immediately see Adam at the fridge looking for the milk.

"Tommy, there's trouble at Pangloss House."

"So? There's always trouble in that fucking loony bin. Why are you telling me? It's one of Gordon's areas now, with the re-structuring. Not my problem."

"Gordon's off on leave and there's no-one else available. I thought John was free but apparently he's taking a training course."

"Bloody marvellous. Adam, this is Alma, by the way. Alma, Adam. But enough of the pleasantries. What is it this time?"

"It's very bad. They're threatening a mass walkout.

Apparently some member of the travelling community took umbrage at not getting his benefit money on time. He's gone and lobbed a bag of rats over the counter and they're running wild."

"That's today's lunch taken care of for our lot," commented Tommy, sipping his coffee. "It'll save them having to go to the Chinky across the road."

"You better get down there."

"Aye. All right. Come on, Adam. I'll drive. I've got the car round the back."

Adam found himself involuntarily shutting his eyes as Tommy Ogdon accelerated round the corner onto the main driveway and sped off. A large orange tomcat, one of the growing population of feral felines that was forever roaming the White House grounds, emitted an anguished miaow of protest at being forced to interrupt its measured macho amble up the middle of the path, leaping several feet in the air and twisting towards the adjoining lawn to avoid the hurtling vehicle. On a bough of a nearby tree a female tabby observed the spectacle with a detached queenly dignity, her reproachful gaze fastened on the speeding car until it became a speck in the distance.

"I don't know if you're familiar with this branch, Adam," Tommy was saying. "They're mad as fucking March hares, the lot of them. The bloody office has only been up and running six months. Branch secretary is Dolly Deacon."

"I don't know her."

"Him. He's a shirt-lifter. But he's all right. Not a bad lad for a poof. The Chairman – or Chairperson, if you're into political correctness -"

"I'm not."

"Thank fuck. He's a big guy called Otto Vage. Mad as a hatter. They're both unreconstructed lefties. Stupid ones. Trots, as a matter of fact."

"Not sophisticated, then."

"Nope. One trick ponies. They think strikes are the answer to everything. Or industrial action, as it's known these days. What a misnomer. They're all white collar for a start, so they're non-industrials. If they stop working, it's stopping action. Non-industrial inaction would be more like it, as somebody or other once said. Or unpaid bloody leave, to you and me and anybody else with a brain in their head."

"What do you think's going to happen here today?"

"They'll walk out. Bound to. So we might as well swan in and take the credit for it while we're here. This is it."

Tommy rushed furiously through a red light and swerved round in a corner into a convenient parking space in a side street adjacent to Pangloss House.

Outside the front door of the redbrick building, situated between a shop and a pub on Belfast's Golden Mile, a huge figure in an American football outfit, complete with shoulder pads, body armour and metal helmet, energetically beckoned.

"Who the fuck's this cunt?" inquired Adam, inadvertently lapsing into the vernacular of his mentor.

"That's big Otto. He's a part-time bouncer in that Gridiron bar down the city centre when he's not working here," explained Tommy, locking the car doors as they got out. "You know that American football theme place? Never was my cup of tea. Too young a crowd."

Otto Vage removed his helmet as he stroke towards them, revealing a beaming cherubic countenance topped with a shock of red hair.

"Yo! Tommy, my main man! Gimme five! What's cooking up at the White House, good buddy?"

"Fuck all. What's with the get up?"

"I was supposed to be off today, so I'd arranged to do the door at the Gridiron for a Budweiser promotion that's running at lunchtime. I'd just got changed when Dolly rang me on the mobile to tip me off about this -"

"Yeah, yeah. So what's the beef?"

"We reckon there were four rats. Three were chased out when all the doors were opened. Another got caught behind a filing cabinet and was beaten to death with an umbrella."

"Right. We better inspect the body. What angle's the management taking?"

"Houston and McKechnie are waiting to see you in room

six. They want to talk to a White House official rather than the local yokels. Most of the staff are up in the canteen for an emergency general meeting of the branch."

"Right. Go and join them. Keep the lid on it until we get there."

As Otto Vage disappeared in the direction of the stairs, Tommy strode through the near deserted office, Adam in his wake. A large sign at the entrance read:

PANGLOSS HOUSE SOCIAL SECURITY OFFICE
Our mission is to delight our customers by acting as pro-active facilitators of a world class quality service based on an over-arching culture of business excellence that is focused on continuous improvement.

"That'll put bread on the table," remarked Tommy. "Here we go – there's wee Maddy from the branch committee."

A small thin woman in a blue dress approached, followed by a gangling youth with thin lank hair and a very prominent Adam's apple. Lurking behind them was a couple of middle-aged men clad in the anonymous attire of everyday office workers.

"It's over here, past those computers," the woman called Maddy said in a harsh, croaking voice. "Luke killed it – didn't you, Lukey?"

The gangling youth nodded morosely, jerking a thumb at the battered body of a giant rodent on the blood splattered carpet by a grey filing cabinet.

"There was four rats, see, and I g-g-got an um-um---" stuttered Luke, "---umbrella, and I g-g-got him, see, that one, over there …."

Tommy poked the corpse inquisitively with his foot, chuckling. "He's a fine old captain of the sewers, and no mistake. Well done, Lukey. Can you put him in a bag, or something? You can? Good. Bring it upstairs to the meeting. We'll be with you in a jiffy. Whereabouts is room six?"

"Down that corridor, Tommy," said Maddy, pointing behind her. "Second door on the left."

"Right. Come on, Adam. Let's give these bastards an education about the meaning of constructive industrial relations."

Adam watched aghast as Tommy turned the door handle, then sent the door flying open with a thunderous kick. Two grey-haired men in their fifties gasped at the ferocity of the entrance as Tommy strode in and thrust his face inches from theirs, banging the table in front of him with a clenched fist.

"What the fuck do you shower of fucks think you're playing at?" he demanded.

"Now, Tommy ..," one of the grey-haired men began.

"Don't you 'now, Tommy' me, you fuck! Why hasn't this building been cleared? Do you want an outbreak of bubonic fucking plague in here? Eh?"

"Mr Ogdon, I'll thank you to moderate your language," the other man interjected icily. "We were expecting to be dealing with Mr McElrath in any event. Not you."

"Gordon's off. You've got me whether you like it or not. Now – are you going to send your staff home or do I have to lead them out of the building for you to get the message?"

"You can't do that," the second man protested. "That's wildcat action. You'd have to call a ballot. There are rules and regulations …"

"Fuck your rules and regulations. Adam – go up to the meeting, try and stop them wrecking the place. I'll be one minute. That's all I'm going to give these two cunts to see sense."

The woman called Maddy was waiting outside.

"Where's the canteen?" Adam inquired. "Tommy's going to be a little while longer."

"Come with me," she said. "I'm going up there myself. Luke's down the corridor, he'll wait for Tommy."

The canteen was a huge cavernous room with tables and chairs packed on top of one another to accommodate the murmuring crowd. Adam estimated that there were upwards on a couple of hundred people present.

At the top of the room in front of a small table stood the bloated figure of Otto Vage in full American football regalia, by now with the helmet back on, and a plumpish bespectacled sybarite with brilliantined black hair, several chins and an ostentatiously effeminate manner whom Adam correctly surmised to be Dolly Deacon, the branch secretary.

"We agwee the following wesolution, then, comwades," Deacon was lisping, holding up a crumpled piece of paper from which he proceeded to read. "This bwanch unanimously condemns the act of aggwession committed in this building today and unequivocally cwiticises management for not sending the staff home, even when the wats were wunning awound the office. It is the view of this bwanch -"

Deacon's ramblings were abruptly cut short as the canteen door was flung open and the florid face of Tommy Ogdon peeked in from behind it.

"Oggy! Oggy! Oggy!" he bellowed.

A huge cheer went up from the crowd as Tommy marched through a group of onlookers close to the door and up to the top table, the youth called Luke following behind clutching a large paper bag.

"I can't fucking hear you!" Tommy shouted. "I said – Oggy! Oggy! Oggy!"

"Ow! Ow! Ow!" the crowd responded enthusiastically.

"Oggy!"

"Ow!"

"Oggy! Oggy!"

"Ow! Ow!"

"Oggy! Oggy! Oggy!"

"Ow! Ow! Ow! Ow! Ow! Ow! …"

Tommy raised his right hand slowly and theatrically to quell the tumultuous ritual barking. Only when total silence had descended did he beckon Luke to his side and take the paper bag from him. Opening it, he slowly removed the revolting contents, holding the monstrous dead rodent aloft by the tail at arm's length away from himself.

The crowd gasped in shock and horror and the initial murmurs of outrage began swiftly to grow to a crescendo.

"Rats!" bawled Tommy. "They fought the dogs and killed the cats! They bit the babies in their cradles, and ate the cheeses out of the vats…and licked the soup from the cook's own ladles! Are we going to stand for this sort of thing, comrades? Are we going to give every buck eejit in this country a licence to come in here and fire rats about the parish and intimidate us in our own workplaces?"

A loud murmur of dissent spread around the audience, many of whom were shaking their heads emphatically.

"Are you? Because if you're not, there's only one answer to give your management here today, you know that. They won't stand up for you. But your union always will. TUNICS will never let you down. Are you with me, comrades?"

The cheers of the crowd reverberated throughout the canteen as Tommy made his way towards the door.

"Everybody out!" he shouted, beckoning the crowd to follow him.

Downstairs, one of the grey-haired men was emerging ashen-faced from the main office. Tommy brushed him aside and casually tossed the dead rat through the open door.

"All yours, McKechnie," he said dismissively. "Get this fucking place cleaned up and maybe - just maybe – your staff might come back in tomorrow."

Outside, a television crew was waiting. Adam could not help but notice the statesmanlike veneer of oleaginous gravitas affected by Tommy on spotting the lurking camera.

"Tommy Ogdon, who is an official with TUNICS, the recognised trade union for the workers in Pangloss House, has just come out," the news reporter was saying into a microphone. "Mr Ogdon, is it true that the staff are staging an unofficial walkout here today in response to the unprovoked attack earlier this morning?"

"That's correct, Seamus," Tommy replied, his voice suddenly low and saccharine and confidential in tone. "I would like to take this opportunity to pay tribute to the courage and dignity displayed by all of our members in taking this principled stance here today. I should add that this is not actually an unofficial strike, contrary to what management here seem to think. This is a health and safety matter. Management has a duty of care towards the workers in a situation like this. They failed to clear the building, I'm sorry to say, and so the union has had to do it for them. The staff here have nothing but the highest regard for the travelling community. But having said that, they will not sit idly by and let themselves be threatened or abused. All they want to do is to get on with providing a much needed service to the public in an environment where their personal safety and wellbeing is not at risk. We don't think that's too much to ask and we hope that the public will bear with us and support this action here today."

As they returned to the car, Tommy confided to Adam that the television crew's presence had been arranged. He'd tipped off Seamus Tate, the interviewer, by a call on his mobile phone on the way up to the branch meeting. He knew that Tate was going to be interviewing members of the public on the Golden Mile about current political events.

It was too good an opportunity to miss for attracting public support for the walkout.

"He's a good lad, Seamus," Tommy said, manoeuvring the car into Great Victoria Street. "Always sympathetic to the unions. He knows all our lot. You'll see him up at the White House a fair bit during the summer – he plays in our wee tennis league. He likes our grass court even though he's a member of one of the local clubs where they have that astro-turf, or whatever you call it. He loves the game. Went to school years ago with that Spirit of Ireland cove, wossname, that won Wimbledon once."

"Jack McGrath. He was a character."

"McGrath. Yeah. He was more than just a character. McGrath was a fucking role model, pal. He knew how to live life to the full."

"The papers are still writing about him, you know. There was an article the other day – one of the Sunday broadsheets, I think. Apparently he's fallen on hard times."

"Makes a change from hard drink."

"He was too fond of that. He still gets called the Spirit of Ireland, even now."

"So he should. That man showed the world what this country is all about, or should be about. So what if he liked a drink? Don't we all, for Christ's sake. He was a man of the people, that's what I'm saying, the people's champion. Am I right or am I right?"

"Right. So – what are we going to be doing the rest of the day?"

"Meeting on Civil Service pay. There's a team of management side reps coming to the White House to talk to us about a new pay system."

"I haven't read any papers -"

"Neither have I. You don't need to bother at this stage, it's only proposals. You just sit there nodding from time to time and saying things like 'I hear what you're saying' and 'I can see where you're coming from.' Drink plenty of coffee, and you'll not nod off. And stroke your beard a lot."

"I don't have a beard."

"You fucking will have by the time you're done listening to these cunts."

Later that evening, Adam felt tired but exhilarated as he made his way to Slattery's. The bar's black exterior and gold signage beckoned a familiar welcome, the apricot coloured walls and wooden surfaces of the interior combining to provide the warmth of a home from home.

Unusually, Adam did not recognise any of the customers, except for an American acquaintance called Everett Nash who was peering short-sightedly at the jukebox as he hovered hesitantly with a coin. A couple of part-time students were doing a shift behind the bar. One of them, whom Adam knew to see, told him that Pat Farland had not been in for some days. He had rung in to say that he didn't know when he would be back. Family crisis, apparently. Adam picked up his pint of Smithwicks, pocketed his change and decided to join Nash at the other end of the bar. He looked round briefly as he walked and spotted Tom Bellingham slouching up to the bar, hands in pockets.

"Cheesy Ring been in?" he demanded.

The nearest barman shook his hand, polishing a glass as he did so and barely looking up. Tom grunted and wheeled off out the door, not noticing Adam. Adam let him go. He didn't fancy being stuck with Tom for the evening.

Everett Nash persuaded him to give the Students' Union a

try. He was a postgraduate student, in his thirties but younger looking in a goofy, boyish way. He had been doing some interminable thesis for as long as Adam could remember and was often seen wandering around the bars in the university area on his own. He was a tall, stooping individual with small rimless glasses and long floppy brown hair. He had a puppyish tendency to look delighted and astonished at any mundane comment that was directed his way.

“There are some American students I know who might be here tonight,” he told Adam as they went into the bar.

The American students were fated never to materialise but Adam instantly recognised Jap Prendergast in the company of two younger drunks, a couple of students called Bunjy Doolan and Squigs Quigley. It was several years since Jap had graduated but he still behaved like he was a youngster just up at Queen’s. Adam didn’t see much of him these days. Doolan and Quigley, a couple of boorish youths from rural backgrounds, were the latest residents of the house in Ireton Street. Doolan, a small rotund figure with a silly fringe and a cigarette stuck stupidly in the corner of his mouth, was standing up squinting and pointing at a passing acquaintance.

“G’wan, ye big tube ye!” he was jeering. “Fukken bate the day, boy! Fukken wan fourteen til fukken wan twelve! Yeeeoh!”

“Some Gaelic football match. Bunjy’s team won,” Adam explained to his baffled American companion.

“Adam Conway! Yo!” Jap shouted, waving. “Get them in, boy! Pints of Harp all round!”

Jap hadn’t changed much. He still had the same gormless grin and irritating Newry accent but the nascent beer belly that peeped over the belt of his trousers lent his lanky frame an incipient incongruity. As ever, his obsession with reminiscing dominated the conversation that night. He recalled the night of Pat Farland’s fortieth birthday down at the Rumour Machine.

“Great night, boy,” he said, lighting up another cigarette and reaching for a fresh pint of Harp. “But imagine being forty! I can’t imagine anything in this world that could be worse than being old.”

“Hey – don’t say that,” protested Nash. “I’m only a few

years off the big four-oh myself."

"Whah?" Doolan stared at him in astonishment. "Fuck off then, ye dying auld cunt! Get the fuck away to a home, before you pop your clogs!"

"Aye. You're not with us, you Yankee fucker," Quigley added jocularly. "Away and die off!"

"We're the boys!" Jap squealed happily. "We've not seen the end of the student capers yet, Conway! Come on, lads – sing! All together now:

You don't get me, I'm part of the union
You don't get me, I'm part of the union
You don't get me, I'm part of the union
Til the day I die
Til the day I die!"

The rest of the company studiously ignored Jap's lusty carolling and took the opportunity to swallow more beer and stare at a group of girls who had just come in. None of them could have been more than twenty at the most, Adam decided, as Jap gulped down his pint and loudly harangued Everett Nash for not being quick enough in getting his round in. The American meekly sloped off to the bar.

"Keep her lit!" beamed Jap. "Here, Adam – you must miss Ireton Street. We've seen some days down there, boy!"

"And some nights," assented Adam, humouring him.

"Of course we have," said Jap ponderously, "and we'll see many more, believe you me."

"What about the old crew?" said Adam, struggling to make conversation that wasn't entirely asinine. "Ever hear from them?"

"Aye. Well, big Farland's still there, though he hasn't turned in for a while. Some family crisis, he told them at Slattery's. More likely he's throwing the dong into some dirtbird up a back alley somewhere."

"What about Dommo and Stevie?"

"Dommo's back home in Downpatrick. Never goes out. Total recluse, boy. Has been ever since that wee dirty from Ardglass had the abortion that time, after he bubbled her. We should go down there and see him some of these weekends. Get him out for a few pints, cheer him up. Stevie's still in Liverpool. He fucking hates it."

He paused to bite the top off a packet of peanuts and take a long draught of Harp before launching into a long repetitive story about Stevie starting a fight in a Liverpool pub by saying that scousers were all a pack of humourless bastards. Nobody understood his accent except for a nearby Glaswegian, who repeated what he'd said and laughed. Some scouser hit him and it started a free-for-all. Stevie was just about conscious enough to get out before he caught one of the punches that were flying.

"Anyhow," Jap was chortling, "Stevie gets a taxi and asks to be taken to Ireton Street. The driver wasn't quite sure where it was so Stevie tells him Botanic Avenue and calls him a stupid cunt for not knowing where he was going. Then he falls asleep, until the driver gives him a dig to wake him up. 'Here we are, mate,' he says, and charges him whatever it is. He's just starting to drive off when Stevie says: 'Is this Liverpool or Belfast?' He was totally blitzed, like.The driver looks at him like he's a total dipso and says: 'Liverpool', then he drives off and leaves Stevie standing there."

"Where was he?"

"Ireton Street! There's an Ireton Street in Liverpool as well, apparently, only it's miles from where Stevie's staying in Smithdown Road. He didn't have a baldy where he was, so he just cowped in a doorway. He woke up in the morning with his pockets empty and found a dog pissing on him!"

Adam had had enough to drink to find the story funny. Not so Everett Nash, who peered attentively at Jap as he spoke but obviously didn't comprehend much of it. It was getting late and the shutters were starting to come down at the bar.

"What'll we do now, boys?" said Doolan.

"Back to Ireton Street. Game of cards, maybe?" suggested Quigley.

"Fuck that," said Jap impatiently. "Come on and we'll go somewhere for a late one."

"Where?"

"Anywhere. What about that new Czech bar down in Donegall Square? I seen a heap of wee dirties heading in there earlier tonight."

"Hey, guys – there's a Czech bar in Belfast?" asked Nash, wide-eyed with wonder. "I guess I didn't know about that."

"Aye. The Velvet Revolution, they call it. Sells only Czech beer. Sound shed, boy. They have those big statues of Stalin and Lenin in the entrance hall – you know the ones used to be in that Northern Whig place years ago? Came out of the old Communist Party headquarters in Prague."

Doolan and Quigley eventually won the argument for a game of cards, much to the chagrin of Jap. Eventually Adam agreed to join them for a hand. Nash made his excuses and left, his exit scarcely noticed by his companions.

As they proceeded down Botanic Avenue, Jap kept going on about Dommo being in a bad way.

"We'll have to see the man, Adam," he said, stopping at the top of Ireton Street to urinate into an alleyway. "Last time I seen him, I says to him, fucking cheer up! Less of the dooming and glooming. It's a wonderful world, boy, and everything that happens, I honestly believe it all happens for the best. True bill. But would he listen? Would he fuck."

Adam paused before agreeing mechanically, then told the waiting group that he'd skip the card game after all.

"Early start tomorrow," he said. "Better not push it. I'm only there a day. See you again."

He watched them lurch down Ireton Street to the familiar doorway, Jap performing an impromptu hopscotch routine outside the door as Doolan fumbled for a key. Adam reflected that his sojourn in Australia hadn't been a total waste of time. If he hadn't managed to get away from that sort of environment he might easily have turned into another Jap, a perpetual adolescent who would never grow up and who would never begin to comprehend the stunted nature of that narrow existence. It would only be on the rare occasions he sobered up that the barren futility and isolation that lay at the end of that road would impinge upon his consciousness. It would be then that the gremlins would get him.

Adam turned and went back the way he had come. He decided on a whim to take a short cut through Botanic Gardens. He climbed the locked gate at the back of Queen's University, not without difficulty, for the night's drinking had taken its toll. The short walk to get there had seemed like an eternity, likewise the nocturnal journey through the unsettling quietness of the park itself. He felt suddenly very tired, as though the events of the day and of the evening had abruptly drained him. Tommy Ogdon had promised him a quiet day in the office tomorrow but he doubted if there was such a thing to be had at White House.

He reached the wall beside the gate at the top of the park at the Stranmillis Gardens entrance, facing the lit-up monstrosity of the Physical Education Centre opposite, then clambered awkwardly over it, leaving him with the shortest of short walks to where he lived. He was halfway over it when the air was rent by the most horrendous scream he had ever heard, way in the distance behind him somewhere. The screaming went on and on in the stillness of the night but faded as he walked and he had put it to the back of his mind by the time he reached his own house.

By the time he had slumped into bed he was oblivious to all, the veil of untroubled sleep swept aside only by chance in the morning by the harsh jangling of the alarm clock he had fortuitously left on a shelf on the far side of the bedroom beyond his blindly seeking hands.

Chapter 14

Turning Japanese

LINES ON THE perceived plight of John Aloysius Prendergast:

Down long-day years that pass so sombre by
The opaque casements of imagined history
There flit the shapes of half forgotten dreams
And fantasies that ne'er will come to pass;
Cracked pavements, broken glass
Stoic streetlights shining dimly – so it seems
And forlorn wasted streets
Still complement Jap's grey sap-dappled sheets
Where meet, intertwined in sleep
The one imbibed, exhaled; the other a vasty deep
Receptacle for troubled recollections –
His constant companions
Beer and a lonely bed.

The glittering illusions that sell
The sophistry of being, in Life's cell
Or chart the boundaries of Heaven – or of Hell
Can never speak the future, merely swell
The groundswell of delusion, of the past
Like the tintinnabulation

Of a ghostly and uncertain bell – one that's cast
In shadows, where its music forms a shell
And fragile but obsessive, sounds a knell
To summon adulation
That will quell
The spirit that, transformed, could make him well
And lift all those who're fallen whence they fell.

Across the pale parabola of pain
Juxtaposed by joy, though yet again
And again will he traverse that dusty road
where once shone hope
And vistas that beckoned, unsullied;
Once more will he embrace a dream to cope
With the insistent tattered beggar of reality
Pursuing the hurried slideshow of the mind
Into a kind of awareness; one that is not kind
To beggars or to choosers. Or the bullied –
More's the shame;
For if all in the end are losers, who's to blame?
Not those who never chose to play that game.

The Union bar and Harp will never change
Nor harp discordant memories in time
The faces as they pass may now be strange
But ne'er will the belles of Belfast cease to chime
In concord with concupiscent design.
Jap's happy when he dreams of being a pappy
Bubbling some wee dirty in her prime
Spending summer evenings changing nappies
Swilling lots of pints and feeling fine
Wallowing in the gross primordial slime
Of Newry, or some shit-hole, where you climb
From the sewer to the gutter, there to fester
And to spend your days enacting Life's dull mime
Your lot is that of a hackneyed old court jester
Whose reason never rose to match his rhyme.

Chapter 15

Ringing The Changes

"WHAT THE HELL was that about?" Max Lovell demanded. "I didn't understand a word of it."

"Neither did I," said Glyn Moxley, pausing to take a hearty draught of ale before rummaging in his inside jacket pocket. "Let's have a look at the programme. Here we are. What sort of an accent was that, anyway?"

"County Armagh, I think. I don't know who John Aloysius is but I think he should sue."

"I thought you enjoyed these 'Poems and Pints' nights, Max."

"I tolerate them. There's too bloody many of them, if you ask me. I don't like the way the English Society has taken this club over. It's supposed to be for everybody."

"It's called democracy, Max. They have a majority of their people on the committee. Why don't you stand yourself at the next AGM? Now…here it is."

Moxley peered intently at the back page of the programme.

"It's a poem from a new collection published by the Meltsonian Institute Press. *Future Echoes Of The Past*, they call it."

"Doggerel, I call it."

"Sub-title is *Observations By A Time Traveller From A Parallel Universe.* Poet is an MA student, School of English. The poems are all about people he's met here during his year on the Creative Writing course. I can't pronounce his name. 'The Bard of Bessbrook', he calls himself."

"He should be bloody barred. He's lucky he's not getting what your man Cinna got."

"Who?"

"Cinna, in *Julius Caesar*. Killed for his bad verses."

Chelsea Hynes sighed with exasperation. Getting stuck in the vicinity of these two had a hideous *déjà vu* inevitability about it; it seemed to be an unavoidable tragedy that her visits to the Queen's University Common Room, mercifully rare these days since her decision to move to London, invariably occasioned., Anne George, who had up to then been staring numbly at the latest collection of fine art prints that lined the wall beside her, had finally had enough.

"If you don't like the piece," she hissed through clenched teeth, "you could at least have the manners to applaud anyway. It's not easy for students to stand up in front of a crowd like this and read their work, you know. It's the first time for most of them. If you don't appreciate it, please don't show your ignorance."

"She's right, Max," Moxley grinned. "Have a bit of grace about you and don't be such a philistine. I told you we should have gone to the BBC Club tonight. I've been hearing some political gossip I'd like to check out with some of the BBC people."

"Like what?"

"Clandestine meetings between the Reverend Ichabod Cairns and some very unsavoury militant loyalist elements, for a start."

"Really? The Ulster Loyalist Defence Coalition, I take it? They're the only ones making bellicose noises these days."

"Not just any old ULDC people. I've heard Cairns has been talking to the New Butchers."

"Those bloody cut-throats? It's time they were wiped out before they start another bloody war. You'd think the other loyalists would take them out. They have still got their command structures and their weapons, for God's sake."

"The ULDC is getting too big for them. They're all afraid of Billy McCaw anyway."

"Well, we can go to the BBC Club later. Let's have another drink here first. Perhaps these young ladies will join us. Ladies…?"

Chelsea and Anne were already on their way towards the door by the time Lovell had turned archly in their direction, his mouth opening and closing like that of a fish as he abruptly realised that they had found the conversation less than enthralling and could not be persuaded to stay for another drink. Anne suggested that they visit A Rainbow In Curved Air, the new bar on the Stranmillis Road.

"It's lovely," she said. "And it shouldn't be too crowded this early in the week."

Chelsea nodded.

"Anywhere but here. Let's take a taxi. I don't want to walk it in these heels."

The bar had the appearance of a surreal modern church, all sombre grey stone and shining glass from the outside, standing tall in the middle of a vast lawn like some contemporary folly. Inside, the kitsch atmosphere created by the furnishings of dark wood panelling and chrome was complemented by angled mirrors on the walls behind each table, twisted metal chandeliers above the winding staircase leading to the Spectrum restaurant on the top floor and high leather upholstered barstools in various hues dotted round the circular bar in the centre of the room. The high ceiling, visible at the top of the staircase, was made of glass; the tinted curves reflected the full band of colours seen in a rainbow. Strange background music reverberated all around them, electric organ and electric harpsichord ebbing and flowing in cyclical patterns in a minimalist *avant garde* tempo.

Chelsea looked absent-mindedly around her as she settled into a comfortable seat in a nearby alcove while Anne went to get drinks. Anne had put on a lot of weight since she had last seen her, she noticed with a slightly malicious satisfaction. Not that that would make a lot of difference to the sort of men who went for big, busty women like her in the first place. A pity she didn't really have the height to carry it off, though.

Looking around, most of the clientele appeared unostentatiously affluent; elegant young women, some beautiful, some horsy types like you often saw in places like the Botanic Inn, all well dressed and immaculately groomed, and a lot of clean-cut young men. Only one couple appeared slightly incongruous – a rugged big man, not handsome but interesting looking in a way, sat facing the pub entrance with a woman dressed entirely in black. The man looked about forty and wore a cheap looking jacket and shirt with jeans and laced up boots. He glanced frequently at the door with a worried frown as the woman talked. She seemed to be doing all the talking. She was maybe ten years younger than him, with ash-blonde hair worn in a bob at the front, striking good looks and a tan that suggested a lengthy spell in a more exotic climate. She chain-smoked incessantly as she talked.

Chelsea thought the man looked vaguely familiar. Suddenly she realised who it was.

"That man over there, I know him. Pat, I think his name was. He used to share a house with Adam Conway in Ireton Street," she told Anne as she returned from the bar. "Did I tell you Enda was Adam's cousin? Their mothers are sisters. It was a while before I knew. It's a small world."

Anne nodded.

"I see Adam occasionally," she said. "He works up the road now. You know that White House place? There. He lives near here too. I think it might be that street you used to live in, with Belinda."

Chelsea smiled. She thought about telling Anne about her last encounter with Adam but decided against it. Anne had been shocked enough when she'd told her about getting her own nipples pierced, after listening to her spending about five minutes making tart remarks about a girl with several facial piercings and multiple ear-rings they'd seen in the Common Room.

It had been no big deal. She'd had it done in London during one of her early visits there, the year she was doing her finals at Queen's. She knew it would delight Enda. She had got to know Enda's preferences very quickly.

"Come with me," Paula had told her one day. "I'll take you to the woman who did it for me. She's really good."

It had been comforting to have had Paula with her when she went to the place, at the end of a narrow cobbled street, where the door was answered by a woman with a strange, crooked smile.

"Come in, my love," she said. "Take as long as you like choosing what you want. There's no hurry."

The woman was in her fifties, with dyed black hair and a deep reassuring voice. She showed the girls a selection of rings which Chelsea spent some time examining, lost in thought. From time to time, she would glance at some of the other esoteric adornments on display in the glass cases on the far wall. The woman seemed to have everything for sale, from enormous chunk rings, facial horns, nipple tridents and jewelled navel studs to tiny stainless steel padlocks, flesh tunnels, nipple trainers and body bolts. The jewellery was in an astonishing array of colours and materials, dayglo plastics and ebony vying with metals such as gold, iron and silver. It was Paula in the end who suggested the silver rings.

"It's up to you," she said. "But I know him. These are much bigger and more obtrusive than the usual, and they'll feel quite heavy to wear at first. These are the ones he'd want on you. He'll love you for it."

Chelsea decided that she would have them. The rings were large, round and silver, more like a gypsy's ear-rings than the sort of thing she would until then ever have contemplated wearing on her breasts.

"I'll take them," she told the woman."Please do the necessary."

The woman nodded.

"An excellent choice, my love," she remarked. "They'll suit you beautifully."

The woman opened a small bag and laid the tools of her art on an adjoining table. She sat beside Chelsea, whom she bade take off her casual cotton shirt, smiling as she noted that Chelsea was not wearing a bra, whilst motioning her to lie down on a nearby couch. Chelsea did as she was requested.

The woman talked smoothly to Chelsea as she prepared her for the piercing, telling her in a low voice exactly what she was doing as she proceeded. After rubbing Chelsea's nipples carefully with disinfectant, the woman selected a fine, long-handled pair of forceps with tiny loops at the end. She used these to grasp the nipples and pull them up. Chelsea tried closing her eyes but in the end could not resist watching, fascinated, as the woman worked.

The long thin needle she produced was lined up against one of the forceps loops holding the nipples in place, first one, then the other, as with strong, practised motions the woman pushed the needle through to line up with the loop on the other side. Chelsea flinched a little each time it was done, as the woman then pushed up one of the silver rings both times and quickly pushed it through the holes she had created before fastening it. The job was done.

The woman invited Chelsea to stand up and take a look at herself in the mirror. Chelsea got up, slightly shaky after the experience, but quickly regained her composure as she posed in front of the full length mirror at the other side of the room, clad only in a pair of tight denim jeans and sandals. She gasped involuntarily at the sight of her reflection. She didn't think she had ever seen such beautiful pieces of jewellery. The rings weighed more heavily than she had realised would be the case when she had handled them: heavy and prominent and so glaringly obvious as they were, they undoubtedly served to accentuate the beauty of her bare breasts, perhaps more perfectly than anything else could ever do.

"I told you, my love. Gorgeous. Just gorgeous," the woman repeated, admiring her own handiwork.

The woman complemented Chelsea on her firm young bust. There was a glint in her eye that made Chelsea feel just slightly uncomfortable.

"They'll heal up quickly enough," the woman told her. "Just follow the advice I gave you earlier. I'd keep them on for at least a couple of months if I were you."

Chelsea replied that she intended wearing them permanently.

Later, on the train back to Arsenal station, Chelsea closed her eyes, pleasantly savouring the dull burning in her nipples, the lingering twinges and discomforts which she knew to be such a temporary and tiny price to pay for the unique ornaments which now so spectacularly graced her breasts, naked beneath her light blue cotton shirt. She was certain beyond the slightest shadow of doubt that what she had done was absolutely the right decision. Enda had often spoken to her of his admiration for girls who wore provocative distinguishing marks, whatever their sorts, be they piercings, tattoos or brandings. And he loved everything daring or innovative that she initiated. She knew his homecoming that evening was going to be special. She didn't anticipate quite how special at the time, though.

She had spent a long time luxuriating in the bath, washing her hair and drying it, brushing it until it shone, before applying just the right amount of make-up, including a new bright red lipstick. She discarded several perfumes on the bathroom shelf before finding Enda's favourite fragrance, using it liberally in the way she knew he liked. It was a hot day and she lay on the bed, nude, for about half an hour, reading a magazine for a while until lapsing into a light sleep.

The sound of the front door opening and shutting woke her up with a start. Quickly, she sprang to her feet and pulled on her tight, low-cut denim jeans, pausing only to brush her hair back with a few perfunctory flourishes. Excited, she rushed through the bedroom door, barefoot and naked to the waist. She gasped with dismay as she realised that Enda was not alone. With him were three other men, two of whom she immediately recognised as Shaun Simpson and Toby Venables; the third man was an older, rather world weary looking individual.

Before Chelsea had time to react Enda was by her side in an instant, clasping both her hands behind her back as she instinctively strove to raise them to hide her breasts, kissing her tenderly on the mouth. He whispered in her ear that she was to stay exactly as she was and not put anything on.

"Go and make us all some coffee," he murmured. "Then come and join us for a cup."

Chelsea felt herself blushing furiously as she served the coffee and biscuits, trying desperately to prevent her breasts, so conspicuously pierced and ringed, from swinging against the faces of the visitors as she leant over to pour the coffee for them. Eventually she sat down, Enda pulling up a stool for her between himself and the elderly man whom he introduced as Ron Mendlicott, a famous sports journalist. Chelsea sat erect and proud, her shoulders back, consumed with a perverse pride at her condition mingled with sudden and overwhelming surges of shame that contrived to keep her cheeks coloured a deep scarlet at the wantonness of it. She was only half listening to the conversation of the men, which seemed to be dominated by talk of forthcoming sporting fixtures and gambling odds. With the exception of Toby, who had smiled at her warmly in his kindly faced way and complimented her on the beauty of her rings, the visitors paid her little or no special attention.

Chelsea marvelled at the unselfconscious and natural way they chatted to her from time to time as they sipped their coffee, as though it were the most normal occurrence in the world to be served coffee by a half naked girl young enough to be their daughter.

"We got a good price on Khusainov for the tennis. There's no doubt about that," Mendlicott was saying. "I'll always trust your judgement when it comes to your own game, Shaun. I hope you'll trust mine on the racing side. Perry is the one man on the inside who's constantly come up trumps for us in the past year. We should pay him the retainer he's asked for. He's well worth it."

"He's right, Shaun, Perry is expensive but he's good. It's an investment that'll pay for itself," Toby said. "I think we should cut down on the football bets for a while. We've been losing a bit lately on the football. We should be investing more in the fight game. The illegal fights as well as the legal ones. All you need is the right information, for any of these one-on-one events."

"More coffee, anyone?" enquired Chelsea, tossing her hair back.

"Thanks, darling. I'd love another drop," said Toby. "What do you reckon, Shaun?"

Shaun was staring at several sheets of paper he had extracted from a cardboard folder, underlining some figures on them with a black marker.

"Makes sense," he said at last. "There's a few big fights

coming up. We can rely on you to tell us what's happening there, I take it, Ron?"

Mendlicott nodded.

"I'll talk to the usual people," he said.

"Good. There's something happening across the pond soon, I hear. Unofficial all-Ireland championship in bare knuckle boxing. Wilson Squires tipped me off about it. He's been asked by some underworld elements to look after some wagers."

"He knows who's going to win, then?"

"Wilson knows everything that's going on in Northern Ireland. He used to be a cop. He's a good man to have over there."

"Over there, is it now, Shaun?" Enda chided him. "Not 'back home' anymore?"

"I'm out of Ballysillan a long time now," Shaun replied. "But it would be a nice little break for you and Chelsea. Go over to Ireland for a few days, talk to Wilson and check out the details. See your respective families and friends in Belfast and Dublin. What do you say? Jenny can look after the shop."

"I'm game for that," smiled Enda. "What do you think, Chelsea?"

"I'd love that."

"Right," said Shaun, taking the cardboard folder under his arm and standing up. "That's that settled. If it goes well, we'll consider it as a possible annual investment opportunity. It would be a pleasant regular jaunt back to the old sod for you. Give me a call when you get back. Hopefully we'll start ringing a few changes soon. This year could still be our best yet."

"You better believe it," grinned Toby.

The men departed, Enda leading them down the stairs as their voices faded into a low chatter.

Chelsea did not tell Anne about that incident. It was too soon for her to assimilate all of the changes in her life that were overwhelming her herself, never mind start analysing them with Anne.

Luckily, Anne had done enough talking for both of them, bemoaning the lack of a decent man in her life for most of the evening. But it had been good to see her again. When they left A

Rainbow In Curved Air they hugged each other and resolved to keep in touch.

"Don't ever get uptight about boyfriends," Chelsea told her. "There'll always be different ones from time to time. But friends are forever."

Chelsea glanced out the window of the taxi as it passed the Stranmillis street where she used to live, then smiled enigmatically all the way home to Glengormley, to her parent's house in the quiet cul-de-sac of the ever expanding suburb.

Her mother was waiting up for her, like she used to do when Chelsea was a schoolgirl.

"Your father's gone to bed. He's tired. He's got an urgent job on this week," she said.

"I know," said Chelsea. "He told me earlier."

Her father, an electrician by trade, had never been out of work in his life and seemed driven to work every available hour possible. But he had been delighted to see her back home, in his own undemonstrative way. Her mother had fussed over her constantly since her arrival, forever making her cups of tea and updating her on news about family, friends and neighbours. She was excited at the prospect of Chelsea's brother and sister, Ivan and Karen, coming home the following day for a family reunion.

"It'll be like old times," she had said fondly. "It's been years since we've all been in the house together, as a family. Where does the time go?"

Later, Chelsea peered through the bedroom curtains at the blackness of the solitude beyond. The world outside her window was as quiet as a tomb, the little cul-de-sac safe and peaceful as she had always known it. Her bedroom was a shrine of pristine cleanliness, pervaded by the light fragrance of a bouquet of freshly cut flowers her mother had thoughtfully placed in a vase on her bedside table.

It was strange, now, to sleep on her own, snuggled up amidst the crisp linen sheets and goose-down duvet and soft pillows, in the familiar sanctuary of the bed that had been her own since childhood. But it was comforting too. Feeling as far divorced from London as she had ever done since her move there, Chelsea closed her eyes and drifted happily into a deep and dreamless sleep, memories ebbing as consciousness faded of a recent age of half-remembered innocence.

Chapter 16

In The Court Of The Crimson King

"I ENJOY THESE little vacations," Enda said. "Long may they continue."

Wilson Squires nodded as they closed the car doors and gazed up York Street, already sparsely populated in the early evening.

"They'll continue as long as we keep picking winners. We'll keep picking winners as long as we keep getting the right information. So we'll follow the money as usual."

He checked his watch and frowned.

"We better start walking. The message was to park as near as possible to the station, then walk towards the city centre."

"Why?"

"The people we're going to meet are very security conscious. Leave the talking to me, by the way. They won't like your Dublin accent. You'll be all right because you're with me. Just don't antagonise them, that's all. They're rough diamonds."

As the men walked, they fell to discussing last year's championship final. It had been a savage road match, held in a makeshift ring formed by a number of cars and jeeps. The fight had gone on after dark, the lights of some of the nearby jeeps serving as makeshift floodlights, with the gipsy champion Hobo Chang Ba eventually biting and head-butting his opponent The China Pig, a prominent Orangeman who had a Mongolian father, into submission. Both fighters had suffered serious head, eye and hand injuries but there were no medical personnel on hand to help or intervene.

The China Pig had later disappeared, left to fend for himself by disgruntled supporters who had gambled heavily on the outcome. He had staggered to a nearby Orange hall where he was found unconscious the next morning by a passer-by, shocked at the sight of a member of the local lodge sprawled helplessly across the crazy paving stones by the blood-splashed palings.

"Why does anybody volunteer for that sort of shit?" asked Enda. "It can't just be for the money."

"It is just for the money. It's a very lucrative business. It's not even illegal in some countries," replied Squires. "There are no conscripts. These people know the rewards are huge, provided they're successful. Ordinary boxing operates on the same principle. Nobody does it for the fun of getting beaten to a pulp. Here are our allies, by the way. Mr Turkington."

A heavily built individual with close-cropped hair stepped grinning from the corner of Molyneaux Street and motioned them to keep walking.

"Mr Hobson."

A youngish bald man with sharp features and shifty eyes wound down the window of a slowly passing car and waved, then wound it up again. A loud whistle came from behind them. They turned back in the direction of Yorkgate and saw a tall, lean, fair-haired man walking towards them, on his own.

"Mr McCaw."

The man came up to them and smiled, showing regular white teeth. He had a thin, bony face with the beginnings of a goatee beard, pale blue eyes that managed to look piercing and vacant at the same time and a muscular body. He wore jeans and a short sleeved shirt which revealed heavily tattooed arms.

"Well, Wilsie!"

He looked at Enda arrogantly up and down, as though

inspecting an object. "Who's your friend?" he demanded.

"This is Mr Storey. A business associate," said Squires. "He's all right."

"I hope he is," said McCaw. He looked coolly at Enda once again. "Because there's a smell of a Fenian about the place."

He jerked a thumb at a taxi which suddenly appeared from out of Molyneaux Street and drew up beside them.

"Get in. We're going to a wee club I know."

"Not the Black Dog, I hope," said Squires. "The word is it's under twenty four hour surveillance. But I'm sure these things still get noticed on the Shankill without anybody having to spell it out for you."

"Right first time, Wilsie. Not the Black Dog. Just get in the taxi and I'll see you where we're going shortly."

Following the example of Squires, Enda did not speak to the driver at any time during the journey. He was not familiar with the route the taxi was taking but assumed that Wilson would be, with his intimate knowledge of Belfast's arcane geography and its multifarious hidden nooks and crannies. The driver in any event kept the radio blaring throughout, the raucous noise drowning out even the roar of the traffic. Enda noticed that the car was slowing as it headed up the Woodstock Road and he took a mental note of some of the streets they passed until the car stopped.

"Down that one," the driver said in a guttural Belfast accent, gesticulating towards the top of the nearest street. He had kept the engine running. "Down the side there, turn right. The Crimson King. You can't miss it."

The two men walked away from the taxi in the direction indicated.

"This area's gone downhill fast," Squires commented, looking around him. "Ten years ago it wasn't a bad place to live, it was on the up and up. Now – well, look at it. There's more atmosphere on the moon. It's like a throwback to the seventies."

"You're the man would know."

Enda thought the Woodstock Road had a melancholy air, the street even more so. The surroundings appeared to get bleaker and bleaker until they reached the Crimson King, which struck

Enda as surely one of the bleakest places on the planet. Outside, the building was a picture of rank, brutal, seamed, rusting, peeling, decaying ugliness. A wooden sign depicting the head of a deranged red-faced ogre creaked alarmingly at the front, thrashed into motion by a sudden vicious squall whipping in around the dusty street. The entrance was a wooden door at the corner of a gable wall, which was flakily decorated with a red, white and blue mural of King William of Orange at the Battle of the Boyne and, in messy black capitals underneath, the words: IRELAND, STAY OUT OF ULSTER.

The two men entered a vast room with a high, pockmarked concrete ceiling, festooned with a multitude of Union Jacks and Ulster flags. One side housed a row of pool tables that was blocked off by a grey partition from the bar area. In the top corner of the bar above a piano, a television blared.

Enda and Wilson Squires sat on cheaply upholstered seats at a table well away from the main crowd, with only a couple of pasty-faced youths drinking pints of lager and arguing about football in the immediate vicinity.

"This is a right tip," Enda remarked. "You'd think they'd spend a bit of money on it, tart it up a bit."

"Times change," said Squires. "Governments stopped throwing money at the paramilitaries years ago. You should have seen some of the loyalist clubs when they were soaking up the hand-outs. State of the art, they were. All done with 'peace' money. Those days are well gone. They're turning back into shebeens now."

Billy McCaw emerged from behind the grey partition carrying a briefcase. With him was another man of similar height and build, with combed back dark hair and moustache and arms covered with loyalist tattoos. He sported a suede waistcoat over a white T-shirt.

"Who's the other ape?" inquired Enda.

"Mark Skelton.You'd better watch your mouth," said Squires grimly. "These men are loyalist icons. You might not like them or what they stand for but they're well thought of in these parts. You've never heard of Billy the Kid and Chopper Skelton?"

"No," said Enda. "Nor they of me, I shouldn't wonder. They sound like something out of the old comics my da used to collect. Korky the Cat. Winker Watson. I've heard of them all right but not these gobshites. They look like a right pair of homos. Look at the struts of them. They'll be holding hands next and doing a twirl."

McCaw and Skelton were traversing the floor with an almost identically insolent swagger, nodding occasionally at familiar welcoming faces amongst the clientele.

"Just watch your mouth," said Squires. "These are dangerous bastards."

"I'm pissing myself."

"You would be if you knew what these people are capable of. It was a mistake for you to come here."

"Shaun said –"

"Shaun's been out of Ballysillan a long time. Just button it and let me do the talking."

McCaw and Skelton pulled up a couple of chairs and sat down.

"First things first," said McCaw. "Let's get some drinks in. Vodka all right for everybody? Good. You – go up to the bar and bring us down a bottle of Smirnoff and some mixers."

The order was directed at the nearby table where the two pasty-faced youths were sitting. Looking slightly distressed, one of them got up.

"Not you. I told him to do it," said McCaw coldly, pointing at his companion. "Are you back yet?"

The other youth quickly jumped to his feet and hurried to the bar.

"I want both of you up the other end of the bar after he comes back," McCaw added, jerking his thumb at a vacant table beside the piano. "There's a private meeting on here. Move it!"

The remaining youth clambered awkwardly to his feet and rushed off, almost knocking his chair over in his haste.

"Well, Billy. You obviously think your man's going to win the fight, then," said Squires genially. "That's what the size of your wager's telling me, anyway."

McCaw nodded.

"Danny Boy's a cert. He's quality."

"Who's he beaten?"

"That gippo that won it last year. Hobo whatever you call him. Other good ones, too. The Blimp. Ant Man Bee. Bigmouth Billy Bass."

"Who's the opposition?"

"Bullhammer Brown. He's good but not as good as Danny Boy. I seen his last two fights. Last one was against Wildchild Willie Hicks in a warehouse up in Coleraine."

"Right. Well, we'll cover the bet, as agreed."

"I saw a recording of last year's final in a bar in Spain last summer when I was on holiday," said Skelton. "As far as we know, the gippos look after the recording end of things. We wouldn't mind a piece of that."

Squires shrugged.

"There's always going to be a market in countries where it's still illegal. Force anything underground and you'll always have a market for it. There's no point in starting a row over the recording rights. You can always clock it on your mobile if you want."

The youth returned to the table and anxiously set down the drinks on a tray. McCaw waved him away and poured a measure of vodka into three of the accompanying glasses. He poured himself a glass of lemonade from one of the bottles of mixers. Squires opined that fight styles came and went but there was a trend lately, in America and Russia particularly, for quasi-gladiatorial contests where the participants had weapons.

"Knives, sharpened bicycle chains, that type of thing," he said. "I don't care for that sort of entertainment myself but tastes differ."

He spoke of the fashion some years ago for the Hocus Pocus, a formalised type of fight ironically named after a popular dance routine of the time and conducted between rival gangs in public streets.

"Those were the days," said Squires, his eyes shining. "Five-a-side, free-for-alls between costumed gangs. Just fists and boots, last team with people standing wins it. I saw one in London once." It had been outside a tube station, he said. He had seen two men, late twenties or maybe early thirties, dressed in traditional clown outfits. They were looking aggressively around them.

"There he is, Charlie," one of them had said, pointing at a big burly youth wearing a Gaelic football jersey who was staring up and down a nearby escalator. "That's him. That's Kieran."

The man called Charlie turned out to be the leader of the Battersea Clownboys, one of the most feared Hocus Pocus teams in London at the time. The pre-arranged skirmish was with the Kilburn Gaelics. "Oi! Irish!" Charlie shouted. "Over here!"

He was a mean looking, beady eyed individual with short thinning curly brown hair and a snub nose. Unlike the other Clownboys, who quickly materialised as though out of thin air, he did not have a red plastic version appended to it. Almost immediately the fight began, the rest of the Kilburn Gaelics lining up beside their leader.

"It was good, honest, no-nonsense stuff," Squires related. "No quarter asked or given. The Gaelics put up a good fight and this Kieran guy took a lot of putting down. He was the last of them left standing. Anyhow, the Clownboys used to have this catchphrase. 'Nurse! Nurse!' they used to shout, whenever they had an opponent down and out. As a sort of a joke, like."

He hesitantly poured himself a second vodka, smaller than the original measure proferred to him by McCaw and added a generous splash of tonic water.

"It just so happened," he continued, "that a couple of nurses were passing by at the time, in full uniform, just as the Clownboys were staggering off covered in blood, holding each other up and cheering and singing. One of them goes over to the nurses – they were smiling nervously, like, at the sight of all these fellows got up like bloodied circus clowns – and goes 'Nurse! Nurse!' One of them turns round and he says to her: 'Do you want to dance to the Hocus Pocus?' The crowd watching enjoyed that. They had a good laugh. There was a bit of community spirit about these things."

Enda emitted a braying guffaw and slapped his thigh ostentatiously before reaching over for the vodka. Brushing aside his glass, he took a hearty swig of it from the neck of the bottle before planting it loudly back down on the edge of the table. Squires flashed him a warning glance. He grinned back.

"There was that," said Skelton grudgingly. "But that Hocus Pocus thing was very English. It never really caught on here."

"More's the pity," said Squires. "It would have given our local lads something to do ...given them a bit of discipline. It definitely gets you in a martial mood watching one. I'm not a belligerent man, you understand, but I was using a public phone shortly afterwards and this heavy looking young cockney wanker started to give me a bit of lip about taking so long. I turned round and told him to fuck off. I was ready for digging him one."

"What this country needs is warriors,"said McCaw. "Soldiers. Not a bunch of fruits horsing about in train stations. The trouble with this country is that it went soft. Most of our politicians would sell us out tomorrow if they got the chance."

"You've no faith in our single unionist party, then?" said Squires. "Not even your friend the Reverend Ichabod Cairns?"

"Cairns is all right," said Skelton. "Most of them are yellow bastards. They hide behind us when it suits them, then they disown us."

McCaw poured himself another lemonade.

"Next border poll, we're fucked," he said. "Unless we fight now, we've had it. We need to make the Taigs scared to walk the streets again. We need more men like your old mate, Wilsie. Men like Lenny Murphy."

"Len was a good loyalist," Squires acknowledged. "He got a bad press but he was well thought of. His funeral was the biggest I've ever seen on the Shankill. His problem was that he was reckless. I was in a certain club one night when he killed some old homeless guy who'd wandered in off the street. Len was only out of jail. He'd done six years, then his first night out, what does he do but put his own liberty in jeopardy again over some harmless nonentity. That business with the man O'Loan in the Black Dog reminded me of that."

"It's easy to be wise after the event," Skelton riposted. "Outsiders don't drink in the Black Dog. He could have been anybody. What were the boys supposed to do? He came into the place in a Lone Ranger suit, for fuck's sake. Turk was doing the bar and he tried to order a fucking tomato juice off him. 'Shot of redeye', he says. He had fucking red eyes all right by the time the boys were done with him."

"I'm not saying there mightn't have been an element of provocation," said Squires. "I'm saying that you over-reacted. Protestants tend to frown on that sort of thing. Maybe you shouldn't be trying to turn the clock back to that way of going. Remember that Lenny and others in his team were whacked or set up eventually by their own side. You wouldn't want the same thing being said someday about Billy McCaw."

"Our own side won't move after that warning we gave Tucker Beattie," replied McCaw. "Anyhow, Billy McCaw couldn't have had anything to do with that job in the Black Dog because Billy McCaw was having a drink in another bar that night. Along with dozens of witnesses."

"Why do you talk about yourself in the third person, you fucking weirdo?" Enda enquired in his soft Dublin accent.

There was a stunned silence following an involuntary gasp by Squires. McCaw and Skelton stared unblinkingly at Enda. He returned their gaze, smiling mildly.

"We've got a real live one here tonight, Billy," Skelton said at last. "Why didn't you tell us your mate was a Fenian, Wilsie? We could have laid on a little entertainment. Just remember you're on British soil now, sunshine. We're all British here."

"You could have fooled me," said Enda. "But I'll say one thing. I've lived in Britain for years and I've never seen as many flags as I have in this tip tonight. Still, I hope you enjoy your holiday here anyway. Sunshine."

Skelton flushed with anger and made to rise to his feet before McCaw hurriedly pulled him back.

"Gentlemen, gentlemen – we're all friends here," Squires said soothingly. "We're all businessmen. Let's just remember we're here tonight for a transaction – one that should benefit us all mutually if all goes to plan. Let's not fall out."

Skelton scowled and poured himself another measure of vodka, promptly swallowing it straight.

"You're right, of course, Wilsie," McCaw said, smiling without humour. "We're all businessmen together."

He stared directly at Enda, looking him up and down.

"There's a certain party in south Belfast who had an unfortunate accident the other night," he said slowly. "He's missing half his face and he'll never see again. Both eyes were literally hanging out of their sockets, from what I heard. Acid burns. Sometimes I don't know my own strength."

"It's a fact that Taigs make more noise when they get a full facial," Skelton added conversationally. "This cunt apparently screamed longer and harder than Tucker did when he got it. Squealed louder than a stuck pig. Or so they say."

"Is that a fact?" said Enda. "I wonder what sort of a pig you think you'll squeal like when your turn comes around."

Squires struggled angrily up from his seat and led Enda towards the door as Skelton was again restrained by McCaw, this time with some difficulty.

"Get out!" Squires hissed furiously. "Sit in the taxi we came in until I get out of here. Give me five minutes. Try not to get yourself killed this time."

Outside, the taxi was waiting, the driver nodding his head to the rhythm of the music still blaring on the car radio.

"How much longer, boss?" he shouted across at Enda. "Are you ready to go back?"

Enda smiled and held up the fingers of one palm.

"Five minutes? Fair enough, boss."

Enda sauntered down the alleyway flanking the Crimson King and looked around him. Some distance away, on a patch of wasteland at the back of the building, a group of youths was standing around a makeshift fire bordered by small rocks. They were swigging from bottles and passing what might have been a bag of glue amongst them, pushing their faces down to it from time to time. Their Belfast accents, harsh and discordant, were indecipherable in the whistling wind that was blowing unseasonally around them. Two skinheads were urinating against a tree at the back of the Crimson King, one of them clutching a large bottle of cheap cider, the other singing loudly and drunkenly.

"Hello! Hello! We are the Billy Boys
Hello! Hello! You'll know us by our noise
We're up to our necks in Fenian blood
Surrender or you'll die …."

A smaller skinhead in a Union Jack T-shirt emerged from the other side of the club.

"It fucking well was him," he said excitedly. "I told you I seen him earlier. It was Billy McCaw himself. I asked a fella coming out and he said aye –"

The singing skinhead paused only for a second before launching into another demonic cacophony.

"There's only one King Billy
That's the Kid
Oh, there's only one King Billy
That's the Kid
There's only one King Billy
Billy, Billy, Billy
Only one King Billy
That's the Kid!"

Enda grinned at the scene and walked towards them, hands in pockets, calculating as he did so the chances of taking all three of them. He reckoned the odds were good. They were all pretty drunk.

"Good evening, gentlemen," he drawled. "Would any of you faggots happen to know any decent songs at all? Like *The Fields Of Athenry,* maybe, or *The Wild Colonial Boy*?"

The three skinheads stared at him, astounded.

"Who the fuck are you?" one of them blustered.

"Korky the Cat."

"What?"

"I'm an icon. I'm well thought of in these parts."

"Where did you come from?" the small skinhead demanded.

"From my mummy's tummy. That's enough questions. Get your fat arses into that club and fetch a round of drinks out here before I have to give you a slap. Mind you don't scrape your knuckles on that concrete on your way in. I'll be waiting at the front."

Enda began to swagger back up the alleyway, determined to mimic the strutting gait practised by McCaw and Skelton earlier in the club. In the background, the skinheads stood transfixed as though a spotlight had been instantly trained upon him. The reason was that he could not maintain the simian posture.

Before he knew it his lips started to curl, the jutting jaw collapsed into a boyish grin, the knotted shoulder muscles and stiff arms relaxed and he looked about him laughing, as though the whole world were nothing but a joke and the three skinheads the funniest thing in it.

The singing skinhead was on to him first, running up and lashing his right boot in the direction of Enda's groin as he turned. Enda moved quickly, but not quickly enough to avoid the kick landing on his upper thigh. The two other youths closed in, circling and stalking around him, looking for an opening. From the depths of the Crimson King came the strains of some light, happy music, a tinkling piano, barely audible, accompanied by seemingly far-off tipsy voices. A cold gust of wind swept through the alleyway and it began to rain.

"You're a Fenian fucker," the singing skinhead said.

"Beats being a Proddy wanker," said Enda.

The second skinhead spat at him. Enda snatched the large cider bottle from the youth's right hand and smashed it over his head, pushing the jagged remains of it into the face of his nearest henchmate and turning it in one swift movement. The smallest skinhead screeched in pain as Enda slashed an elbow into his face, then punched him in the throat. As the rain began to turn to curtains of hail Enda dragged him to a nearby drainpipe and smashed his face into it several times.

He ran swiftly back up the alleyway and kicked the leader of the trio ferociously in the face as he started to get up off the ground, then, as the hail shower subsided as quickly as it had begun, punched his companion to the deck and stamped repeatedly on his head. Panting, he strode straight up the alleyway and into the back of the waiting car. Squires was heading towards it from the entrance of the Crimson King, where the lone figure of McCaw stood.

"Remember what I told you, Wilsie," McCaw was saying.

"Nothing stands still in politics. Everything changes. We're sailing very close to the edge. We only have to get lucky once, as the republicans used to say, and it's on again. Only this time we're going to win."

Squires eyed Enda suspiciously as he got into the car but didn't speak until the taxi had dropped them back off in York Street.

"What the hell happened you? You're covered in blood."

"A couple of young lads were being cheeky. I had to give them a bit of a cuff."

"You're a liability. I can't leave you alone for five minutes."

"Sure it was only a bit of fun. They enjoyed it as much as I did. It must have been all that talk about fighting that put me in the mood. Anyway – I take it that's the wager in that briefcase."

Squires nodded.

"It's the biggest I've seen since we started this game," he said.

"Where would those tossers get their hands on that sort of money?" asked Enda.

Squires shrugged as he started the car.

"The usual. Drugs. Extortion. The odd armed robbery. Front organisations like pubs and clubs. Places like the one you've just been in. McCaw's influence is growing by the day. He's eliminated most of the other serious contenders on the loyalist side. All the old guard."

"So how are you going to handle that bet?"

"I'll discuss that with Shaun. We'll probably lay some of it off, get some of our own money on first. We should do very nicely. Don't worry about it. Just you have yourself a nice night in with your girlfriend."

"I can't. She's spending the night with her family in Glengormley. I'm heading down to Tallaght tomorrow myself, to see my own folks."

"Very well. I'll be seeing you, then."

Enda got out of the car, wincing slightly at the pain in his thigh, then hobbled briskly across the car park to the Hilton hotel.

He grinned cheerfully at the door staff and the receptionist, a pretty young girl with glasses, as they took in with professional detachment the contradiction presented by his blood-stained clothing and his status as a paying guest who was generous with his tips.

Shutting his bedroom door, he thought about having a shower and a change of clothes and taking in some of Belfast's more civilised nightlife. He decided against it as he had told his mother he'd be getting an early train to Dublin in the morning. Instead, he had a pleasant bath, sipping a cold beer from the mini-bar as he did so and reflecting on the day's events. Before he went to bed he started to watch a movie on television, an old martial arts film called *Kickboxer* starring Jean Claude Van Damme as a character seeking revenge for his brother who was crippled in a fight. It was standard fare, the absence of a plot not detracting in any noticeable way from what passed for the action. He tired of it about halfway through and tried some other channels. There was nothing much. A documentary about the Indian doctor who had pioneered the new 'magic bullet' cure for lung cancer. A news item about the latest space mission to Mars. An interview with someone called Keith Dalkeith, of the Meltsonian Institute. A pornographic film. The latter caught his attention. The female lead bore a striking resemblance to Chelsea.

He checked his mobile phone, which he had left in a drawer. She had sent him a text message to tell him she was safe home and missing him already. He sent her a message back, telling her he'd had a quiet night but that he was thinking of her. Grinning, he lay back in the bed and intently watched the rest of the film.

PART FIVE

The World Turned Upside Down

Chapter 17

Portrait Of A Lady

"I LIKE THIS place," said Heather Lockhart. "It's kind of comfortable. You don't feel like you're in Belfast."

"That's probably why you like it," said Pat Farland.

A Rainbow In Curved Air was a venue he had chosen after much deliberation. Since moving to Balfour Avenue he had scarcely been out of the house and had not visited any pubs or public places beyond the lower Ormeau Road. But knowing that Heather was back in Belfast eventually proved too much for him. He searched for her mother's address in the telephone directory but couldn't find it.

Undeterred, he inspected an electoral register at a post office and found it there. He called round to the house, in a quiet terraced street near a primary school, one afternoon. No-one was in but he posted a note through the letterbox inviting her to ring him. When she did, she had seemed genuinely pleased to hear from him and readily agreed to meet up with him.

"I can't get over how beautiful you still are," Pat told her.

He meant it. He had often thought about her, frequently even dreamed about her. She now sat beside him, sipping a glass of Heineken, looking uncannily like the girl who had come to his flat all those years ago after her rift with Jim Butler. She was dressed entirely in black just as she had been then, a look that lent her an air of austerity. And she was beautiful; her ash blonde hair had been fashioned into a girlish bob and she was as slim and striking looking as ever, her high cheekbones and dazzling smile unaltered by time. If you looked closely at her you could see she was a bit older, but it was as if ageing a little actually suited her, if anything transforming her condition from that of an immature beauty in a transitory stage of life to that of a confident and assertive woman. She had a natural tan that advertised her years of exile.

"You mean to say you'd forgotten?" she said, smiling widely. "You must have a short memory. Do you think I've picked up an Aussie accent, by the way? My mother says I have but I think I revert to Belfast whenever I come back here."

"A bit," said Pat. "Just a bit."

She noticed him frown slightly as she lit a cigarette. She quickly put a hand on his arm.

"I know you hate these things," she said, "but please bear with me for one night. This is my last night on them. I'm giving up tomorrow, for good."

"That's what they all say."

She looked at him sharply and a little angrily.

"You don't understand," she said curtly. "These days, when I decide to do something I always do it. I've changed in a lot of ways since we last met. I don't care what 'they' all say. If I say I'm doing it, I'm doing it. I've set myself a timescale and I'm going to stick to it. Tonight's the last night."

"All right. I believe you."

"Why do you keep looking at the door? Are you expecting somebody?"

"No. But there's a new Shankill Butcher gang on the loose. Nobody told them the war was over. It's a long shot, but they might just come bursting in here armed with meat cleavers at any minute."

"I'm surprised you can still joke about things like that after what happened you. Don't you ever have nightmares about any of it?"

"All the time," said Pat. "But it's all over now."

He said that he regretted ever getting involved but that his intentions were honourable at the time, as he saw it. Most of the people he knew from that era had no regrets.

"I don't think Rhett ever had any regrets, for instance. Though I haven't seen him since he got out."

Heather shook her head impatiently, exhaling smoke.

"He was always reckless. He's not what anybody would call a leader … he was always a follower, but he was very reckless," she said. "I couldn't believe it when I heard about Jim going on hunger strike. I mean, why would anybody …don't get me wrong, I'm glad he's alive and well now. I just wouldn't be keen on ever seeing him again now. That phase of my life is over. I was very young."

"But you're happy enough to see me?"

She smiled and clasped his hand.

"You're different. You're a nicer person. And you were always much deeper and more intelligent than a lot of people gave you credit for. You made the effort to find me, too. How did you know I was back?"

"A friend told me. Nobody you'd know. But you're not back for good – you're only visiting?"

She nodded.

"There's no way I would ever come back here to live. You know I always wanted out. You and I could still have been in Blackpool if I'd had my way that time."

"Sometimes I'm sorry I did come back."

"Don't look back," she said. "Never go back. Always forward. I fell in love with Australia. It's funny – when I was a young girl I used to think the world was turned upside down there, because it was on the other side of the globe."

She told him she had gone to Sydney with her boyfriend of the time, Darryl. Darryl was English but had family in Sydney. They'd done various casual jobs around Bondi beach for a while and spent most of their spare time swimming, sunbathing and surfing. Then Darryl's grandfather died and Darryl inherited a lot of money.

"His grandfather was very wealthy. He owned businesses

all over Sydney. Souvenir shops in The Rocks – that's the main tourist area. A couple of restaurants in Manly, over on the North Shore. OTB, as the Aussies call it. Over the bridge. And a few private hotels. Everything started to go wrong once Darryl came into his inheritance."

They had gone to live in his grandfather's former house in Point Piper, an affluent eastern suburb.

"When I call it a house," she said, "it's really more like a mansion. Fronting the harbour. It's really too big for me on my own. And it's weird for someone with my background to be paying other women to come in and clean the place. I'm living the life of a lady."

She had married Darryl and they'd had a child, a baby girl, the following year. But things already had started to go disastrously off the rails.

"Darryl couldn't handle money," she said. "We were much happier when we had nothing. Then Chloe was born and he just wasn't ready for the responsibility … he was never there for her, or for me. He started getting into drugs in a really serious way. He'd dabbled a bit before but now he suddenly found that he could afford absolutely whatever he wanted, whenever he wanted it."

She stubbed out her cigarette and promptly lit another one, inhaling deeply.

"He killed Chloe."

"What? What happened …?"

"He killed her. He let her die. He was on drugs, he didn't tell me what he was doing. He said he wasn't but I know he was. He let her drown in the bath. We were away on holiday at the time. She was only a baby."

Pat put a protective arm around Heather as she wiped some tears away from her eyes with a tissue.

"It's all right. Don't make a fuss of me. Please."

She had divorced Darryl. She couldn't bear looking at him again or having him anywhere near her after what had happened. She had got to keep the house in Point Piper and he had disappeared out of her life. She didn't know where he was now and she didn't care.

"I didn't know where to turn at the time. I've got friends over there who were very supportive. But I've never been religious or anything like that. That might have helped. But things like the death of a child …I don't think you ever can get over it. All you can do is get through it."

One of her neighbours, a Mrs Moore, told her about the Meltsonian Institute. It was run by a famous mystic called Keith Dalkeith, who had bases all over the world including one on the outskirts of Sydney. Mrs Moore told her that this man's teachings had been of immense benefit to her when her husband had died. He'd told her that there was really no such thing as death because the spirit lived forever.

"He told me that there are spirits all around us at any given time," she had said. "Some people can see them naturally, including people who have been diagnosed as being clinically insane. He told me that he knows of the existence of parallel universes where the dead are still alive but that the world wasn't ready for that sort of knowledge yet."

Mrs Moore claimed that he had put her in touch with her dead husband and that she had been at peace with herself ever since. She offered to take Heather to see Dalkeith. Heather thought that she had nothing to lose.She was just about getting by on prescription drugs at the time and ready to grasp at any straw.

The Sydney branch of the Meltsonian Institute turned out to be a large private house in a secluded area. Mrs Moore introduced her to Dalkeith, who seemed a warm, enthusiastic man. He told her that his work was what motivated him as a person; he had made enough money from his philosophy phone-line business alone the previous year to retire, but he wanted to help people.

He was currently working on two new books. One was a project on time travel, the other a definitive proof of the existence of multiple universes and their infinite expansion. He said that he believed he could help her but that she would have to follow his instructions to the letter.

"Needless to say, I agreed," she told Pat, lighting yet another cigarette from the packet. "Who's that blonde girl over there, by the way?"

“Which one? They’re both blondes.”

“The pretty one. She’s been giving you the eye but you haven’t noticed. Do you know her?”

“I don’t think so. Must be my animal magnetism. I’m with the best looking blonde in the place anyway.”

She smiled at him and squeezed his hand.

“You still know how to say all the right things.”

“I just never know how to do all the right things. So what happened with this Dalkeith guy? I’ve a notion I might have heard of him.”

“He told his assistant to prepare something he called the Blue Lodge. His assistant was a beautiful looking long-haired girl called Miranda. She was wearing a white robe with some symbol on it, I don’t know what it was. She was nice but very odd. She had this sort of low, expiring voice and a faraway look about her, like she was on something.”

The Blue Lodge turned out to be a room full of mirrors at the back of the house. The ceiling and floor were an identical shade of blue, an extraordinarily luminous shade.

“I looked around the room,” said Heather, “and all I could see was me.”

Eventually Dalkeith joined her, followed by Miranda holding out some sort of wooden cup. Dalkeith asked her to stand in the middle of the pentangle mosaic in the centre of the stone floor.

“There are certain things you must do,” he told her. “You must trust me implicitly. And don’t deviate one iota from what I tell you to do.”

He said that what she was going to see was a product of old magic. He said that he had learned it from an Albanian sorcerer he’d met once when he was on tour in Tirana with an organisation he referred to as Vice Versa. “I prefer the old magic to the new magic,” he told her. “The new magic is very much a parody of the old. But it’s what people want these days. Self-help books. Motivational courses. Philosophy phone-lines. The old magic is much more difficult …much more enervating.”

He offered her a drink from the wooden goblet. She asked him what it was.

"Just water. But the cup has special powers."

He claimed it was carved from witchwood, from one of only six trees in the world with the magical properties necessary for what was about to happen. She drank it obediently. He told her that she'd had a dog that died, not long before the death of her child. A black and white dog. A collie. She almost dropped the cup in shock.

"Prince," she'd said. "He got run over by a car…."

"He's going to be with you very shortly," he'd replied. "He's a very old spirit. A splendid one. Just do exactly what I tell you to do. This can only be done once."

He was looking into her eyes and speaking very slowly and deliberately. He told her to look into the mirror directly in front of her.

"Whatever you do, don't take your gaze away from the mirror. What you're about to experience is coming from the mirror. Lose concentration for even one second and the spell will be broken. Prince is coming to you now."

She did as she was told, keeping her focus straight on the mirror. She felt an incredible shock at the sight of her dog coming bounding towards her in the reflection.

"You can stroke him," Dalkeith said, "but don't look down. Whatever you do, don't look down."

It was the strangest experience of her life; she was stroking and cuddling her dog, who was happily and eagerly clambering all over her. She could see him, touch him, smell him. To the left of her reflection a vision started to materialise of a young child in a playpen.

It was unmistakably Chloe. She was happy, she was smiling and laughing.

It had been too much for Heather.She had turned involuntarily to her left and nothing was there. She looked down to her right, where the dog she had been stroking was no longer in evidence to any of her senses. She looked back into the mirror and saw only her own distraught reflection. Dalkeith and Miranda moved swiftly to usher her out of the room as she began to sob uncontrollably.

"You did fine," Dalkeith told her later as they drank tea in the downstairs living room. "I didn't tell you in advance for obvious reasons, but everyone looks down. No-one can help doing it. You held it better and longer than most."

He suddenly looked very old and very tired. He explained that the old magic was very draining and involved a huge psychic effort on the part of the facilitator to establish a bridge between two worlds.

Pat was shaking his head perplexedly as Heather spoke.

"This man sounds like a dangerous charlatan. Did he take money off you for this?"

Heather shook her head and took another fresh cigarette from the packet.

"No. And I don't think he was a charlatan."

"The drink he gave you," said Pat. "There could have been something in the drink. Some tasteless substance. That stuff about the dog – that's a standard line for fairground clairvoyants and hoaxers. Everybody's had a dog, or a cat, at some time."

"Well, he was able to describe Prince. And when he passed away."

Pat took a long draught of his Guinness, which he had barely touched up to then.

"Did he hypnotise you? Can you be sure? The power of suggestion could account for all of what you saw. He didn't describe Chloe, did he?"

"No. He had none of the paraphernalia... no swinging pendulum, or anything like that. He did have a very soothing voice. There was some unusual music playing. Not unlike the background music here tonight. Electronic music. Very repetitive..."

"I don't like this music much."

"I like it."

She told him that she had found the experience comforting and reassuring rather than terrifying. Mrs Moore had stayed on for several hours and they'd discussed all sorts of things with Dalkeith. She hadn't understood much of it. She'd subsequently tried reading some of his books but she'd found them too difficult for her, too metaphysical.

She'd been more at home with one called *Managing Your*

Mind, a self-help manual on which a hugely successful business course had been devised and used by companies throughout the world to motivate their staff.

"It's cognitive psychology," she explained. "I'm using it for all sorts of things. Like giving up smoking. I only started when Chloe died. The idea is you set yourself goals, write them down … stick to them. Visualise what it is you want and go and achieve it."

"And what is it that you want?"

"All sorts of things. I miss never having had a proper education. I left school far too early. I'm doing all sorts of educational courses now. I'm going to do a degree in Business Studies someday. I want to get married again. To the right man this time, and have more children. Four would be ideal. Two of each."

She stubbed out her cigarette.

"That's the last time you'll ever see me smoking."

"I hope it's not the last time I'll ever see you."

"It doesn't have to be," she said, inclining her head and looking at the floor. "That's up to you. I'll be here for another few weeks. You know my mother's on her own now …David's working in England and doesn't get home much. Shirley's married to a Lurgan man. She visits when she can."

She added that she intended to sell the house in Point Piper and move to a smaller one for the time being, maybe in a slightly livelier part of Sydney. Pat said that he intended getting out of the country himself, probably sometime soon. She was surprised.

"Really?" she said. "I thought you were a perpetual homebird. But I've been talking about myself all night. Tell me about you."

Pat complied with her request carefully and selectively. He told her about his steady job in Slattery's, which he had now given up. She appeared interested and attentive when he told her about the play he had written, the one that had been performed during the Arts Festival and received encouraging reviews.

"That's brilliant!" she enthused. "I always knew you had it in you."

He said that he'd like time to concentrate more on creative work like that. There were other reasons, too. He didn't like the political drift that was taking place at the moment. He feared it would degenerate into more violence, possibly another extended period of futile conflict. Another working class war, one that would achieve even less than its predecessors. But most of all, it was boredom that was getting to him.

"I was sharing a house until recently with a bunch of blokes. They were nice enough guys but … well, a bunch of wankers. It's a bit of a pain being surrounded by young lads. You feel you have to carry on like them all the time. I need to do something different. Get out of Belfast. Maybe go to America again."

Heather held his hand tightly and told him he was right. She said that she sometimes had nightmares about Belfast and was never wholly relaxed about coming back, even for brief visits. She said it was a dark, brutal city even now and would never shake off that threatening aura in her lifetime or in his.

"I turned on the news this morning," she said, "and the first item on it was about some young man getting acid thrown in his face when he went to answer the door in the middle of the night. No motive, apparently. No reason. A car was chased and found burnt out on the Shankill. I mean, in the name of God – who on earth would do a thing like that? That's the sort of thing I mean when I say this city's diseased. There's a sickness - "

"Where was this?" demanded Pat. "I haven't been watching the news."

He had put down his pint glass. His face had grown pale. "Near here. Or near enough. Botanic Avenue – one of the streets down there. I don't know this side of town very well."

"What was the name of the street?"

"I can't remember. Something beginning with 'I', I think. 'Ireland Street', maybe – something like that."

"Ireton Street?"

"Yes. That could have been it. Something like that."

"Was the victim named?"

"No, I don't think so."

They were among the last of the customers to leave A Rainbow In Curved Air that night. Pat absent-mindedly looked around for the two blondes Heather had pointed out earlier but they were gone. He hardly spoke during the taxi journey back to her mother's house but Heather didn't notice, she was chatting away throughout the journey.

She told him as he kissed her goodnight that he should maybe think about Australia instead of America.

"I could help you," she said. "I'm going to need help sorting out my affairs. I just want to simplify everything. Live a simpler life. Think about it."

Pat said that he would. He went back to Balfour Avenue and listened to the late night news on the radio. There were no major incidents that night. He went to the chest of drawers in his bedroom and hurriedly dug out the telephone number of Wilson Squires from a sheaf of other papers. He hesitated only for a moment before dialling it.

Chapter 18

A Victim Of Circumstance

"SCOUSERS ARE JUST horrible," said Stevie Marlow. "I told you they were the pits. All the bullshit you hear about the marvellous Liverpudlian sense of humour – it's a load of bollocks. They can't fucking talk right, either."

He kicked a stone vindictively out of his path as the procession trudged back along the wet streets.

"They talk about 'sarnies', for sandwiches. And 'elecky' for electric. And 'pressies', for presents, and 'lippy' for lipstick. A 'scally' is anything from a thieving bastard to a murderer. They ask for a 'portion of chips' instead of a chip. They say 'Go on, then' when you're buying them a pint, like they're doing you a big favour letting you buy it in the first place. Then they don't buy you one. Or it takes them a fucking hour to drink it. If they're ordering one, they'll say 'I'll have a pint of bitter,' or some shite like that. 'Please' and 'thank you' don't come into it. No, it has to be 'I'll have', like anyone who's serving them is a fucking skivvy. I'm not kidding you."

"Why do you stay there, Stevie?" Dommo asked.

Stevie shrugged his shoulders."Dunno. It's a job, I suppose. I'd be back home like a shot if I could."

"Come on," said Adam Conway. "Let's get a drink."

The funeral cortege had dispersed in all directions after the graveside prayers at Carrickcruppin cemetery. It had been a dull day to begin with, the rain falling steadily from the grey skies as the crowd emerged from the chapel into the gathering gloom after the service.

"Outside," the priest had intoned to the numbed congregation that packed the aisles, "the light is fading dimly and the sky is crying. Throughout this land, the sky is crying. And inside this church, the family and the many friends of John are crying. And throughout this land, the people are asking themselves why, why was this terrible deed allowed to happen? And the people are crying. The people are crying out for justice in this land!"

The mood was sombre as the trio walked into Camlough village.

"I always thought Jap was an out and out Newry man," Dommo said. "He would never have imagined himself ending up buried in south Armagh."

"He was an out and out Newry man," said Adam. "Newry's only a few miles down the road, remember. His father's from around here originally. That was the family plot they buried him in."

"I remember him talking about Camlough," Stevie said. "In the old days, there were apparently more pubs than houses in the place. He would wax lyrical about south Armagh the odd time. All the green fields, the mountains, the lakes. That's when he wasn't giving off about the colchies."

They stopped outside one of the small bars dotted around the main street.

"This one will do," said Adam."This is the one that doubles up as an undertaker's."

Inside, the small bar was packed with mourners from the funeral, the preponderance of Belfast accents instantly dispelling the mild country pub paranoia habitually engendered by the disdaining glances of bucolic regulars resentful of their personal comfort zones being usurped by strangers. Adam immediately recognised some familiar faces, amongst them a number of barflies from Slattery's. Bunjy Doolan and Squigs Quigley were there, both looking as white as sheets and nursing tumblers of whiskey. Tom Bellingham stood in a corner sipping a glass of stout, talking to Terry Parcury and Cheesy Ring. There were others he couldn't immediately put a name to, including a sturdy looking youngish man whom he recognised as a former boyfriend of Chelsea Hynes.

"It could have been any one of us, boy," Bunjy Doolan said to Adam. "It just happened to be Jap."

"It should have been me," said Adam. "I was going with you that night, remember? It was pure chance that I changed my mind. I always used to sit on that chair nearest the door during the card games. I heard the screaming that night when I was in Botanic Gardens on the way home. It never registered at the time."

"If only we'd gone to that Czech bar like Jap said," said Squigs Quigley moodily, staring at his whiskey. "If only we'd gone anywhere …."

"He was a good man," said Doolan. "A hell of a good man."

"He was a Slattery's man," said Tom Bellingham drunkenly. "There's no higher accolade than that. One of the old school. Put it this way – he was a character …"

The old woman behind the bar said that there wasn't a finer or more decent family than the Prendergasts in the country. A copy of that morning's *Irish News* lay face up on the bar counter, showing a photograph of Jap flanked by both of his parents on his graduation day at Queen's. His father, a local doctor, stood tall and proud; his mother, a small woman with a fond smile and an adoring look sweeping her face, looked even more delighted than Jap, who was sandwiched between them and beaming awkwardly.

A VICTIM OF CIRCUMSTANCE was the headline in the paper. It was a comment attributed to a senior policeman investigating the case, who had bemoaned the narrow escape made by the assailants on the night of the attack. There, too, was an interview with a neighbour from across the road in Ireton Street, a woman who did not want to be named. She had seen it all from an upstairs window. Two men, gloved, balaclavas pulled over their heads, knocking fiercely at the door; the tall young man answering it being pulled roughly onto the ground, then smashed over the head with some club-like object; then kicked over until he faced the sky, moaning. One of the men produced a bottle and poured the contents over the victim's helpless face before smashing it against the pavement. The neighbour claimed that she would be haunted by Jap's shrieks of agony to her dying day. He had rushed, screaming and screaming and screaming, waywardly across the road, running full tilt into a passing car which had swerved to try to avoid him but could not, both eventually smashing into a parked car on the far side of the street.

There had been some speculation for a few days that he might make it, might somehow survive the horrendous ordeal. The ambulance had been quickly to the scene, the police even quicker, chasing the dark coloured car used by the assailants through the streets of Belfast only to lose it in the depths of the Shankill Road where the vehicle was soon spotted ablaze, its erstwhile occupants having vanished into the night. A follow-up search had produced nothing but the police were said to be following a definite line of enquiry. There was talk of the New Butchers, a ruthless cabal within the loose paramilitary alliance that called itself the United Loyalist Defence Coalition, being involved. There was talk of the group's leader, an infamous individual who modelled himself on the late Lenny Murphy, being personally involved in the attack; the intended target was alleged to be a known republican, but the philosophy of the loyalist leadership was said to be that 'any Taig would do' in the event of the target not being available. There were rumours of random retaliation presaging a return to war.

"He was everybody's friend, missus," Terry Parcury was muttering to the old woman behind the bar. "Everybody's friend. That's the truth."

The old woman said that it was a mercy that John had died. She said that it would have been more terrible for a young fellow like that, with his whole life in front of him, to have ended up blinded and disfigured and crippled, undergoing the torments of hell for the rest of his days. It would have been more than his poor mother could have borne. There were whispers going around that his father had been instrumental in what some said was a mercy killing. His father was a doctor who would have known about these things. His mother had been heavily sedated since the incident but had still cried and screamed incessantly throughout the funeral mass.

"He was some character, boy," Doolan was mumbling, a pint of Guinness settling slowly on the counter beside him. "The stories I could tell about that man …"

"Do you mind th'on night in the Rumour Machine with th'on hape of big English rides from Manchester?" Quigley demanded, peering absent-mindedly through the nearest window of the pub. "Whah? Some steam that night. What was Jap like?"

"Fukken magic, boy!" Doolan spluttered, a moustache of foam from the head of his Guinness attaching itself to his upper lip as he sipped. "Fukken here's Jap – 'C'mon and we'll get the hole the night, boys!' Here he was, cool as a cucumber, to this big dirty in the middle of them – 'Yo, ye girl ye! Who's for the buckin' the night?' Fukken here he was til her: 'C'mere – fuckface! You and me on the floor – right now this minute!' "

"Jap always did have a way with women," said Stevie. "Did he get off with her, then?"

"Well – no. She bate the gob off him for being a slabber, come to think of it. But the crack was good."

Adam edged away from the company to have a word with Dommo, who was standing morosely on his own drinking a pint of beer in a series of long thirsty gulps.

"One of the last things he ever said to me," Adam told him, "is that we'd have to go and see you, cheer you up. He said you were depressed."

Dommo laughed hollowly and continued to stare into his pint glass.

"Me? Depressed? I suppose that's one way of putting it. Jap could never have seen me again anyway, even if he'd lived. Not after what those bastards did to him. He's better off dead."

He finished his drink and promptly lifted another full pint off the counter.

"I'd rather be depressed than dead," he said to Adam. "I know what some people say about me, that I'm a recluse and all the rest of it. But I'll tell you what, Adam. Abortion for me is murder. Anybody who'd do a thing like that is every bit as bad as the scum that killed Jap. At least Jap had a life first. That child was as much mine as hers. I'll never forgive that bitch for what she did as long as I draw breath."

Adam decided he'd had enough. He pushed through the crowd to the doorway, watching the rain pummelling the dead street from the gloomy sky. He wondered where he'd get a taxi to Newry train station from such a godforsaken place. He turned as a hand clasped his shoulder from behind.

"Adam, isn't it?"

"Yes. I think I know you, don't I? You used to go out with Chelsea Hynes."

"You and me both."

The young man smiled and shook hands.

"She blew me out, too. Dropped me like a stone, if it's any consolation. I'm Alastair O'Loan, by the way. Ally O to most people."

"Adam Conway. I saw you at the funeral. How did you know Jap?"

"I knew him from the Students' Union mainly. John lived in the same house as a guy I know from Queen's, he's in my year. He's in there – Squigs, everybody calls him."

"Quigley. Yeah. Jap never really got away from the Students' Union scene. He was working, though."

"I know he often talked about getting a job back in Newry, settling down there. Then something like that happens. Do you want a lift back to Belfast, incidentally? I've a car parked back up the road a bit."

"Thanks. Thanks a lot. Let's hope they get the bastards who did it. Everybody's saying it was that New Butchers gang the papers are always going on about."

"You better believe it. The same ones that murdered my uncle. Thompson O'Loan."

"He was your uncle? I knew him. The Lone Ranger – I'm sorry."

"It's all right."

The young man pulled a set of car keys from his pocket as they approached a row of unevenly parked cars.

"I know he used to go out in that cowboy suit sometimes. But uncle Thom was a good man. He would never have hurt a fly. I'd do anything to get back at those bastards."

"So would I," said Adam quietly. "Jap was a mate. It could so easily have been me, instead of him …"

He turned, inquisitively, as a man approached them, walking with a long, swinging stride and a one-sided gait. He had a cap pulled down over his forehead, long grizzled locks of hair straggling downwards from beneath it, heavy framed glasses and a chin sunk into a tartan scarf which he wore with an old black overcoat.

"It was me they were after," he said.

Adam looked at him closely, astonished.

"Pat …?"

"Excuse the outfit. I didn't want to miss the funeral," said Pat Farland, removing the glasses from his face. "I overheard your conversation. It might interest you to know that there might be an opportunity coming up soon to do something. I'll tell you about it if you're interested. I was their real target, not Jap."

"I'd worked that much out myself," Adam said. "You better tell me the full story."

"It's not going to stop raining," said Pat. "If you're heading back to Belfast, maybe you could give me a lift and we can talk in the car."

Alastair nodded and opened a back door of the car.

"Get in," he said. "If there's anything you know about these people, I want to hear it too."

The three men clambered silently into the car and banged the doors shut behind them, the journey back to Belfast in the driving rain spent in an intense discussion.

Chapter 19

Love Is Strange

IN THE END it had not been a difficult decision for Chelsea. She had talked it through at great length with Heavenly and Paula; it was their opinions and experiences she felt driven to divine, for she knew that Enda would need no persuading at all. It was something about him that she was unable to understand.

"Didn't you ever get jealous, or possessive?" she wanted to know. "Paula told me you encouraged her."

"I did encourage her," he replied. "I'd encourage you as well if you were interested. I know you're curious."

"But … you were going out with Paula, she was your girlfriend … didn't you love her?"

"Of course I loved her. I loved her very much. I still do, as a friend."

Enda told her that love is strange. A lot of people, he said, take it as a game.

"Once you get it," he said, "you're in an awful mix. Once you've had it, you never want to quit."

He said that he knew a lot of call girls on Toby's books and that they were no different, by and large, than anyone else pursuing a lucrative career. It was other people who had a problem with what they did for a living, not them.

"Maybe people," he said, "don't understand. They think loving … is money in the hand."

He told her that her sweet loving was better than a kiss.

"When you leave me," he added softly, "sweet kisses I miss …"

He told her the decision was hers and hers alone. That she could see Toby herself or arrange something through Heavenly or Paula. That she could tell him about it before, or afterwards, that he didn't mind. That he thought she'd make a first class whore. She slapped him indignantly after the last observation but he just laughed, pulling her on top of him and kissing her long and hard until she was breathless and dishevelled.

It was Heavenly who told her about the appointment with Styx Hendricks.

"You're joking!" Chelsea protested. "What would one of the most famous film stars in the world want with …"

"With hookers? You've got to be kidding, honey. Most of them love hookers. Why not? They can afford us."

Heavenly showed her a magazine article on Hendricks, one which featured an in-depth interview with the star as well as a standard spread of posed photographs. A startlingly handsome man, in an arresting, quirky way, his small blue eyes registering a perpetual look of challenge, he spoke in the interview of the failure of his marriage due to his wife's obsession with Scientology and his own belief in a more personal spirituality. He mentioned the teachings of Keith Dalkeith as a major influence and there was a small picture of the renowned professor at the launch of a recent book, *Business Class On An Astral Plane*. Chelsea admitted that as a schoolgirl she had once had an enormous crush on the actor since she had seen him in a film called *Love Beach* with Cassandra Claybrooke. She had even had a poster of him on her bedroom wall at home.

"Well, here's your chance," said Heavenly. "If you want to get a bit closer to him, just follow your leader."

She told Chelsea that she would square things with Toby Venables. Toby often hired girls on a trial basis, to see if they liked working for the agency and if they were good enough to interest the clients. Some girls worked on a part-time basis, like Paula did now; others were former employees who were virtually retired, having made as much money as they'd wanted or married or got other jobs, but volunteered their services on an occasional basis. There were very rich pickings to be had, Heavenly confided: all of the agency's full-time staff also had the cover of *bona fide* employment on the books of Toby's public relations firm, so that their illicit earnings simply topped up what to all extents and purposes was a normal salary from a regular job.

Chelsea said that she was willing to give it a try. Just this once.

"Sure, honey," Heavenly said with a mischievous smile. "Just this once."

Heavenly chose the outfit for her to wear. She took her to her house in Holland Park, watching with amusement as Chelsea murmured her awed appreciation of her surroundings. She was enthralled at the spaciousness of the living room, the deep carpet, the expensive white and gold wallpaper, the marble-top tables, the luxurious sofas and chairs, the ultra-modern hi-fi equipment. There was a strange clock on one of the bookshelves, its appearance so puzzling that Chelsea could not resist asking what it was.

"It's called a Timisis Life-Clock," Heavenly explained. "It was a present from a guy with a very obsessive personality. This thing doesn't just show you the hours and minutes passing. It tells you how many you might have to look forward to. Say the average life expectancy is seventy six years, right? Well, this ticks off how many seconds you have left to live, how much longer your marriage might last, if you're married … apparently the average span is seven years. It even tells you how long you have left before you retire, if you're in a regular job."

"It sounds rather morbid."

"Yeah, well, it is. The guy who gave it to me is pretty morbid. He's a management consultant. I guess the moral of the story is this – don't waste time. Life's short, seize the day, and all that. Anyway, let's check out some outfits."

As they ascended the stairs Heavenly explained that the

girls on the agency's books received an allowance for what she called their working clothes.

"It's good," she said, smiling broadly. "Full-timers get more than part-timers. Length of service gets you more again. Toby starts all the full-timers on a six month contract to begin with."

Heavenly led her into the spare bedroom, sparsely decorated but bright and clean, slide robes running from wall to wall on all sides. She threw them all wide open and laughed delightedly at Chelsea's shocked reaction. Adorning the rails within the slide robes were some of the most stunning and provocative outfits Chelsea had ever seen: topless dresses, split skirts, see-through blouses; skimpy, clinging outfits in silk, in satin, in leather, in rubber, in PVC; exotic lingerie, some of it in unlikely combinations of straps and chains; an abundance of suspender belts and stockings and, on the floor and on shelves above, row after row of shiny thigh length leather boots and dozens of pairs of stiletto-heeled shoes.

"When you're entertaining a guy," Heavenly said, "it helps if you know in advance what he likes. The guy I was with last night always goes for the same thing. He likes to take a girl out wearing just a light raincoat. Nothing else, just shoes and stockings."

"Now that's what I call kinky," said Chelsea.

Heavenly looked at her quizzically.

"No, honey," she said gently. "Not really. This guy is very much a gentleman. An absolute lamb, you can do anything you like with him. He just gets turned on at the idea of a woman being out in public with him, naked underneath her coat, always available, just for him, nobody else knowing. That's okay."

She asked Chelsea if she'd told Enda about it yet. Chelsea shook her head.

"He's fine about it, though," she said. "He's working late tonight but I'll tell him about it when he comes home."

Heavenly smiled. She told Chelsea that she'd pick her outfit for her, if that was okay.

"There's lots of these clothes will fit you," she said. "There are all sizes here. Besides, I know what Styx likes. He likes his whores to look like whores. His agent's completely different, a guy called Seth Bernstein. He likes a woman to wear an evening dress, act like a lady. He'll not be there tonight, though."

She told Chelsea to take her time in the jacuzzi and spend as long as she liked doing her hair and make-up.

"There's another bathroom on the other side of the house – that's where I'm going," she confirmed. "One of life's little luxuries. I'll see you later and we'll sort out something to wear."

Chelsea would later remember the evening as an almost dreamlike experience, with everything simultaneously baroque but yet intensely real. Heavenly chose for her an ultra-tight black leather mini-skirt, with black fishnet stockings and the highest spiked shoes she could find in Chelsea's size. For a top she offered her a shiny red PVC jacket, short enough to leave her midriff bare but with only two buttons at the front so that a generous portion of cleavage was open to view. She set the outfit off with a peaked black leather cap, perched jauntily over her blonde hair and tilted slightly to one side. For herself, Heavenly selected a black skirt split high at the back so that with every step she took an alluring expanse of bare thigh was visible, a pair of knee length shiny black leather boots with high heels which served to exaggerate even further her Amazonian bearing, a transparent blouse under which a minimal gold satin bra was clearly visible and a short black jacket spangled with silver sequins. Chelsea brushed her hair lightly and nervously in front of a mirror as Heavenly rang the taxi.

"It's one of Shaun's businesses," she confided. "Centre Court taxis. They take us everywhere."

As the taxi crawled through the London streets she told Chelsea that she could expect a huge bonus for her first assignment.

"Styx always doubles the fee," she told her. "We've only got an hour tonight but he'll treat it like a full night anyway. That's the way he is."

She explained that Styx usually had an entourage with him when he was in London and thought nothing of having his manager hire a dozen or more girls at a time.

"But not tonight," she said. "His personal assistant will be there and that's it. Davina Caldwell. She's a very feminist, difficult, tough woman. She doesn't like sex, apparently, and doesn't find him attractive but he doesn't care about that as long as she's good at her job. I guess she must be."

Chelsea found herself blushing furiously in anticipation as the taxi pulled up at the front of the famous hotel. The two women attracted a multitude of stares and a chorus of wolf whistles from a group of passing men even on the short walk from the taxi to the hotel entrance. The doorman nodded respectfully at Heavenly as they went in.

A woman approached them as they looked around the reception area. She was slim, sharp-eyed and unsmiling, with light brown hair worn very short. She wore an immaculately cut navy suit with a light white blouse, black stockings and plain black shoes.

"Hi, Davina," Heavenly greeted her. "Sorry we're a little late. Traffic."

"Come along. We don't have much time," the woman said abruptly.

The woman avoided their gaze in the lift, looking straight down at the floor. Heavenly spent some time adjusting her hair in front of the mirror in the lift, encouraging Chelsea not to be inhibited as she did so, urging her to relax and enjoy herself, telling her that Styx would love everything about her.

"I love actors," Heavenly was saying as the lift door opened. "They appreciate performance art, it's what they do too."

When the woman called Davina knocked the door and opened it, it was Heavenly who went in first, walking very straight, her shoulders pulled back, her breasts straining against her blouse, tossing her long blonde hair seductively and smiling her dazzling smile.

"Hi, Styx," she purred. "How's every little thing?"

"Fine, Heavenly. Just fine."

Chelsea was immediately struck by the different appearance of the actor in real life compared with his cinematic persona. He was much smaller and skinnier than he appeared on the screen, his face small and bony and unremarkable. He wore a silk dressing gown and a pair of sandals.

"Who's the lovely lady with you tonight?"

"Her name's Chelsea. She's a big fan of yours, Styx. She

loved you in that film – what was it?"

"*Love Beach*," said Chelsea shyly. "With Cassandra Claybrooke."

Hendricks laughed uproariously and suddenly looked more like the famous actor he was, his eyes twinkling with genuine humour.

"That was the worst movie I've ever made, bar none," he said. "I hated it."

"But … didn't you have a real life affair with Cassandra?" Chelsea asked breathlessly. "It was in all the papers at the time …"

"Don't believe everything you read in the papers. Cassandra was a pretentious cow. Still is. She was a nightmare to work with. Can I offer you ladies a glass of champagne, by the way? Or maybe a line of coke?"

Heavenly said that they'd pass, they knew that he was a little pushed for time. Davina Caldwell had by this stage silently disappeared out of the room, closing the door quietly behind her. Hendricks was looking at Chelsea appraisingly when Heavenly suggested that she should get stripped.

"Come on, honey," Heavenly said impatiently. "I'm sure Styx doesn't want to sit here all night looking at you with your clothes on."

Chelsea had never felt quite so self-conscious – even, she thought, on the night in Belfast when Enda had persuaded her to give herself to Adam one last time before he left for Australia. She had taken a lot of persuading; it had been quite a shock even discovering that they were cousins. Needless to say, the whole scenario at Stranmillis that evening had been orchestrated by Enda.

"Why not?" he had coaxed her, stroking her hair and looking directly into her eyes. "I know you, remember. I know about your fantasies – you've told me. What better way of acting them out? If you want to know what it's like with two men, why not two men you know? You told me you'd always like Adam."

Enda insisted that no-one would ever know, because Adam was an extremely private person who always kept things to himself. He always kept secrets, even when he was a child growing up in Poleglass. Enda said that he used to visit his aunt's regularly as a youngster and Adam used to come down from time to time to stay with his family in Tallaght. They still kept in touch, just about. The last time they had spoken, Adam told him about Australia.

"I don't think he'll ever be back," Enda surmised. "It is a beautiful country. There's so much to do. So many opportunities. I told you about that season I had in Melbourne, didn't I? I wouldn't have come back that time only I had to."

Enda told her it would be a wonderful send-off for him. Adam had told him about some girl he was totally cracked about a while back; he hadn't mentioned her name at the time but from the description he was convinced it must have been her. And it was Enda who suggested the handcuffs and the blindfold, so that Adam would have the option of acknowledging her or not, depending on his own wishes. Later, Chelsea had been forced to admit that she had thoroughly enjoyed the experience. Adam did not reveal himself to her, either by speaking to her or removing the blindfold. But he had taken her repeatedly during the time he had spent with her, using her much more roughly and wantonly than had ever been his customary way when he was her boyfriend. She had never told anyone about it except Belinda, her best friend at the time, who had shared the house with her and asked her the following day what all the noise was about. To be fair to Belinda she had got over her initial shock fairly quickly and had eventually come round to the idea of trying something similar herself one day, just for the experience.

But this was different. Standing in front of the idol of her teen years, Chelsea felt momentarily frozen, unsure of what to do. Heavenly stepped over to her side and slowly took off her jacket for her, smiling wickedly as she noticed a perceptible expression of instant interest flit across Styx's impassive features as he saw the gleaming silver rings dangling from Chelsea's nipples. As Heavenly pretended to make a fuss of folding the jacket up neatly, she ordered Chelsea to get rid of her skirt and let Styx have a good look at her, front and back. Chelsea promptly undid her skirt and slipped it off, revealing her nudity, finally standing inches away from the actor, her hands behind her back, wearing only her fishnet stockings, stiletto heeled shoes and black leather cap. She turned round slowly, letting his gaze linger over her for a full minute before resuming her previous full frontal stance.

"You're very pretty," Hendricks said quietly, looking her up and down. "You're very young, too."

"Thank you," replied Chelsea, looking him boldly in the eye now and smiling.

He told her that he'd like her to lie on the bed on the other side of the room. She nodded obediently. He put his hand on her waist as they walked side by side to the bed, a hand which descended as they walked to glide over her bare behind. He seemed to be feeling the movements of her buttocks as she walked beside him on her high heels. She lay down, her legs flung open at his request, her labia and the inside of her thighs exposed lasciviously to his intent inspection.

"Wider, honey," Heavenly encouraged her. "You can open wider than that, you know you can."

To facilitate his view Chelsea opened her legs even further, then raised her knees and held them wide apart, sliding her own hands down to her labia and opening them with her fingers. Heavenly meanwhile was undoing his dressing gown and easing if off his body with practised hands, until he stood totally naked, then she herself began to strip, slowly, tantalisingly.

"You don't know which way to look, do you, honey?" she teased him, tossing aside her blouse and unhooking her gold satin bra before pulling it away from her magnificent breasts, the globes swaying as she moved, her nipples erect. She lifted her breasts in her hands to display them lewdly to him, inviting him to come close. She pulled his head to her chest and kept him there for some minutes before grabbing him by the hair and forcing him down on his knees, his head now between Chelsea's wide flung thighs.

"Go on, Styx baby-Chelsea's been dreaming about this moment since she was a schoolgirl," Heavenly exhorted him, standing over him like some beautiful dominatrix. "Don't disappoint her."

Chelsea would later remember the exquisite lightness of the actor's touch as he caressed her all over, kissing the insides of her thighs gently before tonguing her furiously until she moaned and felt the first shuddering spasms of orgasm. She moaned again when he mounted her, gasping as he penetrated before thrusting deep into her, sending her into shudders of ecstasy as he went rhythmically to work, savouring her yelps and moans as she dug her fingernails fiercely into his buttocks, pushing him onwards as he drove himself deep into her until eventually he abruptly quit, having shot his load far into her in momentous bursts, his belly pounding up and down against hers, until at last he was completely satisfied.

"Well done, honey," Heavenly was saying. "I told you you'd love it. I bet you're a little tired now, Styx. But don't worry, it won't be for long. I won't let you refuse me. Why don't you take a shower, Chelsea, then come back and watch us?"

Chelsea obeyed, casting aside her cap, stockings and high-heeled shoes as she walked naked to the bathroom. Heavenly was completely nude now, as impressive looking a woman as Chelsea had ever seen. She was so much taller than Chelsea, her breasts and her buttocks were more substantial, her curves delightful, her long, shapely legs seemed to go on forever. Her lush blonde fleece matched the natural colour of her flowing tresses.

By the time Chelsea emerged from the shower, a towel wrapped lightly around her waist, Hendricks was once again stiffly and fiercely erect, Heavenly removing his sex from her beautiful, gaping mouth before settling on top of him, straddling him. Chelsea marvelled at the way she controlled his every movement, lightly massaging him with her fingertips, telling him exactly what to do, tuning him into her own wants gradually and meticulously, like some absorbed maestro manipulating a priceless Stradivarius. Heavenly took her time, before finally rolling her hips in a slow, sensual motion, telling Hendricks he was allowed to come now and it wasn't very long before he did, shouting out loudly as he climaxed, Heavenly pinning him to the bed by the arms as though participating in some erotic wrestling match, squealing exultantly all the while.

"Just watch me perform with this guy, honey," Heavenly had told Chelsea beforehand. "I'm real good to look at."

Chelsea had to admit that it was true. Heavenly's face was so naturally expressive, her body so curvaceous and so beautiful, and it seemed that the throes of orgasm intensified her very essence, transforming her by her own extreme lust and passion into an uncontrollable exotic animal, thrusting about wildly and with an unrestrained abandon. Chelsea knew that she was seeing something utterly exceptional. Silently, she pledged herself to learn as much as possible from Heavenly whenever the opportunity arose. Later, Enda wanted to hear every single detail of the evening. He smiled widely when she told him about Davina Caldwell coming back into the room, looking at her watch, just as Chelsea and Heavenly were preparing to get dressed. She had given both women a hard, cold-eyed stare, her eyes lingering reluctantly on the silver rings that pierced Chelsea's nipples. She had curtly informed Hendricks that he was expected downstairs in the restaurant in fifteen minutes before handing the women a large plain envelope each. Enda whistled when he heard how much it contained.

"Heavenly suggested that we go down to Knightsbridge tomorrow and spend some of it," Chelsea told him. "Harrods, Harvey Nicks, some of the designer shops."

Enda said that she should do that. He mentioned a pub in Sloane Square he liked and suggested that he could meet them there after work. He told Chelsea he was proud of her and that he loved her. She asked him if he was sure.

"Hold me close," said Chelsea, "and tell me how you feel. Tell me love is real."

She asked him to let her hear him say the words she wanted to hear.

"Darling, when you're near …," she murmured.

Enda held her in his arms and whispered soft and true: "Darling, I love you …" and throughout the night, and into the brightness of the early morning, his words of love reverberated through her heart and into the depths of her very soul.

Chapter 20

Barker At The Tree Of Life

THE INITIAL MEETING with Wilson Squires had not been particularly auspicious. It had taken place at Malone House, a Georgian mansion set among the rolling meadows and parkland of Barnett Demesne off the Malone Road. Sited on a hilltop, the building commanded a superb view over the landscape of the Lagan Valley Regional Park, surrounded itself by magnificent mature trees and woodland. Pat knew the place was open to the public, for functions and weddings and the like, though he had never been inside it before. He was enjoying afternoon tea in a room looking out on the entrance driveway when Squires arrived. He was fifteen minutes late.

"That's an impressive disguise, Mr Farland, but it doesn't fool me. I'm an ex-policeman, remember."

"You're late."

"Better late than dead. I'm surprised you're still about. If you had any sense you'd be back in America by now."

"I'm not going to America. I thought about it. I've decided against it. Various reasons. What happened to Jap was what clinched it."

"Yes, young Mr Prendergast. That was very unfortunate."

"Unfortunate? Is that what you call it? Why did they do it? Jap was never involved in anything."

Squires shrugged.

"Why not? They were annoyed that you'd disappeared. They'd watched the house and the bar. So why not whack one of your friends, teach you a lesson? It'd be a warning to others and anyhow, a Taig's a Taig. That's the long and short of it. They'll not expect you to show your face in Belfast again."

"These people are scumbags."

"You're all as bad as each other."

"A plague on both our houses, eh? That's an original philosophy."

"It's not original. But it is my philosophy. I can tell you what I think because you've come a long way from what you were and you've worked a few things out for yourself. But I don't have time to sit here debating semantics. Just listen, and listen carefully."

Squires told him tersely that time was of the essence. He said that the mainstream loyalist paramilitaries were ready to move against McCaw. He was attracting too much heat on the Shankill and too many recruits to his faction, most of them young men, and he was viewed as being totally out of control. But McCaw was smart. Very smart.

"He had his team take the Black Dog apart the other night. They got every bug in the place. Six microphones. A very sophisticated phone bug. A hidden camera behind one of the eyes in a big portrait of Lenny Murphy they have hanging up in the bar."

Squires asserted that the surveillance techniques available now were among the best in the world.

"It's not just closed-circuit television these days. Though we have more of those than any other country I know."

Squires spoke dreamily of technological wonders, modern marvels that were being enhanced and developed all the time. He spoke of something called an IMSI catcher, a machine in a car that could fool your mobile phone into thinking they were base stations on your network. They could even tell your phone not to use any form of encryption, so they could listen to every mobile call you made. There were other man-made miracles, remote sensors that picked up voices from vibrations of the glass in ordinary house or office windows. There were the celebrated Van Eyck devices, instruments that could read everything on your computer screen from a street away from your house. And tiny airborne devices the size of butterflies that could watch every move you made. But it was an old fashioned car tracer that had almost snared McCaw the night of the Ireton Street attack.

"McCaw ordered a couple of his foot soldiers to hijack a car and have it ready for himself and Chopper Skelton that night. These guys weren't the brightest. They stole a car the previous night and the police had twenty hours to get to it and get it fitted up. It was a good job. A linear device, colour coded – "

"Why weren't they caught?"

"They very nearly were. Why do you think the police were on the scene so quickly? It was pure luck on their part that they got away. But it's bolstered their reputations even more amongst their own people. Once they'd made it to the Shankill, there's no way they were going to get caught. And of course they both had alibis."

The fact that two of the top men in that wing of loyalism had done the job themselves and escaped against all the odds had glossed over the appalling nature of the deed, adding to their leader's legend of invincibility.

"But he's not invincible," Squires said as the two men walked outside into the Malone House grounds. "Nobody is. There may be an opportunity coming up soon. I'll try to get you some photographs of McCaw from one of my police sources. And I'll speak to a leading loyalist I know who'll work with you if you need assistance. I rather think you will."

Squires said that he would meet him again on Sunday. He waved a hand expansively to his right.

"Over there. The other side of the road."

"Where? Clement Wilson Park?"

"Further down. Do you know that sculpture, the Tree Of Life? It's in a field between Lagan Meadows and Belvoir Forest Park."

"I know it. Why there?"

"Just call it an innate caution. It's served me well over the years. A lot of my contemporaries are dead or in homes. I'm still alive and kicking."

"You're sprightly enough for your age, I suppose."

"I hope I am. I have a lot of interests. And I take plenty of exercise. I do a lot of walking. I gave up smoking years ago and I drink very little."

"I've noticed. I've served you in Slattery's, remember."

"Sunday evening. Make it seven o'clock."

With that, he was gone. Pat strode purposefully back to Balfour Avenue, deep in thought. The lower Ormeau Road was busy as usual, traffic zipping up and down, shoppers hurrying here and there and small groups of youths loitering on street corners. Men wandered in and out of the pubs and the betting shop down the road as the sun broke through the clouds and swathed the surroundings in a benign heat.

He went straight to his room and checked all his personal possessions. He had made the journey back to Ireton Street just once since he had received the warning in the Ulster Museum; he had gone there on foot at dawn one morning, piling most of his clothes and personal effects into a bag and exiting swiftly and as quietly as he could, locking the bedroom door behind him. None of the inhabitants of the house had stirred. If any of them had heard anything, they would have assumed it was one of the others. He didn't think anyone saw him, though he passed a couple of drunken men shouting nonsense into the air at the junction of India Street and Wolseley Street.

The attack on Jap took place the following night. The first Pat had heard of the incident was Heather's comment about it in A Rainbow In Curved Air. He had been too preoccupied with thoughts of America prior to that to bother listening to the news or reading the papers. The shock of it affected him badly, the guilt even more so. He cursed himself repeatedly for not warning the others, for not realising the sheer propensity for random viciousness of his adversaries. Squires did not answer his mobile phone that first time he rang him.

Eventually, feeling drained and slightly nauseous, he had crawled into bed. He slept fitfully, troubled images trapping him in a twilight world between sleep and consciousness.

Bernie, the woman who lived alone in the house, came to his bed that night. She wore only a negligee and a pair of slippers. She was a women in her late thirties, maybe, or early forties, average height and on the thin side. She had dyed black hair, a direct way of looking at you and a commonsensical manner. A native of the New Lodge Road, she had lived in the lower Ormeau area for years, Farnham Street for a long time and then Balfour Avenue. She had married very young and her two sons had grown up and left home. Her husband, Liam, had been shot dead by loyalist paramilitaries years ago. She had spoken little to Pat since he had moved in, cooking and cleaning for him, keeping busy around the house and generally respecting his privacy. But now she was leaning over him, soothing his hair back from his sweating brow.

"Are you all right?" she asked. "You've been shouting out. You woke me up."

"I'm sorry. I'm fine. I'm just feeling a bit tense."

"You've no need to be, you know."

She smiled at him and slipped off her negligee, leaning over him again. She looked self-consciously at her bare breasts.

"Before you say anything, I know they're just bee strings. But I'm not bad looking for an old doll with two grown up kids, am I?"

Pat told her she wasn't at all bad for an old doll and that she'd do him any time. He took her by the hand, laughing with release. She cuddled up beside him in the bed, pausing only to switch off the bedside lamp. He made love to her avidly throughout the remainder of the night and, when the alarm clock sounded the advent of morning, they both ignored it and lay entwined without speaking for several hours longer; eyes shut tight, each imagined they were in the arms of another, he with Heather, she with Liam, and neither one cared.

The solace that Bernie provided temporarily kept the bad dreams at bay, the flashbacks of previous troubled times during the conflict, the memories of operations gone right and gone wrong, the tearful faces of grieving widows and relatives in the aftermath, the boundless depths of depression that time on remand had sent him hurtling into; most of all, she kept his psyche guarded from thoughts of Jap's horrific end, dissipating for the time being those chilling images he had experienced of his former friend standing at the foot of his bed in the dead of night, hideously disfigured, pointing mutely and accusingly at him and mouthing words he could not hear before fading slowly and despairingly into the blackness, leaving his consciousness frozen in a miasma of panic and paralysis.

The second meeting with Squires was more productive. It was a pleasant summer evening and Pat enjoyed the walk up the towpath from its beginning near the River Lagan's edge at Stranmillis. Waterfowl were plentiful along the river, with the occasional swan floating serenely amongst the moorhen, grebes and mallard; to the other side lay the damp grassland of Lagan Meadows. When time allowed, he liked nothing better than to ramble through the meadows and woodland for hours on end, taking with him for sustenance a bit of bread and cheese and a bottle of beer, finding some secluded spot and noting down in a jotter he carried with him any ideas that came to him for the new play that was slowly taking shape in his mind during leisure hours spent in tranquillity.

The Tree Of Life was a strange piece of work, nestling at the back of a field surrounded by trees over a bridge that led from the towpath towards Belvoir Forest Park on the other side. Created by someone call Owen Crawford back in 1993 as part of some sponsorship exercise promoting awareness of trees, it consisted of a dozen totem poles carved in a variety of striking images hooped together in a circle; inside of the circle, several more protruded outwards, seemingly shaped in the likeness of a spear, a canoe paddle and a large cross. Pat did not know what it all meant.

Squires approached from amidst the trees behind. He was carrying a rolled-up newspaper.

"Well," said Pat. "At least you're punctual. Have you got the photos you promised me?"

"No."

"What? Why not?"

"Things have changed. Have you seen this?"

He unrolled the newspaper, which Pat recognised as *The Island On Sunday.* It was a trashy tabloid he had never much liked, much given to lurid tittle-tattle and sensationalism at any cost.

ENTER THE KOMODO DRAGON was the vast headline that dominated the front page, with a footnote exhorting readers to turn to pages six and seven for the full story. The few paragraphs tucked below a terrifying picture of a brutish figure in a balaclava, gloves and combat gear brandishing a machine gun, hinted darkly that the current fragile peace was hanging by a thread as a loyalist leader prepared to unleash a ferocious internal feud more bloody than any ever previously experienced.

"What's this bullshit?"

"Just read the story."

Pat turned to pages six and seven, where the banner headline read: THE GRUDGE FIGHT OF THE CENTURY – UNFORGETTABLE BECAUSE IT CAN NEVER BE REPEATED! BILLY THE KID VERSUS THE KOMODO DRAGON

It was the paper's flagship Dog In The Street column, which purported to have exclusive inside knowledge of matters political and paramilitary. It was written by an apocryphal journalist rejoicing in the appellation of Rex Barker, whose name appeared every week beneath the picture of a doleful-eyed bloodhound attired in a trench coat and deerstalker hat, peering at the readership through an old fashioned magnifying glass. Pat read on as Squires had requested.

Storm clouds are gathering over the Shankill Road following the recent tragic death of young Newry man John Prendergast, who suffered fatal injuries following a barbaric attack on him at his south Belfast lodgings. The attack, in which John Prendergast had sulphuric acid thrown in his face after an assault with a heavy weapon, bore all the hallmarks of the brutal Shankill Road gang known as the New Butchers. This gang, modelled on the original Shankill Butchers, carried out an almost identical attack on a leading loyalist some time ago when he dared to challenge their activities. Since then there has been no let-up in their brutal murder campaign, designed to plunge the province back into savage civil war. But there is no mystery as to who is responsible for this depravity. Even we dogs in the street know that this campaign, orchestrated by the loyalist splinter group known as the United Loyalist Defence Coalition, is aimed at provoking the republican movement back into conflict and shattering the fragile political institutions which separate the progressive present from a bitter past. And The Island on Sunday can today reveal that the ULDC is led by the Master Butcher himself – the bearded Svengali who has masterminded these cruel and cowardly attacks is none other than the terrorist overlord known throughout Ulster as Billy the Kid.

"How exactly do you need to be a mastermind to cut somebody's throat or throw acid in somebody's face?" Pat enquired. "Who writes this drivel? Who is this Rex Barker?"

"It doesn't matter," said Squires. "Nobody in particular, as it happens. Whoever has the hottest story at time of going to press does the Dog In The Street column. The word is that wee Marty Simmons did this one. He'd better watch himself. Just read on."

Rumours are sweeping the loyalist heartlands that the New Butchers have gone a step too far with the murder of John Prendergast. Protestants generally have reacted with anger and disgust at the gang's frenzied spate of killings. Whatever their political sympathies, they have viewed these brutal murders as a throwback to uglier and darker days when anarchy reigned. Billy the Kid and his cohorts further embarrassed the loyalist cause recently by the vicious torture and murder of Thompson O'Loan, a former teacher and Methodist lay preacher whom they mistook for a Catholic.

But time is running out for Billy the Kid. The people he purports to represent are in reality sickened by the mindless acts of violence he has perpetrated in their name. His victims have been for the most part innocent Catholics: one abduction attempt in central Belfast on a high profile republican, a former hunger striker, ended in failure.

The death of John Prendergast has opened up an unforeseen prospect of nemesis for the Master Butcher.

Prendergast, a Catholic, was attacked because he lived on the same premises as the gang's real target, a former republican activist known as The Ice Man because of his cold and calculating demeanour when on so-called 'active service' duty. The Ice Man is thought to have led a gun and bomb attack on the Shankill Road some years ago which resulted in the death of Billy the Kid's brother, himself a well-known loyalist terrorist.

Pat looked up.

"I take it they mean me. The Ice Man."

"Yes."

"I've never been called that in my life."

"Nor has Winkie Kirk ever been called The Komodo Dragon. He'd lamp you if you talked to him like that. Any idea what a Komodo Dragon is, by the way?"

"It's a monitor lizard, as far as I know. So called because when you see one you know there's going to be crocodiles about. They're monstrous big lizards the size of a horse, totally poisonous. They'd eat anything, including their own young."

"Yep. Sounds like a pretty accurate description of Winkie, all right. A bit too many syllables for your average lumpen Prod, though."

"What?"

"Mad Dog or King Rat they could handle. Or the Jackal. Even Bald Eagle, or the Border Fox. Billy the Kid, Chopper. But this … I don't know. I just don't know."

"You don't have much of an opinion of your own community, have you?"

"No. Nor you of yours, from what I hear. It's one of your few saving graces. Just read the article."

Pat shook his head and cast his eyes back to the printed page.

Although John Prendergast was a Catholic, he was a product of a mixed marriage. His mother, Vera, currently on a life support machine after taking a drug overdose following the funeral of her only son, is a Protestant from Sandy Row. She met her husband Donal thirty years ago when they worked together in Belfast City Hospital, he as a doctor and she as a nurse.

In the parlance of the crazed bigots who make up the ranks of the ULDC, John Prendergast would have been dismissed as a 'fifty-fifty' – a product of a mixed marriage who, in their eyes, would have been no better than a 'Taig'. What they didn't know is that his mother is a cousin of one of the most feared figures in mainstream loyalism – the south Belfast paramilitary commander known as The Komodo Dragon. It is now increasingly unlikely that the tensions within loyalism can withstand any more provocation from the New Butchers gang led by Billy the Kid. Already it is known that The Komodo Dragon has issued an edict that the ULDC must disband – an edict that Billy the Kid has rejected outright. The stage is set for a bloodbath unprecedented in any loyalist feud in living memory – that is if republicanism is not drawn into the conflict first. Even the dogs in the street are heading for their kennels as the province stands poised on the brink of a momentous disaster.

"All right," Pat said, handing back the paper. "The punch line is that he's gone too deep underground to get at, I take it."

"Don't you want to read the rest of it? There's more on the next page."

"No. I get the gist."

Squires paused and stared at him.

"There's one thing I don't understand, Mr Farland. Why exactly didn't you get out of the country when you had the chance rather than take this job on?"

"I told you. I have my reasons. They're none of your business but there's another reason anyhow. You know what it is. I'll not be safe anywhere if I don't do this job."

"And you think you will be if you do?"

"Yes. If you can cut a deal with Jimmy it'll always stick."

Squires smiled humourlessly and nodded. He jerked a thumb at another story beside the Dog In The Street column, some grim morality tale about a rapist being found hanged in prison. The name struck Pat as exceedingly odd: the dead man was called Lloyd George Taylor.

"You're prescient enough," Squires commented. "This was no accident, you know. Don't get me wrong. McGuinness deserves to fry for some of the things he's done. But he's led republicanism out of a morass of its own making and he doesn't want any backsliding. He's astute enough politically. He'll end up running the country one day."

"Some would say he already does. You think he's right about McCaw, then? Take him out of it and all's well with the world?"

"Oh yes. Quite right. Cut off the head of the hydra …."

"And two more grow in its place. Who's his second in command?"

"Chopper Skelton. Equally as brutal as Mr the Kid but a fool. Not capable of lasting very long. Beyond him, nothing but rubbish. No leadership material whatsoever. They'll sink out of sight faster than the Titanic, believe me. They'll waste a few people first, of course, but that's politics."

"What if McCaw's faction comes out top in this internecine feud?"

"The future is very, very bleak if that happens. Unfortunately Winkie Kirk and his friends won't be available to assist you, as I'd hoped. They'll be busy watching their own backs."

"So what exactly am I supposed to do? You've brought me nothing. I don't even know what McCaw looks like."

"I'm bringing you information. Just listen to me."
Squires had lowered his voice even though there was no-one within sight. He pulled a mobile phone out of his inside pocket.

"Have you got one of these?"

"Sure."

"I'll need your number."

Squires told him that there was one chance and one only, for him to succeed in his mission. He told him to watch the local news the following Wednesday and to buy the local papers the next morning.

"Why?"

"There's going to be a rally in support of McCaw on the Shankill Road. He's going to have some interesting company on the platform. The Reverend Ichabod Cairns, for one."

"What? That hillbilly headcase?"

"Or democratically elected voice of Ulster Protestantism, according to your point of view. He'll be there. Some Orange Order backwoodsmen as well. I'm not suggesting you attend the rally. I'm suggesting you watch the news and keep the photographs from the papers."

"Then what?"

"Then do nothing until you get a call from me. You'll need to give me a contact number, like I said. Have your team on stand-by, if you have a team. The one chance you're likely to get will present itself on the first day in June."

"That's not far off. What's so special about it? Here's my number, by the way, I've written it down for you."

"There's a bare knuckle fight on in County Down. Newcastle. All-Ireland championship. One of McCaw's foot soldiers is the favourite for it. Young hood by the name of McDaniel, fights under the name of Danny Boy. He used to be a very promising heavyweight boxer before he fell in with such bad company."

Squires explained that he had arranged to meet McCaw to give him his winnings from a bet that day provided McDaniel won the fight.

"He might not turn up," he said. "But I think he will. I don't know the venue yet and I won't until the last minute. That's the way he works. You'll need to be in Newcastle on that day and be ready for any eventuality. You'll need to keep in touch with me. We'll have to work out some sort of code in the meantime, to be on the safe side."

Pat said that he would keep in touch. As Squires turned to go, Pat called him back.

"You're a strange sort for an ex-peeler," he said. "Tell me one thing. How did you ever survive in Lenny Murphy's inner circle all those years ago?"

"I wasn't in his inner circle. Or his outer circle. I was on the fringe."

"Didn't they know what you were?"

"Oh yes. They knew that I was a cop. But the right sort of cop, in their book. A true blue RUC man who looked after his own and knew who the enemy was. And they only knew that when it was expedient for them to know. Most of the undercover work I did on the Shankill then was before I joined the police, as far as they knew. In other words they knew nothing about the undercover work."

"I don't buy that. Why would Murphy have trusted you then? Or McCaw now? You must have had blood on your hands at some time. A lot of blood. For all your sanctimonious crap about terrorists, you must have been in it up to your neck yourself."

Squires smiled thinly and looked up at some passing clouds.

"It's a beautiful day," he remarked. "I've seen a lot of days that weren't so bright. Or so beautiful. I've been around a damn sight longer than you, remember. We're all products of our time, Mr Farland. Special Branch did whatever Special Branch had to do in those days. Seeing as we're such wonderful friends now, maybe there's one little thing you wouldn't mind telling me."

"Maybe."

"Your name. It's not Pat, is it? Why are you called Pat?"

"It's a nickname."

"It's a funny sort of a nickname. A false name for a real one."

"It goes back to my school days. I liked cowboy films. My favourite was an old one called *Pat Garrett and Billy the Kid*, starring Kris Kristofferson and James Coburn. Most of my school friends identified with the Kristofferson character. They liked the outlaw chic. It was fashionable at the time. I didn't. I identified with James Coburn. He played Pat Garrett."

"So 'Pat' comes from Pat Garrett?"

"Aye."

"You're winding me up."

"I'm not."

Squires looked at him sardonically and began to stride off across the field in the direction of Belvoir Forest Park.

"Well. Just be careful you don't end up like the Lone Ranger," he said over his shoulder.

Pat gazed after him, silently, until he had disappeared from sight. He watched a young couple across the way on the towpath, walking hand in hand as they enjoyed the glory of the summer's evening. The sun was shining brightly and the sky was smiling. He contemplated the only means of escape available to him from the empty room his life had become and the darkness of his thoughts obliterated the light as he began his own slow journey back to the safety of Balfour Avenue.

PART SIX

Closing Time

Chapter 21

<u>*Here Come The Drums*</u>

"HERE COME THE drums," said Pat Farland.

It was an old television, almost an antique. Bernie had a sentimental attachment to it because it had been a wedding present from her grandmother. The pictures came eventually. The first sight was that of a flute band, a strutting configuration of uniformed bullies with pit bull eyes and cruelly barbered skulls; the Orangemen behind them formed a motley concourse of bilious recusants whose crepuscular meandering bore little resemblance to marching. The cameras unerringly focused on the worst of the faces underneath the surreal proliferation of bowler hats: the greasy-haired, the heavy-jowled, the scowling, the twitching, the raddled features blotched by alcohol. As the sound was turned up the thunderous battering of the Lambeg drums intimidated the cosy insularity of the little living room of the house in Balfour Avenue.

"He's certainly attracted a crowd," Alastair O'Loan commented. "You have to give him that."

"I intend giving him a lot more than that," Pat said grimly. "Just drink your beer and listen."

Adam Conway re-appeared from the kitchen with three more cans of lager and handed them round as the camera switched to the platform where the Reverend Ichabod Cairns was exhorting the crowd to participate in a rendition of *Rock Of Ages*. Some of the crowd joined in as the preacher, as well known in some circles for his gospel singing as for his apocalyptic politics, crooned the hymn into the microphone with a pop-eyed, bat-eared, open-mouthed intensity, his voice glutinous with synthetic piety in the fungal night. On the platform were a number of prominent figures from the area, including one leading Orange Order dignitary.

A huge cheer went up from the crowd as the singing ended and the camera picked up Billy McCaw striding confidently towards the platform, hand in hand with a young woman with short dark hair and pretty features. Surrounding them were a number of shaven-headed, heavily tattooed bodyguards, their bodies preternaturally bloated by years of weight training combined with anabolic steroid abuse.

"The young man who is with us here tonight," the Reverend Ichabod Cairns was quavering into the microphone, his voice rising to a shriek to make himself heard above the ubiquitous din, "is a young man whose only crime is loyalty. A young man who was born and bred here in the Shankill Road. A young man who's well thought of in these parts. A straight talker and a man of his word. An evangelical young man. One who walks with the Lord. Who opposes the erosion of our culture and traditions. A young man with a stake in this country. A young man who has been picked upon, demonised and threatened, not only by republicans but by his very own people. Why? For daring to express a political opinion – for nothing more and for nothing less! Neither I nor my party condone people being forced to take the law into their own hands. But we understand the frustrations and anger of the Protestant people who do not want to go down the Dublin road that others are trying to cajole, threaten and force them down. As a political representative, I can understand why a counter-terrorist group like the Ulster Loyalist Defence Coalition was formed – as a last resort, as an organisation to defend the people of this country, against treachery and sell-out and betrayal! The ULDC represents a political point of view, one that is largely shared by myself and others in my party, that the day may be coming soon when the people of Ulster will have to defend themselves by taking the war to the enemy, to those who would deprive us of our birthright. On that day, the enemies of Ulster will reap a terrible harvest! I make no apology for defending free speech here tonight. I make no apology for endorsing William McCaw's right to voice his political analysis of the situation we face and take a stand without being pilloried for it. I make no apology for utterly condemning those who seek to stifle free speech and the legitimate political opinions of others by violence and by threats of violence!"

Adam shook his head in despair.

"This man's certifiably barking. An absolute fruitcake," he opined. "He should be in an institution."

"He is. It's called Parliament," Alastair quipped.

"Quiet. McCaw's going to speak," Pat said. "Listen to this."

The noise from the crowd rose to a crescendo as McCaw shook hands with the Reverend Cairns and took the microphone. He cut a statesmanlike figure in an immaculately cut black suit, crisp white shirt and grey diamond patterned tie. His hair and goatee beard were trimmed short and neat. He stood tall and erect as he faced the crowd. When he spoke, his voice was firm and authoritative.

"I wish to thank the Reverend Cairns for his support here tonight, also the District Master and all the good people in the Orange Order who have come here tonight to support free speech."

He raised a hand to quell the spontaneous outbreak of cheering and clapping below.

"Make no mistake about it, the threats that have been made against me are real. I answered my phone a couple of nights ago and a man said to me: 'We are going to get you, William,' and put the phone down. It's a sad state of affairs when a threat like that can be made to a citizen of this country and nothing can be done about it. The police did not want to know about it when I contacted them. The saddest thing of all is that I don't know whether that threat came from a republican or from a so-called loyalist."

He paused to sip from a glass of water sitting on a lectern beside him, then continued.

"I know the ULDC has its critics. There's even been a smear campaign about a number of executions of republicans in recent times. There's been propaganda about the ULDC being involved. I make no comment whatsoever about that except to say that no-one from the ULDC has been charged with anything arising from those executions. It could have been anybody, it could even have been republicans who carried out those operations. But things have come to a bad way when loyalists like me are hounded and harassed by fellow loyalists. The same organisations who make a big virtue out of holding their ceasefires have told me I have seven days to get out of the country. I say to them, I will not be leaving the land that I love to appease traitors. The republican movement never succeeded in gagging me or stopping me from openly stating my political opinion and I can tell you here now, tonight – no so-called loyalists are going to do it either!"

The news item swiftly switched to an interview with the station's political affairs correspondent, an earnest young reporter who seemed preoccupied by the possible electoral damage the Reverend Ichabod Cairns might have incurred in the light of the night's events, given the likelihood of an autumn general election. He was of the view that the fiery clergyman had made a huge mistake in associating with such a notorious paramilitary figure. Pat turned the television off.

"There you have it," he said. "You'll know his face the next time."

"I'm surprised he's gone public," said Adam. "Everybody knows about his reputation. Now everybody knows what he looks like too."

"Exactly," said Alastair. "I thought you said McCaw was smart?"

Pat shrugged his shoulders.

"I've been told he is. I don't understand what he's at," he said. "He has a lot of enemies with scores to settle. Maybe his ego got the better of his judgement."

"Surely his days are numbered now?" Alastair asked. "That sort of celebrity is short lived, surely."

"All celebrity is short lived," Adam said. "And everybody's

days are numbered. The question is, do we have to go after him now, Pat? Why not leave it, let somebody else do it?"

Pat shook his head.

"No. There's no guarantee he won't come out on top in this loyalist feud, whenever it gets off the ground. The consequences of that are incalculable. It doesn't bear thinking about. The other thing is, his security is going to be iron tight from now on. It always was tight. It'll be even tighter now. There's just one chance. It's coming up soon. I need to know whether you boys are with me or not."

He explained that the opportunity would be likely to arise in Newcastle, on the first of June. It all depended on a Shankill Road hoodlum winning a bare knuckle fist fight and McCaw turning up in person to claim his winnings on a substantial bet. They would only know of his exact whereabouts at short notice so the operation would have to be planned and timed to perfection. He had his ideas as to how the thing could be done.

"I know you boys have emotional reasons for wanting to help me," he said. "You don't have to, though. If you're having second thoughts about it you'd probably be better just forgetting about it. I'll be leaving the country afterwards, come what may. You still have to live here."

"Count me in," Adam said quietly. "I'll do my bit. I'll be in Newcastle that week anyway. My union's annual conference is on there. I'll be staying at the Slieve Donard hotel."

"What about you, Ally?"

"I'm in, Pat. I don't want to get emotional with that bastard. I just want to get even."

"All right. I'll be in touch."

Bernie came down the stairs and looked briefly through the door. Pat got to his feet and went to talk to her out in the hallway as Adam and Alastair finished off their cans of Harp. They heard the front door shut and Pat came back in.

"I've been getting very fond of Bernie," he told them. "I'm sorry I'll be leaving her behind soon. It's not a bad life around here."

He told them that there was a sense of community about the lower Ormeau Road. You could live there comfortably, drinking in the local street corner bars, working somewhere convivial. Bernie had a job in an off-licence, just a few minutes' walk from the house.

It was shift work, not well paid but very handy. She kept herself to herself most of the time but had a cordial relationship with her neighbours. She came from a big family and a lot of her free time was spent visiting her brothers and sisters and their families.

Adam said that he and Ally had arranged to meet a couple of girls down in the Velvet Revolution.

"It's a pity you're lying low," he added. "You'd like the place."

Pat said that he was sure he would, he'd always liked Czech beer. He told them to enjoy themselves and not to worry about him. As they walked briskly up the street he stood just outside the door, looking around him.

At the far end of the street, a dozen or so children were playing. One of them, a boy about ten years old, was strutting along the middle of the road with an orange scarf draped over his shoulders in the manner of a sash. A tin drum was suspended at chest level by a piece of rope he wore around his neck and he was banging it noisily with a couple of sticks. Two capering urchins cavorted on either side of him, jeering and making impassioned five fingered gestures at the others, some of whom feigned looks of outrage and unbridled aggression. Several others sat stony-faced in the middle of the road, as though to block the drummer's swaggering march.

Pat observed and was silent. He shut the door behind him and went to the fridge for another can of beer. Opening it, he sat lost amid his own thoughts and quietly awaited Bernie's return.

Chapter 22

Room Full Of Mirrors

CHELSEA WAS NOT particularly enamoured at the way Enda had chosen to decorate the bedroom. She did not share his obsessive interest in *The Story Of O*, the classic erotic novel about the wilful debasement of the eponymous heroine, a young Parisian fashion photographer who consents to be brought by her lover to a remote chateau where she is kept naked and in chains, regularly whipped and raped at will by various members of a clandestine society. Enda often told her that O was every man's perfect woman and that she should try to be as much like her as possible. She was never quite sure how serious he was when he made comments like that.

Certainly, his choice of prints that now adorned the bedroom walls indicated a growing preoccupation. They included works by artists such as Stefan Prince and Lynn Paula Russell directly on the theme; there, too, were others with imagery of a similar bent, by the likes of Allen Jones, Graham Bingham, Gunther Blum and China Hamilton. Above the bed, Enda had inserted a long row of metal hooks from which hung an exotic assortment of whips, canes, tawses, riding crops, chains, masks and handcuffs. Whenever she told him it all reminded her too much of work he would just throw his head back and laugh.

One whole shelf of the bookcase beside the bed was taken up with paraphernalia. As well as *The Story Of O* and *The Story Of O Part Two*, both by the original author Pauline Reage, there too were the graphically illustrated comic book version of the original by the Italian, Guido Crepax, a book of hyper-realistic drawings by Loic Dubigeon and a volume of photographs by Doris Kloster with a French language commentary; beside them lay film and television versions, which Enda liked to watch from time to time with Chelsea naked beside him throughout the duration. He particularly liked the original uncut French language film version starring Corinne Clery, filmed in sumptuous soft-focus golds and browns. He told her that Toby Venables had been commissioned to assist with the casting for a new underground film version where the sequences were not fantasy, but involved a literal acting out of the entire storyline. Toby had been inundated with offers from stunningly attractive women wanting to play the part of O, some of them even volunteering to do it for nothing.

Intrigued, Chelsea re-read the book, her mind lingering on some of the more intense scenarios of formalised subjugation. It was exquisite, in its own way; great attention was paid by the author to the heroine's inner feelings, to her clothes and to her surroundings, creating an almost equally fetishistic counterpoint to the detailed description of her continual degradation. She'd had to admit to Enda that the novel filled her with a mixture of sexual excitement, horror, anxiety and envy.

"I can see what you like about it," she had said. "It appeals to deep instincts in men and women. Most women like being dominated … but it's really a male fantasy, isn't it? No woman would possibly put up with all of that."

Enda told her she'd be surprised. He said that he would take her to some clubs he knew sometime so she could see for herself.

"Anyway," he added, "Pauline Reage was a woman. I think she was a literary critic in real life. Some say she wrote the whole thing to keep her husband interested in her, but I don't know. I wouldn't be surprised if she wrote a lot of it from experience."

Idly, Chelsea had picked up the first book to hand on the shelf below as she was putting the novel back with the other works.

It was *The Picture Of Dorian Gray* by Oscar Wilde. She flicked it open and read a little of chapter eleven, where the hero had found himself compulsively reading a novel, an extraordinarily decadent piece of work which had held a horrible fascination for him and had exerted a powerful influence on his life. The final sentence in the chapter perturbed her somewhat: '*Dorian Gray had been poisoned by a book.*'

Paula had shown no surprise when Chelsea had told her about that incident the previous day. She readily admitted that Enda had whipped her on occasions when he was her lover but insisted that it had never got out of hand.

"It was always consensual," she had told her. "I was never really into that scene and Enda will never take you places you don't want to go."

That he took genuine pleasure from having a partner who worked as a call girl, she never had any doubt; he had often told her that he found it exciting to envisage her being used by other men, men who would and did pay her handsomely for the privilege.

Chelsea said that she thought her relationship with Enda was changing rapidly and that she'd need to talk to him about it soon. He didn't seem to understand that prostitution was just a phase for her; she didn't intend to make a career of it like Paula and Heavenly had.

"Well, it is a career for me," Paula had shrugged. "It gives me greater independence than anything else could. You know what I mean. Heavenly's different again. It's wealth and status for her."

Chelsea nodded. The more she had got to know Heavenly, the more she had been struck by her insatiable desire to make huge amounts of money. She had a hardness about her that many of the other girls in the agency lacked, perhaps because they had been cosseted by Toby Venables and had never experienced what she called the rough trade end of the profession. Heavenly had worked as a whore since her teenage years, starting off in a cheap bordello in New Orleans. She sometimes talked of setting up her own agency but claimed that she would never do it in London because she didn't want to compete with Toby. She felt she owed him for running such an efficient operation, running it the way these things should be run. Paula thought she was probably rich enough by now never to have to work again but as far as she could see she enjoyed it and got her sense of self-worth from excelling at what she did. She never liked to take too many days off, on the grounds that she often got bored when she did.

Chelsea said that she had realised that she didn't want to do it anymore only very recently, during an episode she referred to as her 'epiphany at Tiffany's.' She had been having breakfast in the hotel with a Japanese client, a courteous and deferential man who smiled a lot but spoke very little English. It had hit her with the suddenness of a thunderbolt that it was absurd that she found herself in this position, that she simply didn't want to be there, doing what she was doing.

Her feelings towards Enda had changed abruptly too. When she'd first moved in with him she felt as though she really needed him, she'd loved him and wanted to service him in every way, not just in bed and emotionally. She even loved going to the supermarket for him, ironing his shirts, cooking him meals. That had changed. He was still her brown-eyed handsome man, she still enjoyed being with him, but the sense of euphoria she had felt initially had worn off. She now insisted on getting the house in Sotheby Road cleaned every day by an outside firm and bringing in caterers every time they had a dinner party, for instance. Enda had jokingly remarked only the other day that she was turning into a raging bourgeois housewife, so furiously had she ranted about the failure of the cleaners to vacuum underneath the new rug on the living room floor. She hadn't been amused at the comment. Enda's attitude to her seemed to be that he didn't want her to change in any way; conversely, she did want him to change, to be more sensitive and romantic and emotional, to be more aware of her own feelings and moods and changing needs, without constantly having to have everything spelled out for him.

She determined to broach the subject with him very soon, to tell him of her plans. She had one last appointment to keep first. She rang Centre Court taxis and ordered a cab, glancing again at the card she had received from the agency. The address was in the Kensington area, a building called the Meltsonian Institute. It sounded vaguely familiar. Toby Venables had told her it was some sort of international foundation, run by a famous bigwig who'd been knighted in a recent Honours list. The clients were a couple of Malaysians, they didn't speak English and they only had about an hour at the most to spare so it was essential that she was on time and ready for them. He said that the receptionist would look after her on arrival.

Getting out of the taxi, Chelsea was puzzled at the appearance of the Institute, which to all extents and purposes was a large detached private house in a quiet street of the prestigious area. Only a metal plate on the door with the name engraved on it distinguished the house from any of the others around it.

She rang the bell and the receptionist opened the door. She smiled and introduced herself as Eva. She was tall, a good head taller than Chelsea, with blonde hair pulled back in a ponytail and a well-endowed bosom straining at the buttons of the white linen blouse she wore with a charcoal business suit. Her face was not conventionally pretty or beautiful but her almond shaped blue eyes, a very defined jaw, unusually thick lips and prominent nose, slightly too long, contrived to lend a touch of masculinity to an otherwise very feminine face. Her voice, when she spoke, was throaty with a slight German accent.

"Please come with me. You're just in time; they'll be here in about fifteen minutes. You're to receive them in the Blue Lodge."

She beckoned Chelsea to follow her down a corridor where a black door faced them. Producing a set of keys, she opened it and asked Chelsea to come in. The walls of the vast, pleasantly air-conditioned room were completely mirrored; the ceiling was painted an extraordinarily luminous shade of blue, as was the wooden floor. A large pentangle with strange surrounding symbols was carved into the middle of the floor. The only furniture was a single plain wooden chair, pine by the look of it, standing beside the centre of the pentangle where a metal ring was bolted to the floor.

"Please undress. They have left instructions for you to be completely nude. I will take your clothes and bring them back to you in an hour's time."

When Chelsea complied, Eva returned with a long silver chain attached to a collar of the same metal by a ring in it. Chelsea sat still as the other woman fastened the collar around her neck. It was about three inches wide, tight enough fitting but flexible and very cold against her skin. Eva then fastened the chain to the ring in the floor.

"I'm going to tie your hair back," she said, producing a red ribbon from her handbag. "You'll look more naked when your shoulders are entirely bare."

Having done it, she smiled at Chelsea and remarked how well the collar and chain complemented the rings she wore on her breasts. Dumbfounded, Chelsea froze as the woman passed her hands lightly over her nipples, before kissing her hard on the lips. Then, without another word, she turned and left.

Chelsea took a few paces in one direction, then another, to test the limitations of her bondage. Eventually, she decided to just sit down and wait. She sat on the chair the wrong way round, her legs opened wide on either side in the classic pose pioneered for posterity by Christine Keeler, a more famous call girl of a previous era.

She smiled quietly into the mirror straight ahead of her, practising looks and poses of seduction for the benefit of her reflection, never for a moment suspecting that her every movement and gesture was being meticulously watched.

"People see all sorts of things in a room full of mirrors," Keith Dalkeith commented. "Every branch of the Meltsonian Institute has a room like this."

"They're all two-way, then?" asked Toby Venables.

"Certainly. The design is virtually identical the world over," said Dalkeith. "It's the same with the observatories. They're all like this one. All soundproofed. All equipped with cameras. The cameras record everything that can be seen in the Blue Lodges."

"They record everything that happens, then."

"Not quite. There are some things they can't record."

"Like what?"

"The paranormal. Inter-dimensional images. Hypnopompic phenomena. Revenants."

"I won't pretend to have a clue what you're talking about, Sir Keith."

"It doesn't matter. Don't feel obliged to indulge me with the nomenclature, by the way. These little vanities are so ephemeral, don't you think? Perhaps we could get down to business. You know who I represent."

"Sure. How come you're so close to the royals?"

"I provide them with certain…insights. All courts throughout the ages have had their magicians. My kind of magic happens to be in vogue at the moment. That's all."

"Do you tell them the future?"

"No. The monarchy hasn't got much of a future. Let's just say I provide them with a service. I help them out in practical ways as well as spiritually, you understand. That's why I contacted you. Another brandy?"

"Thanks. Don't mind if I do."

Dalkeith got up from the black leather sofa, went to an adjoining table where several bottles and glasses rested and poured another two glasses.

"Palace sources have to be discreet. I chair a certain committee … there are eight of us altogether. We have been tasked with selecting women to help – how shall I put it? – launch the young royal males into their future lives."

"Right. I understand. Well, I reckon Chelsea would be as good a girl as you could get for a job like that. She's been a marvellous find for the agency. Star quality. It was her lover who recruited her for us – a young Irish lad, Enda. Works for Shaun Simpson. Premium rates would apply, of course, plus maybe one or two other little favours …."

"If I decide to select her," said Dalkeith, " and if she agrees to do it –"

"Why wouldn't she? It's her job."

"If my conditions are satisfactorily met, then a small package of value will be coming to you shortly. I must emphasise that she must agree to it and that total confidentiality will be demanded."

"Of course."

"Very well. Let us enjoy the spectacle. I can let you have a recording later, if you like."

"Great. I'd appreciate that."

In the mirrored room, the door opened and the two Malaysians were ushered in, grinning, by Eva who promptly left. Chelsea got up from the chair and stood, arms akimbo, chained and naked in the middle of the floor, glad the waiting was over, smiling a greeting.

Behind the glass, the two men watched intently and the cameras whirred.

Chapter 23

The Operation

ADAM CONWAY STRODE purposefully away from the front entrance of the Slieve Donard hotel, its great redstone presence looming in the background at the north end of the great sweep of the beach, which led in the other direction to the small harbour, onwards to Donard Park and Tollymore Forest Park on the slopes of Slieve Donard mountain.

He loved Newcastle. The Mountains of Mourne really did sweep down to the sea, as in the words of the old Percy French song; Slievemartin, Eagle Mountain, Pigeon Rock Mountain, Hen Mountain, Cock Mountain, Slieve Muck, Butter Mountain, Slieve Bernagh, Slan Lieve, Luke's Mountain – he knew all of them, some old names, some misread, some mistranslated, named after ancient long forgotten incidents, long forgotten heroes.

Some seagulls soared wailing overhead as he watched a long green wave washing over the beach, gleaming like curved glass in the bright sunlight. It was a perfect June day, the air throbbing with a faint, blue, shimmering haze and an all-enveloping warmth.

Adam stood at the top of Railway Street as arranged and glanced at his watch. He looked round nervously as a small stone came skimming around his feet from behind him. Pat Farland grinned, striding towards him with the idiosyncratic walk he had affected as part of his now habitual disguise.

"Well," he said. "Are you enjoying the conference?"

"It's good in parts."

"I'll let you get back to it shortly. What about Ally?"

"He's fine. He knows where to meet us. He'll be there, all right."

"Right. We won't have long to wait. Here's Squires now."

The figure of Wilson Squires emerged from the corner of the nearby Golf Links Road, carrying a briefcase. He looked gaunt and worried and very old.

"Did it all go to plan?" asked Pat.

"Not quite," said Squires wearily. "Danny Boy won all right. Just about. Caught the Bullhammer with a haymaker just when it looked like he was going to get battered to bits. He broke his right hand very badly. I doubt very much if he'll fight again for a long time."

"Whatever. He won, didn't he? That's the main thing. Presumably McCaw will turn up to collect his winnings."

"Two hours from now. At the Bar A Gogo."

"I know it. Are you sure he'll be there?"

"I'm not sure of anything anymore. He might just send somebody. He wasn't at the fight."

"Where was it?"

"In Donard Wood. There was a big crowd. I recognised several of his henchmates but I didn't see him. I'll tell you who I did see, though."

"Who?"

"Marty Simmons. You know, Rex Barker out of the paper. He was down to do an undercover story on the fight."

"So?"

"He told me he spotted Winkie Kirk in town this morning. I'm getting a bad feeling about all of this. Do you see that man over there? He's from the CIA."

He nodded obscurely at a man walking some distance up along the beach, a mobile phone glued to one ear, head down. He was a tallish man with long floppy brown hair and a serious expression.

"That's Everett Nash, for God's sake!" Adam exclaimed. "I know him. He's a postgraduate student at Queen's. I didn't recognise him for a minute without his glasses."

Squires looked at him sharply.

"He doesn't wear glasses. His name is Wallace. He's from the CIA, all right. I've met him a couple of times in the American consulate. I don't know what cover he operates under in Belfast but I can assure you he's CIA. Turn around."

The three men turned around unobtrusively as the American walked off into the distance in the other direction, still concentrating intently on the mobile phone.

"What the hell would the CIA be doing here*?"* Adam demanded. "That's Everett Nash, I'm telling you! He's been a student for years."

"The Americans have an interest in our local politics," said Squires. "They don't want the peace to collapse. They've invested a lot of political capital here, never mind the economic side of things. McCaw is seen as a major problem on every front right now. If you want to abort this operation, I wouldn't blame you."

"No," said Pat. "There's no time for that now. Adam – I'll see you later. In an hour's time, okay? Go back to the conference for a while."

On returning, Adam opened the door at the back of the conference hall. Tommy Ogdon and Derek Greenslade were standing at the back wall with their arms folded. Hundreds of delegates sat with their backs to them while up on the stage the union's Executive Council sat in rows behind long wooden tables. At the lectern below, John Lennon was speaking into a microphone, his image caught on two giant screens at either side at the top of the hall and on several television screens around it.

"At the end of the day," Lennon was saying in a dreary monotone, "there are no instant solutions, but there is, in a sense, a danger that some of us perhaps can't see the wood for the trees. What is important is that we do not close the window of opportunity that now opens before us onto the level playing field that we all know, when push comes to shove, and Hardy comes to Hardy, out there in the real world -"

"John's talking some shite today," Adam observed. "Has he been on the beer, or what?"

"Shush. He will be if he gets away with this," Tommy whispered. "Derek's bet Bignose a case of stout that he can't deliver a speech composed entirely of clichés without anybody noticing."

"What's it supposed to be about?"

"Privatisation. He hasn't mentioned it once. Looks like the cunt's won it."

"And so we know," Lennon finished triumphantly, "at the heel of the hunt …and when all's said and done … it's a game of two halves. The first half and the second half. And I'll tell you this, delegates – the door to progress, to moving the situation forward, to the return of democratic accountability, has not yet been closed. I can say without fear of contradiction that there's a cautious optimism afoot. A cautious optimism that in a very real sense is only the tip of the iceberg. That we can, at last, detect a ray of light at the end of the tunnel. Because in the final analysis, we all know that the second half isn't over. And it won't be over until the fat lady sings!"

There was a polite ripple of applause from the audience as Lennon departed straight-faced from the podium, ceding his place to the next speaker on the motion. A rabble rousing cheer went up from one section of the crowd as the portly figure of Paul Stomper became visible, waddling arrogantly up the aisle.

"Comrades," he began in a high pitched whine of accusation, "I have no difficulty with any of what I've just heard. I agree with every word of it. But we need to go further than that, comrades! What we need now is a mass campaign, one involving industrial action –"

"Fuck these Free Radical wankers," said Tommy. "At least Bignose was taking the piss. These cunts come out with the same shit every time without even realising it. They never change the fucking record. What fucking millennium do they think they're living in?"

"Relax, Tommy," Greenslade said. "None of this is meant to be taken seriously. You know that, I know that, the audience knows that. It's all froth. Talking of which, I hear the Bot is putting on a real ale festival at the weekend. You interested?"

"Aye, I'd be up for that all right. Saturday night, maybe."

Adam sat down in a chair at the back, closing his eyes as the gruff chatter of the two officials beside him mingled with Stomper's affronted diatribe. He came to with a start when he recognised a familiar voice at the microphone as a new speaker was called.

"Conference delegates, distinguished guests," the voice was saying solemnly, "the previous speakers were right about the responsibilities of our politicians. Those of them who take note of TUNICS policy – and I know that many of them do so assiduously – must ask themselves where they are going to be standing when the levee breaks and the floods of oblivion start to wash inexorably over vital public services in their own constituencies. It will be too late then to shout at the wind and to order the waves to go back. They cannot ask then for whom the bell tolls, when the chimes of public sector fiscal freedom that have been endorsed by the trade union movement and those of a similarly enlightened egalitarian ethos are but a distant echo across a sea of tears!"

"Who is this vexatious popinjay?" enquired Tommy. "Have you a bet on with him as well?"

"He's all right," muttered Greenslade. "He's on the Beige Antelope wing. He's not in the Service long. Bit of a windbag. The name will come to me."

"Eaves," interjected Adam. "Dorian Eaves."

"You know him?"

"I knew him years ago. He's an asshole."

On the platform, Dorian Eaves stood imperiously and glanced at the typed speech in front of him before looking straight ahead, focusing on the audience with an expression of the deepest sincerity.

"Conference," he continued, "you know that even in our darkest hour, when wholesale privatisation stared us in the face, trade unionists of vision did not lose sight of the first faltering rays of sunshine penetrating the darkened skies over the boulevard of broken dreams the public sector had become, disturbing the voracious predators of dogma and destruction even as they hovered, vulture-like and malevolent, over the softly beating heart of the body politic."

He paused momentarily to clear his throat and cast another eye over his notes before continuing.

"Some on the management side will always possess a perverse nostalgia for that sad, bleak and unattainable past, a time when such errant philosophies were rife. Even now there are those who will queue up to tie themselves to the mast of this ship of fools rather than cry freedom from the myths of corporate populism, the myths that decree that all that is private is good and all that is public is bad. But the winds of change are blowing, delegates! The role of the trade union movement as harbingers of light will continue unabated. We will banish the crooked shadows of deception and outmoded management theory from this, our public domain! For there are, as the previous speakers have intimated, promising new alternatives and enticing possibilities in the latest political soundings that have been taken. There are, in short, angels in the architecture – celestial visages now gaze forth into the roseate vista of a brand new dawn, where once foul gargoyles cast their baleful glare!"

"Fuck this," commented Tommy. "I'm going to the bar for a pint."

"I'll join you," said Greenslade. "I've had enough of this crap myself. Coming with us, Adam?"

Adam shook his head. Greenslade shrugged and followed Tommy as he stroke off towards the exit. The audience appeared convulsed in paroxysms of raucous hyena-like laughter at some witty sally that Dorian Eaves had just vouchsafed in the interim.

"And so," Eaves concluded, picking up his papers and turning to leave the podium, "on that note I will close. Remember that the opportunity still exists for our politicians to act with good moral authority. If they take that opportunity, the angels will sing. And pigs may sprout large, powerful wings and learn to fly. But we all know what the alternative is to moving forward, delegates. Let us hope - and, indeed, pray – that we do not have to take two steps backwards for every step that we take forward!"

Adam got to his feet and hurried through the door, walking briskly through the corridor at the back of the hall and nimbly skipping up the hotel stairs two at a time until he reached his room on the second floor. He changed quickly into some old clothes he had brought with him and put on a baseball cap and a pair of sunglasses. He saw few people in the hotel foyer on the way out but cursed silently when Alma Walker stepped out from behind a noticeboard beside the reception area casually scanning a message that had been left for her on a postcard she was holding.

"Conference that bad, is it?" she said good-naturedly.

"I'm feeling a bit sick. I had a few beers last night," Adam explained. "I'm going for a walk, see if some fresh air helps."

The walk to the apartment took less than ten minutes. It was one of a block owned by Wilson Squires, Pat had told him. Squires had assured him that the adjoining apartments would be kept empty for the duration so that they would not be disturbed by inquisitive holidaymakers. It was Pat who answered the door when he rang the bell.

Inside, Ally O'Loan was looking daggers at another man who was visibly sneering at him. The man was a thin, dapper individual of average height, short slightly greying hair brushed to one side. He had the nonchantly cheap dress sense of those who care nothing about such things. He looked about mid-thirties, with the unhealthy etiolated look of someone who had served a long prison sentence. In fact, according to Pat, he had served five years of an eighteen year sentence before the last amnesty was declared for political prisoners. Dennis Linden had enjoyed a daunting reputation as a bomb maker in republican circles. A motor mechanic by trade, he had developed an outstanding expertise over the years with explosives of all descriptions, from the blockbuster bombs that turned huge buildings into car parks to deadly accurate home-made mortars and ingeniously innovative car bombs. Pat had warned Adam that he was not a likeable man. He was the type who could start a fight in a lift, so persistently did he rub people up the wrong way. Pat had reluctantly decided to avail of his services for two reasons. One was that he could supply what was needed. The other was that he was a good operator. Whatever else might be said of him, he was totally reliable under pressure.

"So this is the other college boy," Linden said, looking Adam up and down mockingly. "You're the man that knows how to put a team together, Pat. We're taking on the fucking New Butchers and you line us up a couple of college boys. Do you know what these things are, college boy?"

He gestured at a case sitting on top of a wooden table to his left. Adam said that he knew what grenades looked like.

"These are special issue," Pat said, running a finger over the metallic blue surface of the nearest one. "Made in Germany. They make nine loud bangs from internal explosive charges. They're sometimes used in military and police training to give the impression of being under fire during exercises."

"So you brought me here just to chuck a fucking grenade?" Linden demanded. "Why? Any cunt could do that."

"Not any cunt could have laid his hands on these babies at such short notice," said Pat. "Only a cunt like you could do that. Now shut up. Time's short. Here's how we're doing it."

He reached into the back pocket of his jeans and produced a tightly folded piece of paper.

"If McCaw shows up today," he said, "it'll be in a pub not far from here. The Bar A Gogo."

"I know it," said Linden. "South Promenade, isn't it?"

"Further on down. Main Street."

"It's a snout bar, if I'm not very much mistaken."

"Yes, Dennis. It is," said Pat, "as you put it in your admirably direct proletarian patois, a snout bar. The owner is one Arthur Gogarty, also known as Gogo Gogarty. He's a loyalist in his mid-forties, originally from the Shankill. He's never done time. He's lived in Newcastle for about five years now, kept his nose clean. He opened up this bar about a year ago."

He unfolded the sheet of paper in his hand and laid it out on the table. On it was traced a rough map of the surrounding area. Pat produced a pencil from another pocket and marked an X on Main Street to denote the approximate position of the Bar A Gogo. He looked intent, purposeful, objective. Adam thought that he had never seen him look quite so focused, almost as if the operation were the very culmination of his life's work.

"Listen carefully," Pat said. "It's like I said. Time's short."

Later, when Adam thought back on it, as he was fated to do every day and more nights than he would have wished, in his dreams, from then on, the one overwhelming impression that lodged in his memory was the sheer sense of speed at which all of the events took place. That, and the inevitability of all of it. Pat had repeatedly stressed both to himself and to Ally that it was going to be a high risk operation, that they could pull out of it at any time they wanted and there would be no questions asked. If things went wrong, they could find themselves facing death or serious injury. That, or spending the best years of their lives in prison with little or nothing to look forward to when they got out. It was entirely up to them whether they wanted to go through with it but he would appreciate their help if they did decide to offer it. Any doubts Adam had were overcome by Ally's resilience. He was determined in his own mind to see justice done, as he insistently put it.

Adam's role was the least dangerous. His job was to phone in the bomb scare. He walked past the Bar A Gogo first, pretending to read the headlines of the sports pages of a tabloid newspaper he held in front of him. He noticed that there were several men sitting in a black jeep parked on the opposite side of the road from the pub and at least one car on either side of it occupied by silent observers. Adam walked on. He saw Wilson Squires pass him, never looking at him, as he drove slowly up Main Street and parked his car several doors down from the pub.

Adam turned into a side street and, glancing over his shoulder, saw Squires walking towards the bar entrance with a black briefcase in his hand. The following ten minutes were the longest of the day. Squires had insisted on it, saying that McCaw and his henchmates would immediately smell a rat if he did not stay to have a celebratory drink with them. But they would not think it odd him only having one, because normally that was all he ever had.

Adam watched the seconds pass by on his watch in a cold

sweat before pulling out the mobile phone. It was a special one that had been obtained for him. Pat had advised him to use it as it was less risky than a public telephone but had told him to get rid of it afterwards.

"Gogo," he muttered into it. His voice sounded hoarse and distant even to himself.

"What?"

"Gogo Gogarty."

"Who is this?"

"This is Captain Kirk of the Ulster Justice League, Gogo. We don't much like the company you've been keeping. Your time is up. There is a bomb on the premises and you have exactly one minute to get out. Codeword is 'Cromwell'."

Adam was trembling and sweating profusely and his heart was beating like a Lambeg drum as he walked quickly down towards the beach. Stooping over, he wrapped the mobile phone in his newspaper, smashed it several times with a large stone and hurled it out into the water. He threw several pebbles after it, skimming them on the surface. He went to a wall nearby and sat on it. Further down, a young mother was playing with her children, two girls and a boy. The boy, little more than a baby, began to cry as he lost his grip on the string of a green balloon he was holding. His sisters played on, unconcerned, shrieking and laughing as they tussled with each other, while his mother comforted him and stroked his hair. Adam watched the child's balloon float off into the blue sky, drifting first one way, then the other, finally disappearing out of sight forever over distant rooftops.

It was several days before he managed to meet up with Ally to find out exactly what had happened. That his companions had escaped safely, he knew; the full facts behind McCaw's assassination did not come out for some time, but it was clear that another loyalist faction had been blamed fairly and squarely for it.

Squires had left the bar after one drink, as arranged. As he drove off, Adam had simultaneously phoned in the bomb scare and Linden had taken up position in a car not far from the back of pub. When Gogarty had raised the alarm inside, some panic-stricken customers had run towards the back entrance, at which point Linden stepped out of the car and lobbed a grenade expertly in the direction of the back wall.

The resultant bangs were so loud that they sounded like machine gun fire, causing serious disorientation and shock to all in the vicinity. Some managed to turn round and scurry desperately towards the front of the bar, where other customers were already spilling indiscriminately out onto Main Street.

There was a consensus later amongst eyewitnesses that two motorcycles appeared virtually at the same time, one speeding down from South Promenade, leading straight onto Main Street, the other emerging from a side street called Beach Avenue. Billy McCaw, wearing a lemon coloured check shirt and blue jeans, was conspicuous as he ran wild-eyed towards the open door of the waiting jeep, followed by several shaven-headed myrmidons hastening in his wake. As the first motorcycle passed by, slowing only slightly, the pillion passenger produced a handgun and shot McCaw between the shoulder blades as he hunched down to get into the vehicle. He managed to turn round, shocked, his shirt rapidly staining from the blood of the wound, only for the pillion passenger of the second motorcycle that then drew up to pull out a sawn-off shotgun from underneath his coat and blast him in the face. McCaw had put his left hand up to his face in an instinctive gesture of self-defence and several of his fingers were blown off as a consequence.

As he fell to the ground, dying, if not already dead, slumped on top of a black briefcase chained to his right wrist, some high velocity missile tore through the air and embedded itself in his torso.

Bedlam ensued. Ally later said that he was operating purely on instinct when he steered the motorbike past the jeep that tried to block him and the waiting car that drove straight at them, eluding both with the sort of breathtaking swerve that he had more often been lauded for on the rugby field. He had accelerated at maximum speed away from the scene, turning to the left up Bryansford Avenue instead of Donard Street as had originally been planned. Pat kept shouting directions from the pillion seat as they went, until eventually they reached Tipperary Wood where they torched the motorbike along with the leathers, gloves and helmets they had worn.

Pat disposed of the handgun in the nearby Shimna River and they made their way on foot to a safe house off Tullybrannigan Road.

The riders of the other motorcycle were not so fortunate. One of the cars managed to ram it and knock both men off it and on to the ground, where they were mercilessly kicked and beaten by McCaw's men. One of McCaw's closest associates, Hedley 'The Turk' Turkington, grabbed the shotgun from the pillion passenger and shot him in the chest before the howling of sirens filled the air and the police surrounded the scene. It was Pat's view that it was no coincidence that the police were so quickly on the scene, nor was it by chance that a number of their cars had come screaming down Donard Street a minute after they had passed. He had always said that Squires could not be trusted, that it would be just too convenient for him if everyone connected with the operation got stung; hence the last minute change of plan.

The incident heralded the most vicious loyalist feud that anyone could remember. That very night, a bloody brawl erupted in a Shankill Road drinking den, with opposing factions using glasses and bottles to inflict horrendous injuries on each other. When those were used up, the broken glass mixing with blood on the floor, chairs and tables were used as the battle raged on. At one point, one of the combatants flicked the switches to plunge the premises into darkness, with only the faint glow of street lights outside illuminating the barbaric hand to hand fighting, the savagery punctuated by the screams of men in agony as glass was smashed into faces and bodies.

KOMODO DRAGON SLAIN was the headline in a number of local newspapers several days later, when leading Belfast loyalist Winston Churchill Kirk was ambushed at his house off the Donegall Road by a sledgehammer wielding gang from the ULDC who battered its way into his bedroom before dousing him in petrol and setting fire to him. He died several hours later in hospital in excruciating pain.

There were dozens more deaths to follow, the Shankill

Road in particular totally polarised by the outbreak of internecine warfare, other loyalist heartlands only marginally less so. The ultimate demise for the ULDC came when its replacement leader, Mark 'Chopper' Skelton, was arrested and subsequently jailed after discharging an illegal firearm. He was apprehended one night outside the Black Dog, shooting a revolver into the air in a display of drunken bravado, a young woman clinging, bewildered, to his tattooed arm. As Wilson Squires had predicted, the organisation, already rudderless since the assassination of McCaw, rapidly degenerated into a rag, tag and bobtail ensemble with no cohesive leadership which in time was crushed out of existence – though not before another fresh spate of killings and an unprecedented number of fire bombings of houses on the Shankill Road.

It was only *The Island On Sunday*, a newspaper that few people took seriously, that sought to link the McCaw murder to renegade republicans and the CIA; it was the Dog In The Street column that pointed out that he had been shot twice, with neither of the weapons used capable of being traced to previous operations, as well as being hit by a crossbow bolt fired apparently from the upstairs window of a nearby building. No-one was ever arrested for the first shooting or the crossbow attack and the assailant who had thrown the grenade at the back of the Bar A Gogo had likewise disappeared amid the commotion.

But McCaw's supporters had harboured no doubts. The two men they had apprehended were, after all, known members of Winkie Kirk's crew; one of them, a seasoned gunman by the name of Abernethy, was killed by Turkington during the melee. Also Arthur Gogarty would have let them know about the nature of the telephone message he had received and the authentic codeword. He wasn't saying much to the media. Adam watched him on television that night, a cautious, leathery faced man, seemingly much older than he actually was, his black hair oiled back from his low forehead. He had a presence suggesting great wisdom and dignity.

"There's not much I can tell you," he kept repeating patiently to the horde of reporters than surrounded him. "I've heard of the New Butchers, of course, but I know none of these people personally. I don't know everybody that walks in here off the street.

Everyone is welcome in my bar, Catholics and Protestants alike. It's a tragedy that something like this should happen in a quiet family town like this."

Adam watched a lot of television that night. He had followed Pat's advice to the letter, staying in his hotel room on the pretext that he did not feel well and resisting the almost insuperable temptation to join the party downstairs that heralded the end of the TUNICS annual conference. Pat had suggested that the last thing he should do was go out and get drunk and maybe start shooting his mouth off. He advised a period of calm and reflection. Adam agreed. He went to the nearest off-licence on his way back to the hotel and purchased a case of Smithwicks ale and a bottle of cheap vodka with a name he had never heard of.

By the time he drifted off into alcohol induced oblivion, the television set still blaring, only his conscience was doing any talking. And it was all pretty incoherent at that.

Chapter 24

A Day At The Races

ADAM HAD NOT intended to go to the races. It just so happened that he did.

He had got up early on the Saturday morning to go to White House and prepare some papers for a series of meetings on the following Monday. There were several letters on the mat in the hall and he stuffed them into the inside pocket of his jacket on the way out.

He sat down shortly afterwards in the White House canteen with a cup of coffee, took out the letters and opened them. Two were bills; the other, in an air mail envelope, was from Australia. It contained a colour photograph of Pat Farland and Heather on a sunny beach, surrounded by people; Pat, looking younger and fitter than Adam had ever remembered him, was smiling broadly and carrying a surfboard. Heather, smiling also, looked tanned and lithe. The accompanying letter was short and succinct.

Dear Adam

I thought I'd drop you a line as I haven't seen you for the last two years. As you'll gather from the address, I settled here in Sydney with Heather.

Picture it as you see it in the photo. Lots of sun, sea, sand and the other.

We're doing all right. Heather used to have money but she gave it all away to an outfit called the Meltsonian Institute. She's working part-time as a hairdresser again – that's what she used to be. I can't say I mind. I made a bit out of my last play – did you know the film version is coming to Belfast very soon? It might already be playing by the time you get this. Go and see it if you get a chance.

Write sometime and let us know how you're getting on. Better still, come over and stay for a while. Make it soon if you do. I can't see all this lasting forever. Nothing ever does.
Pat

Adam smiled and put the letter back in his pocket. He'd heard of the Meltsonian Institute; Ally O'Loan had joined it some months ago, as his late uncle Thom had once done, eventually going to work for one of its branches in Mexico and joining some elite group within it called the Vice Versa Society. Adam had not heard from him since. Ally had gone through a religious phase after the Newcastle operation, latching fretfully on to one organised religion after another before taking up with a succession of cranky New Age groups.

"We didn't really get away with it," he often said to Adam during that period. "We thought we did. We were all elated about it. But we have to live with it now for the rest of our lives. I'm sorry I ever got involved."

The previous night had seen the film of Pat's play *Parallel Lines* open at the Queen's Film Theatre. Adam had gone to the early showing. He had thought it reasonably good, though it was clearly a commercial rather than an arthouse take on a work that might have been better suited to the latter approach. He was more than familiar with the story line.

Adam wandered through the White House grounds when his morning's work was done. He strolled past the fountain at the front down to the four-square layout of paths further down. A bewildering profusion of flowers served to offset the familiarity of the water garden: hop hornbeam on the east-west axis, pink and white Judas trees trained over iron tunnel arbours on the shorter north-south axis. The quadrants were planted with small trees in grass, dwarf box hedges surrounding each quadrant, while the deep perimeter borders housed shrub roses in groups. Many of the double borders, as far as the eye could see, had a dramatic colour scheme provided by contrasting foliage, magnificent in the summer sunshine, while a goosefoot of narrow avenues extended in one direction from an ornate stone arch through a splendid grove of cedars.

Adam sat on a wooden bench and idly flicked through a copy of the union newspaper, *TUNICS News,* which he had lifted on the way out. The White House View, the lead column penned by Reg Hetherington, was to be his last before his pending retirement. He had written the column for ten years, his full tenure as General Secretary. In the early days a full facial photograph accompanied the column; as time wore on, this was replaced by a picture of Reg's eyes looking through his square black glasses; in the final few years this had been superseded by an image of the glasses only.

Pending the election of a new General Secretary one of the senior White House officials, a Galway man called Graham O'Shaughnessy, had been earmarked to take over the column.

He was a loud, rumbustious individual who lacked Hetherington's sharp intellect and ascetic ways but he'd made his name as a redoubtable organiser and was respected for his negotiating skills. He antagonised a lot of people, not least Tommy Ogdon who invariably referred to him as "that fat-arsed Galway ponce."

But then he had repeatedly criticised Tommy, who had got himself in a lot of hot water recently. He had caused great consternation a few weeks back by interviewing a woman about an alleged sexual harassment incident with a white cat, one of the ferals that inhabited the grounds, sitting purring on his shoulder.

"Don't mind Sooty. He's a good lad," he had told her cheerfully. "He usually drops in for a bit of breakfast around this time of morning. Now – what can I do for you?"

It turned out that the woman was allergic to cats and she

had run screaming and sobbing from the room, tripping over an empty sardine can and a saucer of milk as she did so.

O'Shaughnessy had loudly proclaimed to anyone who would listen to him that Tommy would have been sacked long ago for behaviour like that if he were working for any other employer. The latest complaint involved a member threatening legal action because Tommy had broken his nose in the Botanic Inn. It happened one Friday night, when Tommy was in a particularly foul mood. He was sinking pints at a furious speed and scowling at anybody who came near him. Derek Greenslade spotted the two youths giggling in a corner, egging each other on. Eventually, one of them sidled up to Tommy.

"Here – Tommy," he said slyly. "Who's this?"

Tommy turned round suspiciously.

"Oggy! Oggy! Oggy!"

"What? What was that you just said, you ignorant wee fucker?"

"Oggy! Oggy! Oggy!"

Tommy exploded, as Derek knew he would. He hated being approached by members in his leisure hours at the best of times and generally gave them short shrift. He particularly detested anyone using his catchphrase.

"Do I know you, you hideous little toad?" he demanded. "Eh? Who the fuck are you?"

"I'm a union member," the youth protested. "I was on a training course you took-"

But by then Tommy had pinned him up against the nearest wall, shouting loudly at him and punctuating his remarks with a series of emphatic head butts.

"Don't you ever," he snarled, "talk to me like that again, you tenth rate little cunt! From now on, if you see me in public anywhere at all you refer to me as Sergeant Majah Ogdon, sah! Got that, sonny boy? Sergeant – Majah – Ogdon – sah!"

He had been barred from the Bot, his favourite pub, as a result but had quickly established himself as a regular down in Slattery's, where he had been persuaded to compere a comedy night twice a week in the upstairs bar.

“That bastard O’Shaughnessy can do what he likes,” he had told the other officials. “I’m not dependent on TUNICS to earn a crust. I can always go back to what I do best.”

Adam decided to go down to Slattery’s for a lunchtime drink. Lots of people he knew would be there; it was Ulster Harp Derby day and the bar always laid on a day out for the regulars at knockdown prices.

As he walked down the road he saw several coaches parked outside the pub, ready to transport the punters to the Down Royal racecourse. Going through the front entrance of the bar, he noticed a new glossy poster featuring a picture of Tommy Ogdon on stage. It read:

WELCOME TO THE OG POUND
An evening with Tommy Ogdon
Comedy the way it used to be
- before the world turned sour
Every Tuesday and Thursday
Doors open at 7.30pm, Upstairs Bar

Inside, the bar was teeming with people, many of them watching the big screen recently erected at the top end of the bar. Stevie Marlow, whom Adam thought looked plumper and more self-satisfied every time he’d seen him since he’d come home from Liverpool, tugged him excitedly on the sleeve.

“There’s Jack!” he yelled, pointing at the screen. “Did I ever tell you that I saved that man’s life?”

“Only about a million times,” said Adam.

Stevie had called an ambulance one night in Liverpool, when he had seen a man lying on the pavement covered in blood and vomit. People were walking past the man, their faces averted, some even crossing the road to avoid having to look at him. Stevie had been shocked at their callousness. It was only later that he found out that the man was Jack McGrath, the former tennis star known as the Spirit of Ireland, and that he had received medical help in the nick of time. Following a recent much publicised liver transplant McGrath looked thin and sallow, a travesty of his former self. Beside him sat Shaun Simpson, the only other Irish player ever to grace the sport at the top level, looking much younger and fitter than his compatriot but distinctly ill at ease. The men were discussing the outcome of the men's singles final at Wimbledon, due to be played the following Monday.

"I've heard it said that Cirillo has only the one shot," Jack McGrath was saying. "I wouldn't agree with that. You need more than that to get to a Wimbledon final. I can't see him being beaten. He has spirit. He can pull all the shots out of the bag when he needs to."

"I wouldn't write off Morgan," Shaun Simpson argued in his strange, quasi-American accent. "Of course Cirillo's first serve is awesome. He's the fastest in the world. But the big serve and volley men don't always win. I think Morgan is the better all round player."

Tom Bellingham walked up behind Adam and clapped him on the back.

"There's a spare seat going on the bus," he said. "Intergalactic Bob can't make it. Are you in or out?"

Adam hesitated only for a moment.

"I'm in," he said.

Slattery's bar staff excelled at organising these outings. Adam thought that it was about time he went on one. It was a serendipitous decision, as far as the race meeting went; the atmosphere on the coach was one of festive anticipation mixed with the noisy hilarity of a crowd that had started early and meant to carry on.

"You should have got down earlier." Stevie said. "You would have got your dinner and a free pint to kick off with."

The racecourse was awash with colour, the women in particular seeming to have made an effort to dress up, their hats and finery mimicking the timelessly lavish excesses of Royal Ascot.

Slattery's had booked a marquee, a large one at the top of the track, where a popular local jazz band was sending strange unlocatable sounds exploding, imploding and zigzagging through sliding trumpets as the crowd milled in and crashed forward at the bar, eager to exchange the beer vouchers they had received as part of the promotion for liquid refreshment. At the start, names of all present were written on tickets for a free draw before the start of every race, with prizes such as free bets, bottles of wine and cases of beer up for grabs. It added to the jovial ambience in the marquee, where everyone knew everyone else and loud cheers and catcalls greeted every beaming winner going up to the front to collect a prize.

Outside, huge crowds mingled at the numerous bookmakers' stalls, where the chalked up prices for the runners were being changed rapidly to reflect the support they were attracting. Adam was struck by the oddity that most of the people who had come did not watch the races on the track; rather, they viewed the big screens strategically sited around the course or surrounded one of the televisions in the bars or the marquees. There was an obvious logic in it, he realised, because standing at any one point facing the track, all you could see was the horses speeding crazily past that one point.

Adam placed his first bet of the day and to his surprise, he won. His luck held for the next few races. Others were not doing so well, as one favourite after another was beaten.

"What are you backing for the big one?" Stevie asked him, slurring his words slightly.

"I don't know. What's the favourite?"

"Equilibrium. Two to one."

"I'll do it. It's near time a favourite won one."

The Derby turned out to be the closest for years, the Slattery's company jumping with red-faced excitement and gesturing wildly as three powerful steeds streaked towards the winning post, neck and neck. The result was too close to call, with even the various angled shots of the television cameras failing to settle the fevered arguments that raged as the results of the photo finish were awaited. There was much speculation about a possible dead heat and the consequential reduction in winnings that would attend such a verdict.

Adam wandered idly out into the grounds and glanced into the champagne tent as he passed, noting that it appeared to be an oasis of tranquillity amid the hubbub. Many of the better attired race-goers were there, sipping champagne from fluted glasses and paying little or no attention to what was going on outside or on the television screens. When he returned to the marquee a loud cheer and a wave of applause greeted him.

"What won the big race?" he demanded.

"Equilibrium at two to one. By a short head from Coal Imp at a hundred to thirty!" Stevie exclaimed triumphantly. "You've doubled your money. So have I. You won the last draw, by the way. That's what all the shouting's about. That case of Harp on the table is yours."

"Right. Well – what's everybody waiting for? Get stuck into it!"

By the time of the last race Adam felt pleasantly drunk. Many of the company did not look like they would remain coherent for much longer. Terry Parcury and Cheesy Ring, in particular, looked glassy-eyed and near collapse.

"What? You mean more so than usual?" Stevie laughed when Adam mentioned the fact. "I can never tell with that pair of eejits. It doesn't matter. Sure we're all going to be bladdered by the end of the night."

Hector Carbon, one of Slattery's regulars, was going round the tables in the marquee urging the company to drink up.

"Hi-ho!" he kept shouting at the top of his voice. "Get it down your necks, folks!"

A jowly individual in his late thirties with a baby face and thick curly hair, he liked to affect the air of a man about town, constantly chattering into his mobile phone when he wasn't fixing some unfortunate with a glittering eye in the manner of the Ancient Mariner and engaging in endless talk about golf, cricket or car number plates.

"You're a dickhead, Carbonara!" Terry Parcury shouted at him. "Fuck away off, curly bap!"

Some ten minutes later everyone had been persuaded to finish or leave their drinks.

"Hi-ho! Hi-ho!" Carbon roared."It's back to the bar we go!"

"Lead on, Carbonara!" someone shouted.

Carbon swaggered off at the head of a swaying conga of Slattery's finest, the chants of "Hi-ho! Hi-ho!" filling the early evening air as the entire party spilled untidily across the fields back into the various coaches.

The momentum was unstoppable, sobriety impossible. By the time Adam threw open the doors of Slattery's the other coachloads had already disembarked and people were swarming around at the bar. Prominent amongst them was Tommy Ogdon, who had brought his wife Charmaine out with him for the day.

"All right, Joanie?" he was shouting at the nearest barmaid. "What colour of knickers you got on today, then, gal?"

"Hi, Tommy. The usual, is it?"

"Aye. Pint of wallop. Vodka and bitter lemon for the wife."

"How did you get on, Tommy?" Adam called over. "Any winners?"

"Just the one. The last race. It was enough for me to break even, so I'm happy enough. Have you met the wife, by the way? Adam – the wife. The wife – Adam Conway."

Charmaine Ogdon said hello and shook hands. She was a small, slim, demure woman with short dark hair, neatly turned out. She had a naturally warm smile.

"It's not often he takes me out," she said. "I'm going to make the most of this."

"Don't worry, love," Tommy beamed, an affectionate arm around her shoulder. "You're going to have a great night. We all are. Even that miserable wee shite there. Isn't that right, Mercury?"

Terry Parcury looked round drunkenly, spilling some of his pint on the bar floor.

"Parcury it is, Tommy. Not Mercury," he mumbled. "I'm not the only one that got a few winners. Cheesy got the first four, for fuck's sake."

"Aye, and he's another tight cunt and all. It's time one of you got a round in, Mercury."

Tommy paid for the drinks and turned to follow Charmaine down to a nearby table where there were a couple of spare stools.

"I'll tell you something, Adam," he said as he passed. "I've been married three times and she's the only one of them who was ever any damned good. The last one was a bloody nag. Never shut up. The first was a menace – tried to stab me with a kitchen knife once. Women, eh? I'll tell you all about it some time."

It was maybe a couple of hours later – he couldn't be sure, in retrospect – that Adam was conscious of Maeve Lindsay's presence. She looked impressive in an expensive looking white dress and matching slingback shoes, her hair dyed blonde. Adam liked Maeve. He'd had a few flings with her in the past and enjoyed them. He noticed her expression of shock mixed with amusement at the inchoate gibberings of Terry Parcury and Cheesy Ring at either side of her and decided to rescue her.

"No muff too tough," Terry Parcury was leering, swaying uncertainly on his feet and ogling her through half closed eyes. "You and me, darling –"

Adam took her by the arm and steered her to the bar past Cheesy Ring, who was starting to hyper-ventilate with laughter as though in the presence of some great comic genius whilst still managing to look supercilious at the same time.

"It's great to see you," Adam told her. "I haven't seen you around for a while."

"I haven't been around for a long time."

"I know. Not since chapter two, to be exact."

"What?"

"Nothing. I hope those two space cadets weren't annoying you too much."

"They're awful! That dwarf – what on earth's he like? He's horrible! And that Cheesy Ring! What sort of a name is that? What's his real name?"

"Roger."

"What?"

"Roger. Roger Ring."

"You're a pisshead, Adam! Seriously, what are those two like? Are they for real?"

"Well, no. Seeing as you ask, they're not. They're padding."

"They're what?"

"They're just padding. They don't actually exist."

Changing the subject, Adam pulled out the letter and photo he had received from Pat that morning. It was Pat who had introduced him to Maeve years ago, one night in the Rumour Machine. Pat had met her there one night when he was on his own and had been greatly taken by her. He'd spoken highly of her, saying that she might come across as a mad young thing now but that she was going to grow up very soon to be an exceptional woman. Pat had always had a way of talking to you like you were an equal, even in those days when he was a man living amongst boys. Adam thought it was an accurate enough assessment. Maeve had mellowed a little and had made a good career for herself as an interior designer but she still had an agreeably wild streak about her.

"That's amazing," she said, shaking her head as she read the letter and examined the photograph. "I was in Donegal last week at a music festival. In Bundoran. I could have sworn I saw Pat Farland in the crowd, wearing that big sombrero he used to have. It couldn't have been him, then. Not if he's in Australia."

The conversation continued for maybe an hour, darting hither and thither. Maeve was fairly drunk. She'd been at the races, travelling on one of the other coaches, and had consumed a heady mixture of wine and lager. She was telling Adam something very personal, speaking loudly and repetitively and holding Adam's gaze close up, when Chelsea came in.

Adam spotted her in the mirror behind the bar with another woman, whom he recognised as the girl called Belinda she'd lived with years ago in Stranmillis. Chelsea saw him and waved, smiling enthusiastically. Adam affected not to notice her. It wasn't difficult; Maeve was demanding his unwavering attention, standing very close and looking straight at him. He felt unaccountably shocked and stunned. He knew Chelsea had broken up with Enda. She'd come home and found employment as a social worker somewhere outside Belfast, giving up what he'd heard was a very rewarding job in public relations in London. She'd lived a jet-setting lifestyle, according to mutual acquaintances he'd spoken to; there were even rumours of dalliances with royalty. She had forsaken all of that apparent glamour and affluence for a more modest and conventional life in Northern Ireland. She'd married someone called Dunne, a quiet, decent sort of a man from what he'd heard, and they were living in Glengormley not far from her family home. There were no children that he was aware of.

Adam could never fully explain what he did next, even to himself. It was a spur of the moment thing at first. The thought flitted through his mind that he was being presented with a unique opportunity, one that would not come round again, to let her know what absolute rejection felt like. He had always been too compliant and predictable with her in the past; behaving outrageously out of character would shock her to the very core and send her a message of a sort she'd never had from him, or he suspected any man, before. One that she would never forget. So he ignored her.

He ignored her when she kept waving at him. He ignored her when she and Belinda came right up behind him, inches away from him, as Maeve was finishing her very personal story.

"So he told all of them that I was a lesbian," she was saying thickly, her eyes slightly glazed. "You know I'm not, Adam – but none of them knew. Imagine that bastard saying things like that about me."

Both Chelsea and Belinda called his name. He ignored them and kept his close range eye contact with Maeve. Eventually Chelsea shouted his full name so loudly that even Maeve could not fail to notice. Adam turned round slowly, as though profoundly annoyed at being so rudely interrupted, and stared Chelsea straight in the face. He did not speak and turned back round again. She tried to hold his hand but he stuck both hands ostentatiously in his pockets. She clung to him for perhaps a minute, then withdrew her hand as he carried on talking to Maeve.

It was maybe another ten minutes before he dared glance in the bar mirror. Chelsea and Belinda were sitting glumly together further down the bar, not speaking to each other. Eventually Chelsea walked over to him, hands on hips.

"Excuse me!" she snapped.

Adam again turned round and looked her directly in the eye, then turned his back on her and put an arm round Maeve.

Chelsea stood for several moments before going silently back to Belinda.

Time passed. Belinda left. Chelsea sat on alone, eyes downcast. Adam conspicuously ignored her. Eventually, she disappeared without him noticing her go.

Maeve was talking in a strained voice now, about a painful time in her life when she had finally been left by a man whom she described as the only man she had ever really loved. Adam did not recognise his name.

"That burned me", she said. "He made me burn".

She spoke of floods and floods of tears. Of messages and reminiscences passed to and fro through third party intermediaries. Of terrible revelations and recriminations. Of words of love and words of hate. Of conciliatory soundings, anecdotes and misunderstandings. She asked Adam if he had ever really loved somebody, really and truly.

"I need another drink", he told her.

He walked away to the far end of the bar where Tommy Ogdon was singing one of his favourite songs, an old Tom Waits number called *I Hope That I Don't Fall In Love With You*, in a gravelly, rasping voice.

"*The night does funny things inside a man*
Those old tomcat feelings you don't understand ..."

Adam got himself a final pint of Smithwicks as last orders was called at the bar. Tommy, well inebriated, was struggling for the right words as he came to the end of the song and asked if anyone else knew it. Jean Creighton stepped forward, slightly flushed. She was a tall girl who had a pert, rather hard face with a mole on her upper lip and a light tan that she'd acquired on a recent French vacation. Adam had never heard her sing before. When she did, her voice was clear and beautiful and filled the bar, silencing the merrymakers around her almost instantly.

"Now it's closing time
The music's fading out
Last call for drinks
I'll have another stout
When I turn around

To look for you
You're nowhere to be found
I search the place
For your lost face
Think I'll have another round
And I think that I just fell in love with you...."

The last thing Adam remembered was the spontaneous outburst of applause recognising the poignancy of the moment before he left the bar with Maeve and took her back to his house.

When he woke up the next morning, severely hung over, he felt shame and horror at the memory of what he had done. Maeve didn't give him much sympathy. She was feeling decidedly rough and didn't much like the idea of getting out of bed. Her breath stank of stale tobacco and alcohol.

"You're a bad mannered bollocks," she told him testily. "Why didn't you tell me what was going on?"

"You were oblivious. Everybody was. Nobody knew what was going on except me and her. Maybe I should find out where she works. Send her an apology."

Maeve looked at him with disgust and contempt.

"Are you mad? You've made your point, whatever it was. You were obviously trying to punish her."

"All the same ...maybe I should do something."

Maeve shook her head as she threw off the duvet and sat up, groping in her handbag at the side of the bed for cigarettes.

"How long ago was it since you and this woman were an item?"

"A long time ago. Years."

"Then leave it, for heaven's sake. Don't be such a wuss. She'll only think you're pathetic if you go apologising to her now. Let it go."

Adam left Maeve over to Botanic train station around lunchtime. He kissed her an affectionate goodbye. He knew that he wouldn't see her again for a long time but that was the way she liked to operate. She enjoyed her freedom.

The following Monday he left work early and walked down to Slattery's, in past the surly resentful stares of two of the bouncers who had been on duty on the Saturday night.

"There he is now," one of them said sarcastically. "So – are you proud of yourself?"

Adam stopped, turned round and faced him.

"Seldom", he said quietly. "Whatever your gripe is."

He went into the bar, ordered a pint and took it down to the table beside the public telephone. He looked up Anne George's number in the directory and rang it. Following a brief conversation, he had the details he wanted scribbled on the back of a beer mat.

He finished his drink quickly and headed back up the Stranmillis Road, pausing at the newsagents to check the availability of a suitable card. There were only two apology cards in the shop, neither up to much. One was so flippant that it would have been interpreted as an insult. The other depicted a woebegone looking cartoon black cat with big sad eyes standing in a large pool of spilt milk, fragments of a broken bottle scattered around it. The message inside in spartan black lettering was: "*Forgive me.*"

Adam decided that it would have to do. He printed Chelsea's name and work address on the envelope and, after crossing the road to the florists on the other side and ordering a massive bouquet of flowers to accompany the card, wrote the first words that came into his head, words that reflected the quixotic nature of his remontant emotions, words of love that he regretted almost as quickly as he'd written them, words that would be the last communication of any kind that there would ever be between them.

It was a pity, he surmised after another drunken night when he had walked the streets up and walked the streets down, drifting ineffably from one pub to another with Belfast in the darkness and the wind and the rain epitomising the monolithic detachment of night cities, that he could not remember what they were.

But that's the way it was, and is. Here's how it ends.

It was approaching midnight when Adam got back to the house on the Monday night. He did not feel much like sleeping. When he closed his eyes, sprawling motionless on the sofa, he thought only of the malevolence of fate.

He remembered Maeve Lindsay telling him she'd been burned by the man she'd loved. He recalled his old friend Dommo

Gray using a similar expression in a pub conversation many years ago, one that had come back to haunt him in later life when a pregnant girlfriend had elected to have an abortion and in doing so had unwittingly condemned him to the existence of an embittered recluse.

In Dommo's monochrome world there was no avenue of escape from the singularly personal retribution that was out there waiting for you, it was simply a matter of time before your turn came around.

It was the destiny of some to be burned literally, Adam reflected drowsily. Like a Vietnamese child covered in napalm. Or others closer to home. Jap Prendergast's blind optimism had constituted no defence against a random acid attack, nor had Winkie Kirk's position of paramilitary prominence prevented unseen antagonists from turning him into a human torch.

As for Ally O'Loan, compassion was the cross he bore; it doomed him to be seared by guilt for the rest of his life. Maeve's independent nature had not protected her from being scorched emotionally by her lover and Chelsea's welcoming overtures had not shielded her from the undeserved torment and humiliation he had visited upon her that black night in Slattery's bar. Even Jack McGrath was a burnt-out case these days, a parody of the Spirit of Ireland he'd once personified, unrecognisable now as the violent, unpredictable, hard drinking maverick whose past glories had inspired in others the fires of envy and admiration in equal measure.

Adam opened his eyes when his thoughts began to drift and he began to envisage before him a huge lake of fire, one with no apparent boundaries, crackling insanely into the infinite depths of eternity. Disturbed, he went to the bathroom and splashed several handfuls of cold water around his face. He felt immediately better. He decided to make a pot of tea and watch a movie.

The previous week Derek Greenslade had offered him the choice of a couple of erotic films he'd got off a former policeman, a colleague in his Masonic lodge.

"Old Wilson's got some amazing contacts," he'd said. "He gets all this sort of merchandise from London. You have to see it to believe it."

One of the films was an underground version of *The Story Of O*, a title that sounded vaguely familiar to Adam. Greenslade insisted that it was the real thing, that there was absolutely nothing faked in it. The other was called *Blue Heaven*, which he said opened with a blonde girl in chains in a room full of mirrors, posing on a chair like a modern day Christine Keeler.

"Then a couple of Malaysians come in," he said. "You can imagine the rest. There's no plot or dialogue. It's just an entertainment."

Adam replied that he felt like someone who'd lost the plot a long time ago and that he wasn't in any mood for dialogue.

He chose the latter.

About the Author

Michael McKeown comes from Bessbrook in County Armagh and lives in Belfast. He is a leading trade unionist with NIPSA (Northern Ireland Public Service Alliance), the largest union in Northern Ireland.

He has previously worked as a personnel officer, teacher, civil servant, factory worker, labourer, barman, salesman, fairground operator and security guard at various times and in various countries.

He holds several degrees from Queen's University, Belfast including an MA in English (Creative Writing).

He has won a number of literary awards for short fiction and had a dozen short stories published. 'The Blue Room' is his first novel.

Other books currently available from David James Publishing:

Eighty Eight

By A. L. McAuley

This is an explosive story of miracles and mayhem, kidnapping and killings, affecting the entire human race.

It begins in the quiet waters of Strangford Lough in Northern Ireland when marine biologist Doctor Eva Ballantine makes an astonishing discovery while studying a unique species of algae. A short time later, ex-priest and former member of the British Special Forces, Hugh Doggett, becomes involved in a bizarre string of events.

Three thousand miles away in Chicago, Valentine Sere is finalising his hostile takeover of BION Pharmaceuticals, his father's multi-national drugs company. When he promotes Kay Kane to BION vice president, no one could have imagined the horrifying consequences.

'88' is no ordinary thriller. It's not about good and evil; it is about events that may change our world forever.

Trying Times

By Janice Donnelly

This is an enlightening and touching story of how you can still come out smiling despite all the trials and tribulations of life.

Take Cassie; she is holding down three jobs to make ends meet. Then there is Jo; she is struggling with university and part time work, while friend, Gail, faces up to the prospects of redundancy.

Meanwhile, young and beautiful Orla appears to have it all, but appearances are deceptive. And with his sixtieth birthday looming, Benny and his wife Deirdre are looking forward to a new found freedom, until a phone call changes all that.

Focusing on the strength and importance of relationships in difficult circumstances, this is a multi-layered contemporary tale that will sometimes bring a smile to your face and other times a tear to your eye.

The Hunt for Black Friday

By David W Stokes

She had been young and beautiful once. She'd had her whole life ahead of her until they took it all away in an instant. He had been born with a burning hatred in his heart and lived a cold and loveless life until he had found a reason to exist.

When both worlds collided, security agent Nick Savvas found himself in a race against time as a suicidal plot unfolded to tear the heart out of the British Establishment. As journalist Lyndsay Mitchell discovered, a very black Friday was to descend on the House of Lords, and the closer she got to the truth the more dangerous it became for those around her.

From the poverty stricken streets of Bogota in Colombia to the halls of power at Westminster and Whitehall, THE HUNT FOR BLACK FRIDAY is the explosive follow-up to the international thriller and top Amazon download, THE ICELANDER.

Printed in Great Britain
by Amazon.co.uk, Ltd.,
Marston Gate.